"You may kiss your bride."

"I'd rather not," Sam curtly replied, echoing Ella's own thoughts, though for slightly different reason: she was all too aware Mr. Carrigan's touch had a strange effect on her.

"A kiss is traditional," Judge Barkley insisted. "I don't know if the marriage would be legal without it."

"A kiss or a dance. A kiss or a dance," the Wilson brothers commenced to chant and were quickly joined by the others. Using his six-shooter as a baton, the sheriff merrily conducted the rowdy chorus.

With a heavy sigh, Sam leaned forward and gave her a chaste peck on the cheek.

"You call that a kiss? You got to kiss her like you mean it or it don't count," the judge chided.

"If that's the way they kiss in the city, I thank the Lord I was born a cowboy," George chimed in.

With a growl, Sam grabbed Ella by both shoulders and pulled her into his arms. She squealed in protest as his lips came down on hers. He expertly moved his lips across hers and Ella could feel the blood heating in her veins. He was taking her breath away and there was nothing she could do to stop him. The kiss went on and on until every inch of Ella tingled with impetuous excitement. He was intoxicating her with his touch. As Ella willingly surrendered herself to the sensation, she clung to him even tighter.

Abruptly setting Ella away, Sam straightened his coat sleeves. "That, gentlemen, is how we kiss in the city."

RENÉ J. GARROD

HER HEART'S DESIRE

ZEBRA BOOKS
KENSINGTON PUBLISHING CORP.

To my brother Glen and my favorite
sister-in-law Glynda

ZEBRA BOOKS are published by

Kensington Publishing Corp.
850 Third Avenue
New York, NY 10022

First Printing: June, 1994

Printed in the United States of America

Prologue

He was lost. Samuel Carrigan nudged his wire-rimmed glasses up the bridge of his nose and scowled fiercely as his eyes searched the expanse of gray-green sagebrush and spindly clumps of darker green bunchgrass stretching out before him. Scarlet Indian paintbrush and lavender asters dotted the landscape, and in the distance, a stand of aspen quivered in the breeze. To the east the craggy peaks of the Wind River Mountain Range rose up from the valley floor like giant granite sentinels.

He squinted his eyes against the sun and methodically surveyed the wild terrain in every direction a second time. There was definitely no sign of a creek, and the map he held in his hand, though faded, clearly showed there should be one.

Shifting on his saddle, he fingered his mustache, and forced the scowl on his face into a mirthless grin. At least he had no one but himself to blame. He found a certain perverse satisfaction in the knowledge. Besides, he didn't consider himself hopelessly lost, just temporarily disoriented. Even now he didn't regret his decision to ride out on his own. He needed time alone with his thoughts to try to sort out his feelings about so many things he couldn't begin to list them.

Up until six weeks ago his life had been as steady and predictable as the ticking of the silver clock that sat on the mantel over the cozy fireplace that warmed his study. Up until six weeks ago he had moved through life a supremely confident man. His every endeavor was blessed by good fortune. Comfort, happiness, success required nothing more than the application of his wits and his innate ability to work single-mindedly to achieve his goals. His life *before the reading of his mother's will* had been as close to perfect as a man could hope to experience this side of Paradise.

But that was before his felicitous world had been turned upside down and wrong side out in the space of a moment. These past few weeks he felt more like the lead player in a poorly written melodrama than a self-possessed New York businessman.

His gaze dropped to the starched, white cuffs of his shirt peeking out beneath the sleeves of the finest wool coat money could buy.

To discover at the age of twenty-seven that one was not the only child of a widowed mother as one had been told all his life was a shock of indescribable magnitude. He had been numb for days. Then the anger set in, warring with the crushing grief he felt at the passing of his beloved mother. The mother he had always admired, respected, and trusted above all others. The mother who had lied to him for twenty-seven years.

He shook his head briskly to set his thoughts in a more productive direction. He was here in the territory of Wyoming to find the father and brothers, up until recently, he never knew existed. His mother's will had requested he do so—she had divided her fortune equally between her three sons—but Sam knew he would be here even if she had not asked him to come.

He needed to meet the man who had fathered him, the man

his mother still professed to love even though she had abandoned him. And, he wanted to get to know his older brothers. "Adam and Joshua," he tested their names on his tongue. He hoped they would want to get to know him as well.

The horse beneath him whinnied and pawed at the ground, impatient to be on his way. His hands tightened on the reins.

"You tell me which direction I should go, and I'll be more than happy to oblige you," he informed his mount.

The horse cocked his head and raised his nose as if pointing to the east.

"I guess east is as good a direction as any I can think to go. Logic says if we travel in an ever widening circle, we will run into something or someone eventually," Sam said. Then, realizing he was carrying on a conversation with a horse, he abruptly clamped his lips together. Folding the map back into a neat square, he tucked it into his breast pocket.

He nudged his horse forward.

One

"I repeat: I am not, I am *absolutely not* going to marry Willie Crumb," Ella Singleton decreed. Clapping her hands over her ears, she frowned at her four younger sisters. "And I don't want to hear another word on the subject."

"But he loves you," Janie pleaded.

"I refuse to be held responsible for his feelings." Crossing the room to the large cast iron stove, Ella shoved several sticks of wood into the fire, then picked up a spoon and began stirring the pot of oat porridge simmering on the stove top. "From the day we met I've made it perfectly clear I'm not interested in forming a romantic attachment. The dullest of wits could not have mistaken my feelings. As a kindness, I've taken to avoiding the man with near religious fervor, but that's all the coddling I intend to do. If he insists on continuing to delude himself . . ." She shrugged.

"You're acting like Willie is the first," Lily whined, her fingers worrying the ends of the new blue ribbon adorning her dark hair. "What about Jacob? And Roger and Henry and Timothy . . . Half the men in the valley have proposed to you, and you've turned everyone of them down in the blink of a squirrel's eye. The least you could do is take the time to consider their offers."

"It doesn't take a lot of time to know what I already know."

"They're good men, every one of them," Janie insisted.

Lifting a skillet from the stove and flipping a half dozen

flapjacks onto a warm plate, Ella crisply replied, "Never said they weren't. It's my pleasure to call them 'friend.' I just don't want any of them for a husband."

"Why not?" Marilee demanded.

After pouring more batter into the skillet, Ella slowly turned to face her siblings. One hand rested on her hip, the other wielded a spatula like a school mistress wielding a lecture stick. "I've told you all at least a thousand times, when I marry—if I ever do—it will be to a man of culture. Someone who is well-educated, knows how to conduct himself in proper society, dresses in something besides buckskin and denim . . ." Her hazel eyes momentarily darkened to a dreamy hue. "The man I marry will have to think reading the classics and glorying in the beauty of a sunset is just as important as turning a tidy profit at the next cattle sale."

"That's just a convenient excuse 'cause you know there ain't any man like that around here," Fern said.

"Isn't any man like that around here," Ella corrected.

"Ain't any man like that around here," Fern repeated. "And I'll thank you to not tell me how to be speaking my mind. Just 'cause you're trying to learn to talk fancy don't mean the rest of us . . ."

"You stop pestering me about marrying some country bumpkin and I'll stop pestering you about sounding like one," Ella assured her, an impish grin teasing the corners of her generous mouth despite her genuine pique with the topic of conversation. She agreed with Fern. It wasn't any of her business how her sisters chose to speak, and the truth was her own grammar was far from perfect, especially when she lost her temper. She just couldn't resist the temptation to aggravate Fern to punish her for persisting to aggravate her.

Fern pursed her lips and threw her sister a withering look before she picked up the thread of her original speech. "As I was saying before you tried to distract me: All your talk

about hankering after some high-minded man is just that. Or
are you forgetting how we all chipped in our money and sent
you to St. Louis for two whole weeks last year for your
twenty-fourth birthday? We sent you to find a husband, and
all you came back with was a trunk full of books. Books,"
Fern repeated the word with disgust. "As if we don't already
have enough of them around here filling your head with high-
falutin' notions."

"I didn't know a soul in St. Louis," Ella reminded. "What
did you expect me to do? Stop strangers on the street and
interview them for the position of my mate?"

"We expected you to come back with a husband," they cried
in unison. "Who cares how you did it!"

Ella sighed loudly. She sympathized with her sisters, truly
she did, but she was soul weary of being harangued on the
subject of marriage. They all acted as if she took pleasure in
thwarting them when the opposite was true, and they knew
it. If she ever met the man of her dreams, she would be more
than happy to accommodate them and marry the fellow. She
just wasn't willing to get leg-shackled to a man she didn't
love *and respect* just to please her sisters. She would cheerfully die for each and every one of them if circumstances ever
called upon her to make such a sacrifice. She loved her sisters
that much. But she couldn't bring herself to share her bed
with some oaf, especially when it was all so unnecessary. She
turned her back on them, brushing a wisp of midnight black
hair out of her eyes with her forearm.

It would be nice, if just once, they would try to understand
her sentiments, but experience told her there was about as
much chance of that happening as there was of her meeting
a man who met her visionary standards.

After sliding the last of the flapjacks from the skillet and
stacking them on the plate, Ella squared her shoulders, took

a deep breath, and again faced her disgruntled sisters. "I tried the best I could to oblige you," she stated flatly.

"Well, you could have tried harder," Fern protested.

"You'll recall, when I discovered how disappointed you all were, I offered to pay back every penny you'd spent on the trip."

"This ain't got nothing to do with money. The trip was your birthday present." Planting her hands on her hips, Fern tapped her foot on the wooden floor. "But that don't excuse your behavior. I said it before and I say it again: you could have tried harder."

"How?"

"I don't know. But I get the feeling in my gut your heart ain't really into finding a husband. You're smart when it comes to just about everything else. Seems to me if you *really* wanted the kinda fella you say you hanker after, you'd figure a way to get him. Why, I bet if we served up your perfect man to you on a silver platter, you'd contrive some way to get out of marrying him."

"That's not true. If ever I meet such a man, I swear to you on Daddy's Bible, I'll use all my womanly wiles to lead him to the altar," Ella argued. She fished in her apron pocket for the old chain watch she carried there, checked the time, and slipped it back into her apron. "The trouble is: I just don't expect I'll ever meet him."

"We're all gonna die old maids, I just know we will," Lily wailed. "It ain't fair. Why should we have to suffer on account of you, Ella? You're muleheaded; that's what you are, selfish and muleheaded."

Ella gritted her teeth and counted to ten twice. "Why don't the lot of you get out of my hair and go badger Grandma Jo. She's the one who won't let you marry till I do, not me. I wouldn't mind being a bridesmaid instead of a bride. In fact,

I can't think of anything I'd like better. So, as you can clearly see, it's her mind you ought to be trying to change, not mine."

"You know she won't listen to reason. She's even more muleheaded than you are," Marilee declared.

"Who's more muleheaded than Ella?" A spry woman carrying a basket of eggs and wearing a wry grin upon her seventy-two-year-old face sauntered into the cozy, log cabin. She pulled off her sunbonnet, revealing a coronet of snow white braids, and hung the hat on a hook near the door.

The clatter of dishes and silver filled the room as the four younger Singleton sisters took a sudden and ardent interest in setting the table. They refused to meet the older woman's penetrating gaze.

Josephine Singleton studied each of her granddaughters in turn. Ella wore a long-suffering expression upon her handsome face and a starched, white apron tied over a red flannel shirt and a pair of buckskin trousers. Janie looked to be on the brink of bursting into tears and drenching her blue Sunday-go-to-meeting dress. Fern sported a rebellious pout and the calico skirt she had just finished hemming the night before. Marilee kept shaking her head and yanking at the lace cuffs of her blouse. Lily chewed her bottom lip like a mouse trying to gnaw its way through a wall.

They took after her in her youth, everyone of them, with their dark hair, hazel eyes, and rosy good looks. Too bad they all seemed to have forgotten how to smile.

"Well?" Grandma Jo prodded. "Who were you girls talking about?"

"Nobody," Janie meekly offered. The others nodded in agreement.

Grandma Jo chuckled. "And here I was getting all puffed up with pride 'cause I thought you were gossiping about me. Damn. Must be getting soft in my old age." Grabbing the pot of coffee from the stove, she retired to her spot at the head of the table and poured herself a cup.

Janie helped Ella serve up the meal; then, they joined the others at the table. After intoning a succinct blessing over the food, Grandma Jo applied herself to the oatmeal porridge and flapjacks with gusto. The others followed suit.

Conversation at the table centered on the upcoming trip to town as last minute items were added to the supply list. Ella followed the conversation with interest, adding her own comments when necessary. She was going to stay at the ranch and work rather than go into town with her sisters, but she wasn't feeling the least bit put upon. Her sisters planned to spend the night at Sally James' boardinghouse, and she could count on them to find a reason not to start for home until past noon the next day, which meant *she* wouldn't have to listen to a soul whine about Willie Crumb for nearly two whole days. The prospect of all that peace and quiet came near to making her giddy.

Though Grandma Jo was as eager as the rest to see her hitched up to some man, and she wasn't the least bit shy about speaking her mind, she didn't peck at her like a flock of hens pulling apart a juicy worm. Grandma Jo could be depended on to say her piece then keep her mouth shut until there was something intelligent to be said. Since they had already "discussed" her refusal to accept Willie Crumb's offer of marriage, Ella was confident she wouldn't have to hear his name until her sisters returned.

Desirous of beginning her holiday as soon as possible, Ella mentally went over the list of supplies one more time. Satisfied she hadn't overlooked anything important, she rose to her feet. "I'm going out to the south pasture to check on Electra. She looks to be ready to drop her calf any minute now. You all have a nice time in town."

"Are you sure you don't want to come with us?" Janie asked.

"Positive," Ella gaily replied as she headed for the door. "See you all tomorrow."

"So, you girls still riding Ella for turning down Willie Crumb?" Grandma Jo wasted no time easing into her subject when the door closed behind her eldest granddaughter.

They nodded.

"Do you any good?"

"She won't even consider him," Marilee glumly replied. A chorus of piteous sighs rang out round the table, echoing her disappointment. Pushing herself up out of her chair, Grandma Jo began stacking the breakfast dishes. Her granddaughters followed her lead, falling to their respective chores without further prompting.

"Didn't reckon she would," Grandma Jo stated matter-of-factly as she carried a stack of plates to the wash tub Marilee was filling with steaming water. "Can't say as I blame her. He's a fine-looking man and sweet as sugar, but even his own mama admits he comes up short in the good sense department. Our Ella would likely get so frustrated with him she'd be pulling out her hair in tufts before the honeymoon was over."

"Well, I for one wouldn't feel the least bit sorry for her. She's had plenty of better offers. I say she'd deserve what she got," Fern said.

"Now, now. Getting spiteful ain't the answer."

"You could let us get married before her. Ella says she wouldn't mind," Janie suggested, her glistening eyes pleading for her grandmother's agreement as she took a handful of silverware from Grandma Jo's weathered hand and dropped it into the hot, soapy water.

"Of course, she does. Says it fifty times a day to me, you, anyone who will listen. What else would you expect her to say?" Grandma Jo gently scolded. "The girl is as addled as a mare who's been nibbling locoweed when it comes to the subject of marriage. That's why it's my duty as head of this family to see to her welfare."

Lily scrubbed at a years-old stain on the table with unaccustomed vigor. "I don't see how denying us our happiness helps Ella in the least," she complained.

"That's 'cause you don't have the wisdom of an old woman to guide your thoughts." Grandma Jo rescued the table from her youngest granddaughter by plucking the dish rag from beneath her hand. "You'll just have to trust I know what I'm doing. The day Ella gets herself married, I'll give my blessing to each and every one of your marriages, but not a day before."

"My Frank says we should all just get married without your blessing. We are of age, after all, and there's nothing you can do to stop us. I for one am thinking of taking him up on his advice," Fern threatened.

Grandma looked her straight in the eye and shrugged. "That's your choice, miss. If you're willing to live with the consequences, no one here will try to stop you."

"You wouldn't really disown me, would you?"

"Sure would," she replied without batting an eye.

"Grandma Jo," Fern wailed. "How can you do this to us? If we marry before Ella, you'll banish us from the bosom of our family, and if we wait for Ella to wed, we're doomed to be spinsters all our lives. It's like something out of one of those books Ella reads. It's heartless; that's what it is. Heartless. It's not right you love Ella better than us."

Josephine Singleton's flashing hazel eyes took on a more commiserative hue. "I don't love anyone one of you girls above the others, and in your hearts y'all know that's true. Before your daddy and mama died, I promised them if anything should ever happen to them, I'd take care of *all* their girls. Men need women and women need men. That's been the way of things since Adam and Eve, and I'm too close to the grave to start telling the Almighty He don't know how to run His own business." She stroked the deep wrinkles time and hard living had etched into her neck. "In the Good Book, if a shepherd loses a sheep, does he shed a tear and stay with the flock or does he go in search of his lost lamb?"

"He looks for the lost lamb," Fern reluctantly answered.

"Well, that's all I'm doing. Looking out for my lost lamb. Ella is different from the rest of you girls, but different don't make her bad. Fact is she's a lot like your daddy, full of dreams and always trying to better herself. I'm not saying there's anything wrong with the men who have been proposing to her. They're good men, every one of them. But that don't necessarily mean they'd be good for our Ella. Either a man sets a woman's blood on fire or he don't, and there's no accounting for the why and wherefore of it. It's obvious to me she just ain't met the right man yet."

"What if he's never been born?" Janie cried.

"Oh, he's out there somewhere."

"How can you be sure?" Marilee asked.

"Faith," Grandma Jo proclaimed. "If you girls really have your hearts set on marrying some day soon, instead of whimpering and whining and thinking ill of poor Ella, I'd figure you'd be putting your heads together and trying to come up with a way to solve our little predicament."

"But how?"

"If I knew the answer to that, I'd have already solved it, now wouldn't I? But I'll scare up an idea eventually. I just know I will." For the first time during their conversation, Grandma Jo appeared less than utterly confident. "Don't think I enjoy denying you girls your hearts' desire. If there was any other way, I'd gladly take it."

"We're doomed," Lily repeated her sister's earlier prediction.

"If you're ready to give up on life at nineteen, you're one

pitiful creature, Lily Anne. Your daddy's blood flows through your veins. And your mama was no quitter either. Where's your spunk? A woman wants something in this life, she's gotta go after it. She don't sit on her thumbs feeling sorry for herself, waiting for someone else to get her what she desires."

"Yes, ma'am," Lily answered contritely.

"That goes for the rest of you, too," Grandma Jo admonished. "There's five of us and only one of her. Ingenuity and elbow grease, that's all we need to find Ella a fine husband. That and maybe a little help from the Almighty."

"We pray for Divine intervention in the matter every night," Janie assured her.

"Good for you. The Lord rewarded Job for his perseverance. There's not a reason in the world we shouldn't expect Him to do the same for us." Picking up a broom, Grandma Jo scooted it toward her granddaughter's feet. "Now get yourselves out of my hair and into town to pick up those supplies like you promised your sweet sister. I reckon y'all want to have plenty of time to flirt with your beaus, and if you don't get going, you'll miss out on your fun."

Every pair of male eyes lit with delight and arms rose to enthusiastically wave a greeting when the wagon bearing the dark-haired, hazel-eyed Singleton sisters rolled into the tiny town of Heaven at half past one. The ladies smiled and waved back with equal enthusiasm.

"How you doing, Ernie?" Marilee called out. "George, that mare of yours foaled yet?" She deftly guided the wagon to the side of the dusty street and reined in their dun gelding in front of Thatcher's General Store.

Instantly, there was a crowd of male hands to help the ladies down from the wagon.

After taking a moment to bask in the sunshine of effusive

male adoration, Janie politely excused herself and hurried down the street to the small log cabin that served as a jail and as the sheriff's office on Wednesday when he came into town from his ranch to discharge the duties of his elected office. Fern slipped into the general store. Marilee remained on the street, exchanging news and flirtations, but it wasn't long before she succumbed to temptation and set off in search of her best friend and would-be-husband Bob McNaught, leaving Lily to preside over their crowd of admirers by herself—a circumstance Lily found much to her liking.

Inside the general store, Frank Thatcher leapt over the counter and met Fern halfway across the room, his arms open wide for an embrace.

She gave him his hug, but when he leaned close to kiss her, she gently pushed him away. "Not in front of the whole world," she admonished in a breathless whisper. "People will start gossiping I'm free with my favors."

Frank dutifully stepped an arm's length away and pretended to tidy a row of bottled apples. "I gotta check something in the back room." He winked at her. "Want to tag along?"

Clasping her hands behind her back, Fern set her skirt to swaying. Her eyes twinkled and her lips stretched into a wide, friendly smile. "Don't know if I should."

"Please. I got a new bolt of lace back there I've been saving 'specially for you."

After pretending to hesitate a moment longer, Fern replied, "I don't see as how I can resist so pretty an invitation, Mr. Thatcher. I guess I'll just have to trust you to be a gentleman." Grabbing his hand, she led the way to the storeroom.

The moment the two had attained more private circumstances, they fell into each other's arms, covering each other's faces with passionate kisses. They indulged themselves far longer than was prudent, but eventually Frank was able to muster enough sense of propriety to tear himself away. Breathing hard, he retreated to the other side of the room and cleared his throat.

"So, what brings you gals to town?" he asked as he straightened his string tie and covertly adjusted his trousers.

Fern hefted herself up on a stack of bean sacks, making a show of arranging herself just so as she gazed across the storeroom with hunger-filled eyes. "We're here to pick up a few supplies and do a bit of visiting."

"So you persuaded that rattlesnake sister of yours to let the pigeons out to play."

"Frank Thatcher, you know good and well we can come to town any time we like. Ella may be mean about some things, but she lets us come to town whenever she can spare us for the day. Mad as I am at her this morning, I'll not hold her guilty for something she ain't done."

"That's mighty generous of you." His mouth curved into a boyish grin. "I knew there must be some reason I love you so much."

Fern blushed, her eyes growing brighter at his words.

"So you gonna tell me what she did to make you mad?" Frank queried.

"Willie Crumb asked for her hand in marriage, and she turned him down. That's the third man this year. Pretty soon there won't be a fella left in the territory who ain't proposed." Her voice took on a desperate tone. "Then, what are we gonna do?"

Frank frowned fiercely. "Don't know. The only thing I do know is I'm getting mighty itchy to marry you, Fern. Don't know how much longer I can wait."

"You wouldn't get so tired of waiting for me you'd ever marry someone else, would you?"

"I wouldn't want to." He ran his hand up the back of his neck and massaged the base of his skull. His brow pleated and his large, brown eyes darkened. "I love you more than a cowboy loves whiskey. But . . . a man has his limits. Why just this morning, I was looking over the latest edition of the St. Louie paper to make it to town and my eyes kept straying to the 'Heart and Hand' column. Some of those gals are starting to look mighty tempting."

Fern paled. *"Oh, Frank, please, say it ain't so."*

"I wish I could, darling, but you know I never lie to you. The truth is a man has certain needs . . . and this courtship of ours has gone on far longer than is natural. I need me a wife. I want you to be that wife. But I ain't willing to wait forever."

Marilee read the note Sally James handed her. Refolding it, she tucked it into a pocket of her skirt and sighed.

"I'm sure he's just as sorry about it as you are, dear," Mrs. James consoled.

"I know," Marilee agreed. "It just kinda takes all the fun out of coming to town if Bob can't be here. I may as well have stayed back at the ranch with Grandma Jo and Ella."

Mrs. James nodded in understanding.

Marilee stayed to gossip a while, working side by side with Mrs. James as the proprietress bustled through her daily duties, but having no great affinity for housework, Marilee excused herself when the news began to become stale.

"Guess I'll just mosey around town till I think of something to do with myself," she mumbled as she started for the door. "See you at supper time."

"Have a nice afternoon, dear." Mrs. James cheerfully waved her on her way.

Stepping back into the sunshine, Marilee glanced up the street. Lily was still holding court in front of the general store. She could see no reason to intrude upon Lily's pleasure just because her day in town was a disappointment, and she started off in the opposite direction.

With no purpose in mind, Marilee wandered where her feet led her, paying no particular attention to the passage of time. Without Bob, there really was nothing to do. Fern would take care of purchasing the supplies. Janie and Lily were occupied with their beaus.

There was nowhere else on earth she would rather live than right here where she did, but Heaven was not exactly teeming with activities to tempt a young lady's fancy. Pete MacDonald's Red Eye Saloon offered the town's only entertainment and respectable females like herself were not welcome inside its doors.

A long walk suited her mood as well as anything else she could be doing at this moment.

Her thoughts returned to Bob. It felt like forever since she'd last seen him even though he'd come to supper a week from last Saturday. After the meal, they'd gone for a leisurely stroll, walking hand in hand. Bob had such big, strong hands. He'd stolen more than one kiss from her lips under the moonlight. Warm, sugary kisses that made her blood pound and her toes curl. His thick, blond mustache always tickled when he kissed her, but she wasn't complaining. Bob McNaught could kiss her from sunup till sundown any time he wanted.

Unleashing a series of mournful sighs, she wrapped her arms around her waist to ward off her present loneliness. She sure wished Bob was here right now. As far as she was concerned, Heaven was hell without him. . . .

"Oh!" Marilee startled to attention and jumped back a step, bringing her hand to her bosom. "Mercy me! I didn't see you sitting there. I didn't mean to almost step on you. I'm so sorry. I oughta been paying more attention."

The man momentarily appeared as startled as she, but he quickly recovered himself. Carefully laying the book he held in his hands on the ground, he rose to his feet, removing his hat and brushing bits of dirt and leaves off his suit as he did so.

"No harm done," he assured her with a genial smile. "Are *you* all right?"

"I'm just fine. . . ." Marilee replied as she studied him from head to toe. Her eyes widened. This was no ordinary cowboy standing before her. In fact, by her reckoning, he wasn't any kind of cowboy at all. He sure didn't dress like a cowboy, and his voice was smooth as cream. He looked to be just the sort of fella Ella might . . .

His voice intruded on her thoughts. "Are you certain you are feeling fit? You look a little dazed. I could escort you back to town if you'd like and find someone to tend you."

Marilee shook her head to clear it and stopped staring quite so boldly. "There ain't no need for that. You're the one almost got stomped on, not me."

"But I feel partially responsible . . ."

"Why? I was the one who was daydreaming. You were just sitting under this here tree minding your own business." Despite her best intentions, her eyes fixed on his face and she gazed into his eyes. Her voice was unnaturally reedy when she continued. "Besides, the longer I stand here talking to you the better I'm starting to feel. Do you always read books and dress so elegant?"

"I indulge myself with good books and fashionable clothing when I can," he courteously replied.

"What a lovely answer," Marilee proclaimed, trying not to squeal with delight. Her breath kept catching in her throat and her heart was pounding so fast she was starting to feel light-headed.

"Are you sure you are all right, miss?" her companion asked, his expression filled with gentlemanly concern. "You appear a little flushed."

"Do I? Oh, dear. That will never do. I best be going. It's been a pleasure meeting you. A true pleasure, indeed," she fired off the sentences in rapid succession. Turning on her heels, she beat a hasty retreat, a joyful grin stretching from ear to ear.

"There you are," Marilee announced with relief. "I've been looking all over for you!"

Janie dropped the weed she was using to tickle the sheriff's chin, and he hastily removed his head from her lap.

"Good to see you, Marilee," Sheriff Rex Johnson greeted, though the pink circles staining his cheeks and the hint of irritation in his voice said differently.

"What are you doing here?" Janie asked, shading her eyes against the late afternoon sun.

"There's something I gotta talk to you about."

"Right this minute?"

"Yes. It's important. Real important. You know I'd never bother you and Rex if it weren't." Marilee did her best to sound calm, but Janie caught the underlying urgency and excitement in her sister's voice. She sat a bit taller and gave Marilee her undivided attention.

"Well?" Janie prodded when Marilee did not immediately commence enlightening her.

Marilee threw a nervous glance in the sheriff's direction, then returned her gaze to her sister. "It's a . . . private matter."

Rex Johnson reluctantly rose to his feet. "I guess I best be heading back to my office to see if anybody stopped by to report a crime while I was out. Doubt they have. Folks around here are so law abiding most times being sheriff feels like a practical joke." He brushed the dust from his trousers. "We still on for supper, Janie?"

"Of course. I'll follow you just as soon as I hear Marilee

out." When the sheriff was out of earshot, Janie addressed her sister, "You better have one fine reason for interrupting Rex and me, Marilee, or I swear I'll . . ."

"I've seen him!" Marilee exclaimed, abandoning all pretense of composure.

"Seen who?"

"Ella's future husband."

"What?"

"Found him sitting under a tree over yonder, like God had planted him there for me to find."

"What?" Janie repeated, her brow wrinkling in consternation. "I reckon you better calm down and start at the beginning. Either you're leaving out the most pertinent facts or I've suddenly become dull-witted."

"All right." Marilee drew in a series of slow, deep breaths; then, she began anew. "I went looking for Bob, hoping he might be in town, too, but he ain't. Left a note at Sally's that he got my message, but he couldn't get away from his ranch today on account of his best wrangler up and quit, and he was expecting some fella from Green River who's coming up to try for the job. Anyway, I was feeling real disappointed and just sort of wandering around feeling low spirited when I practically tripped over this fella leaning against a tree reading a book." Her eyes sparkled and her breath quickened as she continued. "There wasn't any polite way of reading the cover to see what it was he was reading, but it was a big, important looking, leather-bound book—like the kind Ella is always reading. When I apologized for almost stepping on him, his response was as proper and pretty as I ever hope to hear. The man oozes culture from every pore, I can tell you that. And he wears fancy clothes and eyeglasses and not counting my Bob is about the handsomest fella I've ever laid eyes on. Hair the color of coffee and thick as lamb's wool. Big blue eyes. A nose that looks to never have been broke. A strong chin."

"And he told you he was here to marry Ella?" Janie asked numbly. "I know we've all been praying for a miracle, but . . ."

"Of course he didn't say he was here to marry Ella, you goose. He ain't even met her yet. The point is: he looks to be just the kinda man Ella has been pining for all these years. I reckon it's our duty as her sisters to sort of check him out, and if we like what we find, arrange a meeting, don't you?"

Rising to her feet, Janie began to pace beneath the tree. It was impossible not to catch Marilee's excitement; however, she was determined not to let her hopes soar too high. "I agree with you . . . but how are we gonna go about checking him out?"

"I've already got Lily asking everybody in town what they know about him."

Janie frowned.

"Don't worry. I told her to be subtle about it. No sense in advertising we're looking this fella over. He might get skittish and bolt if he hears wind of it."

"What about Fern? Have you talked to her yet?"

Marilee nodded. "I've got her hiding behind a tree, keeping an eye on him."

Janie's gaze met Marilee's. "What do you want me to do?"

"I thought you should be the one to take a stroll past him and strike up a conversation. The rest of us have already walked by once. Me on accident, Fern and Lily so they could get an up close look. I wish they'd have waited till I'd come up with some plan, but I couldn't persuade them. They're as excited as I am. If any of us go strolling by again so soon, he might get suspicious, so that leaves the task to you. I figure you're the best choice anyhow 'cause you seem to understand Ella a little better than the rest of us. You'll know the right questions to ask. After you have your little chat, you can report back to us. We'll have to keep ourselves hidden in the brush, but we'll be close enough we can keep an eye on you in case he tries anything funny. I don't reckon he will, him being a gentleman and all, but a body never can be too careful with strangers."

Janie lowered her gaze to the toe of her boots while she contemplated the plan. "It all seems rather sneaky."

"I know it does, but I ain't getting any younger and neither are you. I've had plenty of time to think this through while I was hunting for you. As I said before, it's like the Almighty planted him there for me to find." Her voice rose in pitch. "What if he *is* the miracle we've been praying for? Grandma Jo would have our hides if she ever learnt about him being here and we didn't even trouble ourselves to find out his name. She'd say we deserved to be spinsters, and she'd be right."

The rustle of approaching petticoats caused Samuel Carrigan to glance up from his book and turn his head in the direction of the sound. He smiled to himself. Another dark-haired beauty was passing his way. Rumor had it the West suffered a scarcity of the fairer sex, but the community of Heaven seemed to boast an abundance of pretty, young women to pleasure a man's eyes.

Perhaps his luck was finally changing. First, his horse had carried him only five hundred yards before he had spotted a wisp of smoke spiralling into the sky. The smoke had guided him to this town—a settlement really. It wasn't even on his map. Though Heaven consisted of less than a dozen rustic clapboard and log buildings on a single dirt lane, the first man he'd stopped was able to tell him exactly where he had turned wrong, and he was delighted to discover he hadn't gone too many miles out of his way. Almost of equal delight to a gentleman used to the creature comforts of city life, he was able to buy himself a bath and a soft bed for the night. Now, he was being treated to a winsome parade.

He'd chosen what he thought was a quiet, out of the way spot to sit and read his book, and this was the fourth young lady to stroll by in the space of less than an hour. He wondered if this tiny backwoods hamlet had been christened with its celestial name by the local men *because* of the ladies living here or if it was the name that had attracted the ladies to settle in the town. Or perhaps one had nothing to do with the other. He'd have to ask someone about it before he left. He liked collecting odd little facts.

Speaking of odd, every woman he'd seen this afternoon was dark-haired and fair-skinned. They possessed an earthy beauty. Even their faces appeared vaguely similar. Generous mouths. Rosy cheeks. . . . It was probably just his imagination, but now that he thought about it. . . .

The lady came abreast him and his conjecture was interrupted by a hesitant, "Hello, you ain't from around here, are you?"

Rising to his feet, he removed his bowler and reached for the hand she offered him. The lady met his hand halfway and shook it with unexpected vigor. "Hello," he replied. She gazed up at his face expectantly but said not a word. "Is there something I can do for you?"

Her color heightened slightly, and she laced her fingers together. "No. Nothing at all. I just thought as long as I was passing this way, I oughta stop and be friendly. Being as you're a stranger to town and all. Grandma Jo says it's important to be hospitable. My name is Janie Singleton. I live on a small ranch southeast of here."

"And I am Samuel Carrigan from New York City."

"New York!" Janie made a poor job of concealing her glee. "I bet a fella from New York knows all about using proper manners and acting cultured and the like."

"My mother did her best to teach me how to behave in polite society," Sam assured her.

"And I can see you like books." She indicated the book laying at the base of the tree with a tilt of her head.

"Yes, I do."

"That wouldn't happen to be what they'd call a *classic*, would it?"

"No, it's not."

"Oh dear." His answer seemed to momentarily fluster her, but she quickly regained a measure of composure. "Don't you like the classics?" she quizzed.

Sam maintained his polite mien with a minimum of effort even though he couldn't imagine what possible concern the woman before him could have in his literary preferences. "I like them just fine. I just happen to be reading something else at the moment."

"Would it be fair to say you're fond of the classics?"

"Yes."

"How fond?"

He could contain his curiosity no longer. "I hope you don't think I'm rude for asking, but is there a reason for all your questions about my reading habits?"

"Yes. I mean, no. I mean, I'm just interested, that's all."

"Are you a lover of books?"

"No. I love Rex Johnson. It's my sister, Ella loves books."

"I see." Sam tried not to smile at her ingenuous declaration. He judged Miss Janie Singleton an awkward young woman but undeniably entertaining, and he was pleased to have finally discovered the purpose behind this conversation. It was rather touching, and he was more than willing to oblige. "Would you like me to give your sister a book or two?" he offered. "I have a couple back in my room I've finished reading."

"Oh no, Ella already has more than enough books," Janie protested.

Sam stared at her, once again totally confounded. "Then, what do you want?"

"Uhm . . . I . . . I reckon I best be on my way. Nice meeting you, Mr. Carrigan. Have a pleasant stay in Heaven."

Before he could respond, she lifted her skirts and hurried into the brush.

Chuckling and shaking his head, Sam settled himself back beneath the tree and opened his book. The contrasts between East and West were many, but one of the most striking was the lack of social constraints he had grown up as thinking a natural part of daily intercourse. No woman of his acquaintance would even entertain the notion of initiating a conversation with a man until they had been properly introduced. It just wasn't done. He didn't think poorly of Miss Janie Singleton for her forwardness. In truth, he found the unreserved geniality of the West rather charming. But it did take some getting used to.

Dismissing the encounter from his mind, he scanned the page before him until he found the place he had left off and resumed his reading.

"Well, what did you find out?" the three youngest Singleton sisters whispered in unison as they pulled Janie behind the thicket of brush where they hid.

"His name is Samuel Carrigan. He's got a good, firm handshake. He's from New York, and he likes all kinds of books. Besides the one he's reading, he's got more back at his room. Oh, and he's real polite and not the least bit shy about sharing."

"That's all?" Fern complained.

"I really like him, and I agree with Marilee. He seems perfect for Ella," Janie added.

"How long is he staying?" Marilee asked.

"I don't know. I forgot to ask."

"You forgot?" her siblings wailed.

"I did the best I could do. Y'all know I'm no good when I'm put under pressure. I get all fidgety inside and my brain seizes up."

"Even a stick would've had sense enough to find out how long he's planning to stay in Heaven," Lily grumbled.

"Well, if you hadn't been so darn impatient to get a look at him, you could've asked him yourself," Janie countered.

"Fighting among ourselves ain't gonna do us a whit of good," Marilee admonished. "I wish Janie had learnt more, but she didn't, so we'll just have to make the best of it. Who wants to take a go at him next?"

"I will," Fern volunteered. "I don't know how much longer Frank is gonna wait for me, and I don't mind admitting I'm feeling more desperate by the minute. You can depend on me to find out how long he'll be staying."

"Good. We'll be waiting right here. Just remember, try to act nonchalant."

Fern nodded and set off at a casual gait.

"Howdy, stranger. I see you're still sitting up here under this tree."

"Yes, I am." Closing his book, Sam again rose to his feet, doffed his hat, and extended his hand when the lady offered hers.

"You look lonely."

"Do I?"

She shifted her weight from one foot to the other, pausing to follow the flight of a meadowlark before her eyes met his once more. "Are you missing someone from back home? Like a wife maybe?"

"I've yet to have the pleasure of making a woman my wife, but I hope to some day soon," Sam genteelly replied.

"Really! That's wonderful news! Some men don't cotton to the notion of marriage. Now my Frank, he's like you. He's chomping at the bit to settle down."

Her initial exclamation caused Sam to step back from her, but her next statements prompted him to relax his stance. The sociable smile returned to his lips. "I take it Frank is your beau."

Her chest puffed with pride. "Sure is and a finer man I could never hope to find."

"I congratulate you on your good fortune."

"Thank you." She continued to grin at him. "I just got the best idea. Why don't you come to supper at my family's ranch tomorrow night. I'll invite Frank and the two of you can meet. We'd love to have you, and you look like you could use a little fattening up."

Western manners were definitely going to take some getting used to, Sam echoed his earlier thought. He hated to deny a lady, but he was unwilling to be swayed from his mission, even if it only meant a day's delay. "I'm sure Frank is a fine fellow and my life will be the poorer for missing the opportunity to meet him. And I appreciate your generosity. But I'm just passing through and will be leaving at first light tomorrow."

"You're leaving tomorrow morning?" Fern repeated, her voice quivering with disappointment.

"Yes, ma'am."

"But I so wanted to have you to supper. My sister Ella is the best cook in the territory. You ought not leave before tasting her rabbit stew."

Ella again? Curiosity overpowered his reluctance to abandon what he had always considered good manners, and he decided to temporarily adopt the western custom of asking candid questions of total strangers. "You don't by chance have another sister named Miss Janie Singleton, do you?"

"Why do you ask?"

He was a bit discomfited when his question seemed to put his companion on her guard, but he didn't retract it. "Not more than ten minutes ago I was chatting with a Miss Singleton and the two of you are remarkably similar in looks and manner. She too has a sister Ella."

"Janie's my sister, all right," she confirmed.

"I thought she might be."

Planting a resolute smile on her face, Fern returned the conversation to the subject uppermost in her mind. "Since you've already met the two of us, you may as well come to supper and meet the rest of the family. A man has as much right to change his mind as a woman does, and we do it all the time. I suspect you've already reconsidered and are regretting your hasty answer."

Sam pressed his lips together and shook his head. "I am sorry to have to decline your invitation. I'm sure the evening would be fascinating, but as I said earlier, I'm leaving at first light."

"Ain't there something I can do to change your mind about staying a day or two longer?" she pleaded prettily.

"I fear not, but again I do thank you for your generous invitation."

"Well," discontent was conspicuous in the lady's tone and on her face, "it's been nice chatting with you. Hope we run into each other again before you leave. . . . Oh, and if you find yourself in the general store, introduce yourself to the man behind the counter. He's Frank."

The moment Fern reached her sisters she filled them in on the disheartening news. "He's leaving first thing tomorrow morning."

"Oh, no. And here I was sure he was a gift from God." Marilee dropped her head into her hands.

Janie slipped a comforting arm around her sister. "I know what you mean. I never met a fella talks so pretty. Ella for sure would have fallen in love with him. It's a terrible pity he's leaving so soon."

"We could try to talk him into staying," Lily suggested.

"I already did. He won't change his mind," Fern informed her.

"Well, before I take no for an answer, I'm gonna have a go at him myself," she announced.

Before her sisters could stop her, Lily was on her feet and had covered half the distance between them and Mr. Carrigan.

"Nice day we're having, ain't it?" she greeted him with a radiant smile. "Bet we'll have one glorious sunset this evening. You do like sunsets, don't you, a fine gentleman like yourself."

Once again, Sam lay his book aside, rose to his feet, and removed his hat. He toyed with a feeling of mild annoyance at these continual interruptions of his solitude, but decided he would rather be amused. His reasons for being in Wyoming might be unsettling, but as long as he was here, he might as well soak up a bit of the local culture. Possibly the experience would leave him better prepared for his meeting with his father and brothers. At the very least, it would provide him with a colorful tale to relate to his colleagues on Wall Street. Shoring up his indefinite smile, he replied, "As a matter of fact, I do."

"I just knew you would." She clapped her hands together. "You look to be the sort who could sit and stare at fine things like sunsets for hours on end without ever getting bored."

"An interesting observation." Sam was tempted to laugh at

her earnest declaration, but he politely refrained. "You can tell all that about me just by looking?"

"Yep. It's the way you're dressed and the book, of course. Shows you have a refined mind. People with refined minds tend to have funny notions about sunsets. Now me, I just can't get all that excited about something that happens day in and day out as regular as a clock, but my sister, Ella . . ."

"Ah, another of Ella's sisters. How many more of you are there?"

"There's five of us all together, counting Ella," she apprised him.

"Somehow, I get the feeling I will have the pleasure of meeting all of you before this day is over."

"Oh, you already have. All except Ella."

Sam held up his fingers. "No. I only count three so far."

"You're probably forgetting to count Marilee. She's the one almost stepped on you earlier this afternoon."

"Ah, yes. And what is your name?"

"Lily," she replied. "Now, about Ella? It would be a sorrowful shame to meet the whole family and not meet her."

"Yes, it would," Sam agreed. He was finding it progressively more difficult to disguise his amusement, but he persevered.

"Well, that's why I'm here. You've just gotta come to supper tomorrow night, so you can meet Ella, too."

"Why doesn't she just stroll on by like the rest of you?"

"She didn't come to town with us."

"I see."

"I'm glad you do." Her cheeks dimpled and she looked half ready to hug him. "So, it's decided. You'll come to supper."

"As I told your sister," he hesitated, searching his memory for a name.

"Fern," Lily supplied.

". . . I appreciate the invitation, but I won't be here tomorrow night."

"We'd have you tonight if we could, but our ranch is a half day's ride from town. We'd all be starving by the time we got there. Besides, it makes Janie skittish to travel after dark."

"Then, we definitely should not ask the lady to travel after dark."

"So, I can tell the others you've agreed to come to supper tomorrow," Lily stated matter-of-factly.

The young lady clearly was determined not to accept "no" for an answer. For the briefest of moments Sam was tempted to indulge her. He couldn't remember the last time he had spent an afternoon in such rare company. Sharing a meal with the Singleton family was bound to be an interesting experience. Still, it wasn't wise to leave his business in the hands of others—no matter how trusted—for too long. If he was going to add any extra days to his trip, they would be better spent getting to know his own family. The Singleton ranch lay southeast and he was traveling northwest. He had no connection with these people. He had already wasted a day getting himself lost. Practicality demanded but one answer. "I'm sorry but I can't accept your invitation."

"Please."

"I'm sorry," he repeated as firmly as good manners allowed. "I must decline. Good day to you." Though he couldn't fathom why, the poor girl looked ready to burst into tears. He hated tears; he never knew what to do or say. In an effort to check them, he abruptly added, "However, if I find myself passing this way on my return trip, I promise, I'll do my best to find the time to accept your family's hospitality."

Acknowledging his words with a nod, she picked up her skirts and hurried off in the direction she had come.

* * *

"I couldn't get him to change his mind either," Lily whimpered when she returned to her sisters. "He may talk pretty, and I can't fault his looks, but he's stubborn."

"Another thing he and Ella would have had in common," Janie sighed. "And now they'll never even lay eyes on each other."

"Even if I unhitched the horse from the wagon and rode hard to fetch Ella, I couldn't get her back here in time to strike up an acquaintance with the man. It just don't seem fair," Marilee protested.

"He promised if he passed this way again, he'd make time for a visit, but who knows when that'll be? For all we know he'll go and get himself killed going wherever it is he's going," Lily lamented.

"He was probably just trying to be polite anyhow and has no intention of setting foot in Heaven ever again," Fern added her opinion to the general gloom.

Janie sniffed back a sob. "Seems our meeting Mr. Carrigan was just a cruel twist of fate."

Silence reigned as they stood in a small circle, their eyes downcast and their hearts constricting with each private thought of what might have been, if only. . . . Fern's bottom lip was set in a mutinous pout. Tears streamed down Lily's cheeks. Marilee rocked back and forth on her heels, while Janie watered the clump of bunchgrass at her feet with her tears.

"Now, wait a minute." Marilee suddenly threw back her sagging shoulders and squared her jaw. "What would Grandma Jo think if she could see us right now, sniveling like a bunch of babies? 'A woman wants something in this life, she's gotta go after it.' That's what she told us this morning, and that's what we oughta be doing. The man said he ain't leaving till first light. We've still got time to try to figure out some way to bring them together."

"But how?" Lily implored.

"I don't know . . . *yet*. But I do know I'm not a quitter. God gave me a brain, and I'm gonna put it to work. I suggest the rest of you sit yourselves down and do the same."

Two

"Ladies," Samuel Carrigan tipped his hat as he came abreast a wagon filled with supplies and the Singleton sisters stopped beneath a spruce tree a mile out of town. They made a charming picture perched in their wagon, the early morning sun reflecting off the highlights in their dark hair and coloring their complexions a pleasant rosy gold. They appeared to be traveling in the same direction as he was, and the thought of asking permission to keep the ingenuous, young ladies company for whatever distance their routes parallelled suited his fine mood. His smile broadened. "You're up bright and early this morning."

"Mr. Carrigan, we didn't figure we'd see you before you left," Marilee returned his greeting, her bright smile echoing his. "And here you come riding along just when we're in need of a man."

Sam's gregarious mien turned to one of concern. "Are you having some sort of trouble?"

"Our back wheel has come loose," Lily announced with a sigh. "We were just sitting here arguing over which one of us oughta walk back to town to fetch some help, and now, if you're willing, we can have you lend us a strong arm, and we can be on our way without the bother."

"I'd be honored to help if I can," Sam assured them as he dismounted.

"Of course, we'll want to repay you for your trouble. We

Singletons don't cotton to charity. You come home with us and let us fill your belly with a hot, hearty meal and we'll call it even," Janie said. Her sisters enthusiastically nodded in agreement.

"Ladies, your persistence is flattering, but I'm afraid I must continue to decline your generous offer to feed me. My time is limited and . . ."

"You don't gotta waste your breath explaining yourself," Marilee interrupted. "Janie just thought we oughta give you another chance in case you had a change of heart during the night and were too polite to say something yourself."

"No, I haven't changed my mind." Sam shook his head. "Now, which wheel is it?"

"The one in back, on the right," Fern replied as they all piled out of the wagon. Lily took the reins from his hands and held his horse while the others gathered round the wheel.

Sam leaned over the axle, studying the spot where the wheel connected. "Are you sure this is the wheel? I can't find anything wro—"

Everything went black as a burlap sack was yanked over his head and tied tight. Simultaneously, he felt a rope coil around his ankles.

"What the . . ." Sam struggled against the aggregation of lace-cuffed arms binding his, grunting in pain as a sharp heel stomped down hard on his instep.

"Ladies! What has gotten into you? I've no desire to hurt you but . . ."

"Get his gun." A voice he recognized as belonging to Marilee shouted. Instantly, he reached for his firearm, but his hand came up empty.

Utter surprise at the ambush and a lifetime of training always to behave as a gentleman had tempered his initial reaction, but now Sam began to fight in earnest. Now, he understood the purpose behind their friendly banter yesterday.

They weren't being friendly at all. They had been staking him out. All last night he had had the vague feeling someone was watching his every move, but he had told himself mental and physical fatigue must be causing him to imagine things.

He had blithely fallen prey to a band of female outlaws. He was as furious with himself for his stupidity as he was with them for their treachery. Chances were they just wanted to rob him and would send him on his way, but he'd misjudged them before and thoughts he might become a victim of murder also entered his mind. He twisted his right arm free, grabbed a waist, and threw off one of his attackers. Whatever these women had in mind, Samuel Carrigan wasn't cooperating.

"Damn! He's stronger than he looks." It was Marilee's voice again. She seemed to be the ringleader.

"Janie!" she shouted.

"I can't!"

"Yes, you can!"

"Mr. Carrigan," Janie wailed in a high-pitched voice. "Please, don't make me do this."

Sam blindly grabbed one wrist and another elbow, flinging them away. With a mighty lunge he managed to escape the other hands binding him, but before he could take a step, the rope around his ankles caused him to trip and hit the dirt with a thud. Jerking at the rope, he freed his ankles and struggled to his feet but was instantly knocked down to the ground again and engulfed in a sea of skirts. Shoving off his assailants, he fought his way back to his feet.

"Janie!"

"Stop being such a coward!"

"He's gonna get away!"

Sam's hands worked furiously at the knot securing the sack over his head as he broke into a sightless run. This knot was more stubborn than the other, and it refused to budge. The sounds of panting women and thrashing petticoats were right at his heels. His left foot hit a stone. Sam cursed as he flew through the air, his epitaphs becoming stronger when his body made impact with the hard ground.

Before he could regain his footing, they were on him again.

"Get off of me, you . . ."

A searing pain shot through the side of his head; then, he felt nothing at all.

Sam blinked at the sun as he gradually regained consciousness. A wagon wheel plunged into a rut and bounced out again, causing his aching head to thump against a sack of flour.

A bead of perspiration began to form on his brow and his heart beat at an accelerated pace as he tried to reconcile his present surroundings. The last thing he remembered was . . . Memory flooded back and with it a surge of outrage so intense it made him tremble.

There they were—the four of them—sitting side by side on the wagon bench. His head whacked against the flour sack again, and he bit back the urge to groan. He didn't want them to know he was awake, at least not until he knew what they were up to.

Sam lay perfectly still, watching them from beneath hooded eyes, taking stock of his situation.

He was trussed up like a chicken, but he could be thankful for the fact they had seen fit to remove the sack from his head. Testing the knots binding his hands behind his back and the second set shackling his ankles, Sam discovered them to be tied far more efficiently than his initial bindings. He was disappointed but didn't give up hope of securing his own release. It might be a long, slow process, but he believed he could eventually pick the knots loose as long as he didn't panic.

The absence of his eyeglasses caused him considerably more consternation. They had probably been broken or lost in the battle, he glumly concluded. Though he could see his immediate surroundings quite clearly, identifying anything in the distance presented a challenge. A man traveling in the wilderness needed sharp eyes. He would have to buy a new pair before he continued on his journey, and he doubted that would be an easy feat.

Sam continued to survey his person and position.

Other than his head, he had sustained no injuries. His horse was tied to the back of the wagon, and they were traveling in the opposite direction he had started out this morning. It occurred to him, during their conversation the day before, one of the sisters—he couldn't remember which—had mentioned their ranch lay southeast of town. It was the direction they now traveled. Why hadn't he recalled that particular bit of information earlier today when he had come upon them in their wagon northwest of town? It should have alerted him all was not as it seemed.

He was in the process of trying to determine the time of day from the height of the sun when two of them began to speak. Sam gave their conversation his full attention.

"I wish he'd wake up. He's been out for a good thirty minutes. What if I killed him?" Janie whimpered.

"You can't have killed him; he's still breathing. Besides, you barely tapped him. He'll wake up when he's good and ready to," Marilee reassured her.

"He's gonna be awfully angry when be does."

"I suspect he will be, but he'll calm down once he sees we have his best interests at heart."

"I still think this is a terrible idea," Janie maintained. "Kidnapping is a hanging offense."

So, they were kidnapping him. Having what he already knew to be happening to him confirmed rankled Sam afresh, and he was forced to clench his teeth to hold back a flurry of furious words. Sternly advising himself that a level head would serve him far better than an emotional outburst, Sam continued to intently follow their conversation.

"Rex ain't gonna hang any of us," Marilee soothed her nervous sister. "The worst he'd do is give us a scolding and throw us in jail for a month or two. . . . And that's only if we get caught, which ain't gonna happen. Not a soul saw us grab him. Besides, I didn't hear you offering up a better plan."

"We asked a powerful lot of questions in town last night when we were trying to figure which way he'd be heading out this morning so we could set our trap. What if someone gets suspicious?" Janie persisted to worry aloud.

"About what?"

"Him disappearing."

Marilee chuckled and patted Janie on the back. "Ain't nobody in Heaven gonna figure he disappeared. As far as they know, he headed out of town just like he planned and is on his way to wherever it was he was going."

Janie's silence indicated she was taking time to think about her sister's words. When she spoke again, she sounded greatly relieved. "I guess you're right."

"Of course, I am," Marilee confidently proclaimed.

They ceased to speak, and Sam used the time to ponder what they'd said. It wasn't a pleasant task. First, Marilee Singleton *was* right. Not a soul in Heaven would suspect he was a victim of foul play. Worse, his newly discovered family had no idea he even existed, so they certainly wouldn't be concerned when he didn't arrive on time. He'd sat down more than a dozen times to compose a letter introducing himself in advance of his arrival on their doorstep, but he'd never been able to find the right words. His business associates didn't expect him back for another two months. And if those thoughts weren't disconcerting enough, there was the mystery of *why* these women had kidnapped him in the first place. Miss Singleton's assertion they "had his best interests at heart" was more confusing than consoling.

Janie began to speak again, and he abandoned his thoughts, carefully listening as he picked at his knots. Her voice crackled with tension. "Marilee, you're forgetting about Grandma Jo. She'll know what we've done."

"No, I ain't forgot Grandma Jo, Miss Fretful," Marilee replied. "She might be a problem. Then again, she might not. She's the one told us a woman wants something in this life, she's gotta go after, ain't she? All we did was take her advice."

"I know what she said. I was standing right there. You don't have to keep quoting her at me every time I don't agree with your way of thinking one hundred percent. I got my own head atop my shoulders, and it don't reckon with any amount of confidence this is exactly what Grandma Jo had in mind."

"Then, why didn't you say something last night?" Marilee asked impatiently.

"I did," Janie protested. "As you'll recall, I was out voted."

"I for one don't see any sense in us fretting about it until we have to face her," Fern stated. "If she makes us put him back, we won't be any worse off than we were yesterday. And if she lets us keep him . . ."

"Do you reckon Ella will be pleased?" Lily chimed in.

"Well, we're bringing her exactly what she says she wants. I don't see how she could help but be happy about it. I reckon the moment she lays eyes on Mr. Carrigan, she'll fall head over heels in love. The man ain't ugly, and he talks even smarter than she does," Fern answered her.

"Do you reckon *he'll* fall in love with *her?*" Janie meekly inquired of her more self-possessed sisters.

"Why shouldn't he? He said he was looking for a wife. I'm not saying Ella ain't got her faults, but there's no reason she shouldn't suit him just fine," Marilee replied. "Now, quit your fussing. It's giving me a headache. We went over all of this at least a hundred times last night before coming to our decision to bring him home to Ella by whatever means was necessary. It's too late to be changing our minds now."

Good Lord, Sam muttered in his head. If he had spent all day speculating, never in his wildest imaginings would he have come up with so preposterous a reason for his abduction. They really thought they could tie him up like a package and make a present of him to their sister? Even having heard it with his own ears, he found it difficult to believe.

He supposed he should feel grateful the Singleton sisters planned no heinous crimes against his person, but the indignity of lying tied up in the back of this wagon, being fetched home from town like a prize rooster precluded any feelings of gratitude. Still, their bizarre revelation did have the positive effect of vanquishing all fear of his captors. There was a good deal of relief in knowing what he was dealing with was a wagon load of crackbrained romantics not a gang of hard-hearted criminals.

His thoughts turned to this Ella person. His bride-to-be, he perversely added the title because doing so fit the pixilated mood of his present circumstances. What was wrong with the woman, no other man would have her? The answer that immediately sprang to mind was that she was probably as deranged as her siblings, maybe even more so, *if that was possible.*

Well, he wasn't going to just lie here like a lamb, docilely waiting for them to serve him up on some matrimonial platter. He had better things to do with his time than humor this bunch of loonies.

"I am not going to marry your sister Ella, so you may as well untie me and let me go now," he stated tersely as he used his feet and elbows to wriggle himself up to a sitting position.

"What'd I tell you," Marilee announced triumphantly. "I knew he'd wake up, and he doesn't appear to be any worse for the bump on his head."

There was a flurry of activity on the wagon seat as Janie, Fern, and Lily turned backwards to face him. They propped themselves on their knees. Marilee remained facing forward, her hands firmly on the reins, guiding the wagon homeward at a steady pace.

"Good morning, Mr. Carrigan. I hope you're comfortable. I made a pillow of the flour sack," Fern greeted him with a sunny smile.

"No, I am not comfortable. I demand you ladies release me at once," Sam commanded in his most authoritative voice.

"I wish we could, but . . ." Lily shrugged. "It would've been so much simpler if you'd have accepted our invitation to supper."

"Why? So you could have knocked me out and trussed me up in the comfort of your own home?"

"What a silly thing to say. If you'd have come of your own accord, there'd have been no need to wrestle you to the ground like a balky steer and keep you tied up. We could've walked you through the door and introduced you proper like," Lily exclaimed.

"My mistake," Sam rejoined.

"Don't take all your anger out on Lily. I'm the one who hit you," Janie confessed, blushing with shame. "I didn't want to, but they made me do it. I hope you won't hold it too much against me."

"The thought never crossed my mind," he drawled. The dull pounding in his head augmented his ire, causing his tone to become progressively sarcastic with each word. "Why back in New York getting whacked along the side of the head by women is my favorite pastime. We have parties on the lawn every Sunday afternoon where the gents line up and the ladies whack away." He impaled her with his impatient glare, his voice lowering to a menacing pitch. "Yes, I plan on holding it against you. That and a whole lot more if you ladies do not stop this wagon at once and release me!"

"But if we release you, you'll never meet Ella. And if you don't meet her, you can't marry her. And if you don't marry her, we're all gonna die spinsters," Lily protested.

Sam shook his head. He immediately regretted the ill-advised motion and squeezed his eyes shut against the pain. "What?"

"Grandma Jo won't let us marry until Ella does, and Frank is getting tired of waiting for me," Fern offered by way of explanation.

"Your grandmother is standing between you and your beaus, so you decided to solve your problem by abducting me so I could marry your sister Ella, thus eliminating the impediment between you and your own matrimonial designs?" he slowly outlined their mode of reasoning to be certain he clearly understood what she had said.

"Yes. I reckon that's what we've done," Fern agreed. "Only I'm not sure 'cause I didn't understand some of those fancy words you used. But don't worry. Ella will understand you. She's read enough books, I suspect she knows just about every word there is."

"You want me to marry Ella, so you can get married yourselves," Sam restated the essentials.

"You got it," Marilee cheerfully confirmed.

Sam didn't know whether to laugh or curse. He resisted both temptations and instead mustered his composure and said, "Let me say it plainly for you once again: I am *not* going to marry your sister."

"Why not? You'd be perfect for each other," Fern argued.

"I don't want to marry her."

"But how do you know?" Lily contended. "You've never even met her."

Patience, Sam schooled himself as he fought off another urge to curse. He tried to smile benevolently as one might do when explaining to a group of mischievous children the error in their thinking, but was forced to settle for a tight-lipped grin and a muted voice. "Be sensible, ladies. You've hit me over the head, trussed me up, and are in the process of spiriting me against my will across the countryside. What on earth would make you think I would even consider marrying into your family?"

"A man needs a woman. Grandma Jo says you can't get by without us. Females are scarce in these parts, and you don't look like the kinda man who would ignore a fine opportunity," Marilee listed her reasons.

Sam couldn't recall ever engaging in so asinine a conversation, and his expression accurately mirrored his feelings. "If your sister Ella is such a *fine* opportunity, why hasn't some other man snatched her up?"

"She's particular."

Peculiar is probably more like it, Sam murmured to himself.

"Anyhow," Marilee continued when she didn't hear his response. "You shouldn't hold it against her. I'm sure she won't break *your* heart. Wouldn't be doing this to you if I thought she'd hurt your feelings. I hope you believe that."

There was little he wouldn't believe at this rather unique moment in his life, Sam thought, but how could she conceive he was sitting here worrying this Ella might break his heart? It was a leap of logic he found impossible to follow. The last thing on earth he wanted was for Ella to like him. He was *praying* she would take one look at him and run screaming with revulsion into the hills, dragging her misguided siblings with her.

His previously high opinion of the female of his species

was undergoing a rapid and radical revision. First, he learned his mother had spent a lifetime harboring a deep, dark secret about his past. Now, these women were trying to dictate his future. It was too much for one man to bear.

Sam shifted his spine in a futile attempt to gain a more dignified position among the sacks, barrels, and paper-wrapped packages. Tempting as it was to sit and wallow in self-pity, he refused to be conquered so easily.

To his way of thinking, he had three promising avenues of escape besides the most obvious one of untying himself and riding as far away from these women as he could get with the single-mindedness of a rabbit with a pack of rabid dogs at his heels. He could nurture Miss Janie's misgivings and persuade her to insist the others let him go. He could hope their grandmother had more sense than they did and instructed them to release him. He could hope Ella didn't think him such a fine catch as her sisters and send him merrily on his way.

He placed the bulk of his faith on the first two possibilities. He'd yet to meet Ella, but it seemed foolish to depend on her to be any more reasonable than her sisters.

Sam had no doubt he would escape the clutches of these marriage-minded females eventually. Logic and the law were on his side. He just preferred it to be sooner than later. To that end, he considered and discarded several courses of action before settling on the one he deemed most efficient.

Earlier he had failed to mention Clara. Partly because his private affairs were nobody's business but his own and partly because he hated to bring her into this mess even if she was safe in her parents' home two thousand miles away. Now, necessity overrode reticence.

His initial inclination was to play his trump card immediately, but Sam decided the unpredictable nature of his protagonists dictated a more cautious course.

It had long been his experience that a disarming smile and

a quiet voice were far more effective than pounding his fist on his desk and shouting when negotiating with temperamental business associates. He called on that experience now, pushing his true feelings far below the surface.

"How much longer until we reach your ranch?" he asked with an air of polite resignation.

"Hours yet," Lily replied.

"How many hours?" Sam courteously requested.

"Four or five, depending on how tired ol' Alexander gets pulling this load," Marilee answered over her shoulder.

Four or five hours, Sam calculated the time in his head. If he couldn't escape these ropes or convince them to let him go en route to the ranch, he was going to lose a minimum of another full day's traveling time. Luckily, he was confident his present plan could not help but succeed to win his freedom.

"Alexander. What an interesting name for a horse," he commented conversationally. A brief digression would keep them off guard and cooperative, allowing him to systematically work himself into the best possible position.

"That's Ella's doing," Fern informed him. "She insists on naming all our animals after characters she reads about in her books. Personally, I think it makes us look odd to our neighbors, but Grandma Jo says there's no harm in it."

"Do you think it makes us look odd?" Lily queried, her youthful face evincing she sincerely valued his opinion on the matter.

"I'm sure your sister's habit does not unduly damage your social standing with your neighbors," Sam reassured her, to himself adding any of their neighbors with a modicum of sense were most certainly giving this family wide berth for reasons that had nothing to do with the names of their livestock.

"Well, I still think Alexander the Great is an ignorant name for a horse that couldn't get more ordinary if he tried, but I'm sure Ella will appreciate your sentiments and that's what counts, ain't it?" Fern said.

"Yep," Marilee agreed.

"You ladies certainly have chosen a beautiful part of the country to call home," Sam eased into his next subject. "It's a pity I can't see more of it." He cleared his throat when they did not take the hint. "Might I trouble one of you to tell me what happened to my eyeglasses?"

"Oh, how horribly neglectful of us. I'm so sorry," Janie exclaimed. "I'd forgotten all about them. I have them right here in my reticule." She pulled them from a black, beaded bag and held them up for him to see. Retrieving a handkerchief, she carefully polished the lenses before leaning over the back of the wagon seat and slipping them onto his nose.

The world immediately took on a sharper edge, and Sam smiled in genuine gratitude. "Thank you, Miss Janie," he took the liberty of addressing her by her Christian name because to do otherwise would elicit nothing but confusion with so many Miss Singletons present. "It was very kind of you to look after them for me."

She blushed at the compliment.

Sam broached his next topic with an equally cordial air. The knots he had been stealthily working on since the moment he had regained consciousness hadn't loosened a hair's breadth. If anything they'd gotten tighter. He judged now as good a time as any to play his card on the table. "Your beau is named Rex, is he not?"

Janie nodded.

"Rex is a very lucky man to have found himself such a remarkable woman."

"Thank you for saying so, but I'm the lucky one to have such a fine man wanting to marry me."

Sam met her gaze, his eyes wide with feigned affinity. "I feel the same way about my fiancée."

"What!" all four sisters cried in unison as Marilee reined the wagon to an abrupt halt.

"I said I am a lucky man to have a fiancée with as many fine qualities as Miss Clara Harrington."

"You mean to say when you told me you hoped to settle down and marry soon you already had somebody specific in mind? Why didn't you say so?" Fern wailed.

"Believe me, if I'd have known you ladies planned to abduct me, I would have, despite the fact it is not my habit to discuss my private affairs with total strangers as some people are wont to do."

"I knew this was a terrible idea," Janie repeated in mournful tones over and over.

Lily began to cry.

Fern stared daggers at him while she murmured curse words under her breath.

Marilee bore their melancholy chorus for several minutes before commanding, "Hush, the lot of you. I gotta do some thinking."

Her sisters fell silent, except for the occasional snivel.

Sam was not so obliging. "There is nothing to think about. You have no choice but to release me. I can hardly marry your sister when I am already engaged to Clara, now can I?"

"How do we know you ain't making this Clara up?" Marilee demanded.

"If you will reach into my left vest pocket, you'll find a miniature of her image."

"Fern, check his pocket," Marilee directed.

Fern did as she was told. She stared forlornly at the tiny, silver-framed oil painting she retrieved from his pocket a long moment before passing it to her sisters.

"She's very beautiful," Janie commented between sniffles.

Lily chewed her bottom lip and looked ready to burst into another flood of tears.

When it came her turn, Marilee gave the portrait a quick glance, then gave it back to Fern's keeping. She sat still as a stone, staring off into the distance.

"Ladies, you have no choice but to let me go," Sam firmly repeated his earlier assertion. He smiled confidently, readying himself to be released.

Flicking the reins in her hands, Marilee set the wagon back in motion.

"What do you think you're doing?" Sam shouted.

"I'm taking you home to Ella."

"Haven't you been listening to anything I've been saying? I couldn't marry your sister even if I wanted to do so! I am already committed to another woman. It is pointless to take me to your ranch!"

"He's right, Marilee." Janie put her hand on her sister's arm. "How can we expect him to marry Ella if he's in love with Clara?"

"He'll just have to fall out of love with her."

"I don't believe that's a nice thing to ask him to do. After all, this Clara has feelings too. It wouldn't be right for us to steal him away from another woman no matter how desperate we are."

"I don't give a squirrel's butt about this *Clara*. She wanted to hold onto him, she oughta have kept him back in New York with her or come with him on his travels. I say, he ain't married to her yet, so he's fair game," Marilee stated defiantly.

"I'm siding with Marilee," Fern announced.

"You always side with Marilee," Janie complained. "Lily, what do you reckon we oughta do?"

Lily hesitated, looking from their prisoner to her sisters and back again. "I reckon we should keep him and let Grandma Jo decide. That way we'll be sure we're doing the right thing."

"That settles it, all democratic like," Marilee declared. "May as well make yourself comfortable, Mr. Carrigan. Looks like you're gonna be keeping us company a might longer."

Three

Wearing a weary yet satisfied smile, Ella Singleton trudged across the field toward the house. She'd been awakened at three in the morning by the sound of Electra bawling and had been with her ever since. Electra had finally had her calf an hour ago. The birth hadn't gone smoothly and she had had to intervene, but thankfully both cow and calf were now doing well. The family would again have a bountiful supply of milk with which to make cheese and butter.

Ella brushed a lock of hair from her eyes with her forearm and glanced at the sun. She quickened her steps. If she hurried, she would have plenty of time to change her clothes and take a bath before dinner. She knew she could depend on Grandma Jo to have a hot meal waiting for her at the noon hour. Cooking was Ella's chore, and one she usually enjoyed, but she was too exhausted today and Grandma Jo would know it. In their family, when someone saw a need, they pitched in without prodding.

Their ranch wasn't a large one, but the six Singleton women had run it successfully for five years without any charity from their neighbors. She was proud of her family.

There was no denying they had their disagreements, but they worked and played together better than most. Love and loyalty abounded. It was a good life she led.

The rattle of wagon wheels caught her attention, and Ella squinted her eyes against the sun. Though they were still some distance away, she immediately recognized Alexander, the wagon, and her sisters. What were they doing home this early in the day, she wondered, her brow puckering with mild concern? She hadn't expected them home till dusk.

Hound Dog stirred himself from his furrow beneath the porch and set to braying as he loped toward the wagon, wagging his crooked tail in greeting. A moment later, Grandma Jo stepped onto the porch.

"I wonder what brings our girls home so early? Most times they gotta be dragged away from a visit to town," Grandma Jo commented when Ella reached the porch.

"I was just wondering the same thing myself," she replied. "Hope no one has taken sick."

Grandma Jo shaded her eyes with her hand. "They all look fit from here."

Ella and Grandma Jo stood side by side and were further perplexed when the wagon came to a halt two hundred yards from the house. Lily climbed down, lifted her skirts and sprinted toward them.

When she reached the yard, she had to pause to catch her breath before she could speak. Her expression became pained as she took in Ella's dishevelled appearance.

"What on earth are you doing dashing across our fields like an antelope?" Grandma Jo greeted when she judged Lily had had time to recover enough to answer her. "And why is our wagon yonder instead of here?"

Lily smoothed her skirt with her hands, gulped in two more panting breaths, and stiffened her spine. "We brought a surprise home for Ella."

"What kind of surprise?" Ella asked, her drowsy eyes brightening.

Lily plowed the dirt with the toe of her boots and worried the fabric of her skirt with her fingers. She met Ella's gaze directly, then lowered her eyes. "I ain't gonna say just yet."

Ella pursed her lips into a mock pout, but the gesture was lost on Lily who continued to show more interest in rearranging the dirt at her feet than Ella's reaction. When she tired of that occupation, she began to rock her weight from heel to toe and play with a wisp of hair at the nape of her neck.

"Why are you acting so fidgety, Lily?" Grandma Jo demanded.

Ignoring the question, Lily raised her head and spoke to Ella. "Now, we want you to keep your eyes shut and your mind open. We've gone to a lot of trouble on your account. You may be a little taken aback at first, but we don't want you jumping to any hasty conclusions."

"You've got me on pins and needles speculating what sort of surprise you could possibly have in the wagon for me. How long are you going to make me wait to find out what it is?"

"Promise you'll keep an open mind?" Lily insisted.

Ella grinned. "I promise."

"Grandma Jo, we're hoping you'll do the same thing. It's kinda unconventional what we've done."

"Young lady, I always keep an open mind." Grandma Jo shook her finger at her, her pretense at affront spoiled by the twinkle in her eye.

"Then, I guess the wagon can come on in." Lily turned her back on them and waved her arm over her head.

Ella clasped her hands behind her back and stood on tiptoe, straining for a glimpse of her surprise as the wagon rolled toward them. Maybe they were bringing home some newfangled invention for her kitchen. Marilee had a weakness for anything modern. Whatever it was—no matter how foolish—Ella was determined to show the proper gratitude. It was sweet of them to think to bring her anything at all, especially when they had been so vexed when they left. Ella lifted herself on her toes a little higher. Lily had her curiosity so piqued, it was difficult not to run out and meet the wagon halfway.

"It's time to close your eyes now and *keep* them closed till

I tell you you can open them," Lily directed as the wagon drew near.

Reluctantly, Ella obeyed.

She heard the wagon grind to a halt before them. There was quite a commotion, as if they were having trouble wresting her surprise from the wagon; then, Grandma Jo's throaty voice resounded in her ears. "Hellfire and damnation! What have you girls gone and done?"

"I'm opening my eyes," Ella announced.

"Don't do it," Grandma Jo admonished in a queer tone of voice.

It took all of Ella's willpower to keep her eyes squeezed tightly shut. There were more sounds—feet shuffling in the dirt, a nervous cough, a muffled growl . . .

"Okay, you can open your eyes," Lily instructed, not a moment too soon.

Ella snapped her eyes open, then blinked hard several times before she could convince her mind her eyes weren't playing tricks on her. Standing before her was a man. A gentleman to be more precise, if one judged him by his clothing. He was bound hand and foot, gagged . . . and he wore the most furious expression she had ever seen on the face of another human being.

He stared at her as she stared at him, his jaw working at the rag in the mouth. Her jaw hung slack.

"Well, what do you think?" Marilee asked, a broad smile splitting her face.

Ella swallowed three times before she could find her voice. "I think you better start explaining yourselves this very instant, because if you've done what it looks like you've done . . ."

"We've brought you home a cultured man, just the kinda fella you've been hankering after all these years," Fern informed her. "We found him sitting under a tree on the outskirts of Heaven. When he refused our invitation to supper, we took him by force."

"Oh, my God!" Ella blanched on hearing her worst fears confirmed. For a second she felt as if she might faint; then, her heart began to gallop and the blood came rushing back into her head. Her wide eyes slowly gravitated back to the gentleman standing in their yard. He was trying to inch away from Hound Dog, who crouched at his feet—ears laid back and teeth bared—drooling on his polished leather riding boots. "I'm so sorry, whoever you are," she mumbled. "Truly, I am. I want you to know I had nothing to do with this outrageous behavior. I would have stopped them if I had known . . ." Her voice rose in pitch. "Grandma Jo, do something!"

"What is it you want me to do?"

Ella turned to her grandmother, disbelieving of the amusement she heard in her voice. The old woman was grinning like a raccoon in a corn barrel.

"For mercy sake, call off Hound Dog and make them untie him at once!" Ella demanded, the heat in her already burning cheeks rising several more degrees.

Shaking with laughter, the older woman cocked her head to one side. "I don't know. He might be dangerous."

"Grandma Jo! This isn't funny! It's humiliating! To think my own sisters would stoop so low! You're horrible! All of you! I'm ashamed to claim you as kin!"

"Ella, you're screeching. It ain't ladylike. What will your gentleman caller think?"

Ella strangled on her own words as she tried to give an answer.

"Oh, settle down," Grandma Jo chided. "I'll admit your sisters may have been a bit overzealous in their desire to find you a husband, but they ain't caused no one any real harm. It's been a long time since we've had any excitement around here, and I intend to enjoy it to the fullest. I can't believe you're so blind you can't see the humor in this situation and allow an old woman a little sport." She turned from Ella to face her other granddaughters. "Now, which one of you thought up this harebrained scheme?"

"I did, ma'am," Marilee confessed.

"And the rest of you went along with it?"

They nodded.

"Why?"

" 'Cause you said if a woman wants something, she's gotta go after it, and we wanted Mr. Carrigan for Ella," Lily proclaimed.

"Hellfire and damnation," Grandma Jo repeated, holding her sides as hoots of glee bubbled up from her belly. "You girls sure took me literal, didn't you? I'd never have guessed you had it in you."

"Then, you're not mad at us for doing what we done?" Janie diffidently queried.

"I oughta be, oughtn't I? I oughta take the lot of you behind the barn and tan your backsides. But I ain't gonna do what I oughta 'cause whether right or wrong I'm proud as can be to see you girls showing a little spirit for a change."

"Grandma Jo, surely you don't approve of what they've done!" Ella cried.

"Didn't say I approved. I just said I wasn't inclined to beat them for it."

"But . . ."

"But nothing. There's a greater sin being committed here. It's high time we stop ignoring our company. Mr. Carrigan, is it?" Grandma Jo addressed him as she shifted her full attention to their unwilling guest. "Mr. Carrigan, I can see you're feeling as irate as a wounded bear, and you've every right to your feelings. A man oughta be able to walk down the street without worrying about being waylaid by a bunch of lovesick females. I'd like to have Marilee remove that rag from your mouth so we can sort this out together, but you gotta promise me you won't try anything rash, 'cause if Hound Dog thinks you mean to hurt her, he'll eat you alive before I can call him off."

Her words were a lie and Ella knew it. Grandma Jo could call Hound Dog off with a snap of her fingers. She started to say so, but Mr. Carrigan was already nodding his head in agreement, and considering his thundercloud expression, she decided it might be wise to keep him ignorant until she was sure it was safe to do otherwise. She was infuriated with her sisters, and might take great joy in pummeling them with her own fists, but she could never allow them to come to harm at the hands of a stranger, even if she judged him completely justified in wreaking a little revenge.

Marilee removed the gag, then stuffed the cloth in her pocket. Grandma Jo stepped forward, shooing her out of the way. The man stood mute as the older woman boldly assessed him from head to toe.

Though her heart was still pounding in her throat and her limbs hung numbly at her side, Ella was able to muster enough presence of mind to really *see* the man her sisters had brought her for the first time.

Though she could fault them with so many sins it would take her a month of Sundays to recite them all, she certainly couldn't fault their taste. Mr. Carrigan's person was as attractive as his clothing. He was nearly six feet tall, with strong shoulders and lean hips. He didn't appear particularly muscular, but if there was an ounce of extra fat on him, she couldn't see it. His face was extremely pleasing to look upon, with its fine bones and trim mustache. His eyes were the color of harebell, large, and fringed with thick dark lashes. The eyeglasses he wore, rather than detract from his superior features, lent them a distinguished air.

"Stop staring at me as though I were a prize horse at the

county fair," Mr. Carrigan demanded, his deep voice rumbling with righteous indignation.

Ella jumped, feeling the beat of a guilty blush stain her already flaming cheeks. She started to apologize for her rude behavior, then realized he was speaking to Grandma Jo not her.

Relief washed over her, lessening her degree of discomfort by a little. The last thing she wanted Mr. Carrigan to think was that *she* countenanced her sisters' scheme. The rest of her family might have abandoned their senses, but she had not.

"If you don't like being stared at, you ought not to have grown up to be so handsome," Grandma Jo's retort halted Ella's brooding. "Fact is, you ever wipe that scowl off your face and replace it with a smile, your face could set even an old woman's heart to fluttering. But I suspect you'd rather discuss your good looks some other time. My name is Josephine Singleton." She instinctively reached out her weathered hand to shake his before remembering his shackles and dropping her hand back to her side. "You can just call me Grandma Jo. Everybody else in the territory does."

"I wish I could say I was pleased to meet you, *Mrs. Singleton,* but I am not."

Grandma Jo ignored his comment. "Well, ain't you gonna tell me your full name?"

"Samuel Carrigan. You may call me Mr. Carrigan," he tersely replied.

"Sam, is it? It suits you."

Ella stood mute as she listened to the exchange. She shifted her stance from one foot to the other, wiping her soiled hands on her pant legs. Although by her reckoning, releasing Mr. Carrigan without delay and sending him on his way amidst a chorus of fervent apologies seemed the only proper thing to do, Grandma Jo clearly had some other course in mind to resolve this crisis, and for the moment she was feeling too rattled to challenge her.

"Well now, Sam, why don't you tell me in your own words how you met up with my granddaughters."

Ella watched the muscles of his jaw constrict. His nostrils flared as he snorted out a breath. "I was sitting under a tree, minding my own business, when they started stopping by one at a time, accosting me with a plethora of questions. Eventually, they began to hound me with invitations to supper. I politely refused."

"And? What happened next?" Grandma Jo prompted.

"I thought I'd seen the last of them. Then, this morning, as I was leaving town, I came upon them on the road. They lied to me, telling me their wagon wheel needed repair. Being a gentleman, I dismounted from my horse and tried to assist them. That's when they jumped me. There was a struggle during which they stole my gun and I was knocked unconscious by some heavy object."

"I hit him with a skillet," Janie supplied the missing information.

"Janie!" Ella shrieked. "How could you? I would have thought you of all people . . ."

"The others made me," Janie protested. "Surely, you don't think I wanted . . ."

Grandma Jo threw a quelling glance over her shoulder. "Stop interrupting our guest," she scolded both of them. Returning her attention to Mr. Carrigan, she lifted the hair from his brow and began to examine the lump on the side of his head.

His expression darkened and he tried to pull away, but Hound Dog discouraged his retreat with a series of threatening growls. "Where's your horse?" she casually questioned as she continued to scrutinize the black and blue swelling.

"They hobbled him near a tree over the rise, out of sight of the house."

"I see." She smoothed his hair back in place and took a half step back. "I've got something in the house that will help take the hurt out of that lump," she reassured him. "Now, let's get back to the telling of your side of this story."

"There isn't much more to tell. When I woke up, I was in the back of a wagon and bound. Your granddaughters informed me they were taking me home to marry their sister. I repeatedly tried to convince them of the futility of their plan, but they refused to listen to reason. Miss Marilee had me gagged when I declined to remain silent on the subject."

"Well, that's quite a tale. You girls want to argue with anything he said?"

"No, he's telling the truth," Marilee affirmed. The others nodded in agreement.

"But even the worst of what we done wasn't as ugly as he makes it sound," Fern emphatically amended. "We treated him as nice as we possibly could under the circumstances, and none of it would've had to happen at all if he hadn't been so stubborn about accepting our invitation to supper. It also would've been real helpful if he'd have told us about having a fiancée a little earlier in our acquaintance."

Ella covered her face with her hands. With every new detail she learned, the more mortified she became. Even calling upon her most potent powers of imagination, she couldn't conceive how her sisters could have ever believed their scandalous scheme might work.

"Do you have a fiancée, Sam?" Grandma Jo's steady voice broke into Ella's grievous musings.

"Yes," he brusquely replied. "So as you can see, even if I was inclined to marry your granddaughter, *which I most assuredly am not,* I am not available. Now, if you would be so kind as to untie me, I will be on my way."

The vehemence with which he rejected the notion of marrying her caused Ella to shrink even further into her skin, but despite a sincere wish to be swallowed up by the earth, morbid curiosity compelled her to raise her head and slowly spread her fingers.

Grandma Jo looked less than happy, but she hadn't lost a whit of what Ella judged to be her maddeningly calm composure. "What is this fiancée's name?"

Mr. Carrigan's eyes narrowed and he stood silent, clearly contemplating whether or not he would answer. When he did, his voice seethed with repressed frustration. "Miss Clara Harrington."

"How long have you known each other?"

"Since we were children."

"Is it a love match or are you wedding each other merely 'cause it's comfortable to be doing so?"

"I don't see how that's any of your concern!" Losing the battle to control his temper, the statement exploded out of Mr. Carrigan's mouth. Ella didn't fault him. Rather, she admired him for being able to hold his wrath at bay for as long as he had.

She cringed at her grandmother's next words.

"So, you're not head over heels in love with your Clara. I didn't reckon you were. You don't have the look of a man in love."

"How dare you presume to know my heart," he sputtered.

"A body dares a lot of things when she's lived as many years as I have. But let's not talk about me. I'm far more interested in you." Josephine Singleton blithely ignored his display of temper. "What brings you to these parts?"

"That is no more your concern than how I feel about my fiancée!"

"True, but I'd like to know just the same."

"Well, I'm not going to tell you!"

"Good for you," Grandma Jo chortled. "Never could abide a man who gabs his business to everyone he meets. Shows lack of discretion. You can tell me later, after we've had a chance to become better acquainted."

"I have no intention of becoming better acquainted! I demand to be released at once so I may be on my way! If you will be sensible, I promise I will not press charges against your granddaughters. However, if you hesitate to do your duty, you will leave me no other choice but to call the full weight of the law upon their heads."

"That's gonna be mighty hard to do here in the middle of nowhere. But never you mind. Your threats don't worry me, young man, so you might as well save your breath. I'll admit if I was wearing your boots, I might be tempted to do a little fussing and fuming myself, but there really ain't any need for it. My girls have put you through a lot of trouble, and all I want to do is make up for a little of it. As long as you're here, you may as well let us fill your belly. I've got a pot of stew simmering on the stove and can whip up a batch of biscuits so fast it'll make your handsome head spin."

"If I agree to share a meal with your family, you will let me go?" Mr. Carrigan asked, his voice and expression haggard.

"I ain't making any promises I might not keep, but I'd be willing to consider it."

"I can't stand another minute of this! How can you tease the poor man so unmercifully? He's done nothing to deserve this. If no one else is going to untie him, I will!" Ella marched down the steps of the porch and stepped between her grandmother and their "guest." "Mr. Carrigan, I hope you'll accept my apologies in lieu of my family's and resist the urge to involve the law in this matter. I know it's a tremendous favor to ask of you, and you owe them and me nothing, but I'm asking it just the same. *I promise,* in the future I'll watch them like a hawk, so there can be no possibility of them repeating their offense." She knelt at his feet and started to pick the knot.

"Ella Marie, stand back." Ella felt her grandmother's hands on her shoulders, and she was forcibly deterred from her task. "I'll say when our new friend has worn out his welcome."

Ella scrambled back to her feet and squared off with her grandmother. "Grandma Jo! I refuse to be a party to this . . . this . . . cruel, imbecilic game. You may think it funny to torment an innocent stranger, but I don't. I'm going to let him go and no one is going to stop me."

"Now, Ella, I know you're tired and not thinking clearly, or you wouldn't be sassing me. You've always been such a respectful girl. There's no reason to let yourself get so upset. I like Sam and you would too if you'd let yourself get passed feeling embarrassed about the way your sisters arranged for the two of you to meet."

"They kidnapped him! We're holding the man against his will! And you're telling me not to be upset? Everyone else in this family may have gone stark, raving mad, but I haven't!" Ella spun away from her grandmother, intent on finishing what she had begun. "I'll have you freed in no time, Mr. Carrigan," she told him. "I apologize profusely for the delay."

"Marilee, Lily, grab your sister and wrestle her into the house," Grandma Jo commanded. "She's taken leave of her senses."

"I've taken leave of my senses?" Ella retorted, while she feverishly worked at Sam's stubborn knot. "Don't either of you dare touch me or I'll season the soup with buckthorn the next time your beaus come to visit. . . . No!" Ella screamed as they clamped onto her and began to drag her across the yard.

Twisting her limbs and digging in her heels, she managed to slow their progress but couldn't prevent it. She tried ramming them with her head, biting, kicking their shins, but they held fast. Their tenacity enraged her and Ella forgot herself completely. Shouting curses at them as they pulled her across the porch, she continued to battle for her freedom, writhing and kicking for all she was worth.

"Grandma Jo, Ella's trying to kill us," Lily whined.

"You just hold on tight, Miss! I'm coming in right behind you—just as soon as I make sure our friend Sam don't give Fern and Janie any trouble. They're gonna have to help him hop up the steps." As she was dragged through the door, Ella flinched when she heard her grandmother shout, "Hound Dog, guard him good now! And if he makes you bite him, mind you don't leave too big a hole in that fine wool suit of his."

Four

His back stiff and his lips taut, Samuel Carrigan sat on the chair where he had been deposited, glowering at the occupants of the room. He flexed his wrists and rotated his ankles against the ropes binding them. Miss Fern, Miss Janie, and the family's vicious mongrel had been left to guard him.

Measuring the distance between himself and the door with his eyes, he pressed his lips tighter against his teeth. Immediately extracting himself from this house was his most ardent desire, but hopping across the room would be not only undignified, in all likelihood it would prove futile. He jerked his gaze back to his tormentors.

Miss Fern bustled to and fro, humming as she set the table for dinner. She answered his scowls and muttered curses with saccharine smiles. The young woman was patently without conscience, and he wasted little time on her.

Miss Janie hefted two metal buckets of water onto the stove and stoked the fire beneath them. She had demonstrated herself an unworthy ally in the wagon, and he sullenly concluded she would continue to do so. She refused to look him directly in the eye, but she was not averse to casting frequent covert glances in his direction. Meeting one of her glances, he fixed her with a killing stare, and she started. Sam smiled. He was glad for any discomfort he caused her. She deserved to be punished.

The last occupant of the room caused Sam the most consternation. The family mongrel rested his head on Sam's lap and stared up at him with large, soulful eyes. Sam wasn't fooled for a minute by the dog's friendly demeanor. Every time he so much as twitched, the beast bared his teeth, emitted an ominous growl, and began to drool in anticipation of the joy of sinking his yellow fangs into his flesh. The manifest vulnerability of a certain tender part of his person persuaded Sam it was in his best interest (and in the interest of any children he might hope to father) to avoid making any sudden moves.

Sam narrowed his gaze and damned the beast under his breath. Without a shred of exaggeration he could say a more repulsive looking canine had yet to be born. The dog was huge, with long floppy ears and jowls to match. His coat was a mottled grey-gold with flecks of black. It was short in some places, shaggy in others. He had one blue eye and one brown eye sunk in his wrinkled face. A crooked tail with a tuft of white fur on the tip sprouted out of his rangy rump.

As if he sensed Sam's uncomplimentary assessment of his appearance, the dog met Sam's gaze and snarled. Sam drew in a deep breath and slowly exhaled it. Warily, he cast his eyes in a less daunting direction.

A thorough survey of his surroundings seemed a prudent task to undertake. Information was a vital tool, and he needed all the help he could get.

The room in which he sat could not be called anything but rustic. The walls were log chinked with clay; the floor bare wood covered by a colorful assortment of braided rag rugs. Open shelves filled with cooking utensils and foodstuff lined the wall near the stove and sideboard. Beside the buckets of water heating on the stove sat a coffeepot and a large iron kettle. The contents of both filled the air with their heavy aroma.

A granite fireplace was centered on the wall at the opposite end of the room. It was surrounded by a faded settee, two overstuffed leather chairs, and a slat-back rocking chair. One corner near the fireplace held a Wheeler & Wilson's sewing machine, a stack of pattern catalogs, and a basket of sewing notions. The other corner was occupied by a kindling box. He sat in the middle of the room at a long, pine dining table of utilitarian design.

Sam dropped his gaze to the dog head on his lap. His trousers were becoming uncomfortably damp with drool, but there was nothing he could do about it without risking worse. Wrinkling his nose in disgust, he consoled himself by conjuring visions of the very unfortunate future he wished upon the slobbering brute before he continued his inventory of the room.

There were two small windows on the same wall as the front door. They were high off the floor and the panes opened on side hinges. The windows were flanked with blue gingham curtains. Someone had taken the time to embroider a row of red tulips across the hem. A man might be able to squeeze himself through those windows, but it wouldn't be easy.

Two plank doors on the back wall led out of the main room. He was certain one led to another room. He could hear footsteps and muffled voices coming from behind it. The other might lead to the yard behind the house, but he thought it more likely when he opened it, he would find a bedroom. Of course, bedrooms usually had windows . . .

Sam carefully noted all possible portals to freedom and estimated the number of strides it would take to cover the space between him and them. Having come full circle, he surveyed his surroundings a second time to be certain he hadn't overlooked anything of import. He was persuaded he hadn't.

Though he had discovered no obvious weapon or promising avenue of escape, one thing in the room had caught his attention. Despite its lack of refinement, the room was exceedingly tidy. This struck Sam as incongruous considering the untidy minds of this home's occupants.

His gaze drifted back to Miss Janie and Miss Fern, and he perused them from head to toe. There was nothing in either of their appearances to alert a man they were crack-brained. Their guise was as deceptive as this room's. How was a man to protect himself if he couldn't tell the difference between innocent women and raging lunatics? The knot in his gut constricted.

If he could pinch himself, Sam knew he would do so in hopes of awakening himself from this fey nightmare. It was unbelievable he was sitting in this house a prisoner of six loony ladies and a savage dog. Unbelievable and decidedly demoralizing. Nothing in his past experience had prepared him for dealing with this sort of situation. If someone had even suggested he might someday find himself where he was today, he would have laughed himself senseless.

Over and over during the long, miserable journey here, he had endeavored to assimilate what was happening to him, but it defied logic. In hopes of attaining his release, he had tried reasoning, cajoling, shouting, begging, cursing. . . . All his efforts had gained him was a rose-scented handkerchief stuffed in his mouth. The Singleton sisters remained determined to see their scheme through. They were as recalcitrant as the knots they had used to bind him.

Deprived of speech and any hope of triumphing over the incarcerating ropes, he had had to resign himself to the fact there was nothing he could do to help himself but methodically dedicate the route they traveled to memory so he could retrace it when an opportunity to gain his freedom did present itself.

Sam mentally reviewed the information he had gathered to be certain it remained fresh in his mind.

The Singleton ranch sat in a grassy vale, nestled in the

mountains above the floor of the main valley. The route was winding, with few distinct landmarks—a craggy rock, a cluster of tree stumps, a patch of creamy-white columbine—but a byway of sorts had been worn into the earth by the Singletons and their visitors. He was confident he could find his way back to Heaven.

Once there he had every intention of pressing charges. He didn't care how many days it delayed his journey, he would see these ladies brought to justice. He owed it to himself and to his fellow man.

Impatience prompted imprudence and he abruptly shifted his position on the chair. His canine warden immediately captured a healthy hunk of Sam's thigh firmly in his jaw and showed no sign of letting go. Sam sat still as a statue. He contemplated demanding that one of the Singletons call off their dog but decided not to risk a vocal outburst lest the dog tighten his grip and draw blood.

As he sat staring at the dog, Sam realized having failed in his initial bids to gain his freedom, he was now faced with a new set of obstructions. The most notable one had a hold of his leg.

He had hoped Mrs. Singleton or, if she failed him, Miss Ella would be his salvation. But in his present circumstance, he could conjure scant reason for optimism.

Mrs. Singleton's behavior was as addlepated as her granddaughters'. She recognized the impropriety of her granddaughter's actions; she was willing to discuss his release; but she refused to *promise* to let him go. Also, she plainly was taking unholy delight in this bedlam. That had him more than a little worried.

He turned his thoughts to Miss Ella Singleton. He could hear her arguing with her family behind the door to his left. Though he could only discern an occasional word, it didn't take any great imagination to guess what the altercation was about.

To her credit, Miss Ella sensibly rejected the idea of embracing him as a husband, and for that he was grateful, but it was depressingly obvious she was no match against the combined forces of her grandmother and sisters.

Recreating the image of the lady in question in his head, Sam shuddered. Never in his life had he seen a female garbed in men's trousers. Worse, not only was the woman scandalously immodest, she was filthy. God only knew what she had all over her. And she smelled—like nothing he had ever smelled before. She was slightly taller than her sisters. In her manly attire her feminine curves were readily discernable, but she was thinner than was fashionable. Half her hair was piled atop her head. The other half hung in strings about her face. Dark circles ringed her eyes and her complexion knew but two shades: ghostly white and florid red. It was little wonder no man would have her.

To his mind Miss Ella Singleton had but one virtue to recommend her: *She alone understood he could not be held against his will and forced to fall in love with her.*

Sam had yet to shift his eyes from the teeth encircling his thigh. The dog stared unblinking, neither clenching his jaw nor relaxing it. Doing nothing in the face of an assault upon his person nearly broke Sam's hard won control over his roiling emotions but he endured—reason and instinct both counseling him that a violent outburst, no matter how enticing, would bring him more harm than good. After what seemed an eternity, but Sam's logical mind knew in fact had been but a minute or two, the dog released his leg and returned his head to his lap.

The voices in the other room were becoming louder, and Sam strained to hear precisely what was being said. Miss Ella was still arguing his cause, but it was clear from Mrs. Singleton's responses, her arguments were falling on deaf ears. The old woman was adamant he was staying for dinner. He couldn't make out what she said next; then, he heard her say, "Marilee, go check the water on the stove. The fire oughta have taken enough of the chill off it. Ella can start getting herself cleaned up."

Marilee entered the room. She waved at him, lifted one bucket of water from the stove, picked up a bar of soap and a washcloth, and exited again. A moment later, she returned for the second bucket and a towel.

At least they were going to do him the courtesy of giving their sister a bath before they forced him to share a meal with her, Sam thought with no small amount of relief.

Though every minute he spent in this house made him doubt his own sanity, he had decided not to attempt to flee before the meal. His decision was purely a matter of pragmatism. He wasn't the least bit enamored with the idea of having their damn dog gnaw off his leg.

Of equal weight was the knowledge that though Mrs. Singleton had refused to promise, she had indicated she would release him after the meal. If he had to battle his way to freedom, he would do so, but being a rational man, he preferred to dredge up a little more forbearance in the hopes he might depart unscathed. It was damnably difficult to remain rational when all those around him were unhinged, but he was determined to persevere.

If, after he cooperated with her senseless charade, the old woman refused to let him go, he'd be no worse off than he was now . . . unless, of course, they meant to poison him. Sam didn't believe they harbored that particular evil intent, but he'd misjudged them before. Just to be safe, he vowed not to touch a morsel to his lips until one of them had swallowed the food first.

Sam continued to occupy his mind with morose musings

as he waited for the meal to begin so it could end. He prayed his presence at dinner would satisfy the ladies and they would let him go immediately after, but he judiciously supplemented this fervent prayer by devising in meticulous detail several contingency plans of escape.

Ella stood naked in the hip bath in the bedroom she shared with her sisters. Dipping the wash rag into one of the buckets of lukewarm water, she rubbed it with a bar of soap, then vigorously scrubbed her skin.

Having delivered her into Grandma Jo's hands, Marilee and Lily wisely kept their distance.

Noting the red finger marks ringing her wrists, Ella scrubbed even harder. Finding herself a prisoner of her own family, outnumbered and for the moment outmaneuvered, was so perturbing she felt ready to explode. At least taking this bath gave her something constructive to do with all her seething energy.

"I swear, I'm beginning to wonder if Electra didn't kick me in the head while I was helping her with her calf and I won't wake up to find myself lying in the field. You all better hope this *is* a bad dream I'm having because if it isn't, I doubt I'll ever be able to muster enough charity in my heart to forgive any of you for this," she tersely informed the occupants of the room.

"But you really do need a bath and a change of clothes, Ella," Grandma Jo replied, her expression guileless.

"You know perfectly well I'm not talking about your insisting I clean myself up before dinner! It was my intention to do so when I came up to the house." Ella resoaped the washcloth and persisted to scour her skin with more zeal than was required for the task. Her voice reflected the agitation of her movements. "I'm talking about Mr. Carrigan!"

"So am I. First impressions are very important, and I'm afraid you may have gotten off to a poor start."

"And that surprises you? They kidnapped him, for mercy's sake! I could have met the man fresh from a Saturday night soak in the tub and dressed in Cinderella's ball gown, and it wouldn't make a whit of difference!"

"I'm sure you're wrong. You're a right beautiful young woman. Look just like I did at your age and I was the undisputed belle of the county. Had beaus standing in line . . ."

"My beauty or lack thereof has nothing to do with this," Ella interrupted. "I have a mirror. I'm well aware I haven't been cursed with the kind of face that frightens small children. And I freely acknowledge any beauty I do possess was inherited from you." She shook her head in exasperation.

"Mr. Carrigan despises me not because I sport an inferior face nor because I am filthy nor even because he caught me in the undeniably disgraceful act of wearing trousers." That thought caused the heat of a blush to spread from Ella's cheeks down her chest; however, she ignored it and continued to lecture her grandmother.

"Under other circumstances being seen by anyone outside this family garbed in such improper attire would mortify me to the core, but I hardly noticed the extra helping of shame because you all have already filled my soul with more shame than it can hold." Having reached her toes, Ella threw down the washcloth, picked up the bucket nearest her, and poured it over her head. She followed it with the second bucket. Stepping out of the tub, she gifted Marilee with a thunderous scowl as she accepted the towel her sister held out to her and began to dry herself with the same vehemence she had exhibited when scrubbing her skin clean. Continuing to address her grandmother, she chided, "Without a shred of doubt, the reason Mr. Carrigan despises me is because he was brought to our doorstep by force."

"I'm sure he don't despise you, dear, anymore than you despise him. You don't despise him, do you? It certainly ain't his fault your sisters fetched him home."

Ella threw another damning glance in the direction of the two siblings who mutely attended her. She was tempted to scald their ears with a few more choice phrases expressing her opinion of what they had done in case any doubt remained in their minds after the litany of curses she already had called upon their heads, but she decided not to waste her breath. She would punish them by ignoring them. Grandma Jo held the reins of the family firmly in her hands. She was the one she must convince to let Mr. Carrigan go. Wheeling away from her sisters, Ella answered her grandmother's question with one of her own. "I don't know the man. How can I have an opinion of him?"

"Good for you. Get to know him first; then, decide what you think of him. That's the sensible thing to do." As she spoke, she ambled over to the clothes chest, pulled out fresh underclothes and stockings from Ella's drawer, and laid them on the bed. "Glad to see you're keeping your promise to your sisters and looking over Sam with an open mind."

Wrapping herself in the towel, Ella starched her shoulders and fixed a steely gaze upon her grinning grandmother. "I am *not* looking him over. I am trying to send him back to wherever it is he came from."

"Why would you want to do that before you give yourself the chance to know him? What if it turns out he's the man you've been saving yourself for?"

"He's not. . . . And even if he was, my *precious* sisters have seen to it a romance between us is impossible. Besides, he already has a fiancée."

Grandma Jo clucked her tongue. "So, you *are* interested in him. I thought as much."

"I didn't say that!" Ella protested.

"Maybe not in so many words, but the way you've been blushing . . ." She let her comment trail off. "I've never known you to be a blusher before you laid eyes on Sam. Profuse blushing is the first symptom of love fever, and I'd say you're coming down with a mighty bad case."

"I am not!"

"Ah, passionate denial. Another sure sign a gentleman has caught a lady's fancy. I admire your tastes, Ella. He's a handsome one. Be fighting you for him if I was fifty years younger."

"Grandma Jo!" Ella yanked up her drawers so hard she almost snapped the drawstrings.

Grandma Jo nodded her head knowingly and smiled. "What, dear?"

"Stop it at once!"

"You want me to stop saying Sam is handsome. Why? It's the truth, ain't it?"

"I want you to stop twitting me about Mr. Carrigan."

"All right, I will . . . just as soon as you tell me—and I'll accept nothing but an honest answer, young lady—if you judge Sam a handsome man."

Sputtering with exasperation, Ella gave her attention to the rest of the clothing laid out on the bed. The only thing she had a mind to tell Grandma Jo would likely earn her a week's worth of penance shoveling dung out of the barn. Anyone with eyes could see Mr. Carrigan's person was without rival. Listening to him talk, she imagined his mind was equally impressive. She wasn't denying the merits of the man. She was expressing her revulsion for what they had done to him. And her.

When she looked up from smoothing her petticoat in place, Grandma Jo was still waiting expectantly. Ella groaned. "Yes, I think he's handsome. But, as I said before, under the circumstances, what I think of the man doesn't amount to a hill of beans. Those two," she gestured toward Marilee and Lily, "and their accomplices destroyed all possibility of any form of friendship between Mr. Carrigan and myself."

"I don't see how."

Ella rolled her eyes heavenward. "Put yourself in his place. How would you feel if a gang of men whomped you over the head, trussed you up, and dragged you home to marry one of their kin?"

"Well, that would depend on the fella they wanted me to marry. If he had a good head on his shoulders and a promising twinkle in his eye . . ."

"You are absolutely incorrigible! I can't believe my own grandmother, a woman I used to respect, has sunk so low."

Grandma Jo patted Ella's hand. "All I'm asking is you get to know the man before you decide whether or not he would make you a suitable mate."

Ella clamped her jaw together so hard it made her teeth ache. Trying to reason with her grandmother was like talking into the wind. She knew her family was keen to see her leg-shackled, but could lovesickness bring on mass hysteria? And even if it could, why would Grandma Jo be affected? Perhaps everyone in the family had eaten something she had not and were suffering from a form of food poisoning that caused irrational behavior. Perhaps this was just some ill-conceived practical joke to get back at her for turning down Willie Crumb. Ella studied their countenances through narrowed eyes, trying in vain to determine which if any of her theories touched upon the truth. She quickly discarded the notion she was the victim of a practical joke, not because of her sisters' countenances, but because the finest actor in the world couldn't have pretended the outrage she had witnessed Mr. Carrigan exhibit out in the yard.

Ella gnashed her teeth in frustration. Whatever was motivating the members of her family to behave like nincompoops she wanted them to cease at once. A body could stand only so much idiocy, and she had reached her limit.

Her narrowed eyes popped wide open at her grandmother's next statement.

"Lily, fetch Ella's green and gold silk dress from the cupboard and find some hair ribbons to match."

"I'm not going to humiliate myself by letting you dress me up like a peacock. Fetch one of my everyday dresses," Ella commanded. Leaning forward she yanked at a wrinkle in her stocking. "On second thought, my black mourning dress better suits my mood."

"Lily, fetch the silk," Grandma Jo sternly repeated.

"I won't put it on."

"Yes, you will. You spent good money so you could buy the pattern and material to make that dress. You say you've been saving it for a special occasion, and I reckon today is mighty special. Besides, you look lovely in it, and after all the trouble he's borne to meet you, Sam deserves to be treated like an honored guest."

"He's not a guest. He's a prisoner," Ella curtly reminded. She tossed the dress Lily lay in her hands on the bed. "There's a world of difference, and I'm not going to pretend I don't know it."

"You want me to make your sisters let Sam go?" Grandma Jo queried.

"Of course, I do."

"Well, unless you start behaving like a proper young lady and do your best to make him feel welcome, he ain't going anywhere any time soon."

Ella paled. "You can't seriously mean to keep him past dinner."

"I can and I will if you don't stop rankling me." Grandma Jo waggled her finger at Ella's nose. "One thing I can't abide is a disrespectful child, and you ain't been showing me enough respect to fill a thimble."

"But . . ."

"But nothing. Sam Carrigan's fate is in your hands. Keep up this caterwauling and I won't be setting him free till the geese fly south for winter. Put on the dress and be a pleasant, obedient girl and you'll find me more than willing to listen to reason." Josephine Singleton's hazel eyes flashed fiery gold, but the daunting lights were tempered by the satisfied grin stretching across her face. "Now, if you'll be excusing me, I've a batch of biscuits to get ready for the oven."

Ella gripped the bedroom doorknob and stopped in mid stride. She didn't want to go out there and face Mr. Carrigan. One look at her and he was bound to jump to the wrong conclusion.

She shouldn't have surrendered, she scolded herself, but that rebellious thought straightaway was followed by the certain knowledge if she had refused to wear what her grandmother had ordered, poor Mr. Carrigan would pay the price, and she judged he had already suffered enough.

Even though he looked ready to murder her entire family on the spot, she reckoned him a good man. Ella searched her mind for solid facts to support her favorable opinion, but found she had none. Nevertheless, she remained firm in her opinion, and believing him to be upright, increased her own agony. If the man possessed some glaring fault, perhaps she wouldn't be so overwhelmed with sympathy for him she couldn't think straight.

Taking stock of her emotions, Ella had no idea which was making her feel the worst: the frustration, the disgrace, the anger, the guilt, or the disbelief this day could really be happening. She wasn't used to feeling so off balance, and she didn't like it one bit. The notion of digging in her heels and refusing to budge an inch held much appeal.

Lily cleared her throat, and Ella frowned. Who was she kidding? If she didn't walk out the door on her own two feet, Marilee and Lily would push her out it. Her family already had made a fool of her more than once this day. She wasn't about to give them another opportunity to do so. If the heroines who peopled her beloved books could face their own deaths with dignity, then she ought to be able to face Mr. Carrigan.

Taking a deep breath, Ella turned the doorknob and stepped through the door.

The wide-eyed, slack-jawed expression that bloomed upon Mr. Carrigan's face when he caught sight of her was enough to convince Ella her worst fears were a pale reflection of the odious truth. It took every ounce of her mettle to resist the urge to turn tail and run back into the bedroom.

"Mr. Carrigan, I want to assure you my change in appearance in no way means I've taken leave of my senses and decided to fall in with my family's scheme to abuse your good nature," she quickly confessed. "They coerced me into this dress."

He nodded curtly in response, slowly running his incredulous gaze from her head to her toes.

Ella felt herself blush under his regard and stammered on, "That's not to say I've an aversion to wearing dresses. I don't. I like them very much. I just don't want you to figure I'm trying to win your favor because I most definitely am not."

"I'm relieved to hear you haven't taken a sudden fancy to me."

"I haven't," Ella earnestly confirmed; then, fearing her statement might be misinterpreted as a slur upon his person, she swiftly added, "Not that I find you in anyway lacking."

"To be brutally honest, Miss Singleton, I don't care a fig

what you think of me as long you remain firm in your opinion your family is wrong to hold me against my will."

Ella met his hard stare without flinching. "You can rest easy they'll never be able to coerce me into changing my mind on that count."

"My gratitude is without bounds."

Bustling across the room, Grandma Jo plunked a pan of hot biscuits on the table. "Well, now that the two of you have all that settled, let's change the subject to something more important. After all, the point here is to give you two a chance to get better acquainted."

"That's why we brought him," Marilee confirmed from the spot near the corner where she stood huddled with her sisters.

Ella glanced in their direction. They were whispering up a windstorm amongst themselves and watching Mr. Carrigan and herself with undisguised expectation. She sniffed in disgust.

She might have no choice about what she wore or about sharing this meal with Mr. Carrigan, but she did have a choice as to the topic of conversation. Raising her chin a notch, Ella's eyes took on an insurgent gleam. "That's right. Mr. Carrigan, let's do get better acquainted. Why don't you acquaint me with the many virtues of your fiancée. I'm sure she is a wonderful woman and you miss her very much." She gazed directly into his eyes and raised a brow. "Please, tell us *all* about her."

"Shame on you, Ella. Sam has already made it clear he don't want to discuss his lady friend," Grandma Jo interrupted before he could seize the opportunity Ella had engineered. Taking Ella by the hand, she led her to the seat next to his and pushed her down on the chair, all the while chattering, "Tsk, tsk, child. Sam will reckon I've failed in my duty to teach you proper manners, and that just ain't fair. Why I've devoted my life to raising you girls up right and . . ."

Squaring her shoulders, Ella cut the speech short. "He also made it clear he prefers to be addressed as *Mr. Carrigan* and that he does not want to dine with us, but you seem oblivious to those wishes."

"Remember what I said about being pleasant and obedient, Ella Marie," Grandma Jo warned. "I'd hate to have to make good on my threat, but you know me well enough to realize if you force my hand, I'll prove as good as my word."

Ella clamped her lips shut.

"Would someone mind explaining to me just exactly what is going on here," Sam demanded. "And while you're at it, call off your damn dog. He's making a puddle on my lap."

"Men ain't allowed to swear under my roof, Samuel," Grandma Jo chided as she carried the pot of stew to the table. "I'll excuse you this once, but in the future you'll watch your tongue."

"You swear," he muttered.

"I ain't a man. The rest of you girls gather round the table, now." She waved them to their places with her arm. "Lily fetch the coffee on your way."

Ella refused to look at them as they took their places at the table. She also refused to look at Mr. Carrigan, but she could feel he was still staring at her.

"Are you or are you not going to call off your dog?" he importuned.

"Hound Dog, lay down," Grandma Jo directed. The dog promptly plopped himself down on the floor next to Sam's chair. "I'll wash your trousers for you before you leave, if you'd like," she offered.

"Thank you, but *no*. I won't be staying that long."

"Suit yourself. Ella, would you offer the blessing on the food today?"

"Certainly," Ella replied through clenched teeth. Folding her hands in her lap, she bowed her head. When the others followed suit, she commenced, "Heavenly Father, we thank Thee for Thy many blessings, and for the bounty on this table.

Watch over us. Guide us back to the path of right thinking when wrong thinking leads us to commit contrary acts against innocent strangers. Forgive the members of this family for the many sins they have committed this day. Plant thoughts of release and restitution in their addled minds. Restore sanity to the members of this household. Smite them with wisdom posthaste. . . ."

"Amen!" Grandma Jo ended the prayer.

"An excellent prayer, Miss Singleton," Sam complemented.

Ella smiled triumphantly. "Thank you."

Grandma Jo snorted and picked up the plate of biscuits. It quickly passed from hand to hand around the table. When it came to Sam, he merely stared at it.

"Dear me," Grandma Jo exclaimed. "We've forgotten to untie your hands, haven't we? Can't have you eating like a hog at the trough, now can we? Ella, why don't you do the honors."

"Gladly." Ella immediately dropped to her knees behind his chair and began working at the knot. Every time her hands brushed against Mr. Carrigan's, a ripple of warmth flowed up her limbs, but she forced herself to ignore the disturbing sensation and concentrate on the continuing conversation.

"I'm depending on you to behave yourself, Sam. Hound Dog don't take kindly to strangers abusing our hospitality."

"Why do you keep calling him that? Doesn't he have a name?"

"Too ugly for a name." Grandma Jo laughed. "But let's not change the subject. I want your word as a gentleman you won't try anything foolish."

"Do you intend to release me as soon as this meal is over?"

"That's my intention. Of course, if a certain young lady don't mind her manners or you get it in your head to misbehave, I might have to change my intentions. A woman always has the right to change her mind."

"If you will keep your word, I will give you mine."

Having released his wrists, Ella turned to the rope binding his ankles.

"He don't need his feet to eat. Sit yourself back down in your chair, Ella."

Reluctantly, Ella obeyed. Mr. Carrigan's expression was grim as he massaged his rope-marked wrists.

"Let Ella rub the life back into your hands for you," Grandma Jo directed. "She'll fix you up in a jiffy. Why whenever my arthritis starts to acting up, it's always Ella I call on to soothe away my pain."

"Thank you for your generous offer, but I prefer to see to my own needs."

"We were the ones that trussed you up, so we oughta be the ones to repair the damage. It's only right."

"Grandma Jo would you please stop trying to push me upon the man?"

Grandma Jo shot her a warning look.

"Here, massage my wrists if it makes her happy." Sam thrust an arm under Ella's nose. "I have my heart set on leaving this madhouse within the next hour, and I would appreciate it if you don't say or do anything to delay my departure."

Planting a false smile on her lips, Ella grasped his hand in hers and applied the pads on her thumbs to his palm. Working efficiently, she kneaded her way up to the tips of his fingers, then reversed direction. When she reached his wrist, she carefully avoided his chafed skin. Dropping his arm, she held out her palm for his other hand.

As she tended it, Ella tried not to notice the warmth of his skin or its smooth texture or its clean masculine scent. Never in her life had she noticed the features of a man's hand in such detail, and she judged now a highly inappropriate time to start becoming aware of such things.

To her chagrin Ella realized her breathing had become shallow and her heart was beating much faster than it should. Her eyes widened.

She absolutely refused to be attracted to Mr. Carrigan's person. To do so was an affront to common sense. It made her feel as though she was somehow as guilty as her sisters of scheming to have him tarry with her.

The instant she finished his second hand, Ella dropped it. Her own hands retreated beneath the table where she clasped them tightly in her lap.

"Feel better?" Grandma Jo asked him.

"Yes."

"Good. Now, let's get at these vittles before they get cold."

While Grandma Jo ladled stew into their bowls, the coffee-pot followed the plate of biscuits around the table.

Ella watched Mr. Carrigan from beneath hooded eyes. At first he didn't seem interested in the food, but after the others started eating, he picked up his fork. Rather than shovel the stew into his mouth, he wielded his fork with grace, taking moderate sized bites. Though he said nothing, it was plain he didn't find the food wanting.

Ella lifted her own fork but, even though she was famished, she couldn't bring herself to do more than rearrange the contents of her bowl.

"Eat up, Ella. Men don't cotton to skinny women," Fern advised.

Ella opened her mouth to deliver a stinging retort, then clamped it shut again. Grandma Jo had said she must be proper and pleasant if she wanted to end this ordeal, so proper and pleasant she would be, even if she had to chew her tongue to ribbons.

"I'm sorry you're mad at us," Janie offered.

Ella shrugged.

"Mr. Carrigan is from New York City," Marilee informed her eldest sister.

"And he likes books and sunsets," Lily added.

"Do you hear that, Ella?" Grandma Jo encouraged.

"Yes, I heard," Ella calmly retorted, though inwardly she wanted to scream.

"What do you do in New York, Sam?" Grandma Jo cheerfully queried.

Ella was sure he wouldn't answer, but after a long pause he gruffly stated, "I am a businessman."

"What kinda business?"

"Investments mostly."

"Are you rich?"

"Compared to a king, no. Compared to a beggar, yes."

"What about your family?"

"I have one."

Mr. Carrigan plainly was becoming increasingly annoyed with each question. Ella wasn't sure why he was answering them, but she suspected it was for the same reason she said nothing: a desire to avoid retribution. She squirmed on her chair.

She wanted to demand her grandmother cease her interrogation, but she kept her tongue resolutely imprisoned behind her teeth.

"How about telling us about your kin," Grandma Jo said next.

"My mother is deceased. I have a father and two brothers."

"Older or younger?"

"Older."

"What are their names?

"Adam and Joshua."

"Biblical names. That's good. Shows your family respects religion. I knew you come from good stock the moment I looked into your eyes. Windows to the soul, you know."

He didn't respond.

"Well, it seems we know quite a bit about you, Sam. What would you like to know about Ella?"

"Nothing."

"There must be something," she prodded.

He hadn't stopped staring at her since she had entered the room. Now, his chin rose and fell as he perused her person. He was making her extremely uncomfortable, and Ella wished he would stop. "No," he said.

"Okay," Grandma Jo retorted. She took a sip of coffee. When she lowered the rim of the cup, her mouth was taut. "If you don't want to ask any questions, I'll just tell you what I reckon you oughta know."

"She's twenty-five years old, sentimental, loyal, the best cook in the territory, smart as they come, willing to work from dawn until dusk without complaining, *and* she thinks you're handsome. Told me so herself when she was getting cleaned up."

"Grandma Jo!" Ella cried.

"Well, you did say so."

"Only after you browbeat me into doing it!"

"You saying you lied to me?"

Ella could feel her cheeks flaming hotter by the moment. She wanted to crawl under the table and right on out the door. There was no way she could answer the question. If she told the truth she would mortify herself. If she lied, she guaranteed Grandma Jo's ire. Her eyes frantically scanned the table for something on which she could safely focus her gaze, and she ducked her head.

"Ain't that just the sweetest thing; she's too shy to admit the truth in front of you. It's okay, Ella. I'll tell him for you," Grandma Jo declared. "Ella thinks you're real handsome. And make no mistake, that's rare praise coming from her lips. Why I've lost count of how many fellas have come begging for her hand in marriage, and not a one of them tickled her fancy. You're a lucky man." When he did not leap at the opportunity to agree with her assessment of his fortune, she added, "So, now that you know what she thinks of you, I reckon it only fair you tell us what you think of her."

"No comment," Sam tersely replied.

"You telling me you haven't a thought in that handsome head of yours? 'Cause if you are, I don't believe it. The way you keep giving her the once over, you must be thinking something."

Laying his fork aside, Sam clenched his fists and grumbled something unintelligible. "I think she is a chameleon."

"A what?" Marilee and the others squinted at him.

"A lizard that is able to change her appearance so completely as to appear a totally different creature," he coolly explained.

Had he just insulted her or complemented her? Ella had no idea, and she wasn't going to ask.

The meal was over. Rising to her feet, Ella began to clear the table. "Well, Mr. Carrigan, it was lovely getting to know you," she proclaimed the blatantly false statement in an overly bright voice. "Have a safe journey to wherever it is you're headed."

"Thank you, Miss Singleton." He leaned down to untie his ankles.

"Hound Dog!"

Instantly, Sam found himself eyeball to eyeball with a pair of feral eyes. The dog bared his teeth and emitted an ominous growl. Sam froze. "Call off your dog," he commanded.

"Sam you best sit yourself back up, you ain't going anywhere just yet," Grandma Jo informed him.

"But you promised . . ." Ella protested.

"No, I didn't and even if I did, you two didn't hold up your end of the bargain."

Having cautiously risen to a sitting position, Sam glowered at the eldest member of the Singleton family, making no effort whatsoever to disguise the breadth of his rancor. "Yes, we did."

"Nope. Oh, I admit you followed the letter of the law, but that ain't enough to satisfy." She shook her head sadly. "Why, I practically had to yank every answer I got out of you with a pair of tongs, and then when it came your turn to do the asking, you made no effort at all to be sociable."

"Why don't you just admit you never had any intention of letting me go," he bellowed.

" 'Cause it ain't the truth. And if you don't want Hound Dog taking a chunk out of you, I suggest you lower your voice."

"Grandma Jo, please let him go," Ella pleaded. "You're embarrassing me and yourself. It's time everyone around here starts behaving reasonably."

"I am being reasonable. It's him who's being stubborn. All he has to do is be sincere in his efforts to get to know you, and let nature take its course."

"You really oughta stay and try to fall in love with Ella," Fern maintained. "If you'd try, I bet you'd find you like her better than your old Clara."

"You did look fine sitting there side by side," Marilee seconded.

Janie addressed her words to Ella. "I'm sure you'd come to like him if you could get over being mad at us."

"She already likes him," Lily apprised her. "Grandma Jo said so when we was in the bedroom."

"Good." Fern sat a little taller. "Then all we gotta do is find a way to talk him into liking her."

"It ain't us gotta do the talking. It's Ella," Marilee counseled. "She hardly said a word during dinner. How's he gonna know how special she is if she don't talk to him?"

"She did rub his hands," Lily reminded. "I imagine that made him feel . . ."

"This is ridiculous," Sam interrupted.

"Life is ridiculous, Sam," Grandma Jo tutored. "The sooner a body comes to understand that, the better time he's gonna have in this old world."

Five

The thought of committing violence against a woman—any woman—was abhorrent to Sam, but as he sat on his chair, staring across the table at the self-satisfied Mrs. Singleton, he was mightily tempted to abandon moral precept and strangle the old girl.

In fact, he'd like to strangle the lot of them, even Miss Ella Singleton. Not that she deserved righteous retribution, but he wasn't in the mood to play fair. If she had had the foresight to wed one of the many men who wanted to marry her, she could have appeased her obnoxious family and saved him this indignity.

Sam spared a glance at the object of his lack of affection. She looked as miserable as he felt.

His initial supposition that the reason Miss Ella had not married was due to an absence of physical charm had undergone a radical revision. The transformation the bath and change of clothing had wrought was nothing short of miraculous. Shadows of fatigue still ringed her hazel eyes, but otherwise she appeared a totally different woman, and an extremely attractive one at that. She smelled nice now, too—rather like Clara but with a subtle difference and without the cloying scent of perfume. Her speaking voice, which he had earlier judged as harsh, was actually rather mellifluous.

Though he was loath to admit it even to himself, when she had kneaded his hands, he had felt a potent stirring of lust in his loins. Only a fool would confuse lust with liking, and he was no fool, but considering the circumstances, he still viewed his reaction as appallingly out of place, and he was determined not to contemplate it. What he needed to focus his mind and energy upon was how to get away. Nothing else was of consequence.

Having anticipated the possibility he would not be released, he had several options from which to choose. It only took a moment to select the one he deemed both the most efficient and the most likely to succeed.

What he required was a few minutes alone so he could untie his feet, and there was one place he could be assured of the requisite privacy. Besides, between the hours spent being jostled in the wagon bed and the coffee he'd consumed with the meal, he genuinely was in need of relief.

Clearing his throat, Sam brusquely stated. "I would like to use the necessary."

"Sure thing," Grandma Jo replied, rising from her seat at the table. "You girls get started on the dishes while I take Sam out back. When we return, Marilee can fetch his horse and bed him down in the barn for the night. Oh, and Ella, fetch my box of medicines from my room, so I can doctor Sam's head when we come back. In all the excitement, I clean forgot to do it."

We won't be coming back, Sam silently amended. And there won't be any need to fetch my horse. He couldn't believe his good luck. With only Mrs. Singleton to contend with, the success of his plan was assured.

"Come on Hound Dog. Nature is a calling Sam's name. Hop right this way." She motioned Sam towards the door from which Miss Ella had earlier emerged.

Pushing himself to his feet, Sam hobbled toward her. When he reached the door, he turned back toward the room. "Ladies." He tipped his head, to himself adding, *Farewell. It has not been a pleasure meeting you.*

Taking his hand and placing it on her arm, Grandma Jo led him out of the room and into the next. Sam gave only cursory notice to the functional furniture, feminine bric-a-brac, and five quilt-covered beds lined up in a row. He was too busy savoring his soon to be won freedom to see any purpose in surveying his surroundings.

The outhouse sat at the end of a well-worn path some twenty yards from the house. His bonds necessitated baby steps and progress was slow, but with Mrs. Singleton's arm for balance, he was managing quite nicely.

Whatever else one might say about them, one thing was certain, none of the Singletons were very bright, else why after going to so much trouble to bring him here were they now making it so easy for him to escape? Did they think he would blithely go along with their plans for him to stay until it suited their fancy for him to go?

He was not forgetting the dog that trailed at his heels, but he judged him a nuisance rather than a threat to his scheme. He looked capable of inflicting grave harm, but allowing him to do so would not serve the Singletons' matrimonial purpose—so he didn't believe they would. He might get bit once or twice before he reached his horse, but that would be the worst of it.

"Here you go," Grandma Jo announced, opening the door for him. "There's plenty of cut up catalogs in the box on the wall if you find yourself in need of them."

"Thank you." Hopping up on the wooden floor, Sam closed the door behind him.

Instantly, he set to work on the ropes shackling his ankles. They were unresponsive. He continued to tug at the knots, pausing periodically to glance at his pocket watch. Just as he was beginning to despair he would never get free, a loop loos-

ened, and half a minute later he dropped the rope down the
shaft of the necessary. He then availed himself of the facility,
quickly reviewing his plan as he did so.

He couldn't fail. All he must do was push past Mrs. Singleton and *run*. She would sound the alarm, but he should
have enough of a head start he could easily reach his horse.
Once on horseback, nothing could stop him. He smiled.

Facing the door, Sam filled his lungs with air and bolted
into the sunshine. His legs flew beneath him. Mrs. Singleton
didn't shout, but she was saying something. He didn't bother
trying to discern what it was. He concentrated on the only
thing that mattered: reaching his horse.

He cut a wide berth around the house.

She was still behind him, and keeping up admirably for
a woman her age, though to his great pleasure her voice
was becoming more and more distant. He thought it odd
she didn't call for reinforcements, but in this family odd
was to be expected.

Sam was in the midst of congratulating himself on a job
well done when he felt himself suddenly propelled forward
by a forceful blow to his back. In the same moment, Mrs.
Singleton's last words penetrated his consciousness.

"Kill, Hound Dog, kill!" she commanded.

Rolling as he hit the ground, Sam found himself face to
face with a row of razor sharp teeth. The dog lunged atop his
chest, expelling the air from his lungs.

Sam struggled to regain his breath as he fought to protect
his neck and face with his forearms. Pitching from side to
side, he tried to dislodge the dog and regain his footing, but
achieved neither goal. The animal had a hold of his forearm,
then a wrist, then he heard the rending of fabric and felt his
vise-like jaws clamp down on his shoulder. It seemed to Sam
the beast had a hundred heads and a thousand paws. The mo-

ment he wrenched one body part loose, another was caught up.

A wave of fatalism washed over him, but he fought on. He had misjudged his opponent, and he feared he would die for it. Mrs. Singleton might appear to be a harmless old woman, but it was painfully clear to him now she preferred him dead to free from her family.

A set of gleaming teeth flashed across his field of vision. Sam balled his fist and delivered a hard blow to the side of the dog's head. It had no effect except to alter the course of attack slightly.

Massive jaw encircled his throat. Sam stiffened. So this was how his life was going to end: lying on his back in the dirt. Unable to bear the sight of his own ignoble death, he closed his eyes, praying God would be merciful when He judged his soul.

"Sam, you've been a very naughty boy. Why just look at your fine coat. It'll take me days to mend it, and it never will look right again no matter how skillfully I wield my needle."

Sam's eyes snapped open at the sound of Mrs. Singleton's voice. She was standing directly above him, wearing a long-suffering maternal expression.

"What the hell do I care about my coat if I'm soon to be dead?" He warily sucked in a breath and croaked out the words.

"There's no reason for Hound Dog to finish the job. What he does is up to you. If you're willing to behave yourself, I've no objection to letting you up off the ground. Of course, you'll end up right back where you are if you start acting up again."

The amiable tone of her voice set Sam's teeth on edge and congealed his conviction Mrs. Singleton's grasp on reality was exceedingly feeble. No wonder her granddaughters were so misguided. With this woman molding their impressionable young minds, what hope was there they could be anything else?

Though the idea of surrender was repugnant to him, given the options of temporary surrender or instantaneous death, Sam had no choice but to swallow his pride. "Call off your dog."

"Say please."

"Please call off your dog," he murmured.

"Hound Dog, let him up, but stick close to him. He ain't as smart as he looks, and he might be needing you to educate him again."

Hound Dog bounded off Sam's chest, furiously wagging his tail as he received a pat on the head from his mistress. Returning to sit beside Sam, he continued to wag his tail.

Sam slowly sat up and rubbed his neck. He counted himself lucky he was by nature an uncommonly pragmatic man. If he wasn't, he doubted he could muster the self-possession to make the insufferable choices necessary to survive this ordeal. And he would survive. If for no other reason, and he had many reasons to value his life, than just to spite them.

"We best be getting ourselves indoors." Mrs. Singleton urged him to his feet. "The girls will start wondering what's taking us so long."

Glowering at her, Sam held his head high as he trudged back to the house.

"What happened to you?" Ella cried, her eyes widening to the size of a full moon when they took in Sam's tattered appearance.

"I tried to escape and she set her dog on me," Sam curtly informed her.

"Grandma Jo!"

"Now Ella, you've got no call to give me a look like that. He brought the trouble upon himself."

"I don't believe that for one second."

"Well, it's true. He tried to leave without even saying good-bye, and you know how I feel about ungracious guests."

Ella scowled. There was no point in wasting her breath wrangling with her grandmother. Grandma Jo was deep into one of her stubborn moods, and nobody—including the Almighty, Ella suspected—was capable of budging her an inch until she was good and ready to be budged. She turned her attention back to Sam. "Mr. Carrigan, I don't know what to say except I'm so sorry. We will pay for a new suit and . . ."

"I don't care about the suit," he growled. "All I want is to be set free."

"And you will be . . . in good time," Grandma Jo avowed. "The trouble with you young people is you're always in such a hurry. Now, if you'd learn to relax and enjoy the fine company Providence has so graciously provided you, you'd find yourself a contented man."

"Madam, it is the Devil's, not Providence's, hand at work here."

"I agree," Ella said.

"Well then, since you and Sam are so agreeable, I reckon you oughta be the one to doctor him instead of me. I'm just gonna sit myself down in my rocker and knit a spell." Sauntering across the room, she plopped herself in her rocking chair and picked up her knitting needles. "Marilee, go get his horse now, and bring me his saddlebags. He's gonna need a clean shirt. You other girls hurry up with those dishes, then skedaddle on out of here. Room is feeling a bit crowded."

Ella rolled her eyes heavenward at her grandmother's blatant stratagems. She would protest, but she knew it wouldn't do her a whit of good. Moreover, considering Mr. Carrigan's present condition, she regarded it her moral duty to keep her family as far from the poor man as possible.

Marilee grinned and threw her a wink as she stepped past Ella on the way to the door. Ella made a silent vow that the very moment she had Mr. Carrigan sent safely on his way, she was going to exact some well-deserved revenge against her sisters.

Starching her shoulders, Ella slowly approached Mr. Carrigan. "If you'll remove your jacket and sit in that chair, I'll see to your injuries."

Sam nodded.

Hound Dog followed at his heel, stationing himself next to the chair when Sam sat down.

"Scat, Hound Dog," Ella commanded.

"Stay," Grandma Jo countered her command.

Hound Dog stayed.

Muttering under her breath, Ella fetched a soft cloth and a basin of warm water and set them on the table beside Grandma Jo's box of medicines.

"I'll tend your head first," she said loudly enough for all to hear; then, leaning close she whispered to him, "I'll find a way to get you out of here. I swear."

He acknowledged her words with a nearly imperceptible upward twitch of his lips.

Ella felt she should say more—like explaining just exactly when and how she intended to fulfill her promise—but at the moment she had no idea. Besides, to her shame, the distressing physical sensation she had experienced during dinner assailed her anew when she lifted his hair to uncover the lump.

The man's hair was as soft as the velvet of a newborn calf's muzzle. It tickled her fingers. She admired the way it curled about his forehead.

She wondered if they had met under different circumstances . . .

Ella pressed her lips together. She couldn't allow herself to have such thoughts. Mr. Carrigan had a fiancée. He would be leaving at first opportunity. She must do all she could to see that opportunity presented itself without delay.

Having cleansed and spread ointment on his forehead, she covered the wound with a bandage, then surveyed the rest of him.

"You'll have to remove your vest and shirt so I can see what damage Hound Dog did," she directed.

Sam threw her a dubious look.

"I promise you, Mr. Carrigan, I won't become unduly agitated by the sight of your person." Her sisters giggled. Ella silenced them with a withering glance. She continued, "I've helped doctor injured ranch hands all my life. I realize where you come from ladies are probably sheltered from the sight of a man's bare chest, but here in the territories pragmatism takes precedence over tender sensibilities. We do what we must."

"Pardon me for ascribing my own prudishness to you."

"I regard your modesty as a compliment not an insult."

Though he still appeared less than comfortable to be doing so, he gingerly removed his vest and shirt.

Despite her promise not to become agitated, Ella felt her pulse quicken and her cheeks warm. Her patient's chest was covered by a thick carpet of curly hair that matched the color of the hair atop his head and tapered as it disappeared at his waistband. His back and arms were similarly impressive—subtly muscled, long, and lean. Scolding herself for giving heed to his manly attributes and reacting like a silly school girl, Ella briskly inventoried his injuries.

He sported a collection of nasty bruises, but nowhere had Hound Dog broken the skin. She announced this with no small amount of relief as she carefully washed the first bruise.

"Of course, he didn't," Grandma Jo spoke to Sam from her rocking chair. "Hound Dog is a smart dog. Once he saw you were gonna be sensible, he decided it'd be bad manners to eat you."

Ella gasped. "I assure you, Mr. Carrigan, Hound Dog would not have eaten you."

"Would have if I told him to," Grandma Jo proudly proclaimed.

"But you wouldn't," Ella argued, tending another bruise. "Despite your current misbehavior, I know you to be a moral woman at heart."

"That I am, but even the best of us sin when provoked beyond our ability to resist temptation, and I don't want to be giving Sam any false impressions." She planted a mournful expression on her face, but her eyes were steely as she addressed the both of them. "I've got my heart set on him keeping us company a while longer, and if he breaks *my* heart, I'll let Hound Dog eat *his*."

"She's twitting you," Ella declared.

"Nope."

"You most certainly are! And neither Mr. Carrigan nor I appreciate the joke."

"Ain't joking."

"You are too!" Ella insisted.

"You'll understand if I'm not inclined to stake my life on your assurances," Sam interrupted their debate, directing his words to Ella. "The very fact that I'm still sitting in this house, gives me little confidence in your perception of how far your family is willing to go to achieve their ambitions for us."

Ella winced. A body couldn't argue with the truth. Setting the jar of ointment on the table, she contritely replied, "Yes, I understand. If I were you, I wouldn't put my faith in me either."

To say the afternoon was hellish was a grave understatement, to Ella's way of reckoning. Only the days she had buried her mother and father were worse. She didn't know how much more she could bear.

Grandma Jo showed no sign of relenting and letting Mr. Carrigan go. She was usually such a sensible woman. Even acknowledging her sense of humor on occasion pushed the bounds of conventionality, Ella couldn't reconcile her present behavior with that of the woman she had heretofore known.

For one thing, this situation wasn't funny.

For another, in twenty-five years she never had witnessed her grandmother commit so much as one cruel act against man or beast. Ella judged using Hound Dog to hold Mr. Carrigan against his will cruel in the extreme. The dog hadn't left his side for so much as a minute, and twice when the man had made a desperate dash for the door, Hound Dog had bullied him back to his chair with a series of growls so ominous they made *her* blood curdle.

She didn't *want* to believe her grandmother would allow Hound Dog to wreak havoc upon Mr. Carrigan's person, but she was fast losing confidence in her own judgment. Despite her having spent all afternoon arguing Mr. Carrigan's cause, he was still here. Every notion she understood to be logic said he shouldn't be.

Her eyes came to rest on the gentleman in question. Naturally, he had given up all vestige of gentlemanly behavior hours ago. Earlier in the afternoon, he had made his own attempts to reason with Grandma Jo, but they had failed as miserably as her own, so now the only words to pass his lips were designed to sting their ears.

His muttered curses, killing looks, and disparaging comments about her family were understandable, but they certainly weren't helping matters.

He was quiet now. She had fetched him a book from his saddlebags, though she wondered if he was really reading it. It had been quite some time since he had turned a page.

Likely, he was using the book as she was using the one she held in her own hands, as a subterfuge to allow her to ponder various solutions to their mutual problem without Grandma Jo continually interrupting her thoughts with some embarrassing comment.

Ella grit her teeth.

For some unfathomable reason, Grandma Jo behaved as though she was convinced Mr. Carrigan and she would make an ideal couple if only they were given a chance to further their acquaintance. True he was handsome, well-groomed, and possessed a sophistication of manner and speech that couldn't be disguised even when he was hurling insults at them. Those were reasons she might admire him, and she did. He owned the most intelligent pair of eyes it ever had been her pleasure to see. But, she couldn't think of one reason he should be attracted to her and could come up with dozens why he shouldn't.

It wasn't that she thought poorly of herself. She knew herself to be a fine woman, worthy of any man who cared to come courting. The trouble was: Mr. Carrigan hadn't come courting. He'd been ambushed.

Even the most starry-eyed optimist couldn't pretend to believe he was going to fall in love with her as her reckless sisters had hoped. So, what was the point in continuing to hold him prisoner? There was no point.

Having exhausted every rational argument, the only means Ella could think of left to secure his release was to fetch the rifle Grandma Jo kept on the rack above her bed and threaten violence. Unfortunately, she knew doing so would prove as ineffective as pleading for the return of sanity to their household. She couldn't shoot a member of her own family no matter how richly they might deserve it. They would know that as surely as she did and be unimpressed by her show of force.

Having no other recourse, Ella resigned herself to doing

nothing . . . for the moment. However, night time was fast approaching, and it would present her with new opportunities . . . as long as she carefully planned what she would do.

Ella lay awake in her bed, listening to the steady inhale and exhale of her sisters' breath. Through the door she could hear the comforting sound of her grandmother's robust snores.

Despite being exhausted from a lack of sleep the night before, she had had no trouble staying awake. She was too worked-up to sleep. A few more minutes to be sure everyone was slumbering soundly and she would begin her rescue of Mr. Carrigan.

Grandma Jo had given up her bed to him, and he lay in the next room, his hands and feet tied to the bedposts. It had taken Grandma Jo, all four of her sisters, and Hound Dog to wrestle him into submission or so Grandma Jo had proudly informed her before commencing a lengthy acclamation of his brawn in an embarrassingly loud voice. The wretches had accomplished their nefarious deed, while she was out back visiting the necessary.

Ella smiled grimly in the darkness. They might think themselves triumphant, but in the morning they were in for a rude awakening.

Slipping her feet over the side of the bed, Ella tied her wrapper over her flannel nightgown, then reached under her pillow for the napkin-wrapped packet of food she had squirrelled into her pockets during supper. She didn't want Mr. Carrigan to get hungry on the long ride back to town.

Her sisters remained soundly sleeping, and she padded on bare feet to the door.

The next stretch of her midnight journey would be the most dangerous. Grandma Jo was sleeping on the settee which meant Hound Dog would be there, too.

Ever so slowly, Ella nudged the door to the bedroom open. Grandma Jo continued to snore. Her rifle was propped beside her. Ella could see nothing of Hound Dog but his tail. Barely daring to breathe, she watched him for several minutes. He didn't move.

The door leading to Mr. Carrigan was ajar. She stealthily covered the distance between her and it, easing it shut behind her. She took a deep breath.

"Mr. Carrigan, don't be alarmed. It's me, Ella," she hissed.

"What are you doing here?" he demanded warily.

"I've come to save you," she whispered into the darkness. The room was pitch black, and she made a slight detour to open the window to let in the moonlight.

"Miss Singleton," Sam acknowledged her propitious presence when she reached the side of the bed. "There are not words to express the extent of my gratitude."

"It's the least I can do." She brushed away his thanks as she began picking at the knots binding his right foot. They continued to converse in low whispers.

"I truly am sorry for all the trouble my family has caused you and that I was unable to secure your release earlier. I've known for a long time they were desperate to marry me off, but never did I reckon them capable of the behavior I've seen today. I just can't imagine what's gotten into them."

"I believe your grandmother may be senile," he stated in sympathetic tones.

"But she was right as rain this morning when we arose. I've witnessed the ravages advanced years can have on the mind, and I've never known it to happen in the space of a moment."

"Perhaps the change was so gradual, you did not notice."

"Trust me, I would have noticed if my grandmother had taken to holding gentlemen prisoner for my benefit." Ella jerked hard on the knot. "It's not as though I've been bereft of callers. Not once has she so much as hinted at the idea of tying one of them up."

"I meant no insult."

"I should have brought a knife."

"What!"

Ella's brows knit as she pondered his tense reaction. When she replayed the last of their hushed conversation from his point of view, she realized where it had gone awry. "Not to use on you; to use on these ropes."

"Oh, thank God. I apologize for assuming otherwise, but you can comprehend why I might be a bit suspicious."

"Yes, it's the easiest thing in the world to comprehend. . . . Who tied this knot anyway?" Ella asked.

"I believe Miss Marilee did that one."

"It figures. She never could tie a proper knot. As many times as Daddy tried to show her . . ." She stared at the door in indecision. "I wonder if I should risk tiptoeing into the kitchen . . ."

"Let's not take the chance. Why don't you see if you can untie my hands; then, I can help with my feet."

"Okay."

The knots binding his hands were tenacious, but Ella was able to pick them loose in a reasonable length of time. She immediately turned her attention to his left foot while Sam applied himself to the right.

"Your horse is in the barn—second stall, but you're going to have to leave your saddlebags here. They're in the next room with Grandma Jo and Hound Dog. I'll bring them to you just as soon as I know you've made it safely back to town. I can't give you your gun either because Grandma Jo hid it and all of ours, too, except for the one she's keeping next to her, and there hasn't been a chance for me to make a thorough search," Ella explained her plan while they worked. She indicated the small bundle she had laid on the foot of the bed with a nod of her head. "That contains a little food in case you get hungry. Also, I brought you this." She stretched across the bed and pressed a wad of bills in his hand. "I know it's not much, but it's all I have."

Sam stared at the money. "There is no need to give me this."

"But I feel you should be compensated in some way for the injustices done you."

"That's very noble of you, but it isn't necessary." He attempted to return the money to her hand, but Ella ignored his efforts. She blushed with contrition and refused to meet his gaze.

"I wish I were as noble as you say, but the truth is: I'm not. The money is really a bribe. Exasperating as they are, I love my family, and I'm hoping to persuade you not to press charges against them. I realize it's not a fair thing to ask of you, and I'll understand if you refuse, but . . ."

He was silent a long time. Ella watched nervously as a succession of emotions played upon his face. He was without question struggling with the decision. "It is against my better judgment . . . but I'll resist a visit to the sheriff . . . as long as you promise to keep a better eye on your overzealous family in the future."

"You have my word."

"And another thing. You have to take back your money. I don't need it, and it would sit better with me if I neglected my duty as a good citizen out of kindness rather than because I was paid to do so."

Ella signalled her consent with a tiny smile. "I've finished." She held up the length of rope before dropping it to the floor. "How are you coming?"

"I've just about got it." A few moments later, he too lifted his rope in triumph.

Slipping off the bed, he quickly donned his vest and jacket, then sat down to pull on his boots.

"You best wait to put those on until after you climb through the window," Ella advised. "No matter how careful a body is, boots make more noise than stocking feet."

"Good thinking."

Ella quietly carried a chair to the window.

"I don't want you to take this the wrong way, Mr. Carrigan, and I most certainly do not approve of the disgraceful way you've been treated, but I'm glad to have met you. You're a gentleman in the finest sense, and I wish you nothing but happiness and good fortune with your future bride and in all that you do."

"Thank you, Miss Singleton. You alone I shall remember with a measure of fondness."

Ella folded her hands and watched Mr. Carrigan climb out the window with no small sense of satisfaction. She had accomplished what she had set out to do, and if she felt a twinge of regret that she couldn't have met him under more fortuitous circumstances, it was assuaged by the gratification of having saved them both from an untenable state of affairs.

He paused to pull on his boots, waved, then sprinted across the yard toward the barn.

"Goodbye, Mr. Carrigan," Ella whispered, before turning from the window.

The exhaustion and the tension of the day that had been kept at bay swept over her like a warm prairie wind. She would sleep in here tonight lest she awaken the household before Mr. Carrigan had put a healthy distance between himself and her family. Ella slipped her arms out of her wrapper and climbed into bed.

It truly was a pity things couldn't have worked out between Mr. Carrigan and herself, she mused as she started to drift off to sleep. Working together to secure his rescue had been exciting. And he had been so kind to her . . .

The silence of the night suddenly was rent by a series of strangled curses and the baying of a dog. Instantly awake, Ella leapt from the bed and ran to the window.

"No!" she added her own protestations to those of the man lying on the ground, doing his best to push Hound Dog off his chest. "Bad dog! Bad dog!" she screamed as Hound Dog pinned Mr. Carrigan's throat to the ground with his mammoth jaws.

A moment later Grandma Jo ambled into her line of vision.

"Hold, Hound Dog!" Grandma Jo commanded, before turning her attention to the dog's squirming victim. "My, you are a stubborn one, ain't you? What am I gonna do with you, Sam?"

"Grandma Jo, don't you dare let Hound Dog hurt him!" Ella yelled across the yard.

Grandma Jo turned to face her. A slow smile spread across her lips. Turning her back on Ella, she again addressed Mr. Carrigan, but she made sure her words were loud enough for Ella to hear. "Oh, Sam." She sighed mournfully. "And here I had every intention of letting you go right after breakfast. Now, you've gone and spoiled my plans. Luring my sweet, innocent Ella into your bedchamber. Why, you've compromised her virtue. Now, I can't never let you go."

Ella felt the blood drain from her face, and she clenched the sides of the window frame so hard her nails left marks. "How dare you accuse him of such a thing! He did not compromise me and you know it!"

"You're standing in his room, wearing nothing but your nightclothes. If that ain't compromised, I don't know what is."

"He was tied up!"

"Ain't tied up now."

"What's all the hollering about?" a sleepy Lily asked as

she wandered into the bedroom, her sisters yawning at her heels.

Ella abandoned her place at the window, grabbed her wrapper from the foot of the bed, and pushed passed them. "Oh, go to perdition," she muttered.

It had been a full week since her sisters had carted home Mr. Carrigan. Ella was convinced no one, man or woman, had ever experienced a level of frustration equal to her own—with the obvious exception of Mr. Carrigan.

She had tried everything she could think of to win his freedom, and the only thing she ever earned him was a fresh set of bruises courtesy of the ever vigilant Hound Dog.

Hound Dog thought it all a great game and was coming to regard Mr. Carrigan as his personal toy.

Though Ella was furious with Hound Dog's behavior, she couldn't rightly hold him responsible. It was Grandma Jo she held responsible. He was only following her orders as he had done with unwavering loyalty his entire life.

Her sisters were no more help than Hound Dog. Janie professed to sympathize with her feelings of chagrin, but her actions proved her to be solidly in Grandma Jo's pocket in this war of wills. Marilee and Fern made no pretense to be anything but one hundred percent pleased Mr. Carrigan was still with them. Lily had taken to giggling like a goose at the slightest provocation. If all that wasn't enough to put up with, the lot of them made no effort whatsoever to restrain their tongues and were given to discussing Mr. Carrigan and her day and night *in front of the man*. Though his personality had deteriorated to that of a bobcat caught in a barrel, their belief Mr. Carrigan would make her an ideal husband became more entrenched with each passing day.

To his credit, Mr. Carrigan had refrained from launching a

physical attack against any member of her impenitent family. True, they kept him tied to his chair during the day and tied to his bed at night which gave him little opportunity. She also recognized Hound Dog's formidable presence had more than a little to do with encouraging his gentlemanly restraint. If he had laid a hand on any of them, Hound Dog would kill him for sure. Still, she had to respect Mr. Carrigan for not exploding in a violent fit of rage. Oh, he exploded often enough, too often for his own good. He'd sit still as a statue and think so hard a body could almost see the wheels turning in his head. It wouldn't be long before he tried something, but always his energies were directed toward escaping, not to wrecking vengeance.

She did what she could to ease him, bringing him books, cups of coffee, and doing her best to deflect the most outrageous statements her grandmother seemed prone to pronounce, but mostly she avoided him by keeping busy with her chores. Her reasons were many, but three were the most compelling.

Every campaign she initiated in hopes of helping him get free miscarried, and she found it increasingly difficult to face the looks of disgust in his eyes. Not that he did any better for himself, or that he was any less critical of his own failed attempts to escape, she just couldn't bear to see any human being feeling so glum.

An even better reason to keep her distance was that despite their insufferable circumstances, the attraction she felt for his physical person persisted to plague her. Worse, Ella knew Grandma Jo was as aware of it as she, so even the teeniest ripple of desire caused her to be engulfed in waves of guilt. Would Grandma Jo be keeping him here if she believed her granddaughter felt nothing at all for the man? Ella couldn't be sure, but at night she lay awake worrying at her inability to hide her discommodious blushes from her keen-eyed grandmother and knew that this was at least partly the cause of Mr. Carrigan's continued imprisonment.

Lastly, she wished to avoid him because whenever he had a chance to whisper in her ear, Mr. Carrigan repeatedly badgered her to solicit outside help. She kept putting him off, but she had no reasonable excuses to offer him, only lame ones, and he was growing more impatient with her by the hour.

Though she had been postponing coming to the conclusion for several days, Ella knew she must accept she was not going to be able to save Mr. Carrigan by herself. Her incessant apologies were beginning to sound hollow even to her own ears. She had hoped to sidestep a public scandal. Too, she didn't want to see her grandmother and sisters locked behind bars. Mr. Carrigan had made it abundantly clear his earlier agreement not to press charges had been contingent on his immediate escape.

Scandal would be unavoidable, but Ella was not without hope her family might still be saved from prison. After all, Rex Johnson was in love with Janie. She would plead with him to let his heart guide him in this matter. She knew her family would have to make some sort of sacrifice to satisfy justice, but maybe it didn't have to be jail time. Perhaps they could make financial restitution or perform some charitable service for the community to demonstrate their contrition.

Whatever the outcome, Ella knew she must set aside her own concerns and do what was right for Mr. Carrigan. He had suffered long enough.

Grandma Jo kept careful watch over her, but only when she was in the vicinity of Mr. Carrigan. Tomorrow, when she went to the barn to milk Electra, she would saddle a horse and ride to town to fetch the sheriff.

Six

"Morning, Ella," Sheriff Johnson greeted. He rose to his feet, his eyes brightening as they focused on the door. "Where's Janie?"

"She didn't come to town with me. I'm here on my own."

"Oh." He sat back down and returned his gaze to the open newspaper atop his desk.

Ella shifted her weight from foot to foot and studied the wall behind him. She had known Rex all her life; he was practically like a brother. She had rehearsed what she would say on the ride to town until she was satisfied with her speech. But now, as she stood ready to confess her family's folly, her tongue wasn't eager to cooperate.

She wet her lips, took a deep breath, and prayed for courage. It didn't help much, but she duplicated these actions twice more. He spared her a glance.

"Did you just stop by to say 'howdy' or is there something you want?"

"I'm always glad to take the time to be friendly, but this is not a social call." Ella was pleased she managed a composed tone, though she was less than pleased Rex appeared to be listening with only half an ear. She wished he would stop reading his paper and give her his undivided attention. What she had to say wasn't agreeable, and she didn't want to have to repeat herself. "I need to talk to you."

"About what?" he asked without looking up.

"Janie and the others."

The mention of his fiancée's name kindled his interest. He finally lay the newspaper aside and gave her his full regard.

Now that she had it, Ella wasn't so sure she wanted it. Belatedly, she realized it would have been easier to say what she must, if he wasn't looking at her.

"They've gotten themselves into a bit of a scrape," she began, preferring to ease into her subject rather than bleat out the awful truth.

"What kinda scrape?"

"Before I tell you, I want you to remember just how very much Janie loves you. She wants to marry you more than anything in the world. As for the others . . . there's no denying how Marilee feels about Bob, and Fern is so in love with Frank she can't think straight half the time, and Lily . . . why Lily loves half the men in town, she just hasn't made up her mind who she loves the most yet. As for Grandma Jo, well, there really is no good excuse to blame for her part in it, but the possibility she may be getting senile has been mentioned. She is getting on in years and . . ."

"Senile?" Rex chuckled. "There ain't a body alive with a sharper mind than your grandma. I ain't saying I always agree with her way of thinking, 'cause I don't, but . . . where'd you ever come up with a fool notion like that?"

"Okay, so we both know her mind is still as sharp as a tack, but I felt obliged to say something in her defense."

"Why?"

"I'm coming to that," Ella vowed.

"Don't sound like it to me. Why don't you quit beating around the bush and get to the point. It can't be all that bad."

"Oh yes, it can. But you're right. I need to just say it and get it over with." Ella expelled a shuddery breath. "My sisters kidnapped a man, and presently they and Grandma Jo are holding him prisoner at our ranch."

For a moment Rex just gaped at her as if she was the town drunk; then, in a dubious voice he asked, "Now, why on earth would they do that?"

It had been difficult enough telling Rex *what* her family had done. Telling him *why* they had done it was so mortifying Ella once again found herself tongue-tied. The temptation to jump back on her horse and run like a hare right on out of town was immense, but for Mr. Carrigan's sake she knew she must bear the loss of face.

"They thought he would make a good husband for me," she blurted out. The heat of humiliation stained her cheeks.

To his credit, Rex did not laugh in her face—a face she knew must be as red as the Indian paintbrush that bloomed on the mountainsides and was getting redder by the second. Instead, he asked in the most sherifflike of tones, "Maybe you oughta start this story at the beginning and don't be leaving out any details."

As Ella stared at his blank expression, her worry for her family's future swelled until it was a crushing weight in her bosom. What if she had misjudged the strength of Rex's affection for Janie and he wasn't forgiving? What if he decided to pitch the lot of them in jail and throw away the key? "Before I do, I have to know," Ella gave voice to her fears, "I have to know, how you intend to deal with my family. I know they have to pay a price for their crime, but I was hoping maybe you could see fit to stretch the law a bit and let them work off their debt to society, so they could still stay home . . ."

Rex gifted her with a crooked grin. "I'm surprised at you, Ella. You know how much I love Janie. There ain't no need to fret about me meting out too stiff a justice to your family. Why I'm practically a member of it. Now, I'm not saying I don't gotta do something. I am the law. But I sure ain't gonna be spiteful about it."

Ella's stiff shoulders sagged with relief. "Thank you, Rex. I thought I could depend on you, but with all that has happened these last days, I find it difficult to be absolutely sure about anything."

"Been tough, has it?"

"You have no idea."

It took a full hour to tell Rex everything that had occurred in the last seven days. When he had said he wanted to hear details, it was no idle statement. Ella answered all his questions truthfully, unsparing of her own feeling when it came to recounting words and incidents she would rather not.

She had failed to secure Mr. Carrigan's freedom on her own, and now she must pay the price. If she viewed Rex's painstaking interrogation as penance for her lack of genius, she was able to endure the whole embarrassing conversation a little better.

"What kinda man is this Samuel Carrigan?" the sheriff demanded after a thoughtful pause.

"What do you mean?"

"Just tell me what sort of character you reckon he is so when I talk to him I'll have some idea who I'm facing."

"It's hard to say. He's been in a foul temper ever since we met. But I don't hold that against him and you shouldn't either," she quickly added, not wanting to give the wrong impression. "I've had glimpses of the man he is, and I know in my heart he's a decent man—honest, upright, and proper as you please. There was a time he was willing to let bygones be bygones and promised he wouldn't press charges. That proves he has a charitable nature."

"Do you reckon he still might let your family off the hook?"

Ella rubbed her brow. "I don't know. I'm hoping he will, but after all they've put him through. . . . Grandma Jo has been absolutely incorrigible."

"So you told me," Rex replied somberly. "I know I for one wouldn't take kindly to having that mutt of hers set on me. I still remember that drifter who tried to steal one of your horses a few years back. There weren't hardly enough of him left to hang after Hound Dog got through with him. No, ma'am. Not a man alive has the chance of a possum surviving an hour in the stew pot trying to gain an inch of ground when he's got old Hound Dog to contend with. But a body has gotta admire this Mr. Carrigan's courage and determination for the way you tell me he keeps on trying."

"Yes," Ella agreed. "To my mind, he has more than his rightful share of grit. But he's not reckless. He's a thinker."

"A thinker, huh?"

"Yes. I don't know where he got his schooling, but just listening to him talk, there can be no doubt he was born with a keen mind, and he wasn't afraid to put it to use. The trouble is he has no experience dealing with someone like Grandma Jo. You know how muleheaded she gets. Mr. Carrigan has reasoned with her till he's gone cotton-mouthed, and so have I, but she's not interested in reason. That's why I had to come to you."

"Well, I guess that about does it."

When he finally ran out of questions, Ella, who had been pacing throughout the interview, sighed audibly and came to a halt in front of his desk. She wiped her sweaty palms dry on her skirt.

"Ella, I know how hard it was for a proud, independent woman like yourself to say what you did, and I appreciate you having the sense to know you were in over your head and coming to me for help." Sheriff Johnson rounded the desk and smiled. "What I want you to do now is ride on home. I won't be far behind you."

"Should I tell them you're coming?"

"That's up to you. I don't reckon it'll make much difference one way or the other."

"I suppose not," Ella commented as he escorted her to the door. She paused at the threshold. "You still intend to be lenient with my family, don't you?"

"Sure enough do. I'd as soon be trampled by a bull as let Janie or those she loves suffer when I could prevent it. We're all guilty of poor judgment at one time or another." He led her to her horse and helped her mount. "You just quit your fretting. You told me yourself Mr. Carrigan is a reasonable man. I can't see how we'll have any trouble bringing this situation to a satisfying conclusion for all concerned."

Ella squeezed his hand. "I owe you one, Rex, and I'll not forget how understanding you have been about all this. I can see now why Janie is so fond of you."

"No need to butter me up with flattery. It's plain to me matters out at your place have gotten out of hand. It's a sheriff's sworn duty to set troubles in his community to rights."

"Duty or not, you have my gratitude. Just as soon as we've freed Mr. Carrigan, I intend to devote my every waking hour to persuading Grandma Jo to let you and Janie wed without delay."

"Well, Ella Marie, I expect we all know what kinda mischief you've been up to," Grandma Jo greeted from her rocker when Ella walked through the door.

"I expect you do." Ella nodded curtly in her grandmother's direction, then focused her gaze on the pot of coffee on the stove. "Mr. Carrigan, would you like a cup?" she offered as she poured one for herself.

"No, thank you."

She continued to direct her words to him. "I would have told you where I was going before I left *had* I been given an opportunity to speak with you privately, but as you know they don't trust me to be alone with you. Anyway, you'll be happy to know help is on the way. I'm absolutely certain before sundown you'll be a free man."

"What kind of help?" Sam questioned, his eyes glimmering with the spark of hope, but the set of his mouth evincing both skepticism and a goodly amount of irritation that she had fore-warned her family.

Ella took a sip of coffee.

"I don't blame you for your lack of confidence in me. Heaven knows, I've failed you so consistently it's a wonder you could have any faith in me at all," she prefaced before answering his question. "I've been to town to fetch the sheriff. He should be here any minute to put an end to this nonsense."

"I reckoned that's what you did," Grandma Jo grumbled. "But don't you reckon I'll be allowing you to untie him a minute before I'm forced to do it. I'm not feeling the least bit kindly toward you or Sam." She snorted. "Mark my words, Ella Marie, when you find yourself a withered old spinster, you're gonna wish you'd listened to me and made more of an effort to win this young man's heart."

"The day I become so desperate for a man I'm willing to chain him to my side, I hope the Almighty has the good sense to strike me dead with a bolt of lightning."

"We didn't chain him. We used the softest ropes we own, and we wouldn't have had to use them if he weren't so dog-gone stubborn. If either of you had made the teeny weeniest effort, you'd both be head over heels in love by now."

Cradling her coffee cup in her hands, Ella faced her grand-mother without flinching. "Think what you will. I know I've done the right thing."

"Yes, you have," Sam agreed. For the first time since they had met, a genuine smile graced his lips. Ella's eyes darkened to a smoky gray-blue hue. Grandma Jo was right, she admitted, turning away to hide her discomfort with her reaction. When he smiled, he was capable of setting a woman's heart to fluttering.

Now that she knew for certain he was going, Ella realized she was going to miss him more than a little when he was gone. It didn't make sense, of course, but she had grown oddly accustomed to having him in the house. She frowned behind her coffee cup. Grandma Jo had accused her of not even trying to like him, but she was as wrong about that as she was right about his smile. She had grown to like him, more than she cared to admit, without even trying. Ella was not at all pleased with herself.

It wasn't that she wanted him for a husband. She didn't, she consoled her aggrieved dignity. She hardly knew the man. True they had lived under the same roof for a week, but no one would ever accuse Mr. Carrigan of possessing the typical male propensity to talk about himself or his pursuits. . . . And she hadn't forgotten he had promised his heart to another. It was just that he was so different from the men she knew.

Setting her half empty coffee cup in the wash basin, Ella schooled her expression to disguise all trace of regret before turning back to face the room. "Well, I best be packing up your belongings, Mr. Carrigan. I'm sure when the sheriff arrives, you'll want to be on your way without delay," she announced a bit too earnestly.

"Yes, Miss Singleton, I do. And with that thought in mind, I will thank you now for all your efforts on my behalf. I wish you would have seen fit to summon the sheriff earlier, but I am capable of understanding why it was a difficult thing for you to do. They are after all your family, and I have had some experience with your dilemma. One tends to love the members of one's own family even when they do contemptible things."

It was the first time he had willingly spoken of his family, and Ella was more than a little curious. She opened her mouth to ask him to tell her more, then clamped it shut again. If he wanted her to know more, he would elaborate without coaxing from her.

Squaring her shoulders, she graciously replied, "I appreciate your compassion. Now, if you'll excuse me, I'll go see to your things so you can be ready when the sheriff comes."

"Well, men, I've called y'all here 'cause we've got ourselves a little problem, and I wanted to ask your advice," Sheriff Johnson stood on the bar and addressed the men crowded around the tables in the Red Eye Saloon.

"What kind of a problem?" Eli shouted from the back of the room.

"I had me a visit from Miss Ella Singleton."

"Them gals are all right, ain't they?" Several men started to their feet.

"Sit yourselves down and rest easy. Nothing has happened to the Singleton sisters. Do you reckon I'd be standing here jawing with you if my sweet Janie was in danger?" The room grew silent and he continued, "Any of you remember that greenhorn who passed through town about a week ago?"

Several heads bobbed, signalling they did.

"Well, according to Miss Ella, her sisters grabbed him, trussed him up, and fetched him home for her to marry. 'Course she's against it. There ain't been the man born she'd willingly march to the altar with. She came to me asking me to help her set him free." He stroked his chin. "But I been doing me some heavy soul searching since she told me about her little predicament. . . . I hear Judge Barkley is visiting over at the Wilson's ranch, and there's more than one of us who is mighty tired of waiting for that gal to settle down so we can hitch up with one of her sisters. I *am* sheriff, and it *is* my sworn duty to look after the welfare of the people of this town. Single men tend to be overly fond of carousing, but a married man, to my way of reckoning, they add prestige to a town. It'd be a good thing for a few of us to settle down with a wife." His eyes took on a golden gleam. "So what do you say, boys?"

"You hinting instead of riding to the rescue we oughta *make* her marry this fella?"

The sheriff grinned. "The notion did cross my mind."

"What if he don't want to marry her?"

"He don't," Rex stated unabashed. "Miss Ella made that plain as could be. Can't say as I blame him. She's too ornery to make a proper wife. When she's not giving some poor fella sass 'cause he was fool enough to come courting, a body would find her with her nose in a book. The man has my compassion, but I don't know why we oughta let a little thing like that get in the way of us getting our own gals. She's a hard worker, and she ain't ugly. Besides, I don't owe this fella nothing. He ain't a friend of mine."

"It would be a neat trick to play on a greenhorn," Willie Crumb opined.

"Him? Who cares about him? Ella Singleton has been strutting around with her chin in the air since the day she learnt to walk. Why there's at least a dozen men in this very room, you and me included, who've asked for her hand, but she can't find a one of us who's good enough for her," Henry Abbot argued. "I say it'd be a neat trick to play on *her.*"

A chorus of enthusiastic "here, heres," burst forth from the lips of many a would-be beau.

Frank rose to his feet. "Now, I'm not saying Ella don't deserve your lack of sympathy, and as far as I'm concerned greenhorns are a dime a dozen, but marriage is serious business." He cleared his throat. "I for one have been seriously trying to get myself hitched to the gal of my dreams for more years than I care to count, and the only thing standing between me and wedded bliss is one Miss Ella Singleton. If we're gonna marry her off, let's do it for the right reason . . . so Fern and me can tie the knot."

"You marry her off for your reasons; I'll marry her off for mine," Henry shouted across the room.

"Jealous, Henry?" George Carson queried with a smirk.

"Hell, no. Y'all know the only reason I proposed to her was 'cause I was dared to do it."

"How many years you gonna keep spouting that tall tale, Henry? Why don't you be a man like the rest of us and admit you were sweet on her, you gave it your best shot, and she wouldn't have you," Tim Fraser gibed.

"We're getting off the subject, boys," the sheriff intervened. "There ain't no reason to bicker over the whys and wherefores. The only thing I need to know is if you're behind me in this."

" 'Fore I'm willing to say one way or another, I gotta know what kinda fella this greenhorn is. I couldn't sleep well at night if I thought we'd leg-shackled Miss Ella to someone who wouldn't handle her kindly," Eli Estes argued.

"That's right," Roger Smith agreed. "I know she ain't been willing to marrying any of us, and that's ruffled more than a few feathers around here, but let's not forget Miss Ella has always treated us good as gold in every other way. She helped you straighten out your account books, Frank, when you got them in a muddle, and she nursed Ernie when he had the fever. And don't forget she bakes everyone of us a pie every Christmas without fail."

"Roger's made a good point, Sheriff," Ernie opined. Everyone except Henry nodded in agreement.

"I would never had mentioned any of this to you if I thought for a minute it'd bring Miss Ella harm," the sheriff assured them. "Everything I know about Mr. Carrigan I heard from Miss Ella's lips, and she didn't have one bad word to say about him and a helluva lot of good. Now, we all know first hand how picky she is about men. In my book, a fella couldn't ask for a more sterling recommendation."

"How's he gonna support her?" Bob McNaught inquired.

"He's a New York City businessman. Don't know the details, but Miss Ella seems to think he's well off."

"She always has had a hankering to see far off places," Jacob Houston asserted.

"His family good people?" Willie demanded.

"Somebody had to teach him manners, and Ella says he's proper as you please, and that's a direct quote." The sheriff grinned.

"What about Grandma Jo? What she think about all this?"

"What do you reckon?" Rex chided. "You know none of them gals can make a move without the old lady's approval. Of course, she's for the match. Fact is: she's insisting on it."

"Must be one fine fella if Grandma Jo figures Miss Ella oughta marry him. She never did any insisting when I was a courting her."

"That's what I've been trying to tell you," the sheriff proclaimed. "What we got here is the makings of a perfect marriage—good man, good woman, and Grandma Jo on our side. So you with me or ain't you?"

"I'm with you." Frank raised his whiskey glass in the air.

"So am I," Henry seconded.

Bob McNaught was next to join them, then Jacob, Roger, and Tim.

One by one, man after man rose to his feet and lifted his whiskey glass. When every man was standing, Sheriff Johnson raised his own tumbler.

"Boys, let's drink to the health of the newlyweds and be on our way. I told Miss Ella I'd be right behind her, and it wouldn't be polite to keep our lovebirds waiting."

Ella turned from the open window. Lines of consternation marred her smooth complexion. "I don't know what could be keeping the sheriff. He said he'd be right behind me," she told Sam.

"I hope he won't be too angry at me," Janie interjected, twisting her handkerchief in her hands so tight the threads were in danger of popping under the strain. "I'm too young to hang."

Ella sighed. All of her sisters now sat in the room . . . waiting. Fern was furious; Marilee stoic; Lily had a case of the nervous giggles; and Janie devoted herself to strangling her handkerchief. Grandma Jo stamped her foot on the floor as she grimly rocked in her chair, alternately giving her and Mr. Carrigan the evil eye.

Ella ignored her and tried to calm Janie. "I told you before, Rex promised me he'd be lenient. The man is in love with you for mercy sakes. He's not going to hang you."

"Well, if he wants to hang *me,* he's welcome to do it," Fern announced. "If I can't marry Frank, may as well swing from a rope."

"Rex isn't going to hang anybody," Ella scolded. "I know you all are just trying to make me feel guilty for riding into town so you may as well save your breath. You brought this on yourselves. I only did what had to be done."

"Traitor," Fern grumbled

"You can call me all the names you like, if it makes you feel better." Ella paced back to the window.

"Benedict Arnold," Lily called after her.

"There won't be any more name calling in this household," Grandma Jo intervened. "What's done is done. I don't want Sam to be leaving us any more than the rest of you, but . . ."

"Finally!" Ella exclaimed. In the next breath she cried, "Oh, no! It looks like he's brought half the town with him. How could he be so thick-skulled? Our family is going to be the brunt of every joke clear into the next century."

"Obviously, he has had dealings with your family before and realizes one man is no match for you," Sam commented.

Ella glared at him. She was too exasperated with Rex to muster the wherewithal to be forbearing. "I know you've been sorely abused, but you could at least pretend a little sympathy for my sake. I didn't kidnap you. I didn't hold you prisoner. I've been on your side from the start. But *I* will be humiliated along with the rest of them. I suppose it was naive of me to think he'd have the good sense to be discreet, but . . ."

Sam raised a brow. "You could not have hoped to keep this crime a secret. Surely, you recognized once I pressed charges, it would be common knowledge."

"I am capable of hoping all manner of things, Mr. Carrigan. Top on my list of irrational hopes was the hope that despite your many threats to do otherwise, once free, you would find it in your heart to forgive and forget."

Before he could answer her, the door burst open and Sheriff Johnson strode in. A dozen men crowded in behind him. The rest peeked in through the open door or stationed themselves at the front windows.

"Afternoon, Grandma Jo, Marilee, Fern, Lily, Janie my love." Rex drew out his fiancée's name, suffusing it with tender affection. Crossing the room, he came to a halt before Sam. "So you're the gentleman Ella told me about. I'm Sheriff Rex Johnson." He held out his hand; then, observing Mr. Carrigan did not have a free hand to offer, shook his forearm instead. "I see you've been enjoying the hospitality of these fair ladies."

"Enjoying is not the word I would choose, but yes, I have

been keeping them company, a situation I have been informed you are here to rectify."

"First things first," Rex cheerfully replied. "As the law, I gotta know just exactly what has been going on in this household. Wouldn't want to jump to any rash conclusions."

"I already explained to you what has been going on," Ella protested.

"I need to hear his version of the story. Then, I'll want to question the suspects."

"Aren't you going to untie him first?" Ella plaintively inquired.

"Sure. Call off Hound Dog, Grandma Jo. I hear you been letting that mutt gnaw on your guests, and I'm not about to have a hunk taken out of my hide," the sheriff directed. "Dog is meaner than a grizzly when he don't want you to do something."

Folding her arms across her chest, Grandma Jo threw him a severe look. "Oh, all right. Just don't ask me to pretend I like what you're doing, Rex. I suspect being sheriff, you gotta do it, so I'll forgive you eventually, maybe, if you get down on your knees and beg like a dog. Then, again, maybe I won't forgive you." She grimaced. "Come on and sit by me, Hound Dog. Looks like the sheriff is gonna take away your playmate."

With Hound Dog safely out of the way, the sheriff pulled out his hunting knife and made quick work of the ropes. The tension in Ella's shoulders slackened immediately.

"Thank you," Sam rubbed his wrists as he stood to stretch his limbs. "And now I would appreciate it if we could take care of the legal formalities with equal efficiency so I may be on my way."

"Sure thing. You can start saying what you have to say any time."

"I would like to press charges of kidnapping against these

ladies, with the exception of Miss Ella Singleton who is innocent of all wrongdoing," he began. "When I am through, I'm sure you will agree, there is more than enough evidence to prosecute."

In a matter of minutes Mr. Carrigan had listed enough crimes against his person that Ella began to fear anew for her family's future. Laid out in so categorical a fashion the events of the past week, dreadful as they had been to live through, sounded twenty times worse. The man had a depressingly precise memory.

When he finished, the sheriff turned from him and without comment said, "Grandma Jo, why don't you go next."

"He's pretty much said all there is to be said," she informed him. It appeared she did not intend to elaborate; then, abruptly, a roguish spark began to glimmer in her dark eyes, "Except for leaving out the part about compromising Ella."

Ella's jerked to attention. "He did not compromise me!"

"You were in his bedchamber in your nightclothes," Grandma Jo reminded.

"I went there to untie him so he could escape. He never so much as laid a hand on me and you know it."

"That true, Grandma Jo?" the sheriff queried.

"It's true," she admitted with ill-humor. "The man has more manners than sense. There he was all alone in the middle of the night with a beautiful gal, and he didn't even try to steal a kiss. Sort of makes a body lose faith in youth of today, don't it?"

Henry Abbot snickered, but a punch in the ribs from his companions shut him up quick enough.

"You gals have anything to add to his story or your grandma's?" Rex turned his attention to the sisters.

Marilee, Fern, and Lily shook their heads. Janie took a tentative step forward.

"I have something to say." She gazed at the sheriff through

tear-filled eyes. "I want to say I'm so sorry for getting involved in all this, Rex. I know it was wrong. I don't know what came over me, and I promise I'll never do anything like it again . . . even if you don't ever forgive me."

Rex slipped an arm around her shoulders and drew her near. "Don't worry about us, honey. I'd never let a little thing like this come between us. In fact, I've got a little surprise for you."

"A surprise?" She sniffed back a tear and smiled wanly.

"Yep. Before riding out here, me and the boys had ourselves a little town meeting and we decided since Ella has been having such a hard time making up her mind about who she wants to settle down with, the only Christian thing to do is give her a little help. Now, standing right before me I see a prime candidate for a bridegroom. Yep. Looks to me like you gals made a fine choice."

"What!" Sam and Ella cried simultaneously, their faces reflecting a mutually felt numbing sense of horror. Peals of hearty laughter rippled on the air as backs were slapped throughout the room.

"At this very moment Bob McNaught is fetching Judge Barkley. We're gonna have ourselves a wedding before this day is over," Rex confirmed with a grin.

"Is this whole community out of it's mind?" Sam demanded, his voice quavering with disbelief. "I am not going to marry anyone today or tomorrow or probably ever considering how I have come to feel about the female of the species these past few days."

"I'm afraid you ain't got any choice in the matter. We took a vote and you lost," the sheriff consoled.

"You took a vote?" Ella mumbled with wide-eyed distress.

"Sure did. And we're all agreed. It's long past time you got yourself properly hitched so the rest of us can get on with the business of starting our own families. We've been as patient as saints, and ain't none of us even close to being saints."

"You can't do this. You're the sheriff. It's illegal," Ella shrieked at him.

"Don't believe it is," he calmly replied. "But if it'll make you happy, I can ease your concern on that count. Boys, all those in favor of adding a law to the books directing the sheriff to oversee the wedding of any marriageable female who's too muleheaded to find her own mate say 'aye.' "

The walls of the cabin shook with the force the chorus of responding "ayes." Grandma Jo sang out her vote the loudest of all.

"Any 'nays?' "

"Nay!" Ella and Sam shouted in unison, their voices nearly matching the volume of the crowd's and far surpassing it in vehemence.

"There you go, all legal like," Rex decreed. "Now, Ella why don't you go get yourself gussied up while me and the boys see to it your bridegroom looks fitting for the occasion. When I cut him loose, I noticed he is starting to smell a bit rank. Grandma Jo, he got any clean shirts? Something Hound Dog ain't ripped to shreds?"

"He sure does. Man has more fine clothes in those saddlebags of his than my husband Nat had in his whole lifetime," Grandma Jo informed him with a broad smile as she bustled to her feet. "Rex, I take back every unkind thought I had about you when you walked through that door. You've done yourself proud. Only thing I could wish for is you'd have given me a bit more notice so I could have baked up a wedding cake."

Sam stepped forward, his head held at an autocratic angle and his hands flexed into fists. "I don't know why you people think you are going to get away with this, but I can assure you, you are not. You cannot force two people who do not want to marry each other to wed."

Gently setting Janie aside, the sheriff stared him dead in the eye. "Just watch me, city boy. You might learn a thing or two."

Seven

Ella stood before Judge Barkley, shackled in place by the steely grips of Henry Abbot and Roger Smith. To her left Mr. Carrigan was similarly manacled between Frank Thatcher and Bob McNaught. His eyeglasses were missing and his face bore a fresh set of bruises earned at the well while he was being stripped, scrubbed, and stuffed into his best suit in preparation for their nuptials. Every time he so much as twitched a muscle, a small army of cowboys stepped forward with raised fists, threatening additional violence should he try to bolt.

Her eyes welled with tears of sympathy, but she quickly blinked them back, unwilling to display any sign of weakness before the unruly mob. Still, her heart cried out her compassion to the man standing beside her. He already had been forced to bear so many indignities at the hands of her family she blushed with shame as the memories flooded her head. How could a merciful God allow more abuse to be heaped upon him?

Ella could not bear to look at him directly, but morbid curiosity compelled her to steal frequent covert glances.

Beneath the black and blue of his bruises, his complexion was so crimson with fury she feared him in danger of escaping their cruel straits by dying of an apoplexy.

He hadn't said a word since they had wrestled him beside her.

Ella had a sinking feeling in the pit of her stomach, he held her personally responsible for this travesty.

She knew she wasn't, as surely as she knew her name was Ella Marie Singleton, but that didn't stop her from feeling culpable. She went back over every word of her conversation with Rex Johnson, trying to determine what she could have said or done differently to prevent this miserable turn of events, but she couldn't think of a thing. How on earth could she have known Rex would play Judas and convince the whole community to join in with him?

Of course, from the looks of them, they hadn't needed much convincing. A party atmosphere pervaded the yard. They assaulted her ears with gleeful hoots and boisterous hollers and enough cackling to drown out a hundred wrought-up hens. More than one whiskey bottle was being passed from hand to hand. The Wilson brothers were entertaining the crowd with an ear-jarring medley of bawdy love songs. *Stupid cowboys!* Ella raged. How dare they make sport with her life! She ought to take a bullwhip to the lot of them.

The only pleasure she took in the sight before her eyes was the split lips and black eyes several men exhibited. At least Mr. Carrigan had had the satisfaction of landing more than a few well-placed punches during his march to the altar.

Her eyes drifted to her own family. They were no better than the rest. They were grinning so wide their faces were in peril of splitting from ear to ear—even Janie, who could usually be counted on to exhibit a modicum of conscience. Ella glared at them. She couldn't hear what they were whispering among themselves, but she was quite certain it wouldn't be to her liking.

Ella couldn't fathom why the whole world suddenly had turned against her. Every time she thought things couldn't possibly get worse, they did. Her head pounded with the effort she made to absorb the unreal reality she faced, and still, she couldn't accept it.

True, thus far she had failed to find a suitable mate on her own. Her lack of a husband thwarted the romantic ambitions of some of the men present. Mr. Carrigan *seemed* to fit the bill. But that didn't justify ruining her life and that of an innocent man. *She* wasn't the one preventing her sisters from marrying. And certainly poor Mr. Carrigan had no stake in their futures. Grandma Jo was the villain.

If the town was hellbent on doing something outrageous, why not hogtie Grandma Jo and the lot of them could marry without her permission? Sure she would kick up a fuss, but she couldn't stay aloof from *all* of them forever. Ella had declared as much as they dragged her before the judge, but her counsel had fallen on deaf ears.

Glancing at her intended bridegroom again, Ella cringed. She didn't have to guess to know what he thought of all this. The man was absolutely convinced he had fallen victim to a pack of devils. And why wouldn't he?

Ella's head whipped face-forward as the judge began to intone the wedding ceremony.

"Dearly beloved, we are gathered here in the presence of God . . ."

Ella wanted to scream that God was obviously preoccupied elsewhere or He wouldn't be letting this ceremony proceed. Instead, she gritted her teeth. It didn't matter what she said. No one would listen to her. The men surrounding her had whipped themselves up into a drunken marriage frenzy and couldn't be reasoned with. Her entire family had betrayed her. Judge Barkley was well known to be sotted more often than he was sober. Even when he was sober, he wasn't a man to be depended upon.

There was no one to depend upon but herself.

Judge Barkley was directing Mr. Carrigan to repeat his vows. The latter remained as stone silent as herself.

"The judge asked you to say your vows," Rex Johnson prompted.

Sam glowered at him. "I'd sooner fry in Hell."

"That can be arranged," the sheriff coolly replied, slipping his gun from its holster.

"You're bluffing," Sam challenged, his eyes shimmering with contempt. "You can't shoot me. If I'm dead, I can't marry Miss Ella which means you can't marry Miss Janie, which I assume is the reason you are willing to forsake the oath you took to uphold the law and promote this criminal farce of a wedding."

Rex shrugged. "That's true. You ain't gonna be much use to me dead. But, if I let you refuse to marry Miss Ella, I can't marry Miss Janie anyway, so I may as well have the pleasure of venting a bit of my prodigious frustration." He cocked the hammer.

The bridegroom remained stubbornly mute.

Sheriff Johnson pulled the trigger.

Ella's scream was echoed by her sisters. The crowd grew still. Frantically straining against the arms binding her, Ella searched Mr. Carrigan's person for a wound. She found none.

"Now, that was just a warning shot," Rex informed him. "You gonna say them vows now, or do I gotta make you look like a piece of Swiss cheese?"

Sam's face contorted with wrath, but his lips remained firmly pressed together.

"Now, Rex," Grandma Jo admonished. "I'm all for him marrying Ella, but I don't cotton to the idea of you shooting him full of holes."

"I ain't hit him yet, now have I? I don't want to see him shot any more than you do. But if he's got his heart set on dying here today, I'm determined to oblige him. I'll try not to hit anything vital 'less he forces me to, but we're either gonna have ourselves a wedding or a funeral."

"Well, see you don't hurt him too bad."

"I ain't making you any promises, Grandma Jo." Rex Johnson was facing her grandmother, and Ella couldn't read his expression, but his voice sounded as earnest as she had ever heard it. He continued without pause. "I'm the law in these parts, and I'm gonna do whatever it takes to get him to comply to the will of the people. Janie and I have waited too long to see this day, and so have the others. I ain't gonna let a pigheaded stranger spoil it. You try to thwart me, and I'll haul you off to jail."

"I guess I've no choice but to bow to your authority. Do what you must," Grandma Jo replied blank-faced.

"Grandma Jo!" Ella protested.

"I'm sorry Ella. All my life I've been a law-abiding woman. I can't go against a lawman."

"Law abiding? Mr. Carrigan wouldn't be standing here risking his life if you were law abiding."

"I'm not the one who brought the sheriff into this. You did," Grandma Jo reminded. "I can't be held responsible for what he does."

Ella refused to believe her ears. Grandma Jo couldn't be saying she was willing to stand meekly by and watch a man be slaughtered. It went against everything . . . before Ella could continue the thought, it was gruffly interrupted.

"Aim for his foot next," someone from the back of the crowd shouted. "It'll hurt like hell, but you won't put a hole in nothing vital." The sheriff readied his gun.

"No!" Ella shouted. Her eyes riveted on her bridegroom, she pleaded with him, "For mercy sake, say the vows."

"No."

"I wish you wouldn't make me do this," Rex complained as he pointed the bore of his gun at Sam's right foot. He nodded

at Frank and Bob. They dropped Sam's arms and took a step
back at the same moment the sheriff squeezed the trigger.

Sam jumped. The bullet grazed the toe of his boot, but his
flesh escaped injury. Before relief could register on his face,
Rex emptied his gun, causing Sam to perform a frenzied
dance. He lost the toe on his second boot; still, he refused to
say his vows. The sheriff reloaded his gun.

He emptied it again. This time Sam was not so lucky. One
of the bullets tore a gash in the calf of his left leg. A bead
of sweat broke out on his brow, but he didn't make a sound.

Sheriff Johnson snorted in disgust. "You do a mighty fine
jig, greenhorn, but I'm running out of patience with you. Bullets cost good money. I hate to do it, but if you'd rather die
than marry that sweet woman standing beside you, I reckon
I oughta just kill you outright and get it over with. Grab him,
boys." Frank and Bob stepped forward and did their duty. This
time when he raised his gun, Rex aimed for the heart. "Best
make your peace with your maker, Mr. Carrigan. You've got
till the count of ten. One, two three . . ."

The blood drained from Ella's face and pooled in her feet,
making them heavy as lead.

"Grandma Jo!"

"Four, five . . ."

"I'm sorry, honey. Rex has made up his mind, and he ain't
gonna let me change it. We'll make Sam a nice grave right
next to your Mama and Daddy."

"Janie, you can stop him," Ella implored.

"Rex, maybe . . ." Janie began.

"Janie, I know how you feel. Your tender heart is one of
things I love best about you, but you gotta leave this to me."

She bit her lip.

"Marilee! Fern! Lily! Somebody stop him!" Ella searched
the faces surrounding her. No one so much as flinched.

"Six, seven . . ."

The world truly had gone mad.

"Rex, no! Please! He's never done anyone any harm," Ella beseeched. "Don't do this!"

"He knows how to stop me. Eight . . . all he's gotta do is open his mouth. Nine . . ."

Ella had never fainted in her life, but she felt herself precariously close to swooning. She admired Mr. Carrigan's mettle, but she couldn't bear to see him die. Especially when it was all so unnecessary. Didn't he realize she would stop this wedding when it came time for her to speak her vows? Rex might be willing to kill a stranger, but he couldn't kill her. At least she didn't think he could. Even if he tried, Grandma Jo and her sisters would surely stop him. They may have turned against her, but nothing could make her believe her family would stand passively by and watch *her* be killed.

Ella heard the hammer of the gun click into place, and if not for the arms holding her, she would have crumpled to the ground. She opened her mouth intending to beg Mr. Carrigan to save himself, but before she uttered her first word her ears were gifted with a blessed sound.

"I Samuel Carrigan . . ." His voice pulsed with enmity, but at last he seemed to comprehend the deadly nature of the game he played.

Ella smiled at him reassuringly. He replied with a brutal scowl. When Mr. Carrigan completed growling out his vows, Judge Barkley turned to her.

After the judge finished instructing her what to say, Ella looked Rex directly in the eye. "Are you going to shoot me now?"

"Why would I want to do that?" he asked, genuinely startled by her question.

"Because I'm not going to speak my vows, and the marriage won't be legal if I don't. So, go ahead and shoot me," she prodded.

"Now, you know I can't shoot you, Ella," the sheriff began.

"That's right," she interrupted. "You can't shoot me. And I'm not going to be saying any marriage vows. So, you may as well release Mr. Carrigan and the lot of you can go home. And if I ever see any of you on our property again, I'll be the one who is doing the shooting."

The crowd groaned in disappointment. Ella smiled triumphantly.

Rex shook his head and scratched his chin while he thought out the matter. "It's true I can't shoot you, Ella," he began after a long silence. "But I'm betting you still can be persuaded to cooperate." He grinned. "See, if you don't say them vows and be right quick about it, I'm gonna be forced to shoot *him* again."

Ella's jaw dropped. "But . . ."

"But nothing. You harbor an ounce of fondness for this fella in that finicky heart of yours, you best be saying your vows *right quick."*

"By God, I reckon he's found a way to get around her after all!" several men crowed in unison.

"Hey sheriff, you're smarter than you look," another shouted.

"Come next election you got my vote for sure," someone else promised.

Ella knew every man's voice, and she silently vowed after this day was over, she would track them down and make them pay for their perfidy. But first she must deal with the sheriff. It had never occurred to her he would use Mr. Carrigan as a weapon against her, and she was as furious as she was taken aback. "Rex Johnson, you so much as harm another hair on his head and I'm going to devote the rest of my days on earth to making you the most miserable human being who's ever been born."

Sheriff Johnson raised his gun and again aimed it at Sam's heart.

"I mean it Rex. I'll hunt you down like the cur you are!"

"You don't want him harmed, you know how to stop me," he calmly replied.

Ella glared at him.

He cocked the gun.

"For God sakes woman! Do as he says unless you want my death on your conscience!" Sam spat the words at her.

Ella cringed. "But . . ."

"But nothing!" he interrupted, his voice a menacing rumble. "These people are beyond reason. As repugnant as the idea of marrying you is to me, I am even less fond of the idea of my own immediate death. Do as he says and do it now before it is too late!"

"I Ella Marie Singleton . . ." Her lips obediently began to form the required words, but Ella's mind was elsewhere. In a few moments she would be married *to a man who visibly despised her.* Oh, she didn't blame him. She despised herself for allowing them to be maneuvered into this hateful marriage.

She was used to being in control of circumstances. She was the one they had always referred to as "the smart sister." When the townsfolk used the title, they rarely meant it as a compliment, but she had taken pride in it nonetheless. So how had an intelligent woman like herself ended up with her life careening over a cliff to perdition?

Try as she might, Ella couldn't come up with a single rational reason to explain it.

Her eyes blazed. The sheriff and the townsfolk may have won the battle, but they hadn't won the war. She would find a way to undo what they had done or die in the effort. There had to be a way. What it was she didn't know, but . . .

"I now pronounce you man and wife."

The words startled Ella back to the present as much as suddenly finding herself released from the burly hands that had held her rooted to the spot and the roar of spontaneous cheers. She started to glance in her new husband's direction, then decided to spare herself the agony and cast her gaze on the ground.

The judge's next words made her temperature rise and her heart skip a beat.

"You may kiss your bride."

"I'd rather not." Sam curtly replied, echoing Ella's own thoughts though for a slightly different reason; she was all too aware Mr. Carrigan's touch had a strange effect on her, and she wasn't eager to expose her vulnerability to their enemies.

"Ah, come on." Judge Barkley threw up his hands. "You're married. Accept it like a man."

"He doesn't want to kiss me," Ella rebuked. "Leave him be."

"The kiss is traditional," he insisted. "I don't know if the marriage will be legal without it."

"I'm sure it is," Ella argued. "Besides, don't you figure it's a bit hypocritical to start worrying about legalities now?"

"Maybe. Maybe not." The judge rubbed his ruddy nose. "Rex, I reckon you're gonna have to shoot him if he don't kiss the bride."

"Ah, come on fella, it ain't gonna kill you to do it," Bob McNaught encouraged.

"But it might if you don't," Henry Abbot advised with a throaty chortle.

"Hey, Rex, if he's too shy to kiss her, make him dance for us again!"

"Yeah! He's one high-stepper. I'd sure like to see him dance again. Maybe I can pick up a few pointers."

"A kiss or a dance. A kiss or a dance." The Wilson brothers commenced to chant and were quickly joined by others.

Using his six-shooter as a baton, Rex merrily conducted the rowdy chorus.

With a heavy sigh and an expression plainly saying: "I am only doing this to shut them up," Sam leaned forward and gave her a chaste peck on the cheek.

Despite its brevity and her resolve not to react, Ella felt the kiss clean down to her toes, and her blood responded accordingly, coloring her complexion a rosy red. She cursed herself for failing to achieve her high-minded goal; still, she managed to maintain a regal posture before the crowd.

"You call that a kiss? You gotta kiss her like you mean it or it don't count," the judge chided.

"If that's the way they kiss in the city, I thank the Lord I was born a cowboy," George chimed in.

"Maybe he don't know how to give a woman a proper kiss."

"Hey greenhorn, ain't you a real man beneath them fancy clothes of yours?" Henry jeered.

"I'm more of a man than any of you will ever be," Sam stated with contempt.

"Then prove it."

"By damn, I will," Sam bellowed, the tattered vestiges of his pride refusing to allow these countrified louts to impugn his masculinity. With a growl, Sam grabbed Ella by both shoulders, he pulled her into his arms. She squealed in protest as his lips came down on hers.

The crushing force of his lips took her by surprise, demanding she respond to him. His lips were hot and moist as they moved with what Ella deemed expert ease across hers. He held her tightly to him, thighs touching thighs, her breasts compressed against his chest. Even in her present frame of mind, even knowing his kiss was an act of wrathful bravado not passion, she was not immune to the physical exhilaration of his flesh pressing against hers. She could feel her blood heating in her veins.

He was taking her breath away, and there was nothing she

could do to stop him. She raised her arms to push him away, but instead found herself clinging to him for balance.

The kiss went on and on and on until Ella's fear it would never end was overwhelmed by the fear it would. Every inch of her tingled with impetuous excitement. She felt deliciously languid and charged with energy all at the same time. He was intoxicating her with his touch.

As Ella willingly surrendered herself to the realm ruled by earthy sensation, she clung to him even tighter.

No longer did she passively accept the kiss, but she gave as well as received. Her partner encouraged her response, stoking the fires building within her until she was sure she would explode in a shower of sparks.

Abruptly, he set her away.

Sam straightened his coat sleeves. "That, gentlemen, is how we kiss in the city," he announced with cold composure. "I assume it satisfies your high standards. If not, I don't give a damn."

Eight

A feral shriek exploded from Sam's new bride's bosom as she hurled herself across the yard and lunged for the sheriff's throat. The assault caught the man off balance, propelling him to the ground. Ella was right on top of him.

She behaved like a wild cat, screeching curses upon his head while she did her best to wring his neck. That aim thwarted, she began to pummel his chest with her fists.

None of the townsfolk stepped in to aid their sheriff, but Janie covered the distance between herself and her fiancée in the space of a breath and commenced tugging at her sister's shoulders.

"Ella stop! You're hurting him," she pleaded.

Without tempering her attack, Ella sputtered, "Good! That's exactly what I'm aiming to do."

"Now, Mrs. Carrigan, there ain't no need to get so riled up," the sheriff counseled as he fended off her blows. "We were only looking after your best interests."

"My best interests? Hah! You call ruining my life looking after my best interests?" She landed an effective blow just below his ribs, causing him to abruptly exhale. "And don't call me Mrs. Carrigan!"

He quickly recovered himself. "We ain't done nothing of the sort, *Mrs. Carrigan*. Mr. Carrigan's gonna make you a right fine husband."

"Ella, please stop," Janie continued to pull and plead.

The crowd rumbled with guffaws as they shouted encouragements to both protagonists without prejudice.

Ella ignored them all, addressing her irate words to the sheriff as she punched him again and again. "He will not make me a fine husband. He only married me to keep from being murdered by you!"

"Nah. I suspect be likes you a little. That weren't no indifferent kiss he just gave you. Besides, I was just bluffing about shooting him through the heart."

"Bluffing!"

"I'm surprised at you, Ella. You've known me all your life. You know I ain't the murdering sort."

"But you shot him in the leg." She punctuated the word "shot" with a hard left to his chin.

"Flesh wound."

"You mean if I had refused to say my vows . . ."

"I'd have been stuck between a rock and a hard place," he confirmed, chuckling despite the blows that continued to fall upon his person. "I don't mind telling you that now that the deed is done. All it took was a wink and Grandma Jo and the others knew what I was up to, but I could hardly have let you in on the joke, now could I?"

"Ooh! You wretched, black-hearted, snake-bellied . . ." Her words trailed off as she directed all her energy to making him pay in pain for his crime.

"Ella stop," Janie persisted to mewl.

Sam watched the entire scene with rising revulsion. Previously, he had been willing to credit Ella Singleton with being measurably more civilized than the rest of her family, but after witnessing this savage display, he was hard-pressed to recall what she had ever done to cause him to form that opinion.

Finding himself married to a woman he did not love was bad enough. Now he must learn to accept his unwanted bride had a penchant for rolling in the dust and engaging in fisti-cuffs? He recognized she was only venting her frustration; he was even willing to accept he might be partly to blame for her present state of mind by further agitating her with that bawdy kiss; still, a lady—no matter how sorely provoked—did not do such things.

What did she hope to accomplish anyway? As the sheriff had said "the deed was done."

They had both been played for fools, and the knowledge stuck in Sam's craw, fueling his already blazing ire. His lips thinned and whitened, and if not for his iron will, he would have roared with outrage.

"Okay, Mrs. Carrigan, I know you feel mighty aggrieved, and you need to get your vexation about this marriage busi-ness off your chest, but enough is enough. I'm an obliging man, but I reckon you've pounded on me plenty long." With amazingly little effort, the sheriff lifted Ella off his chest and set her on her feet. Janie immediate wedged herself between her sister and her beau, spreading her arms protectively and jockeying from side to side to prevent her sister from stepping around her. The sheriff casually brushed the dust from his shirt and buckskin trousers before turning to Sam. "Mr. Car-rigan, looks to me like you're gonna have your hands full teaching your wife some manners." His tone was serious, but his eyes twinkled mischievously. "Yes, sir. I don't envy you the task, but think of the satisfaction you'll have when you finally bring her to heel."

"No man will ever bring me to heel, Rex Johnson. I am a . . ."

"Regardless of what you *think* you are, you are acting like a ill-mannered street urchin," Sam interrupted his bride. "I don't like this marriage any better than you do. In fact, I guarantee you I like it even less, but cursing like a longshore-man and rolling around in the dirt isn't going to undo it. If it would, I'd be right there rolling in the dirt with you. You are embarrassing yourself and me."

Sam smiled a tight-lipped smile when his chiding had the desired effect of silencing his wife. She stood staring at him with wide, plaintive eyes and moved not a muscle.

His eyes scanned the crowd, who had fallen as silent as his bride. Everyone was staring at him expectantly. He returned his gaze to his unseemly wife. Her lips twitched with the apparent need to speak, but she remained gratifyingly mute.

Gratifying except that he hadn't the slightest idea what to say or do next. He had always assumed when he found himself a married man it would be an occasion for celebration not sorrow. As he tried to catalog his options, the only thoughts that filled Sam's mind were thoughts of escape.

The town had their marriage. They had satisfied the letter of Mrs. Singleton's matrimonial law. Everyone was now free to wed whomever they wanted. There was no reason he shouldn't be able to mount his horse and be on his way. No reason except the gut-felt knowledge these backwoods people would never let it happen.

Still, he felt compelled to test his theory.

Without uttering a word, Sam started to limp toward the barn. The pain in his left leg was daunting, but he did his best to ignore it. He would dress the wound *after* he had put a healthy distance between himself and this place. Nor would he take time to gather his belongings. He could wire his lawyer for money to buy fresh supplies and a new set of clothes in Green River, where he planned to return before continuing his journey.

His lack of a firearm was more of a worry, but Sam reasoned he could do without that too until he could buy another. Besides, having been divested of his eyeglasses during the battle to drag him to the altar and being unwilling to risk requesting they be returned to him, his chances of hitting his target were scant.

Sam had limped halfway across the yard and no one stepped forward to block his path. He couldn't believe he had made it as far as he had. He could feel every eye riveted on him.

A spark of hope he might actually be allowed to leave flickered to life in his breast.

Before it could grow, he was stopped in mid-stride by a familiar female voice.

"Where you going, Sam?"

"To the barn," he answered noncommittally, keeping his gaze firmly affixed on his goal as he privately cursed his luck and Mrs. Singleton in the same breath.

"There ain't nothing you need in the barn. What you need is a new pair of boots and gentle hands to tend your wound. Rex can give you the boots. His feet look to be the same size as yours, and being as he's the one who shot yours up, he oughta be the one to give his to you. As to those gentle hands, why they're hanging on the end of your pretty new wife's arms. You best turn around and make your way up to the house."

Sam grit his teeth. "I don't want to go to the house. I want to go to the barn."

"Ain't nothing you need in the barn," Grandma Jo repeated.

"Yes, there is."

"What?"

"The means to return to the sane world," he muttered.

"You ain't figuring on deserting your bride at the altar, are you? 'Cause you know I can't let you do that. I've grown rather fond of you, as you well know, and the Lord don't look kindly on wife deserters. Christian duty demands I protect you from doing something that might consign your soul to the fiery flames of Hell."

Still refusing to turn and look at the dread woman, Sam

curtly replied, "I'll take my chances. Somehow, I think the Lord will be forgiving."

"That's what all sinners say, and they're wrong ten times out of ten. No, I'm just too fond of you to let you go do something so foolhardy."

Sam calculated there were about twenty yards remaining between himself and the barn. Reason told him his injured leg would never allow him to outrun his enemies, and even if by some miracle he did reach his horse, they were sure to give chase.

He glanced over his shoulder. They were all watching and waiting to see what he would do next: Mrs. Singleton, her wayward granddaughters, the sheriff, his speechless bride, and enough fist-ready rustics to make a lesser man's blood run cold.

Philosophizing since everyone around him had abandoned reason he may as well, too, he resolutely stated, "I'm leaving," and resumed his journey to the barn.

"I got a yard full of cowboys saying you ain't."

Every man present confirmed her words with a boisterous, "She sure does."

"You hear that? These are a smart bunch of boys. They know I can't be counting Ella married if this little love match don't stick."

Sam lost the battle he waged to suppress his roiling emotions. He spun to face Mrs. Singleton, every muscle taut with indignation. "What are you? Some kind of witch! How is it you've managed to convince an entire community to do your bidding without complaint?"

A guileless grin stretched across her weathered face, and she patted her bun. "I know how to sweet talk, and I bake a mean chokecherry pie."

Lowering his voice to a fulminant growl, he accused, "You are also holding your granddaughters for ransom."

"That, too," she admitted without shame. "Best way I know to control a man is through his," she cast her eyes to the region below his belt, *"heart."*

"They may think with any part of their anatomy they choose. *I* do my thinking with my head."

"Then your head oughta be advising you are out numbered by about fifty to one and the only smart thing to do is save your hide another beating and give up any notion of running out on my Ella."

Before Sam could think of a suitable reply, the conversation was interrupted by a man who had earlier introduced himself as Bob McNaught.

"Damnation, Grandma Jo. What are we all doing standing here jawing when we oughta be starting the wedding celebration? Since I'm sure Miss Ella's wedding wasn't exactly what every girl dreams it will be, I figure we owe it to her to make her wedding party the best that ever was."

"I don't reckon Ella is much in the mood for celebrating right now, Bob," Grandma Jo cast a glance in her granddaughter's direction. "Why don't we postpone the celebration a day or two. Say this coming Thursday? Y'all meet back here at noon. I'll provide the food, and you boys provide the fiddles. . . . Also, the newlyweds are gonna need some privacy, so I want you to give my girls a ride into town and take them to Sally's. I'm sure she won't mind putting up with them. Bring them back with you when you come Thursday. Oh, and just to be sure my new grandson-in-law don't come down with another case of itchy feet, I'm gonna need me four or five men to stay and guard the cabin. Hound Dog is getting tired of doing all the work himself."

Ella stood before her husband, her lips pressed tightly together. Her eyes moved from him to Hound Dog, who lay a few feet away feigning sleep, then back to him. They were alone in the house. It was the first time they had been alone since the night she had tried to help him escape. She hadn't said a word since he publicly had rung a peal over her head, and she wasn't much inclined to start talking to him any time soon. In her present state of mind, anything she said she would probably regret.

His eyeglasses lay folded on the table. He picked them up, scowling as he bent the frame back to its proper shape. He glared at her while he polished the lenses.

Ella glared right back. It wouldn't hurt him to show a little regard for her feelings. After all, he had her whole-hearted sympathy. *He* was the one who had demanded she say the vows that sealed their fate. *She* had been inclined to offer further resistance. If he hadn't bullied her, she would have had time to think things through and realize Rex was hornswoggling them. So, this marriage wasn't *all* her fault.

If a person looked at the situation logically, none of it was her fault. She hadn't kidnapped him nor held him prisoner nor threatened death if he didn't marry her. She was as much a victim as he. Why couldn't he see that?

Probably because he found her the most undesirable woman he had ever met, Ella blackly mused. His wintry reaction to what had felt to her lips to be a scorching matrimonial kiss was certainly more than enough proof of that. Grandma Jo had often counseled her sisters and her that men, being lustful creatures, didn't have to like the women they kissed to enjoy kissing them. Ella believed her. Her own observations bore witness such was the truth. A man didn't even have to know a woman at all to be consumed with lust for her. The presence of a bevy of soiled doves in every town attested to that sad reality.

That left only one possible explanation for Mr. Samuel Carrigan's cold response: he hated her with every fiber of his being.

Ella tried to hate him right back, but she couldn't. She was furious at him for his lack of understanding and his mistreatment of her. She blamed him for pressuring her into falling victim to Rex's deceit. Her vanity was mortally wounded he hadn't found kissing her even the least bit pleasurable. But she couldn't hate him because if she were in his place, she knew she would feel exactly as he did.

The knowledge deepened her already crushing depression. Unwilling to sink into total despair, she stalwartly attempted to cheer her spirit by reminding herself at least he had had the good sense to take Grandma Jo's advice and spare himself another beating. His poor face already sported more than enough unsightly black and blue swellings.

A body had to admire the manly way he had marched into the house, his head held high. She couldn't have managed such self-possession if her life had depended on it. They had had to drag her, peel her fingers off the doorframe, and shove her through the door.

"Well, what do you suggest we do now, wife?" His voice startled Ella out of her bleak ruminations. She said the first thing that popped into her head.

"I probably ought to take a look at your leg."

"I can tend to it myself, thank you."

"That's agreeable to me," Ella proclaimed with utter sincerity, having no inclination to feel her blood course wildly through her veins, which it was sure to do if she was obliged to touch him. "I'll just heat some water and fetch the medicine box." Without waiting for him to reply, she busied herself doing just that. It helped having something to do. Unfortunately, it only took a few moments to light the fire and retrieve the necessary items from the bedroom. When she returned, he was stepping away from the window.

"I suppose you didn't think to check the exits at the back of the house," he commented.

"Actually, I did. There's a guard at the door and both windows."

"I assumed as much." Hobbling to a dining room chair, he sat himself down with a thud. Ella paced between the window and the stove.

"Would you like some coffee?"

"No."

"I could fix you some tea if you'd rather."

"No."

Ella clamped her lips together.

"I hope you know I had no idea things would turn out the way they did," she feebly offered when the silence between them stretched beyond the coping abilities of her frazzled nerves. "I really thought Rex would . . ."

"Don't waste your breath on explanations. Regardless of what you thought, we're married. Unless what you have to say is going to change that oppressive truth, I don't see any purpose in discussing what you did or did not think."

"Well, excuse me for daring to open my mouth. I suppose you prefer we sit and glare at each other for hours on end."

"No. What I prefer to do is mount my horse and ride hellbent for leather away from here, but as you well know I am being held prisoner."

"In case it has escaped your attention, I am, too."

"They're your friends and relatives."

Ella turned her back on him. "I'd appreciate it if you'd refrain from reminding me of that fact."

"Why should I?"

"Because making me feel more wretched than I already do isn't going to make our situation one bit better."

Ella could feel his eyes burning holes in her back, and she resumed her pacing.

A long moment passed before he morosely admitted, "You're right. It doesn't help our situation. Though it does help me feel meagerly better to rail at somebody."

"If it makes you feel better, then by all means rail away. It's the least I can do." Striding to the stove, Ella tested the temperature of the water, then picked up a pot holder and carried it to the table. After returning the pot holder to its hook by the stove, she walked back to the table and plopped herself down on the chair opposite his. Folding her arms across her chest, she stiffened her shoulders and steeled herself for a barrage of insults.

He propped his injured leg on the chair next to him. When he began to roll up his tattered trouser leg, Ella furtively peered over the table edge. The moment she was certain the wound was not grave, she averted her eyes and didn't look at him again . . . until she heard him cry, "Ouch!"

"Are you okay?"

"I'm fine. I just pressed too hard." He did his best to appear stoic as he continued to cleanse the wound, but the perspiration beading on his brow betrayed his efforts.

"Are you sure?"

"Yes."

"You don't look fine. You look all pale and sweaty."

"If my countenance offends you, there's not a thing I can do about it," he retorted. "I fear I lack experience when it comes to dressing gunshot wounds, having had the singularly good fortune not to have ever been shot before visiting your charming community."

Ella chose to ignore his sarcasm. "Then you best let me doctor it," she advised, moving around the table to do just that. When he resisted relinquishing the soap and washcloth to her hand, she planted her fists on her hips. "The bullet may not have done much damage, but infection can easily take your whole leg if it's not treated properly. Stop acting

like a cornered bull moose and hand over the rag!" He did
as she said. Ella dropped to her knees. While she finished
cleaning the wound, she tried to distract him from the pain
by making idle conversation. "I suppose people don't carry
guns in a big city like New York."

"No, they don't, unless they're criminals, and I move in
higher circles."

Ella had no doubt of that. His good breeding had impressed
her from the start of this whole rotten affair. His good breeding had been what had attracted her sisters to him in the first
place.

Soaking the washcloth, Ella carefully dabbed at the crust
of blood that had dried over the wound. Despite the grisly
nature of her task, her heart insisted on beating at an accelerated rate. Ella was thoroughly annoyed with herself. Keeping
the conversation going was the only defense that came to
mind.

Ella knew she was risking his wrath; he had bluntly refused
to answer when Grandma Jo had asked him; but she decided
things couldn't get much worse between them and she might
as well ask the question that had been on her lips for days.
"I know it's none of my business," she began tentatively, pausing to rinse and dry his leg. "And I'll understand if you prefer
not to tell me . . . but what *are* you doing so far from home?"

His eyes blazing, he opened his mouth, but before he uttered a word, he snapped it shut again. As he studied her, his
expression tempered slightly. "I suppose I won't do myself
any harm if I tell you."

"I would never use anything you said against you," Ella
assured him.

"Not on purpose, anyway." He gave her a hard look, but
relented when she began to squirm beneath his censorious
gaze. "I came to Wyoming to visit my father and brothers."

"Really? I wish I had known that from the start. It would

have saved me a mountain of agony," Ella exclaimed reaching for the jar of antiseptic. "I've been racking and racking my brain since that dreadful moment Judge Barkley declared us man and wife, trying to figure a way to save us from this marriage and . . ." She smiled. "Your family is probably already riding to the rescue. Nobody around here can keep a secret, and a juicy bit of gossip like the news of our wedding will travel through the territory fast as lightning. Your family will be able to find you in no time at all, and since they'll be forewarned of the type of trouble you're in, they'll come prepared."

Her scenario sounded delightful, and would have been flawless except for one small detail. His expression accurately reflecting the darkness of his soul, Sam stated, "I hate to dampen your enthusiasm, but there is something important I neglected to tell you."

Ella looked up at him.

"My family doesn't know I was on my way to visit them. The unvarnished truth is: they don't even know I'm alive."

"What!"

"It's a long story." He reached into the medicine box and handed her the roll of bandaging material. His lips set in a grim line, he focused his gaze across the room.

It was clear to Ella he had no desire to elaborate. She wrapped his calf, secured the end of the bandage, and pulled his trouser leg back in place while her curiosity battled with her reluctance to rekindle his temper. Curiosity won. Rising to her feet, she faced him squarely. "Unless you've got some secret plan to get us out of this house, neither of us are going anywhere any time soon. A long story will help us wile away the hours."

"I'd rather not discuss it," he stated the obvious.

Ella was not so easily put off. "It's not enough you dashed

my hopes? Now, you're just going to sit there and let me be eaten alive by curiosity?"

Sam sighed loudly. He really didn't have a good reason *not* to tell her. And though he acted to the contrary, deep down he knew she was doing the best she could under very trying circumstances that were not wholly her fault. It was difficult to commiserate with anyone else's needs when he felt so misused, but he forced himself to show her some consideration. "All right. I'll tell you enough to satisfy your curiosity, but that is all."

"Please do." After bringing him a clean bowl of water with which to wash the fresh bruises on his face, Ella returned to the chair she had earlier occupied and leaned slightly forward, giving him her undivided attention.

"Don't stare at me."

"Sorry." She shifted her position on her chair so she was facing to the left.

Sam tended his bruises with slow, deliberate movements. When he finished his task, he had organized his thoughts to his satisfaction. Clearing his throat, he began, "A few weeks ago my mother passed away."

"I'm so sorry. I didn't realize her death had been so recent." Ella's eyes met his. She instinctively reached for his hand. "I know how difficult it is to lose one's mother. You have my deepest sympathy."

Sam pulled his hand away. "I appreciate your concern. Now, as I was saying . . . when my mother's will was read I was given quite a . . . shock. It turns out she was not a widow as she had always led me to believe. She had left a husband and two sons behind in Wyoming territory."

"Your mother told you your father was dead when he wasn't?" Ella queried in disbelief. "How could she do such a thing?"

Adjusting his eyeglasses, Sam gave her a killing look. "If

you insist on interrupting me every other sentence, I have no intention of continuing this conversation."

"Sorry."

"And would you stop saying you're sorry every time you take a breath. It's an extremely annoying habit."

"Sor . . ." Ella caught herself, and quickly rephrased her reply. "Yes, I'll try not to do it again."

"Thank you. Now, where was I?"

"You were telling me about your mother's will."

"Yes, I was. My mother, being an only child, inherited a sizable fortune from her father which, through intelligent management, increased substantially during her lifetime. She in turn divided her accumulated wealth equally between her three sons. I came here to see that my brothers receive their rightful inheritance . . . and to satisfy *my* curiosity." He closed his mouth, his expression unreadable, except for the set of his jaw which conspicuously communicated he had said all he intended to say on the subject.

Without pausing to calculate the consequences, Ella immediately began to quiz him. "Did her will tell you why she did what she did?"

"No, but her diaries did. She found life in the territories too hard to bear."

Ella was surprised and pleased he had answered her question without protest, but she decided against telling him so. Instead, she tested her luck with another question. "Couldn't she persuade your father to move back East with her?"

"She never tried. Though they were both born and raised on the east coast and came from similar social and financial backgrounds, for some reason she was convinced he would be as miserable living in a city as she was living in the country."

"But her children?"

"She left them with my father to assuage her guilt for abandoning him."

"And you?"

"She was with child when she left. She knew, but my father didn't."

Heavens! When she had asked why he was in Wyoming, Ella had assumed his answer would be simple: he was here on business or to visit friends or to pay a family visit of a conventional nature. It had never occurred to her his reason would be so complicated. She was grateful he had answered her many questions without balking, but now that she had the information, she had no notion what she should say.

Again the silence between them stretched to the point of suffering, but this time it was Sam who broke it. "Have you become bored with interrogating me or has the horror of learning my family's unpleasant little secret rendered you mute?"

"I'm hardly in a position to pass judgment on your family's behavior, now am I?" Ella demurred.

He dropped the wash rag into the bowl. "I guess not."

"Then please exercise the courtesy of not accusing me of such a thing. Besides, *I* have enough intelligence to realize it would be unfair to hold you responsible for events over which you had no control."

"Your barb lacks subtly but your rebuttal has some merit. However, in my own defense I must say I don't believe my behavior toward you has been excessively bad-mannered."

"What about that, that *kiss* you gave me?" Ella blurted out. "You practically ravished me in the yard. If that wasn't excessively bad-mannered, I don't know what is."

"They called my masculinity into question," he stated matter-of-factly.

"So what?"

"You expected me to just stand there and do nothing?"

"Yes. Why not? If you can endure being beaten to a pulp *and* shot, a little twitting shouldn't cause you to lose your composure."

"I did not lose my composure. I was in full control of myself at all times. I merely proved a point."

Her eyes narrowed and she impaled him with her gaze. "And what point did you prove? That you are capable of coming near to consummating our marriage before a crowd without breaking a sweat? I would think your lack of feeling would confirm rather than belie their poor opinion of your virility."

"Is that what this is really about? You're upset because you ended up blushing and breathless and I didn't?"

"Yes. I mean no! What I mean is: it wasn't a very nice thing to do, embarrassing me in front of all my friends, and if your manly pride demanded you kiss me so provocatively, the least you could have done is pretend you enjoyed it."

"So you chide me for defending the prowess of my sex in one breath, then claim I have gravely insulted your feminine pride in the next? I believe the proper term for one who argues your position is: hypocrite."

The cursed man was right, Ella realized, blushing to the roots of her black hair. Why had she opened her mouth in the first place? She had never intended to bring up the matter. What could she have possibly hoped to accomplish? Hadn't she suffered enough humiliation today without adding to her agony by heaping on more? Because her mood was as vile as the circumstances in which she found herself, Ella bluntly answered her string of rhetorical questions in sequence: Stupidity. Nothing good. More than enough, thank you.

Having finished tormenting herself, she clasped her hands tightly on her lap and willed her voice to sound as aloof as his. "Let's just drop the subject, okay?"

"Fine with me. I wasn't the one who brought it up."

"I never said you were."

Ella focused her gaze on her hands, the walls, the stones of the fireplace, anywhere but on the man who sat across the table from her. One minute ticked into two, then three . . .

Her brow puckered and the corners of her mouth sagged. She wished Grandma Jo would come inside. She was so furious with her grandmother, Ella doubted she could manage a civil word, but someone was needed to fill these unbearable stretches of silence, and Grandma Jo's gift for gab was renowned. *She* certainly had no inclination to fill the breach. Likely, she'd only succeed in putting her foot in her mouth again. Until she was prepared to present a viable plan to undo what had been done, she preferred to keep her lips safely sealed.

Haplessly, Ella knew her grandmother well enough to realize she would make herself scarce until well after dark. There were plenty of outside chores to keep her busy, and if she tired of industry, she always had their guards to keep her company. Ella's only hope was hunger would compel her grandmother to come indoors, and that hope was slim. Grandma Jo was a resourceful woman. She'd probably light a campfire, butcher a hen, throw in some wild greens, and cook up a hearty soup for herself and the men.

The thought of her grandmother having a lovely evening while she sat here imprisoned in the house wishing herself anywhere else on earth deepened Ella's frown. How dare Grandma Jo picnic in the starlight when she was the one responsible for every miserable minute . . .

"I hate it when women pout. I liked kissing you. There I've said it. So, you can stop looking so forlorn."

"What?" Ella nearly jumped out of her skin at the sound of his voice. She was sure she couldn't have heard him correctly.

"I said: there is nothing wrong with the way you kiss."

Ella could feel a hot blush spreading across her face and down her neck. What was wrong with the man he felt compelled to make such an unwelcome and absurd statement? She made no effort to hide her annoyance. "I thought we agreed not to talk about that."

"We did, but you didn't tell me you were going to sit there all pursed-lipped, looking like you're about to burst into tears at any moment. So I'm telling you the truth, unwise as that may be. There is nothing lacking in the way you kiss a man."

"I know that. Just because you didn't find me . . ." She left the rest of what she was going to say unsaid. Straightening her spine, she continued, "One man's poor opinion is not enough to throw me into a fit of despair. I am twenty-five years old. It's not like you're the first man who ever kissed me. I appreciate your concern, but I most definitely have not been sitting here fighting back a flood of tears."

"You sure could have fooled me," he argued, plainly upset his pathetic excuse for an apology had not been well received. His words fed Ella's vexation.

"I'll have you know I almost never cry. Besides, I wasn't even thinking about you."

"Then, what were you thinking about?" he demanded.

"What Grandma Jo is going to cook for supper."

He shot an angry, disbelieving look across the table. "Now, there's a useful occupation for your mind."

"I don't see how it's any more inapt than languishing over your kisses, which was your original assumption."

"At least it made sense."

"To your overactive masculine imagination perhaps, but not to me," Ella tersely informed him. "Despite what circumstances might have led you to believe, I have not spent my days pining for a man to love me. I was perfectly content to be a spinster. I'm not saying I'm opposed to sharing my life with the right man. If the *right* man ever comes along, I'll be more than happy to give up the single life. *But* I most definitely will not waste a moment of my life pining if he never shows up."

"A brilliant lecture, worthy of Miss Anthony herself, but aren't you forgetting something important?"

"And what is that?"

"You can't have two husbands and you already have me."

"I don't consider our marriage a permanent state of affairs. We were both coerced so as far as I'm concerned, we have no moral obligation to honor our vows. I just haven't figured a way to get us out of it yet."

"We need to obtain an annulment."

To Ella's mind his statement was the first constructive thing he had said since they had found themselves married. He had only stated the obvious, but the opportunity to change the current direction of their conversation was like manna from heaven. She didn't understand any better than he did why she had gotten so riled with him for telling her he liked kissing her. Yes, she did, a twinge of insight caused her to amend her thought. He was lying to her because he pitied her and pity was something she could not abide—not when she was the object to be pitied. His ill-conceived attempt to make her feel better had rallied the remnants of her pride to her defense.

Having discharged a portion of her pent-up aggravation, Ella was pleased to find she was able to regain command of her faculties and deal with their situation logically again. "Yes, I know we need to obtain an annulment," she earnestly agreed. "But the question is: how are we going to do that when we are both being held prisoner?"

Apparently, he had decided he too was ready for a truce for when he spoke his voice was low and even of tone. "They can't watch us every minute of every day forever. Sooner or later one or both of us will find a chance to escape."

"And we'd be hunted down like deer the moment Grandma Jo caught on to what we were up to. This is the territories. It's not like we have a judge in every town. Mostly they travel around, and if you want one you just have to wait until he passes your way; then, like as not, you'll find he is of Judge Barkley's ilk."

"Are you telling me I can expect everyone I meet in Wyo-

ming to be as wrong-minded as the people I've already en-
countered?"

"If you had asked me that question two weeks ago, I would
have answered you with a resounding *no*. But after living
through the last few hours, I fear I've lost all confidence in
my ability to accurately take the measure of my fellow man."
Ella combed her fingers through the hairs at the nape of her
neck. "But that really is not all that important. What is important is for you to comprehend our finding a sympathetic
judge won't be a simple task. With the best of luck, it will
take at least a week, and neither of us has been having any
luck to brag about of late. It could take as long as a month.
And while we are trying to find the judge, the whole town
will be trying to find us, and they would. Why all by himself
Bob McNaught could track a snowshoe hare in a blizzard."

"Don't you people have anything better to do with your
time than harrow innocent strangers?"

"Of course, we do. But . . ."

"But . . ." Sam impatiently prompted.

"There's nothing cowboys like more than a contest of wills,
with the possible exception of a good joke," she explained.
"Keeping us married qualifies on both counts. Just because
they've admitted they won't kill you doesn't mean they won't
hunt you down and beat you senseless on a regular basis, if
that's what it takes to keep you with me. And with Grandma
Jo egging them on . . ."

"What if instead of wasting time looking for a judge, I ride
straight to Green River City. I could send a telegram to my
lawyer and . . ."

"I've already thought of that, and it won't work. Green
River is too far, and they'll be figuring you'll ride that direction. You'd be caught so fast it wouldn't be worth the effort
of saddling your horse."

"Thank you for your expression of confidence."

"You've no call to be testy. I wouldn't get anywhere worth getting either."

"Are you trying to convince me I have no recourse but to resign myself to the idea of being stuck here with you for life?"

"Certainly not," Ella protested. "I'm just saying when we make our escape, we have to do it in a way no one will want to follow us."

"And how do you propose we do that?" he demanded.

"I haven't come up with a workable plan yet, but I will. I promise you, I will."

"I'm sure you'll understand if I prefer to put my faith in my own abilities to come up with a plan."

His indictment of her competence was uncharitable, but Ella was honest enough to admit his experience to date completely justified his opinion. Still, there was no reason he had to state his desire to put his trust in himself so acrimoniously.

"Unlike you, Mr. Carrigan, I try not to allow my emotions to cause me to lose sight of the fact we are on the same side and share the same goal," Ella echoed his acidy tone, finding a certain satisfaction in tweaking his patrician nose. "I enthusiastically welcome any and all help you are willing to give me. It makes no difference to me which one of us figures out a way to get us out of this loathsome marriage, just as long as one of us does, *and the sooner the better.*"

Nine

Rising to her feet, Ella tidied the medicine box and returned it to its proper place. Upon reentering the room, she strode to the table and commenced to wring the moisture from the bloodied washcloth with excessive vigor. She didn't spare a glance for the man sitting at the table.

After hanging the cloth to dry so it wouldn't mildew the other laundry waiting in the basket for wash day, she poured one bowl of water into the other and headed for the door.

George Carson was sitting on the top step of the porch, chewing the end of a weed. Ella gave him a menacing smile, but in the end resisted the urge to exact a bit of vengeance and poured the water on the row of wild geraniums she had transplanted along the edge of the porch.

Her head held high, she marched into the house, slamming the door behind her.

Ella's eyes scanned the room. When they fell upon the feather duster, she seized it like a sword and began to attack the dust in the room.

Think, think, she admonished herself. There has to be a way to get out of this marriage. Though she was exceedingly irritated with Mr. Carrigan, she considered his suggestion they ride directly to Green River and contact his lawyer a laudable one. To her mind, soliciting outside help was definitely preferable to taking their chances with the locals. They both agreed an annulment was the proper course, so how to best deal with the legalities was not a problem. What was a problem was how to escape the ranch and get to Green River.

Ella entertained several ideas in succession, but each had to be rejected for the same reason. Devising ways to get off the ranch wasn't difficult. It was the getting *to* the telegraph office in Green River part that left her stymied.

A little divine inspiration would certainly not go unappreciated, she informed the Almighty. Ella cast her gaze heavenward and stifled a sigh. Lowering her eyes, she glared at the back of her churlish husband's head. Several unflattering descriptions of his character readily came to mind; then, she caught herself noticing the winsome way his dark hair curled at the nape of his neck. Jerking her head away, she vent her displeasure on a nonexistent cobweb in the corner.

The only thoughts she intended to allow to enter her head were thoughts directly pertaining to how best to get rid of the man sitting at her table.

Having dusted everything in sight, Ella traded her duster for a broom, applying it to the floor with the same fury with which she had wielded the feather duster. There had to be a way to buy enough time for one or both of them to get to Green River. But how?

"Sit down." The sound of Sam's voice caused Ella to jump, but she didn't cease her activity.

"I think better on my feet," she brusquely informed him.

"I can't imagine how anyone can think while scurrying about like an overwrought scullery maid, but I'll take you at your word." His tone had lost its acerbic edge. It sounded almost contrite. He continued, his mien at once both commanding and compassionate, "However, I would still like you to sit down. I have something I need to say to you."

Ella stood her ground.

"Please."

Shrugging her shoulders, she did as he requested, but her expression remained chary.

"I have been doing some thinking myself," he began, "and I believe I owe you an apology. Actually, several are in order. I know my behavior toward you has not been that of a gentleman. I should not have kissed you in so provocative a manner. Nor should I have allowed my rage to cause me to choose the solace of bellowing like a schoolboy over good sense. You are absolutely correct when you say we are on the same side and should join forces against our common enemies. I also want you to know I appreciate your willingness to obtain an annulment."

Though she was quick to caution herself not to expect too much, Ella was heartened by his sensible change in attitude, and her anger at him gradually dissipated. She wasn't really all that angry with him in the first place. It was the rest of the world that had her hopping mad. *Frustrated* was a better word for what she was feeling toward him. Considering the circumstances, it was unthinkable not to forgive him, and if he was willing to be equitable, she was determined to do all that she could to foster the fledgling spirit of cooperation between them. "Our fighting isn't all your fault. I haven't exactly been at my best these past few days, and I do seem to have a talent for getting on your nerves."

"It isn't you personally," he apprised her. "It's this damnable situation that keeps my temper on edge. I am not by nature an irascible man. It is just I am used to living an orderly life. Where I come from everybody conducts themselves by an agreed upon set of rules, and those who don't are censured by society not abetted. I offer this information not as an excuse for my conduct, but in hopes of making my sometimes boorish behavior a little more comprehensible. I want to assure you I intend to conduct myself more reasonably toward you in the future."

Ella was powerless to stem the rush of admiration flooding her mind and heart. Here was a man who was sincerely sorry for his mistakes and not afraid to admit it. That required a kind of courage Ella deemed far more manly than the boisterous feats of daring the local men had employed to try to impress her. Sternly reminding herself that Mr. Carrigan had no desire whatsoever to impress her, she tamped down her feelings. Now that she had his cooperation, concentrating all their efforts on finding an expeditious solution to their dilemma was not only the most sensible thing to do but far less disconcerting than contemplating her messy emotions. Too, who knew how long his circumspect mood would last? "I know you will find this difficult to believe, but social pandemonium isn't the usual way of things around here. I'm as confounded as you as to why my family and friends have taken leave of their senses," she lamented.

Sam winced as he shifted his injured leg to a more comfortable position. His mouth then settled into a thoughtful frown. "I was hoping you could offer me some significant insight into the workings of the Western mind."

"Not really. People around here tend to be independent and stubborn of nature, because those who aren't either die off or pack their bags and head back home. Otherwise, as a group they're not any different from other folks."

"They also share the common trait of being unrepentant busybodies," he added.

"I appreciate why you'd think that, but usually they go out of their way not to interfere in other people's business. It's just in our case, marrying me off directly benefits a good number of them, so they see it as much their business as ours."

"I see. And if I understand what you said earlier correctly, what you believe we need to do is find a way to leave the ranch that will put anyone off following us, at least for a time."

"Yes."

"How much time?"

"If we follow your suggestion and contact your lawyer by telegram, which I think we should, we'll need a minimum of two days head start before they come after us. Our horses are fine farm animals, but they're no match for a good trail pony. Of course, I've never put him to the test, but by the looks of him, the buckskin you were riding is no race horse either."

"No. He definitely is not a race horse," Sam concurred. He rubbed his brow. "Two days. . . . All right. Let's put our heads together and see if we can come up with a way to escape this ranch and secure the requisite two days."

Marching shoulder to shoulder for a common cause was a huge improvement over lobbing accusations and insults at each other, to Ella's way of reckoning. The tentative bond of camaraderie forming between them was pleasant. When he wanted to be, Mr. Carrigan could be a very charming and intelligent man.

Realizing the danger of allowing herself to think such thoughts, Ella stiffened her shoulders and adopted a business-like air. "Getting off the ranch won't be hard to do, at least for me," she addressed the first requirement.

"I should be the one to ride for help. A woman should not be alone in the wilderness," Sam argued.

Ella bristled at his statement. "I can take care of myself far better than you."

"I wasn't decrying your competence," he advised. "I was merely expressing my innate abhorrence for putting a woman in peril. I can't help what I am. Either I go or we both go, but I wouldn't feel right about sending you on so long a journey by yourself."

Put that way, Ella had a hard time pursuing the argument.

She might find umbrage a more comfortable emotion than admiration, but it was neither fair nor productive to make him suffer for the wanderings of her wayward mind. Not that she agreed with him. She didn't. But his motives were admirable even if his concern was misplaced. "We can discuss the matter later," she announced. "There's no point in either of us going anywhere unless we figure out a way to keep them from coming after us."

Propping her chin on her hand, Ella pressed her lips together and applied all her cognitive abilities to the task she had set them. Sam leaned back in his chair and did likewise.

Five minutes passed, then ten.

"Have you come up with any ideas yet?" Ella queried hopefully.

"No. What about you?"

She shook her head. "I told you, I think better on my feet."

He waved her back to her feet.

Ella paced the perimeter of the room, while Sam remained seated. At length, he opened his mouth, scowled, and snapped it shut again.

"What?"

"It would never work," he informed her. "Your grandmother is too wily to be taken in by so convenient a lie."

Ella, knowing her grandmother far better than he, saw no reason to quiz him further.

They persisted to ponder their dilemma. The only sounds filling the room were the thumping of Hound Dog's tail against the leg of the table and the steady clomp of Ella's boots upon the floorboards.

The first shadows of dusk were beginning to fall when Ella's rhythmic footfalls suddenly slowed. Sam looked up, and accurately read her expression. "You've thought of something," he stated, a note of expectation in his voice.

"I have had an idea," she hesitantly admitted. "But I don't like it, and I figure you'll like it even less."

"I don't care if either of us likes it. If it will work, I want to hear it."

"I can't say for sure it would work." Ella refused the seat he offered with a gesture of his hand and continued to pace.

"Why don't you tell me what it is, and let me judge for myself," Sam suggested, a tinge of exasperation creeping into carefully controlled speech.

"Okay," she reluctantly acquiesced. "But . . . I know you won't like it. If I could think of any other way . . ."

"You haven't and neither have I. At this point any plan is better than no plan at all."

Ella stopped pacing and cleared her throat. She took two steps toward the table, then reconsidered. Noticing with disgust her hands were fidgeting with the sides of her skirt, she clasped them behind her back, then cleared her throat again. "Since the only reason we ended up married in the first place is Grandma Jo's stupid decree I must marry before my sisters, it seems to me if we were to get Rex and all the others happily married off, there wouldn't be any incentive for them to meddle in our lives. They'd be too busy spooning to pay us any attention at all."

Sam nodded, his countenance grim. "What you say makes sense, but I can see why you have reservations. Arranging four weddings could take months."

Ella's eyes widened. "Oh, no, not anywhere near that long! I never would consider, even for a moment, a strategy that would take that long, especially, knowing how impatient a man you are."

"I'm not impatient," Sam declared.

It took a goodly amount of tongue biting to refrain from refuting his statement with enough evidence to satisfy any jury in the land, but in the interest of harmony, Ella contritely replied, "I've been so upset lately, I must have you mixed-up with someone else."

He accepted her explanation and returned to the matter of her sisters' marriages. "If it won't take months, how long do you estimate it will take?"

"Janie, Fern, and Marilee have their hearts settled and could easily be married within a week's time. . . ."

"That quickly," he exclaimed in amazement. "I keep forgetting I am not in New York."

Ella rocked her weight onto her heels. "Lily might take a little longer, but if we prod things along . . ."

"We'll prod," he promised. "Could all the marriages be accomplished in two weeks?"

"Probably."

"All right. Let's assume we can succeed in distracting the lovesick sheriff and his friends with your sisters. Since we'll be asking them to do what they are obviously desperate beyond reason to do in the first place, I think that's a sound assumption." He drummed his fingers on the table, and his countenance sobered. "But what about the rest of our wedding 'guests'? You only have four sisters. What is to prevent them from interfering?"

"They have their ranches to run, and without Rex inciting them for his own purposes, they'll lose interest in us. Even if they don't, nobody around here is going to form a posse to hunt us down without Rex's permission. I've saved some money over the years and I thought, just to be on the safe side, I'd send Rex and Janie on a little honeymoon trip as a wedding gift."

Sam elevated a brow and smiled broadly in admiration of her logic and meticulous attention to detail. "That still leaves your grandmother and him." He cocked his head toward Hound Dog.

"We can outrun them. Hound Dog is too old to keep up

with a horse for more than a few miles, and Grandma Jo is stuck with the same stable of horses we are. She'll be at an even greater disadvantage because you can bet we're going to take the best of the lot when we ride out of here."

Systematically running the details of her plan through his mind several times, Sam searched for some defect that would explain her lack of heart for her idea. He found none, other than the investment of time involved. Certainly, he preferred to be on his way immediately, but only a fool ignored reality. Everything they had tried so far had ended in abysmal failure. A change of tactics was definitely in order.

"I don't understand why you are so uncomfortable with your scheme," he declared. "I don't *want* to stay here another day, but what either of us wants has never been given any consideration or we wouldn't be having this conversation. I am sure I am capable of enduring another week, even two if I must, and so are you. Knowing there will be an end to the ordeal will make it bearable. Besides, it is possible we will think of an even better plan while we are waiting out our sentence."

"I've only told you the part that was easy to say," Ella divulged.

"And what have you left unsaid?" Sam petitioned.

"The time involved in getting my sisters married is a significant drawback," Ella stated, stalling for a little extra time to compose her explanation in a manner she judged least likely to provoke his outrage. Deeming the task futile, she took a deep breath and continued, ". . . But the real drawback is how to handle Grandma Jo. You heard what she said out in the yard. She isn't going to count me married if we don't stay together. If she finds out about our plans for an annulment . . . For my plan to have a chance of success, we'll have to convince her we have resigned ourselves to our marriage. No," Ella resolutely corrected herself. "I may as well be completely truthful. Pretending resignation wouldn't be enough. We'll have to convince her we are *happy* about being married to each other, that we have not only come to like each other but have fallen in love just as she believes we will."

Sam looked at her hard, his eyes darkening to the hue of a twilight sky. His mouth pulling into a thin line.

It was all Ella could do not to cringe under his censorious stare. "I told you you wouldn't like it. It's a terrible plan. We'll have to think of something else."

"What?" he demanded.

"I don't know. I was hoping you might."

"Well, I don't," he curtly informed her. "Don't you think you could pull it off?"

"Of course I could." The confidence that imbued Ella's statement was due less to a faith in her theatrical talents than the miserable knowledge she felt an honest attraction to her husband. He, on the other hand, would have to rely solely on his skill as an actor. "It was you I was thinking about. I should think it impossible to hide your dislike of this marriage, let alone act as though you enjoy my company."

"You underestimate me," he proclaimed. "I am a successful businessman. On numerous occasions I have been called upon to bury my true feeling in order to bring about a worthy result, and I regard extracting myself from this marriage a far more worthy goal than any other I have pursued."

"I've married a practiced liar?" Ella drew back, stunned and disillusioned.

"No, you have not. Disguising my dislike of a man's hobbies or his wife's taste in clothing behind a polite smile does not constitute lying. It is simply good manners and good business."

"But we *would* be lying," she reminded.

"Yes, we would. It is a sad day when a man is reduced to a liar in order to regain the reins of his fate, but I see no way to avoid it. One cannot deal forthrightly with people who have no scruples."

"Are you saying you think we should commit ourselves to my scheme?" Ella asked, her expression jaundiced.

Sam rested his head on the heel of his hand while he somberly inventoried his options. He found them in short supply. Knowing the threats to kill him were a malicious bluff was of no benefit to him now. *They* were no longer a family of misguided females and an overzealous dog. *They* were an entire community of able-bodied men. He wouldn't make it past the front door, if they didn't want him to, and surmising otherwise was absurd. Self-restraint had prevented him from gambling his life earlier, and the miscalculation had cost him dearly. Brute force was no longer a viable option.

Playing Romeo to this backwoods Juliet was only slightly less unappealing than being mauled by a dog or beat to a pulp by a bunch of rowdy cowboys, but not much. However, if doing so would get him out of here, and objective reason told him it should, it would be illogical not to try it.

Lifting his head from his hand, he stoically replied, "Yes . . . as long as you are confident you can cozen your grandmother into believing you harbor tender feelings for me. I don't intend to waste my time or energy, if you cannot. There is an art to acting and . . ."

"It won't be a problem for me," Ella replied, privately vowing she'd be damned before she admitted to him the true reason for her conviction.

"Good."

"Are you certain you won't mind being 'nice' to me?"

There was something about the way she asked the question. He wasn't sure what it was, but it suddenly occurred to Sam his new bride might not be as guileless and cooperative as she seemed. She *had* managed to bungle every attempt to secure his freedom. Perhaps their marriage was not the result of bad luck and unforeseeable circumstances. Perhaps . . . his eyes narrowed and his chin rose to a forbidding angle. "I won't mind as long as both of us recognize we are only pretending to . . ."

"Naturally, we will be pretending!" Ella exclaimed her cheeks growing hot with indignation. "This isn't some ambition on my part to trick you into being an agreeable husband! The only reason I'm willing to even consider adopting this plan is because you say we should. I don't like it any better now than when I first thought of it!"

"I only had a twinge of doubt and you have thoroughly squelched it," Sam told a half truth. He was ninety-nine percent persuaded, but prudence demanded he reserve the right to a whit of skepticism. "I would not have said anything at all, except my record of discerning the motives of others has been far from brilliant of late."

He sounded so sincere *and calm*. Ella winced at the thought her own guilty affection may have caused her to misinterpret and overreact to an imagined accusation in his response. Studying his face, princely despite an abundance of ugly bruises, she glumly concluded such was probably the case.

Sternly reminding herself just because she thought well of Mr. Carrigan didn't mean she was guilty of any other crime, and in fact made her willingness to let him go all the more admirable, Ella forced herself to maintain eye contact. It was important she make a suitable reply, important she say something that wouldn't make an even bigger ninny of herself than she already had done.

Taking a deep breath, she smiled wanly. "It's okay. If my nerves weren't so frazzled I assure you, I wouldn't have screeched at you."

"As you said earlier, neither of us are at our best. In the future we will both have to do better or our plan is doomed to failure, but for now let's concentrate on mapping out our strategy."

"Yes," Ella agreed.

Approaching the matter as he would a commercial transaction, Sam advised, "There should be lots of hand holding, ardent looks, the occasional husbandly peck on the cheek. However, we'll have to be careful not to overdo it, especially for a day or two. If we do it up too brown, she's liable to get suspicious."

"I agree. If we're going to err, we ought to err on the side of discretion. It wouldn't be wise to overact our parts." Ella preferred there not be *any* physical contact between them, but if she told him that, he would likely ask why, and her cheeks were already warm enough.

"Do you have any suggestions to further the illusion of a growing romance between us?"

Not a thought entered Ella's head she cared to reveal. She found her mind's tendency to wander down undesired paths extremely vexing. Almost as vexing as her cheeks' penchant to flame in response to those unbidden thoughts and the interminable pauses that tortured their conversations. In desperation for something to say, she detoured from the principal subject. "I want you to know I intend to write a letter to your fiancée absolving you of all responsibility for this marriage."

"That's a fine idea but hardly one we can use to impress your grandmother with your devotion to me. Why don't we deal with one predicament at a time," he firmly suggested.

She couldn't stand here like a stoic soldier, while he perused her like a general inspecting his troops and found her wanting. Not if she hoped to be of any use to anybody. She needed to pace. She didn't care if it wasn't dignified.

Moments later Ella was able to offer what she judged to be two satisfactory suggestions. "I'll cook you fancy meals, and I'll sew you a shirt. That should be a persuasive show of wifely devotion. Besides, we owe you more than one suit of clothes, so I'll be accomplishing two tasks at once."

"You needn't worry about my clothes. If I make it out of here with what skin I have left intact, I'll be more than content. Still, they are both good ideas. Do you have any more? Perhaps something a bit more sentimental?"

After some thought, she proposed, "I could read you poetry."

"Excellent." His tone continued to be matter-of-fact. "Walking in the moonlight is well-suited to our purpose, too, assuming they let us out of the house."

"Can you sing?" Ella asked.

"Tolerably."

"Good. Grandma Jo is always telling us how romantic she thought it was when Grandpa Nat sang to her. She says that's what she misses most about him."

"I'll do my best."

Though Ella found it beyond her capabilities to discuss engaging in activities such as hand holding and moonlight strolls with cold logic, it was obvious her husband had no trouble doing so. She wasn't sure if she admired his ability or was disapproving of it, but she did deem it helpful to their situation.

When no further suggestions were forthcoming, Sam cleared his throat. "There is something else we need to discuss. Our days will be amply filled with the routine tasks of living and arranging your sisters' weddings. What are we going to do about the nights?"

"We can't consummate the marriage or we'll destroy all hope for an annulment," Ella announced with far more volume and vehemence than she had intended.

"I realize that. That's what we need to talk about. How do you suggest we handle the details?"

Silently cursing him for his effortless ability to remain coolly detached when she could not, Ella did her best to regain her composure even as she felt the dread heat of another blush creeping up her neck. "I'm not sure I know what you mean."

"We are going to have to share a bedroom or all the playacting in the world isn't going to fool your grandmother or anyone else into believing we are a happy bride and groom," he stated.

"I'll sleep on the floor."

"That's very generous of you, but totally unnecessary. I will sleep on the floor."

"That doesn't seem fair since . . ."

"The matter is not open for discussion. As a man, it is my duty to bear any physical discomforts that must be borne. We can take care of the difficulty of dressing with equal ease simply by turning our backs."

"What else is there to worry about?"

"This is a small house. I realize this is a very indelicate subject to bring up, but if we hope to persuade your family we are . . . intimately acquainted . . . we are going to have to arrange a certain amount of," he hesitated ever so slightly, "moaning, creaking of bed straps, and the like."

"Are you sure?" Ella squeaked, too dismayed to even attempt to hide her reaction to his suggestion.

"If we want our charade to be convincing, yes."

Ella wasn't about to ask how he had come by his knowledge. She was certain she didn't want to know. She retreated to the other side of the room.

"I am sorry if my bluntness makes you uncomfortable, but if we are going to go forward with this plan, I intend to see we do everything necessary to guarantee we are successful. Half measures rarely bring about the desired results."

Pursing her lips, Ella scrutinized his determined expression. It was rather off putting, the way he had taken over her plan and made it his own. And she couldn't say she approved of his latest embellishment. But, she also couldn't say he wasn't right. She turned her back on him. "Well, since you seem to have settled all the others details so capably, I'll let you take care of this as well."

"I can't do it all alone or it won't be convincing," he pointed out.

"Fine. When the time comes, just tell me what I have to do, but in the meantime, let's just not talk about it."

"Agreed. Now, there is one more thing. It's probably not worth mentioning, but just to be safe, I think we should both be clear on where we stand on the matter."

Ella slowly turned to face him. He stared at her expectantly, waiting for her to respond. When it was obvious she was going to be required to say something, Ella did so with as much grace as she could muster. "Go ahead. It can't be any worse than what we just finished discussing."

Sam judged her last statement inaccurate. Discussing stratagems for playacting for others wasn't nearly as discomfiting as facing the very real and private seductions of the flesh. He might be a gentleman, but he was human, and his "wife" was amply endowed with physical charms to make a man lose his head.

"Even though we have agreed consummating our marriage would be wrong-headed, since we will be living in such close proximity, it is possible one or both of us may have concerns about the other's ability to control his or her carnal urges," he stated without preamble.

Ella turned crimson. "There is no danger I might decide to throw myself at you. Despite what you may think, the only reason I reacted the way I did to your kiss was . . . well, I was blushing with embarrassment and I became breathless because you practically sucked the breath right out of me. It had nothing to do with feeling any uncontrollable passion for your person."

"I'm reassured to hear you say that, but the reason I brought

the subject up was to *reassure* you that I will not be tempted
to take advantage of our awkward situation."

How gallant, Ella inwardly seethed as she forced a thin
smile. As if there could be any doubt in her mind on that
score. It wasn't that she wanted him to try to take advantage.
She didn't. The truth was, she didn't know what she wanted,
except for this marriage to be over so she could go back to
worrying about simple things like why the cow didn't give as
much milk one day compared to another or how to get a stain
out of a skirt or if the summer season's profits would be
enough she could afford to buy an extra book or two to help
see her through the long winter months.

After considerable effort, she squeezed out a weak "thank
you," following it with a stiff, "If there's nothing more to
discuss, I believe it is past time I get our supper started."

Sam stared at her back as she busied herself at the stove.
There was no doubt in his mind she was angry at him, but
he couldn't fathom why. All he had done was state his intention to behave himself.

If he was a cad, he would make no offer to restrain himself.
There were many pleasures he could afford himself without
jeopardizing the annulment. For that matter, he could have his
way with her, then swear to the judge he'd never laid a finger
on her. Many men, in fact most, would not condemn him.
They would regard whatever liberties he chose to take as just
compensation for the trouble her family had caused him.

Perhaps she thought him as much of a sprig as the men in
the yard. His eyes darkened and he clenched his jaw. Her
willingness to believe him unmoved by that kiss supported
this offending theory. It was true he didn't love her, but he
was perfectly capable of feeling lust for her. She was a physically attractive woman and he was a healthy man. If she
thought him some kind of eunuch, she was grossly mistaken.

The temptation to rise from the chair and prove to her just

how very mistaken she was nearly overwhelmed him, but a stern reminder that if he did so, he could not leave here with his honor intact kept him in his place.

It might be satisfying to fantasize about doing such a thing, but he knew himself well enough to know he wasn't capable of so gross a violation of his own code of ethics without paying a terrible price of conscience.

Too, it was possible he was wrong. Who knew what she was thinking? He wasn't a mind reader. He would be wise to concentrate on facts rather than conjecture.

The facts were: She didn't want him for a husband. He didn't want her for a wife. They had agreed on a plan and how to implement it. There was no reason they couldn't deal with each other in a rational manner for the remainder of what he fervently prayed would be their exceedingly brief acquaintance.

It was nearing ten o'clock when Grandma Jo entered the house. She frowned at them as they sat on separate seats across the room reading.

"Ella, I'd like to have a private chat with you in the bedroom." She didn't wait for Ella to answer her request. Entering the bedroom, Grandma Jo left the door open behind her.

After exchanging an unsettled glance with Sam, Ella closed her book, rose to her feet, and followed her.

"Shut the door and sit down." Grandma Jo motioned toward one of the beds.

Ella sat.

"I can see by the look on your face, you ain't feeling too charitable toward me at the moment, but I want you to listen to me just the same. I love you. Always have, always will. I want you to have the same kinda happiness I shared with your Grandpa Nat. That's why I've done what I've done."

"If the purpose behind forcing me to marry Mr. Carrigan

was to secure my happiness, you have failed miserably. Words cannot express how wretched I feel," Ella stiffly replied.

"It's not me who has failed but you. You have failed to see the truth sitting right in front of your nose. Samuel Carrigan is your soul mate. The two of you were made for each other, and if you search the whole wide world over, you'll never find another to make you as happy as you can make each other."

"I can believe you believe that, but what I can't fathom is where you got this insupportable notion."

"Here." Grandma Jo lay her hand upon her heart. "And here." She pointed to her head. "I've lived a long time and have had plenty of opportunity to observe my fellow man and woman. I've seen couples who came to the altar reckoning themselves so much in love they were weak in the knees tumble into lives full of heartache. I've seen couples marry who showed no more emotion than two trees standing side by side rise up to live glorious lives. *And* these old eyes have witnessed everything in between. Through the years I've become a mighty accurate judge of which direction passion will go. With you and Sam it's gonna soar clear to Paradise. I'd stake my life on it."

Ella met her grandmother's determined gaze with melancholy eyes. "You're wrong."

"No, I ain't. You never saw me push you with any of your other beaus, now did you?"

Ella shook her head negatively.

"That's because in my heart I knew they weren't right for you. But Sam is different. He possesses every quality you've always said you desired in a man and more. I've seen the way you look at him when you think no one is watching, and I've seen the way he looks at you. When you talk to each other, I hear the breathlessness beneath your words. Since the day your sisters brought him home the air in this house has liked to set the place on fire it's been so charged with the bottled up passions sparking between the two of you. Neither of you may be willing to admit it to the world or yourselves, but it's there—that special magic between a man and a woman that comes by once in a lifetime and for some poor souls never comes at all. God gives you such a gift you grab it and hold on tight, and if He gives it to someone you love and she's too proud to see it, you hold onto it for her."

"We don't react to each other any differently than we react to everyone else," Ella argued, though she knew for her part what she said wasn't strictly true.

"Oh, yes you do," Grandma Jo contended. "Sam is the man for you, and you are the woman for him. If I wasn't one-hundred percent sure of that, I'd never have forced you two to marry. You can fight this marriage and make yourselves heartsick, or you can be wise and enjoy your good fortune. I brought you in here to ask you to be wise."

"You are asking me to put my faith in something I adamantly disbelieve," Ella protested.

"I am asking you to put your faith in my love for you which you've believed in all your life and to trust me to know what I'm doing. If you can't do that just yet, at least promise me you'll consider I might be right."

Ella sighed. "I'll think about what you've said, but . . ."

"There's no need to say more. You've got a warm heart and a fine head on your shoulders. If you listen to them, they'll lead you to the truth. Now, I came in here to fetch some blankets for the boys." She shooed Ella toward the door. "You go back in there with that husband of yours and see if the two of you can overcome your indignation and give your marriage a chance."

Ella returned to the parlor, the grim expression on her face mirroring her inner turmoil. She wanted Grandma Jo to be right and herself to be wrong. She wanted to believe if for no other reason than to ease the agony of her situation. But no matter how hard she tried, she couldn't make herself believe it. It was possible, with far less effort than she cared to contemplate, to imagine her own heart succumbing to Mr. Carrigan, but Mr. Carrigan's heart succumbing to her was an entirely different matter. That was impossible to imagine. This was real life not some silly fairy tale where outrageous deeds led to happily ever afters. She couldn't let Grandma Jo's rosy expectations sway her or this marriage would wound far more than her pride. It would leave her heart bleeding.

Plopping herself down on the settee, Ella set her jaw and folded her arms across her chest.

A few moments later Grandma Jo exited the house, her arms loaded down with blankets.

"Is she coming back?" Sam asked.

"She's just taking blankets out to the men."

"Then perhaps I should join you on the settee."

Scooting to one end, Ella made a place for him. He ignored the generous spot provided, positioning himself so his thigh was a hair's breadth from hers.

"What did your grandmother say to you in there?"

Ella kept her eyes focused on the book in her lap. "She thinks we should surrender to her superior wisdom and learn to appreciate this marriage."

"What did you say to that?"

"That I would think about it."

"Good. When we start pretending we like each other, she will think you are taking her advice." Opening his own book, Sam terminated the conversation.

When Grandma Jo returned empty handed after a brief absence, she wasted no time commenting on Sam's change of location. "Now, that's much better. Though I would reckon a couple of intelligent souls like the two of you could think of something more appropriate to be doing than reading books at this late hour on your wedding night."

"I'm not sleepy," Ella demurred.

"Didn't say a word about sleeping, now did I?" she chortled. "Sleeping is for old women not the newly wedded. But I suspect you know that. Likely, you're both just feeling a little shy." Grandma Jo ambled to the cupboard and pulled out a bottle of brandy. She set the bottle and two glasses on the table. "This oughta help. I've decided I'm gonna give you two my room," she continued to converse without expectation of receiving any reply. "Sam's belongings are already in there. You can move your clothes in the morning, Ella . . . I don't mind telling you I envy you, Ella, and you, too, Sam. Starting out in life is just about the most exciting time there is." She sighed wistfully, before turning away from them. "I'll be moseying off to bed now. The boys will escort you to the necessary whenever you're ready to make the trip."

Ella watched her grandmother step into the room Ella shared with her sisters and shut the door. Sam glanced in disgust at the dog at his feet.

"You'd have thought she would have had the decency to take *him* with her," he grumbled. "I'm sick unto death of that mutt staring at me."

"Hound Dog won't tell no tales," Grandma Jo called through the closed door.

Sam threw Ella a meaningful glance.

"Okay, I'll moan," she whispered under her breath. "But I'm going to feel like the biggest fool who ever was."

Retreating back to the safety of her book, Ella tried to concentrate on the page before her with little success. He was sitting too close. She could feel the warmth emanating from his body and smell the fragrance of his skin. Merciful heavens, even the unremarkable sound of the man's breathing incited her senses. She wanted to tell him to move, but reason counseled her she was going to have to learn to deal with his close proximity in a mature manner if their plan was to work and postponing the inevitable was impractical and cowardly.

Ella grasped her book tighter in her hands. All that was needed was a good dose of mind over matter. Mr. Carrigan was just a man after all. Men were as plentiful as bunch grass. Why get excited about one over the others? No reason in the world. She was merely suffering from the common human frailty of craving something she knew she couldn't have. Mr. Carrigan was like cocoa. If there was plenty in the house, it rarely crossed a body's mind to have a cup, but let the can be empty and you'd find yourself ready to sell your soul for a sip. She covertly glanced in his direction.

Cocoa, she repeated. I'm sitting next to an empty can of cocoa. I don't really want any. I'm just being perverse. Her private lecture had about as much effect on her overheated blood as spitting did on a wildfire.

How on earth was she going to sleep in the same room with the man, when she couldn't even sit next to him for five minutes without losing her mind? If he ever found out what she was feeling, she would die of embarrassment.

Mr. Carrigan had an elegant life in New York City, complete with fiancée. She couldn't compete with that. She didn't want to compete, not under the conditions her family and friends had thrust upon her. Even if she was of a mind to woo him, she couldn't stoop so low. She'd lose all respect for herself. . . . Besides, lust wasn't love, and God forgive her, it was lust, earthy and acute, from which she suffered.

At least she had the comfort of knowing she could depend on him to protect her from herself, Ella smiled grimly. Since she was far too proud to throw herself at any man, and he most definitely had no desire to pursue her, she would be saved the agony of a repeat of her disgraceful behavior in the yard.

Ella postponed retiring to the bedroom as long as she could, but after a time her eyes became so fatigued the words on the page blurred beyond recognition, and no amount of blinking remedied the condition.

"It's past midnight. We can't stay up forever," Sam advised, startling her to her feet.

How long had he been watching her and how much had he seen? As the familiar heat of another burdensome blush crept relentless across her face, she damned herself under her breath.

"Perhaps you *should* have a glass of your grandmother's brandy to help settle your nerves."

Ella stared at the bottle a long moment before replying, "No, thank you." If she was going to survive the night without making a complete donkey out of herself, she couldn't risk impairing her wits, no matter how tempting a little liquid fortitude might be.

The routine tasks of brushing her teeth, washing her face, and a trip to the necessary earned Ella a little more time, but not nearly enough to make her happy. Eventually, there was nothing left to do to avoid the bedroom.

Opening the door to the room they were to share, her husband stepped aside, motioning her through the door with a sweep of his arm.

Reluctantly, she entered. Sam and Hound Dog engaged in a brief skirmish at the door, which Hound Dog inevitably won. He trotted into the room, her muttering mate at his heels.

Sam clicked the door closed behind him.

As Ella steeled her nerves to face him, a cheerful voice called out from the other bedroom.

"Good night, lovebirds."

Ten

Just as he had surmised she would, the interfering old woman had her ear to the wall. Sam grit his teeth. He had been hoping, at least for tonight, fate would smile on him and she would be asleep when they retired, saving them the chagrin of feigning a passionate performance. His bride did not appear up to it. The woman was already so jittery, he couldn't help but feel a twinge of sympathy for her.

He refused, however, to allow sympathy to stand in the way of progress toward his goal. He had spent the evening analyzing her plan from every conceivable angle, and he was more convinced than ever it would work—*as long as they played their parts persuasively.*

Sam was rather disappointed he hadn't furnished so obvious and logical a solution himself. His disconcerted mental state was no excuse. When a man was under duress was the very moment he needed his wits to be their keenest. He would not fail himself again. Ella Singleton had graciously supplied the plan, but he would be the one to make certain it succeeded.

After lighting the lamp on the bedside table, Sam slowly turned to face again the other occupants of the room. His old nemesis Hound Dog had curled himself into a ball in the corner and was softly snoring. His reticent wife looked ready to bolt the room.

Sam accepted her discomfort with their sleeping arrangement. Any woman with a drop of moral sensibility would be discomfited, and this was but the first night of what could be many. He fervently wished he had a more immediately rewarding and dignified scheme to offer her and himself, but he didn't.

If he was dealing with rational people, he might have other options, but his gut told him no other avenue—short of murder—promised half as good a chance of achieving the aspired end.

Strong as his desire was to escape, it was not so overwhelming he would stoop to the level of these backwoods misfits and shoot whoever got in his way. They may have taken away his freedom, but he still had his self-respect. If he resorted to shooting women, he would lose that as well.

Since Mrs. Singleton was the ring leader of this circus, and she held the belief men were readily controlled by their lusts, lust was the logical tool to use to dupe her he was falling in love against his better judgment.

Put bluntly, he had no choice. He would do what must be done, no matter how it chafed his patience and pride. Ella Singleton was going to have to do the same.

His eyes flared when she started for the door. Crossing the room, he blocked her path. His face inches from hers, Sam whispered, "Where do you think you're going?"

"I just realized I forgot to fetch a nightgown," Ella murmured in a voice that matched the chary hush of his own.

"You'll have to do without."

"What!" Though the word was spoken no louder than a breath, it didn't fail to communicate the extent of her distress. They continued to converse at close range, using guarded voices.

"Do you or do you not want to circumvent this marriage?"

"Of course, I do."

"Then, it's better you don't arouse your grandmother's suspicions."

"Surely a bride isn't expected to . . ."

"Under normal circumstances, no, I doubt it is expected, but our circumstances are far from normal. It would be unwise to make an avoidable mistake. For tonight, you'll just have to abandon modesty and sleep in your underclothing. Tomorrow, when your belongings have been moved into this room, you will not be so hindered."

Ella's breath was as warm as the heat rising off her cheek, which flamed a not unattractive shade of scarlet. "I suppose you're right."

She began to pace between the door and the window, wearing the expression of a lamb trapped in a pen with a wolf. The trouble was: this particular lamb's hips had the unfortunate habit of swaying provocatively whenever she moved. She didn't do it on purpose. She just did it.

This wasn't the first time he had noticed, but it did qualify as the most inconvenient.

"I am not going to try to take advantage of you," he whispered his earlier assurances in hopes of halting her.

"I know."

Sam suppressed his initial inclination to demand why, if she knew she could rely on his self-restraint, she was so apprehensive. Instead, he decided to distract her and himself from their immediate situation by asking a less disconcerting question, but one that had been niggling him ever since he had awakened in the wagon and learned he was bound for her arms. He had more than an inkling, but it would be prudent to be certain he understood the whole matter. Softly striding across the room, he captured her arms to stay her. When he was certain she would remain still, Sam released her. "Do you have any idea why everyone in general and your grandmother in particular is so unshakable in their belief I will make you a perfect mate?"

Sam watched several emotions play across her face, and he

knew she was struggling to decide how much she was willing to tell him. After a moment her features settled into an expression of resolve and she quietly replied, "Because you are exactly the kind of man for years I have been saying I want."

When she didn't offer more, he gently prodded, "I'd appreciate it if you would elaborate. You have said no more than what, in essence, your sisters and grandmother have already told me."

She hesitated a moment, then began to speak in a barely audible voice, the volume of which he sensed had more to do with embarrassment than the necessity not to be overheard. "Maybe it is wrong of me to want more than a roof over my head and a hard-working man by my side and this," her arms encompassed the room, "is God's way of punishing me. I've never made a secret of my feelings and . . . I have tried to be compliant, but the world is filled with so many wonderful things. I read about them in books."

"You didn't read about me in a book."

"Yes, I have, or rather men like you. You've had an education. Your speech is sophisticated. When your temper is in check, your manners are impeccable. You live in an elegant city. In short, you are a gentleman."

"I have already deduced the reason your sisters 'selected' me was because they judged me a gentleman. But why choose me? Surely, some other city born and bred men have passed this way. Why didn't they lay hold of one of them?"

"That I can't tell you, except to say to my knowledge very few gentleman have passed this way."

"So, I was simply in the wrong place at the right time?"

"Probably. At least in regard to my sisters' interest. We had argued about my refusing to marry Willie Crumb that morning. Grandma Jo is a different matter."

"How so?"

"If she didn't like you, for reasons that have nothing to do with the trappings of a gentleman and everything to do with who you are beneath your skin, she would have let you go." Ella wrinkled her brow. "She is sometimes given to taking notions in her head that this or that must be or some catastrophe will follow, and you and me being married is one of those notions."

"How often is she right?"

"More often than not, and that's the trouble. Every time she *is* right, she gets more stubborn about admitting sometimes she is wrong. We are a perfect example. Refusing to let my sisters marry before me is another."

Sam nodded in heartfelt agreement. "Earlier you said you had quarreled with your sisters. May I ask why you refused this Willie Crumb?"

"I told you, I want to see the world. I want a man who stimulates my mind as well as my . . ." Ella cast her gaze to the floor and swallowed. "Here, men are interested in two things: cattle and horses. It's enough for them. It's enough for my sisters. But it isn't enough for me. I didn't ask to be different. It's quite possible I'm overreaching my lot in life. I've been told as much by more than one person. But to settle for less when there is so much more . . . well, I just can't make myself do it. Selfish or not, someday I want to go to a theater, sail on a ship to some ancient land, meet a poet, dance in a ballroom . . . I want to do everything I have read about and so much more."

"But you live on a ranch now, and this afternoon you claimed to be content with your life before I came."

Ella pursed her lips. "I am not unhappy here. There are many things I wouldn't change about my life for the world. I simply crave new experiences." She clasped her hands tightly together. "When a woman marries, her life is limited by her husband's ambitions. As a single woman I have the freedom to nurture my own dreams, to embrace my own ambitions."

"Had," Sam corrected.

"Yes, *had*. But I will have it again."

"As soon as you unburden yourself of me."

Ella's eyes darkened to a pensive green. "You are not a burden. You are a . . . never mind."

"I would like to hear what you were going to say."

"You are a . . . complication."

Sam was certain she hadn't said what she originally intended, but he didn't speak the suspicion aloud. She had told him what he had asked concerning his selection as her mate, and that was sufficient to satisfy him. She was a woman after all and by nature better equipped than he to understand the convoluted thinking processes of the fairer sex. Besides, he had come to essentially the same conclusion himself.

It didn't make sense to him why her family persisted to pretend he would make her an exceptional husband if coincidence, convenience, and an old woman's fallible intuition were their only sources of motivation, but very little of what had happened to him of late made sense. Perhaps he was suffering from an excess of masculine ego, as his bride had earlier accused, and was imagining there was something more going on here.

Though the object of his ruminations was far from a picture of calm, he had avoided the inevitable as long as he could. Sam cleared his throat. "Are you ready?"

"For what?" Ella asked a little too loudly. He pressed his finger to her lips to remind her to speak softly.

"Our performance."

"No, but I never will be, so we may as well get on with it."

"I'll turn my back so you can get undressed for bed."

"I prefer to sleep fully clothed."

"Your grandmother will notice your rumpled appearance in the morning."

A dismal expression settled upon Ella's features. "I hadn't thought of that."

"You best start thinking about such things or you'll ruin our scheme."

"I'm sorry. I've never slept in the same room with a man before, and I am finding it difficult to think clearly."

"Then, I'll do the thinking for us both." Presenting his back to give her privacy, Sam listened to her make the necessary preparations. It took several minutes before she whispered permission for him to turn around. The sight that greeted him did not please him.

"I told you, I will be sleeping on the floor," he rasped, his eyes taking in the quilt-wrapped figure on the floor.

"I'm fine where I am," she assured him.

"I am not going to argue with you about this. Get in the bed."

Ella sat up, being careful to keep the quilt wrapped securely about her. "Sleeping on the floor is the least I can do . . ."

He had never seen her with her hair down, and Sam was startled by how attractive his wife looked dishabille. Her hair was much longer than he had imagined it to be. It framed her face, calling attention to her eyes which unaccountably appeared larger and decidedly more seductive than he remembered. He felt a perturbing tightening in his loins.

"Please, take the bed."

"No, thank you." She shifted her position slightly. The quilt slipped a little, revealing the lace edge of her chemise.

"You will sleep in the bed," he muttered.

She shifted again and the quilt slipped another inch. "I am more than comfortable where I am."

"Please, take the bed now," he repeated between clenched teeth.

"I know you are a gentleman, but my conscience insists I remain . . ."

"I said, get in the bed, woman!" Sam commanded, his rapidly escalating and highly inappropriate sexual agitation causing him to forget to keep his voice low. He immediately realized his error.

Clamping his hand over Ella's open mouth before she could utter an equally reckless reply, he forcible lifted her onto the bed. "Maybe, she'll just think you're a reluctant bride," he hissed in her ear, holding her down on the mattress.

His wife was clearly not used to being manhandled. She thrashed about on the bed, moaning and mewling and resonant animal cries rising from her throat, as she wrestled to escape his hand. This went on for several torturous minutes, before she suddenly went deathly still, staring up at him with eyes filled with both fury and alarm. She seemed unaware the quilt had fallen away, but he was not. He was painfully aware of the fact her nearly bare breast lay mere inches from his lips. They glowed golden in the lamp light.

Taking an iron grip on his raging carnality, Sam exhaled a hot breath and masked his unwelcome passion with vinegary words. "You have chosen an intriguing way to make the necessary marital music, but I dare say it should convince anyone listening through the walls. However, next time, I would appreciate an advance warning before the curtain rises on our little stage."

Ella jabbered convulsively beneath his hand.

"Yes, sweet wife," he cooed with exaggerated breathlessness. "I felt it, too. Thank you." Lowering his voice, he spoke for her benefit only, "I will be happy to remove my hand from your mouth and release you from the weight of my person, if you will give me your word, you won't allow your temper to do our cause harm."

Ella nodded her head in agreement, but he waited until he read compliance in her eyes before setting her free. In the same movement, he covered her with the quilt and extracted himself from the bed.

"I thought you said we shouldn't do it up too brown," Ella accused, giving just enough breath to her words to make herself heard.

"You took me by surprise, and I was forced to extemporize," he whispered back.

"I didn't throw you on the bed."

"No, you didn't. You forced me to throw you on the bed. A battlefield is no place for insubordination."

"I didn't realize we were at war."

"We are. It's us against your family and the town of Heaven. Since we are plainly out-manned, our only road to victory is to exercise superior wit."

With lips trembling, she darkly stated, "And you have appointed yourself general."

"Yes." Removing his boots, Sam quietly set them on the floor. He extinguished the lamp. "I learned long ago to never delegate power in matters where a positive outcome is critical. I hold my future very dear."

"As do I, if for no other reason than because your future affects mine. But I don't see how my sleeping on the floor instead of you is of any importance at all."

"The issue isn't where you or I sleep," Sam counseled, naming himself a raving liar in his mind. Staying out of her bed was going to prove a great deal more difficult than he cared to ponder. A vision of Clara floated into his head, causing his mind—though regrettably not his body—to recoil from his disloyal desires. He glared at the moonlight streaming in through the window, illuminating his wife's too pretty face. "The issue is obedience. In the next days, there will be numerous occasions when one of us must follow the lead of the other without question, or we will be found out. Your previous

attempts to deliver me from the clutches of your family and
friends do not recommend you for the task."

"But . . ."

"But nothing," he interrupted, slipping off his glasses. He
set them on the bedside table. Shrugging out of his jacket,
Sam neatly folded it and lay it next to him. His hands moved
to the buttons of his vest. "Now, unless you plan to watch
me completely disrobe, I suggest you close your eyes. Tomorrow will be a long day, and we both need some sleep."

Ella covered her mouth to stifle another yawn; then, she
pulled a cake from the oven. The only way she could stay
awake during the day was to keep on her feet.

For three nights she and Mr. Carrigan had shared the same
bedroom. What little sleep she got was caught in brief
snatches and did little to refresh her. She knew Mr. Carrigan
was faring no better. He tossed and turned on the hard floor
all night.

Several times she had offered to change places with him,
but he always refused. She thought he was being ridiculous.
She wasn't able to sleep anyway, so one of them might as
well have a good night's rest.

Until Mr. Carrigan was out of the house, Ella despaired of
ever sleeping again. His intimate physical presence kept her
body in a constant state of distraction. Her heart beat too fast.
She felt overly warm even when the air was cool. She had to
concentrate to breathe in a sensible manner. But most disconcerting were her breasts. They had taken to puckering to attention day and night. This untoward behavior would invariably be followed by an awareness that the most private part
of her person was moist and as hot as an August afternoon.

She could not claim the sensations tormenting her were unpleasant. She had been raised by sensible parents, who saw

no purpose in burdening their daughters with repressive notions about the physical side of human nature—as long as that nature was expressed within the confines of marriage. If this were a true marriage, she would find her feelings intriguing. She would judge this yearning for her husband's touch quite felicitous. She would joyfully explore this heretofore unrecognized aspect of her own character. However, this was not a true marriage.

She was suppose to be *pretending* to be overcome with attraction to her husband. She most definitely was not supposed to become genuinely overcome.

Ella had known this part of her plan would be hard to endure, given her previous reactions to the man who was now her husband, but she had never reckoned on it being this hard. Before she had been able to evade his presence for part of her day and all of her nights. These respites enabled her to regain her balance. Now, she was allowed no relief.

So, every night she lay awake unable to sleep because despite every effort on her part to banish them, discommodious, unladylike sensations evoked discommodious and unladylike thoughts, and neither allowed her a moment's peace.

Luckily for them both, Grandma Jo reckoned her exhaustion the result of too much love play. Mr. Carrigan made sure of that. Every night they took turns bouncing on the bed and making all manner of highly humiliating noises. No matter how crimson her cheeks bloomed, the man was relentless. If she possessed a suspicious nature, she might wonder if their nightly ritual was his way of exacting a measure of revenge for the wrongs done him.

During the day, he was equally diligent. Whenever they had an audience, he cast hungry glances her direction. Twice he had called her sweetheart, but he was mindful to follow his *intentional* unintentional slip with an appropriately startled expression and a disgruntled comment. Last night, they had gone on a moonlight stroll under the watchful guard of Eli Estes. Her husband held her hand and touched her hair. The evening before that, he had pronounced her supper the best he had ever eaten.

The man was one fine actor. If not for the fact each night they planned out their strategy for the next day, even she might be swayed he was reluctantly coming to accept having her for a wife was agreeable.

For her part, Ella confined her efforts to preparing the most scrumptious meals their larder allowed. Grandma Jo was a staunch believer in "the way to a man's heart is through his stomach" school of thought, judging food only second to lust when it came to effective tools for managing a man. Best of all, spending extra time in the kitchen gave her a legitimate excuse to keep her hands occupied and her person a relatively safe distance from her overly stimulating husband.

Ella popped another cake into the oven and turned her attention to the bowl of dried apples. They had been soaking in water flavored with a tablespoon of dark rum all night and were now ready to be mixed with flour, sugar, and spices and baked into pies.

She glanced at her husband. Grandma Jo had given him permission to write a letter to his lawyer in New York after he claimed his financial affairs would suffer if he didn't tend to several urgent matters. He was doing so presently. Ella knew he planned to solicit help, but she also knew Grandma Jo's promise to see the letter posted was contingent on his permission for her to read it first. Her requirement necessitated a coded call for assistance, and Ella wasn't hopeful. Too, when one took into consideration the speed with which letters traveled, if all went well, their marriage would be history before help arrived.

"By the time we're through we're gonna have more than enough food for tomorrow's party," Grandma Jo pronounced as she stepped through the door and surveyed the scene. She set a basket overflowing with eggs on the table, motioning Roger, who followed at her heels, to place the bucket of milk he carried on the stool in the corner. "How's that letter coming, Sam?"

"I should be through within the hour."

"Good. Ella might be needing your help later on. Gonna have some heavy pots to lift up on that stove. I'm sure you won't be wanting to risk having her strain something vital or get too tuckered out before bedtime." She laughed gaily as she shooed Roger out of the door.

Ella made a disgruntled face at her back, swearing under her breath if her outspoken grandmother made one more bawdy remark she would cut out her tongue and nail it to the side of the barn. Her cheeks flamed plenty often of their own accord without Grandma Jo undertaking to embarrass her to death.

Sam cast her a cautioning look.

Shoving her hand in the sack on the sideboard, Ella pasted a tolerant smile on her tight lips as she measured out the flour for her pie crusts.

Another sleepless night, left Ella ill-prepared to face what promised to be a trying day. She wouldn't be afforded the opportunity to hide behind an apron, but would be forced to stand smiling by her husband's side.

As she methodically pulled her brush through her hair, Ella watched him through the reflection in the mirror. He was sitting on the edge of the bed, lacing his shoes, watching her.

They had spent a full hour last night strolling hand in hand under the moonlight so they could attain the privacy required to map out their strategy for today without the necessity of whispering every word. Mr. Carrigan—*Sam,* she sternly corrected; he had told her she should start referring to him by his Christian name to establish an affable tenor to their relationship. *Sam* felt they had laid a firm foundation and were ready to increase their public displays of affection.

He had tautly assumed the reins of their marriage, and she didn't argue with him—partly because she had discovered he possessed a stubborn streak as wide as the Missouri River and when he decided to do something his way, debating with him was a waste of time, and partly because he was able to maintain a detachment she was not and she reckoned him more competent to make sound decisions. Also, only a featherbrain argued with success, and there was no denying following his counsel was leading to success.

Grandma Jo, Roger, Eli, George, Henry, Jacob—all of them appeared absolutely persuaded Sam and she were becoming fittingly fond of each other. The lot of them high-stepped about the ranch with satisfied grins stretching across their faces.

Ella lay her brush aside and smiled wanly as she twisted her hair and secured it into a chignon.

Their guests were suppose to arrive at noon, but Bob had arrived before dawn with a steer on a spit. The smoky aroma of roasting meat filled the yard and wafted in through the open window. She took a deep breath.

She had been awake when he arrived, but she stayed in bed with her eyes closed, pretending not to hear the commotion in the yard. If she was suppose to be exhausted from a long night of lovemaking, she couldn't very well rise before the rooster. Besides, lying abed with the covers pulled over her head was less taxing than facing Grandma Jo's randy remarks and speculative stares.

Giving her appearance a final critical perusal, Ella smoothed her green silk skirt and pinched some color into her cheeks.

"You two lovebirds finally decide to crawl out of bed?"

Grandma Jo greeted when they emerged from the room. "Why it's well past ten o'clock."

"Good morning, Mrs. Singleton," Sam responded, one corner of his lips twitching into a self-satisfied smirk and a guilty twinkle in his blue eyes. "I hope we didn't disturb you last night, and you were able to get a good night's sleep."

She grinned. "Best a body could have."

Ella accepted the need to foster the misconception of intimacy, and she was willing to forgive her husband for encouraging her grandmother's delusions, but sometimes she felt he went beyond necessity. "I'm sorry we overslept," she lied.

"No call to be sorry. You got better things to do than carry pies to the yard. Me and the boys got everything under control. Just let me clear a spot on the stove, and I'll stir you up some breakfast."

"I can do it," Ella insisted.

"Not today. You just sit down at the table and let me take care of you. Don't want you to risk soiling your dress. Guest of honor can't come to the party looking like a three-day-old dish rag," Grandma Jo admonished. Both Ella and Sam started to do as they were told. "Better yet, Sam why don't you carry a couple of chairs out to the porch, and I'll bring your breakfast to you. With all this cooking, it's hotter than Hades in here."

The last thing Ella wanted to do was sit idle, but she had no choice but to acquiesce. . . .

They had barely cleared the breakfast dishes away when a wagon escorted by Rex Johnson and Frank Thatcher and filled with her sisters pulled over the horizon. Ella wasn't surprised to see them, even though she knew they would have had to start out in the dark of predawn to get here this soon. Likely, they were eaten alive with curiosity for days and couldn't wait to be filled in on what had been happening at the ranch.

She stood on the porch, Sam by her side as the wagon rolled into the yard.

"Morning Mrs. Carrigan, Mr. Carrigan." Rex tipped his hat. Frank did likewise. Her sisters scrambled down from the wagon, enthusiastically calling out their own greetings. All except Janie who offered a meek hello.

"Ella, you look good," Marilee proclaimed. "You, too, Mr. Carrigan. Bruises are healing up right nicely."

Sam ignored her comment and politely acknowledged their greeting. "Good morning, Miss Marilee, ladies."

"You still mad at us?" Fern questioned.

"Yes, I am. We both are." He reached for Ella's hand, clasping it gently in his own, the scowl he wore for the others dissolving into a warm smile.

The gesture elicited the heady reaction it was designed to evoke.

"Things been going pretty well around here, have they?" Rex drew himself up an inch. "I told Janie she was worrying herself into a twitter over nothing."

"Rex, I can't help worrying about people I love."

"I know you can't, honey. Don't really bother me, 'specially since you worry about me, too."

"I just want them to be happy."

"If it will make Miss Janie feel better," Sam stiffly proffered, "I will confess, *reluctantly,* and after emphasizing I still find the means to your end unforgivably barbaric, that married life agrees with me more than I originally assumed it would."

"Have you fallen in love with Ella?" Janie asked hopefully.

"Love takes more than a few days time to blossom; however, I am man enough to admit, I may have been wrong to so strongly reject the possibility we might suit each other."

"See, Ella, he don't despise you like you said he does," Lily remarked.

Before Ella could respond, Sam intervened. "I have never

despised your sister. I despised the situation you forced upon us. It would have been better if you had allowed nature to take its course."

"We would have, if you'd have let us," Fern reminded.

Sam allowed a moue to crease his forehead. He exchanged a quick, commiserative glance with Ella. Then keeping his voice modulated to reflect just the right mix of irritation and acquiescence, he stated, "There is no point in arguing about what cannot be changed. It will only put us all in a foul mood. Ella should be allowed to enjoy her wedding party, and she will not be able to if you insist on constantly reminding us how we came together. We are both trying to forget that part of our lives, so it will not taint our future."

"Speaking of Ella, she's being awfully quiet. What's going on in that head of yours? I can tell by the look in your eye you're thinking up a storm," Rex cautiously coaxed her into the conversation. "You ain't figuring on attacking me again?"

"No. I was thinking about marriage," Ella replied.

"Good thoughts or bad?" Frank quizzed.

Frank offered the opportunity Ella had been hoping to engineer, and she seized it without hesitation. "I wasn't thinking about *my* marriage. I'm learning to accept it. I'm even trying to learn to like it, because I am too sensible to spend the rest of my life being miserable just for spite. I was thinking about your marriage to Fern and Rex's to Janie and Marilee's to Bob and Lily's to whomever. Since I'm no longer standing in your way, I want to know when you all are going to tie the knot."

"The sooner the better, I say." Frank enthused.

"Today? Tomorrow?" Ella petitioned, echoing Frank's sentiment in her head. "You all have already waited what must seem an eternity. I reckon you're more than a little anxious."

"That I am. Today is your special day, but if you don't mind us stealing a little of your thunder, it sounds like a fine day for a wedding to me," Frank declared. "Today okay with you, Fern?"

"Today would be wonderful, so wonderful I'm likely to faint from joy."

Sam and Ella smiled.

"What's happening today, that's gonna make you faint with joy?" Grandma Jo stepped out on the porch, her arms laden with more food for the makeshift tables lining the yard.

"I'm getting married," Fern announced.

"Fern Susanne, I can't believe how selfish you can be sometimes. Today is Ella and Sam's day and we ain't gonna be discussing anybody else's matrimonial ambitions."

"I don't mind," Sam and Ella proclaimed in unison.

"That just shows how generous-minded you are and makes me all the more determined the two of you are gonna be King and Queen for a day. We cheated you on the courting end of this romance. We ain't gonna cheat you out of nothing else. Tomorrow is plenty soon enough to start planning our other weddings."

"Grandma Jo is right," Janie said. "I for one am gonna think of nothing but Ella's happiness all day long."

"Me neither," Lily chirped.

"You won't hear any grumbling from Bob or me," Marilee concurred.

"We've waited this long. Another day ain't gonna kill us," Frank spoke for Fern and himself.

"Good." Grandma marched on to her duties in the yard.

Ella and Sam exchanged covert glances of disappointment and frustration.

Within the hour, the yard was filled to overflowing with neighbors from as far away as forty miles, and a few from even farther.

No family came empty handed. The households blessed with the presence of a wife, brought baskets of food to add to the table and practical gifts of household items such as canning jars, a straw broom, and linen. Sally James brought a quilt Ella had admired when she was in town for a visit.

Not to be outdone by the ladies, the men were equally generous. Frank gifted them with an entire set of brand new pots and pans. Timothy Fraser brought a butter churn. Willie Crumb offered a hunting knife in addition to the embroidered pillow slips his mother had given. Several cowboys had chipped in for a pair of silver spurs for Sam and a matching locket for Ella.

Other gifts were obviously motivated by the stirring of consciences. Rex gave Sam an expensive pair of new boots and Ella three leather-bound books. The Wilson brothers had bought the biggest jar of liniment available at Frank Thatcher's store and tied it with a yellow ribbon to a bottle of expensive whiskey, announcing both were to be used to ease Sam's pains. There were several shirts and more than one pair of trousers in Sam's size.

Sam and Ella accepted their wedding gifts with good grace if not enthusiasm. It was hard for Ella to feign delight when she knew, with the possible exception of the boots and one pair of trousers, they would be returning all of the gifts before month's end. Too, it was difficult not to wonder what this day would be like if she was a true bride.

Ella knew curiosity about her husband had motivated more than a few of their guests to attend, but she also knew their generosity and well wishes were genuine.

Nobody besides her sisters and their beaus—and they were now silent on the subject as well—mentioned the circumstances leading up to her marriage.

She supposed it was the Western custom, borne more out of necessity than a nobleness of spirit, of expecting the best no matter what disasters life thrust upon you that allowed their friends and neighbors to treat Sam and her as they would any other newly wedded couple. They wanted them to be a happy couple, so it didn't occur to them they might not be.

It was a simple-minded philosophy, but highly useful when one was trying to survive daunting situations. Unfortunately, Ella found it impossible to employ the philosophy of her Western heritage to adapt her own emotions in this particular daunting situation.

"It appears the neighborhood turned out in force," Sam whispered in her ear when they had a moment's respite from greeting their guests. "I feel like the prize bull at a county fair."

Ella could not deny her husband was the recipient of enough overt perusals to make a statue start to squirm, so she answered him with a piece of advice. "Put yourself in their shoes. Could you contain your curiosity?"

"Yes. It's bad manners to stare. But so is coercing a man into marrying, and that is why we are here, so I'm sure I'll survive this lesser indignity. Where is your grandmother? I don't want her sneaking up on us and overhearing some comment she shouldn't."

Ella scanned the yard twice before she spotted her grandparent. "She's standing beside Pete Wilson, over by the table nearest the house. They're probably discussing when to strike up the band and begin the dancing. Tradition demands we lead the first waltz, but after, we can use your leg as an excuse to avoid the dance floor."

"I have no desire to avoid the dance floor. My leg only pains me a little, and I judge a little pain well worth the price considering the benefits to our cause to be gained on the dance floor. It is common knowledge many a gentleman and lady, who had no intention whatsoever of pursuing a relationship, have had their good sense stripped from them while engaging in the activity of dancing. I believe it greatly to our advantage to become 'over stimulated.' "

Ella's cheeks pinkened. "I hope you aren't planning to do anything too mortifying. When this is over, you'll return to your life in New York. I have to live among these people."

"I will exercise restraint," Sam promised. "Now, in the interest of avoiding being found out by eavesdropping ears, I propose for the rest of the day we do not discuss strategies. Nothing but congenial comments will pass our lips. Agreed?"

"Agreed."

Sam slipped his arm around her waist. "When you feel yourself adequate to the task, I think a bit of mingling with our guests is in order. The couple over there." He gestured to a blond-haired couple sitting on a blanket. "The one with the two little girls. They look relatively harmless."

"David and Pamela are fine people," Ella confirmed. Her smile was perhaps a bit too broad, but she didn't want him to know how disconcerting she found the casual intimacy of his encircling arm.

"Then, why don't we stroll over and strike up a conversation."

As soon as they arrived at David and Pamela's blanket, Sam dropped his arm from Ella's waist. She sent a silent prayer of gratitude winging heavenward.

They spoke with David and Pamela briefly; then, playing the role of attentive hosts, they moved on to another group of guests. On the way to each new group of guests, Ella filled Sam in with a few basic facts about each person with whom they were about to talk. They never stayed more than a few minutes with each gathering.

When, as they wandered toward them, Ella mentioned Charlie and Agnes Rutherford must have been passing through Heaven on other business or they wouldn't be here because their ranch was located too many miles to the northwest for them to have heard the news and gotten here on time, she caught Sam's earnest interest.

"Let me have charge of this conversation," he instructed. "I may be able to do us some good."

"Okay," Ella agreed, though she had no idea why he should think the Rutherfords of special importance.

She didn't have to wait long to discover the reason.

After taking a moment or two to exchange the usual pleasantries, Sam coolly commented, "Ella tells me you live some distance northwest of here. I have family up there. Perhaps you would be willing to carry a message to them from me. I'm eager to share the news of my wedding."

"We'd be glad to oblige," Agnes offered. "Just tell us their names and what you want us to say for you."

"Their name is Carrigan, just like mine," Sam stated, being careful not to reveal his excitement. "The father's Christian name is Barnett. He has two grown sons named Adam and Joshua."

"I don't recall there being a soul within two hundred miles of us with the name Carrigan." Charlie scratch his head. "If there was, I would've made the connection when we was first introduced."

"Are you certain? Perhaps if I give you the exact location of the ranch it will jog your memory?"

"It might help," Charlie agreed.

Sam described the location as accurately as he was able using the information from his mother's map.

When he was finished, Charlie scratched his head again. "I know the ranch, but ain't no one by the name of Carrigan lives there. A fellow by the name of John Sawyer owns it. Least he has for as long as we've lived up there."

"That's true," Agnes confirmed. "Been awhile since you seen that branch of the family, I take it."

"Yes."

She smiled sympathetically. "Well, either someone's pulling

your leg about where your kinfolk live or they moved on. Wish I could tell you which, but I can't."

Ella could see the disappointment in Sam's eyes, but he kept a congenial mien pasted on his face. He engaged the Rutherfords in a little more small talk, then excused them to see to their other guests.

"Do you believe them?" he whispered in her ear as they strolled away.

"What reason would they have to lie?"

"To keep me here," he suggested darkly.

"I don't think so. They weren't involved in making us marry, and Agnes has a reputation for being a stickler for honesty."

Sam pressed his lips together, a pensive expression settling upon his face. "My impression was they were being honest as well, but I still intend to travel to the ranch and see for myself. *When I am able.*"

"Yes. I think you should. It's too important a matter to not go."

"Anybody in the mood to kick up their heels?" Grandma Jo called out the question, bringing an end to the conversation. "I got me a fine dance floor provided by the sweat of the brow of one George Carson and one Jacob Houston, and some fellas itching to make a little music. All this food, we're gonna need to work up some hearty appetites."

On cue the band, a make-do collection of the local musical talent, shoved their fiddles under their chins and struck up the strains of a waltz.

Ella's sisters and their beaus were the first to the dance floor.

The remaining single men rushed to grab hold of the few available ladies, engaging in a fair amount of good-natured wrangling before the final couples were formed.

"Sam, Ella step on up here." Grandma Jo waved them forward.

Sam reached for Ella's hand. His hand felt so warm against hers, Ella knew hers must be as cold as ice, and she wasn't thrilled to have him know how truly nervous she was. She had conducted herself with dignity while they mingled amongst the crowd making neighborly talk, and she was hoping he would assume she was as calm and collected inside as she outwardly appeared to be.

Her feet felt like lead, but she forced herself not to drag them as he escorted her to the dance platform. Ella was so assiduous in her effort, she ended up surpassing him.

"Don't appear too eager," Sam counseled in her ear.

Blushing, Ella slowed her pace.

The dance floor was a hastily assembled twelve foot by twelve foot wooden floor a board's width above the ground. They stepped to the center, and the band stilled.

"Friends and neighbors, it's my immense pleasure to present Mr. and Mrs. Samuel Carrigan," Grandma Jo crowed. "May they have a long and joyful life together."

The crowd erupted into cheers. The band commenced to play. Sam took Ella into his arms, expertly leading her in a turn around the dance floor. After a few minutes, the boisterous well wishes faded to burbling chatter, and other couples joined them in the dance.

Sam was so delightfully light of foot, Ella found it impossible to hide her bliss. She loved to dance and had spent many a stolen moment practicing steps with imaginary partners. She looked forward to every community dance every bit as eagerly as her sisters.

However, dancing with Mr. Samuel Carrigan hardly qualified as the same activity, the experience was so superior to spinning about the cabin floor alone or dancing in the arms of men who substituted enthusiasm for skill and were wont to step on a body's toes with painful regularity. Heaven boasted several men who qualified as good dancers, but none of them came close to Sam in grace.

In fact, he was so graceful, she judged putting up with an irregular heartbeat and too pink cheeks a small price to pay for the pleasure dancing with him afforded her.

"You dance well," Sam complemented.

"Thank you."

"I'm curious. Where does a lady learn to be so fleet of foot living so far from any center of culture? I can't conceive their mothers hire dance instructors as we do in the city."

"My parents taught all of us to dance soon after we learned to walk," Ella apprised him. "Wyoming winters are long and cold. We use to hold family dances every Saturday to wile away the hours and keep our limbs from getting stiff." She danced through the next measure of music. "Where did you learn to dance so well?"

"My mother hired a dance instructor. No son or daughter escaped the tutelage of *the dread dance master.* Oh, how I hated him. In all the years since, I have yet to meet a more consummate prig." The light of rebellion faded from his eyes, and he was again the cool-headed gentleman. "But the man knew his trade, and I have to admit the skills he taught me have served me well."

Ella leaned back slightly, smiling up at his handsome face. "I can't imagine you as a little boy."

"I wasn't any different than other boys. Perhaps a trifle more overindulged than most, but . . ."

"You miss your mother, don't you?"

He was silent a moment before he spoke. "Yes." He spoke the word staidly, but it held a note of despondency and a clear message he did not wish to pursue the subject. Ella respected his wishes and changed the topic of conversation.

"How is your leg?"

"It has felt better, but I'll survive." Sam led her through a series of rapid turns and on to another subject. "I want to commend you on how well you are playing your part today. Your face displays exactly the right amount of ambiguity. Anyone watching—and everyone is—should be absolutely convinced your feelings for me and our marriage are in flux.

Ella didn't think it wise to tell him it was easy to project an ambiguous mien, because her feelings were exactly that. The more time she spent in his company, the more often she found her head filled with wistful thoughts concerning him and their marriage. She rejected them out right, feeling positively immoral for entertaining even fleeting wishes some miracle might occur and they might both decide they wanted to stay married after all, but try as she might, she couldn't prevent these irresponsible thoughts from entering her head.

It was ironic but her chief difficulty in maintaining her absolute abhorrence to their marriage was the strategy designed to end it. Her husband's kindness and attention might all be an act, but she couldn't help but believe a wife of his own choosing would be treated with the same regard, only it would be genuine, of course, and that would make it all the more appealing.

The physical side of marriage went without saying. It was rather startling to discover at the age of twenty-five that one possessed an uncontrollably lusty nature, but she had, and her temporary husband was the object of her lust. If her sisters' physical feeling for the men in their lives echoed her own in intensity, it was little wonder they were driven to the madness of kidnapping a mate for her so they could find relief.

Ella looked up into the deep blue eyes of her dance partner. Even with his complexion tinged a greenish yellow from the fading bruises, he was still too handsome. It was just her luck to finally meet a man she *could* fall in love with, only to have circumstances prevent any hope of winning his heart. Grand-

ma Jo might be convinced they were fated for some grand
love, but Ella wasn't brash enough to consider trying to exercise her charms upon her reluctant husband. Her conscience
prevented her. There were many things she might be willing
to do to have a man she truly loved, but violating her conscience was not one of them.

"Why are you frowning?"

"I let my mind wander," Ella answered with a polite smile.
"I won't let it happen again."

"Perhaps we should sit out the next dance."

"Whatever you say."

As soon as the music ended, he led her away from the other
dancers and fetched a glass of lemonade. "It's going well,
don't you think?"

"Everyone appears to be having a good time," Ella agreed.

"Yes, especially your sisters and their beaus. Have you noticed Lily has danced with our friend George Carson three
times already. Do you think we could get her to marry him?"

"Maybe." Ella knew it was silly but somehow knowing
while her thoughts were occupied with foolish dreams their
marriage might endure, his were consumed with ways to end
it as soon as possible, made her feel despondent.

"You don't approve of him?" he queried.

"He's fine."

"Then, why the dark look?"

"Shoot! Carl and Bethany Hubbard are heading this way. I
can't stand either of them, and they can't stand me. Can we
go back to the dance floor?" Ella deftly evaded his question.
"Unless of course, your leg hurts too much."

"Would you stop worrying about my leg? I am perfectly capable of informing you when and if it is no longer functional."

"Fine, then let's dance." She led the way.

When they were comfortably settled into the rhythm of the

dance steps, Sam asked, "What do the Hubbards have against you?"

"I wouldn't marry their son."

He raised a brow. "Just how many marriage proposals have you had?"

Ella took a moment to added them up and replied, "Twenty-three."

"Twenty-three?" Sam choked.

"I know it sounds like a lot, but I didn't receive them all in one day. It has been seven years since I turned eighteen."

"All right," he didn't argue the point, though his expression said he still thought the number excessive and always would. "They dislike you because you refused to marry their son. Why do you dislike them?"

"Because after I turned down Clement's proposal, his mother and father sat down with a piece of paper and cataloged all my failings; then, they posted it on a tree in the center of town. Rex took it down as soon as he found it, but I was not amused. They said some very unkind things about me, most of them untrue."

"Then I think we should avoid them." Sam struggled to contain his mirth.

"Go ahead and laugh," Ella urged. "Everybody else did, and I confess if I hadn't been the victim of their spiteful trick, I would have laughed, too. Besides, most folks say it made them look worse than me, so the joke was really on them."

"People around here certainly find unique ways to amuse themselves," he observed.

"Busy hands, idle minds." Ella grimaced.

The next dance didn't allow for conversation nor did the one after. Ella was both relieved and disappointed.

It was a pleasure carrying on a conversation with her husband, but she wasn't suppose to be having a nice time. Their private dialogues were designed to foster the illusion of intimacy. She must never forget, even for a moment, that everything they did, though it might appear spontaneous, was part of a precisely prepared plan.

The biggest drawback to the absence of conversation was it allowed her mind too much opportunity to analyze and savor her physical reactions to her dance partner. Due to the severe shortage of females, the other women, even the married ones, changed dance partners with the frequency of hummingbirds sampling flowers, but not a masculine soul approached her.

Having been to more than one wedding celebration, Ella knew leaving the bride exclusively to her husband was not traditional. She suspected her lack of a variety of partners was Grandma Jo's doing. . . .

Rather than a formal meal, lids and napkins were lifted off pots and baskets around five o'clock and guests were free to fill their plates whenever and as often as they pleased. The men from Bob McNaught's ranch took turns at the barbecue spit, slicing off thick juicy slabs of beef.

As was the custom, everyone had brought their favorite dish, and the food was as delicious as it was plentiful.

Ella was too nervous to eat much, but Sam ate with gusto. He seemed especially fond of her spiced apple pies.

As the dancing went on into the night, his limp—which had been slight at the beginning of the day—became more pronounced, but he refused to sit out more than a handful of dances. It saved them the necessity of carrying on too many carefully rehearsed conversations with their neighbors, and certainly established them as a couple, but the hours of close physical contact were taking their toll on Ella's ability to resist her husband's charms.

It didn't help to have him whisper in her ear and laugh and—though he had only forgotten to warn her once—place the occasional husbandly kiss upon her hand or cheek.

It was too easy to be taken in by the spell cast by his

superb acting abilities. If he weren't already a successful businessman, without hesitation, she would recommend he seek a life on the stage.

By the time their guests began to wander back to their wagons, some to take up lodgings with their closest neighbors, others to roll out blankets and sleep under the stars, Ella was so overwrought with pent-up desires there was room for only one rational thought in her head.

Her sisters must marry *and marry without delay,* for if Mr. Carrigan did not remove himself from her presence soon, she would rip off her clothes and behave no better than the prostitute who lived above the Red Eye Saloon.

Eleven

A man who spent night after night lovemaking wore a self-satisfied expression upon his face and strutted about like a rooster in a yard full of hens. Samuel Carrigan acted more like a penned-up bull sniffing a breed cow on the other side of the fence, Grandma Jo mused as she sipped her second cup of morning coffee.

She saw the circles of fatigue ringing the couple's eyes, heard the bed creak and enough moaning to cause a body to blush, but she'd lived too long not to trust her instincts when they whispered things weren't right and her instincts were positively hollering.

Oh, she realized the casual observer would never suspect anything was amiss, and she had been shamming she hadn't noticed either. But she had. It was little things she kept noticing. When he thought no one was looking, Sam had a habit of squirming like his britches were too tight. Ella had the house so clean a body could serve supper on the floor. When a couple held hands, they usually looked cozy. Sam and Ella looked ready to jump out of their skins. Then, there was the funny way they looked while dancing at their wedding party. Half the time they appeared ready to bolt out of each others' arms. The other half they acted like they couldn't get enough of each other—which was a sure sign they weren't.

Grandma Jo drained the last of her coffee from her cup and sighed. Nothing was easy in this life. She'd thought her work done when she'd heard Sam order his balky bride to bed, but she realized now it had just begun. She should have known from the start two stubborn young people like Sam and Ella wouldn't give up without putting up a good fight. Didn't matter that they were wrong, and in their hearts they both knew it. Only thing that mattered was showing the world they couldn't be pushed around.

Yep. Whatever was going on in that room of theirs, it wasn't conjugal communion. She'd bet her last chicken on that.

Rising to her feet, she chuckled. Poor Ella and Sam. They really thought they could outsmart her. She had experience, human nature, everybody in the county, and the Almighty on her side. The arrogance of youth was without bounds.

Though both Sam and Ella did everything in their power to persuade Grandma Jo to let the three sisters who had their hearts settled marry that morning, Grandma Jo remained adamant it couldn't be done that soon, reciting a litany of reasons from the fatigue in her old bones to not wanting to impose upon their guests' Christian natures by thrusting another celebration upon them when many of them were suffering mightily from the after effects of too much partying the night before.

By noon the last of their guests were headed home. Sam and Ella wasted no time gathering her sisters around the table. Ella took the lead. "Well, let's get started planning your weddings. I figure it would be lovely if you all get married this Sunday in one monumental ceremony. Just imagine, four sisters wed on the same day. Why you all would make history in the territory. Folks would be talking about the wedding into the next century."

Sam raised a brow in salute of Ella's shrewd suggestion.

"I'm agreeable," Fern said. "How about the rest of you?"

"Sounds good." Marilee nodded.

4 FREE BOOKS

TO GET YOUR 4 FREE BOOKS WORTH $18.00 — MAIL IN THE FREE BOOK CERTIFICATE T O D A Y

Fill in the Free Book Certificate below, and we'll send your FREE BOOKS to you as soon as we receive it.

If the certificate is missing below, write to: Zebra Home Subscription Service, Inc., P.O. Box 5214, 120 Brighton Road, Clifton, New Jersey 07015-5214.

FREE BOOK CERTIFICATE

4 FREE BOOKS

ZEBRA HOME SUBSCRIPTION SERVICE, INC.

YES! Please start my subscription to Zebra Historical Romances and send me my first 4 books absolutely FREE. I understand that each month I may preview four new Zebra Historical Romances free for 10 days. If I'm not satisfied with them, I may return the four books within 10 days and owe nothing. Otherwise, I will pay the low preferred subscriber's price of just $3.75 each; a total of $15.00, *a savings off the publisher's price of $3.00.* I may return any shipment and I may cancel this subscription at any time. There is no obligation to buy any shipment. (A postage and handling charge of $1.50 is added to each shipment.) Regardless of what I decide, the four free books are mine to keep.

NAME

ADDRESS   APT

CITY   STATE   ZIP

TELEPHONE
(   )

SIGNATURE   (if under 18, parent or guardian must sign)

Terms, offer and prices subject to change without notice. Subscription subject to acceptance by Zebra Books. Zebra Books reserves the right to reject any order or cancel any subscription.

ZB1694

"If Rex likes the idea, and I reckon he will, I do, too," Janie chimed in.

"What about you, Lily?" Ella prodded.

"Well . . . I did get three proposals yesterday, and adding them to the six standing ones I already had, that's ten men to choose from. I don't know if I can make up my mind that quick."

"Maybe I can help," Sam entered the conversation. "I'll be back in a moment." Returning to the room with a piece of paper and pen in hand, he rejoined them at the table. He gave both paper and pen to Lily. "List the names of your prospective husbands on the paper," he instructed.

"Okay," Lily replied skeptically. When she was finished, she handed the paper and pen back to him.

"All right. First question. Are all of these men gainfully employed?"

"Everybody but Harlin. He just got fired from the Kelsy ranch for losing his temper and cussing out the foreman."

"Harlin is definitely off the list." Sam drew a line through his name. "Any tipplers?"

"Every man in the territory takes a nip or two at the Red Eye Saloon on occasion," Lily argued.

Scanning the list, Ella pointed to two names. "Cross them off and that one, too. His temper is even worse than Harlin's."

"We're making good progress. In less than five minutes we've already narrowed the field to six names," Sam announced.

"You can cross Denny Miller off. He snorts when he laughs. I just can't see myself listening to that snorting the rest of my life."

"Five. See how easy it is to come to a decision when you approach it systematically." Sam gifted her with an approving smile. "Are there any others who possess annoying personal habits?"

Lily thought a minute. "Nope."

226 René J. Garrod

"Any womanizers?"

"No."

"What about Bret Jensen?" Janie reminded. "He's proposed marriage to everyone of us at least once. I don't figure you should marry a man with a fickle heart."

"Cross his name off," Lily reluctantly accepted her advice.

"I don't want you to marry Ralph Kincaid," Fern asserted. "He's too old and he's already killed off two wives."

"He didn't kill them," Lily rallied to his defense. "Hannah died of the flu just like Mama and Daddy, and Mary died in childbirth."

"Okay, maybe he didn't kill them, but he has bad luck with wives, and I'd just as soon you didn't take the risk."

Sam crossed off Ralph Kincaid. "That leaves us with three suitors." He turned over the paper and made three columns, each headed with one of the three remaining names. "Now that we have a manageable number of names, I want you to list all the qualities of each man. When you're done, whoever has the longest list is the man you will marry."

"What are y'all so busy doing around the table?" Grandma Jo questioned as she ambled into the house from the yard. "I hope it's important 'cause y'all still have chores to do outside."

"Mr. Carrigan is helping Lily decide who to marry come Sunday," Marilee explained. "We're all gonna get married at the same time."

"Are you now? I don't remember giving my permission for a Sunday wedding."

"You said we could marry as soon as Ella did," Fern firmly reminded.

"That's true and I stand by my word, but I'm not gonna let anybody be rushed into anything. That's how mistakes are made, and marrying the wrong fella is about the worst mistake a woman can make." Grandma Jo rebuked the gathering at the table with a stern frown, waggling her finger at them. Ella could not prevent herself from rolling her eyes at the hypocrisy of her grandmother's words. "Now, I'm not saying I dislike the notion of y'all marrying up at the same time, 'cause I don't. There ain't no one on earth loves doing things up on a grand scale more than me. All I'm asking is you give your little sister time to make up her mind proper."

"Three marriages would be almost as grand as four," Ella interjected, hoping to salvage what she could of her scheme.

"Yes. Three would be more than satisfying," Sam seconded her opinion.

Grandma Jo's frown deepened. "No, now that the suggestion has been made, the notion of *four* brides is too lively to resist. Besides, if your sisters are gonna get married in a herd, they oughta wear matching dresses, and even with us all working day and night, we'd never get them stitched up before Sunday. We haven't even bought the material."

"I can appreciate your attention to aesthetics, but you must appreciate, now that I have a wife, how irresponsible it would be for me to neglect my business overlong. If the wedding can't be held forthwith, Ella and I will have to leave for New York. We prefer not to miss the joyous nuptials, but if we must we must."

"I suspect you're already a hundred times richer than my Nat ever was, and we got by as cozy as you please," Grandma Jo contended. "Still, I don't want you accusing me of interfering in your business, so I vow I'll see this wedding gets accomplished just as fast as my old bones allow. That should satisfy you, and if it don't, I'm sorry. I can't let Ella miss her own sisters' wedding day." She turned from him to her granddaughters. "It's too late today, but first thing tomorrow morning, I want you girls to hitch up Alexander to the wagon and head into town. Buy everything you need for your dresses, and we'll set to sewing up a storm. You're gonna have the finest, most stylish wedding that ever was, and Sam is gonna witness the glory of the Western can-do spirit."

Laundry was Ella's least favorite chore. On cold days the moisture froze your hands and on hot ones the steam from the laundry pot came close to cooking you alive. Normally, she dreaded her turn, but today she had welcomed it. Josephine Singleton had a good notion the reason was because it got her granddaughter out of the house and away from the constant temptation of her husband.

And Ella found him a powerful temptation, there was no doubt in her mind of that. The poor girl was half crazy with desire. Sam was in no better shape.

Those two foolish young folks were their own worst enemies. All that hand holding, reading poetry to each other, the spirited discussions of authors they admired, the winsome looks, the moonlight strolls; they played at being lovers for her benefit, but their game was keeping their fires stoked as good as most anything she could stir up to further the course of true love.

She hadn't been witness to this much bridled lust since Nat's and her courting days. It only proved how right she was to finagle the two of them into marrying each other. Once they came around to being sensible, they were gonna have a marriage every bit as body and soul satisfying as the one she and Nat had shared.

With that purpose in mind, she kept watch through the window, waiting for Ella to finish boiling the clothes and to begin hanging them on the line to dry.

"Sam, will you go out and ask Ella what she did with the baking powder? I've searched high and low, and I still can't find it." Grandma Jo planted her hands on her hips and a perplexed expression on her face. "There ain't no hurry, but

I would like to know in time to stir up some biscuits for dinner, so the sooner you could do it the better."

Sam didn't know why she just didn't open the door and ask her herself, but he was growing restless. "I'd be glad to," he replied.

Stepping out onto the porch, he came to an abrupt halt. Ella was leaning over the laundry basket with her delectable posterior sticking in the air. He swallowed the hard lump of desire clogging his throat, but could do nothing to relieve the tightness in his loins.

She stood up, pinned a petticoat to the clothesline, then bent over again. Even as he cursed himself for behaving more like an animal than the gentleman he had always believed himself to be, his mouth went dry with lecherous longing. There were certain moments of his adventures in Wyoming he had no intention of sharing with Clara, and this was definitely one of them.

His wife stood up and bent over two more times. Every time she did, he was undone a little bit more. The woman possessed the finest pair of hips he had ever seen, and if she didn't stop waving them at him . . .

He cut off the thought and took the porch steps two at a time. "Here, let me help you with those." Sam lifted the next item from the laundry basket. Regrettably it was a corset, *her* corset judging by the size of the bodice which his pertinacious mind did before he could stop it.

Ella snatched the garment from his hands. "I can do it."

Sam glanced down at the laundry basket. The whole damn basket looked filled with nothing but feminine underthings. It shouldn't have startled him since this was a household of six females, but it did.

He had only one recourse: beat a hasty retreat back into the house.

"Where is it?" Grandma Jo queried when he burst through the door.

"Where is what?"

"The baking soda," she reminded.

"Uh . . . just a minute." Sam performed a speedy about-face and stepped back out the door.

"Ella, your grandmother wants to know where you put the baking soda," he called, keeping his eyes focused on anything but his wife.

Ella frowned. "It's on the bottom shelf next to the salt where it always is."

"She says she can't find it."

"That's ridiculous. No one has used it since I put it there myself last night."

"I'm just telling you what she said."

"Well, tell her for me, I'll come in and look just as soon as I get the rest of this laundry hung up."

Sam marched back into the house. "She says she'll come find it when she's finished hanging the laundry. Listen, I'm not accustomed to sitting idle for long stretches, and I've exhausted every useful occupation for my time I am capable of conjuring. Do you have some wood that needs to be chopped or a fence that needs mending?"

Grandma Jo smothered a grin. "The corral has a couple of loose boards. Ella can show you where we keep the hammer and nails if you're of a mind to bang on something for awhile."

"She's terribly busy and I'd hate to interrupt her again. I'd prefer you show me where to find them," Sam declared.

"I'm sorry. My arthritis is acting up, Sam. I hate for you to bother Ella, too, but I just don't reckon I'm up to another trip to the barn today."

* * *

When he approached—Hound Dog wagging his crooked tail at his heels—and asked for her assistance, Ella showed Sam where they kept the tools in the barn; then, she returned to her laundry. She hadn't noticed any loose boards, but a board or two could easily be loose without her knowing about it, so she didn't give it much thought.

Since having her husband in plain view defeated all purpose of prolonging the laundry, Ella finished the chore as quickly as she was able and returned to the house.

The first thing she did was search the pantry shelves. When she could find no trace of the missing baking powder, her brows knit and she scratched the back of her head. "I know I put it right here." Ella pointed to the blank spot on the shelf.

"I know that's where it oughta be," Grandma Jo confirmed. "But it ain't."

Her sense of order offended, Ella began a search of the entire kitchen. Several minutes later she was on her knees, reaching under the stove. "Here it is," she triumphantly announced holding up the tin. "It must have fallen off the shelf and rolled under the stove. It's a wonder no one heard the thud."

"That it is." Grandma Jo turned away, hiding her mischievous grin.

With her husband out of the house, Ella could think of nothing she wanted more than a much-needed nap, and after straightening the mess she had made of the kitchen shelves, she started for the bedroom.

Grandma Jo stopped her a few feet from the threshold. "Before you get busy doing something else, I reckon you might oughta take a tall glass of lemonade out to that husband of yours. We've got just enough lemons left to make a pitcher.

Hot as it is today, I'm sure he's working up a sweat, and you look as if you could use a glass yourself."

A cool glass of lemonade held much appeal; the suggestion she deliver the same to her husband did not. However, Ella was too kind-hearted to ignore his needs. Without comment, she returned to the kitchen to do her duty.

Grandma Jo squeezed the lemons while Ella fetched cool water from the well. Soon, they had two glasses and a pitcher full of lemonade ready on a tray.

"Put your feet up and sit a spell," Grandma Jo admonished as Ella stepped out the door.

At first Ella couldn't see Sam, but as she rounded the corner of the barn, he came into full view. She almost dropped the tray. The wretch had removed his jacket and vest.

His sweat dampened, white linen shirt clung to his back and chest like a second skin, leaving nothing to imagination. Having seen him bare-chested, and being possessed of the discomfiting skill to recall every inch of him in minute detail at the most inappropriate times, she could not claim modesty caused the erratic rhythm of her heart. Rather she knew with unnerving certainty the cause of her affliction was hopeless infatuation with his fine figure. Every time he moved a muscle a trill ran down her spine to her toes, and he had yet to be still.

In fact, from the exceedingly earnest way he was pounding nails into the fence rails, the corral must be in much worse shape than anyone reckoned.

As she continued to gaze at him, Ella pondered her plight. The first time she had stared at her husband's naked chest, she had only had to contend with an intense physical attraction. Now that she knew him better, her situation was so much worse. Hers was not only an attraction of the flesh but an attraction of the mind. Samuel Carrigan's estimable intellect was infinitely more seductive than a pair of well-muscled arms.

Why did there have to be so many things about him to like? If Providence was determined to thrust her into such a untenable marriage, he should have provided her with some means to resist temptation. He could have made the man ugly or stupid or at the very least given him one or two vexatious personal habits. She was not so fanciful to reckon the man perfect, but he was the closest thing to a perfect man she had ever seen.

Ella stifled a groan. With dogged determination she cheerily called out, "I've brought you some lemonade."

"Thank you," he responded in measured tones. "That was very kind of you." Though she was not sure what she would judge it, the expression upon her husband's face as he set his hammer aside could not be called appreciative.

"Grandma Jo thought you might be thirsty," Ella feebly offered, feeling a need to fill the silence.

"I am."

Ella poured him a glass of lemonade and handed it to him. Quickly stepping away, she clasped her hands behind her back.

"I see you brought a glass for yourself," he commented unenthusiastically.

"Yes."

"Are you going to pour yourself a glass or are you just going to stand there watching me drink mine?"

"Are you angry at me?"

"No, I'm angry at myself."

"I don't understand."

Sam drained his glass in a single draught. "I'm not in the mood to explain myself. Why don't you go back to the house?"

"Yes, I will," Ella readily agreed. "I'll just leave the pitcher in the shade in case you get thirsty again."

* * *

Young love was definitely in the air. Janie, Fern, Marilee, and Lily finished their outside chores in record time each morning, then spent the rest of the day chirping like chickadees while they gaily pinned patterns and cut bolts of fabric and lace into pieces for their wedding dresses. Most every evening one or another of their beaus took turns sleeping in the barn, so they could spend a day or two courting. Sam and Ella were so randy for each other these days they could hardly sit still five minutes at a time, and that was just how she wanted them—so hot and bothered with longing they couldn't think straight.

Grandma Jo made no effort to suppress the spring in her step.

She hadn't lost a minute's sleep feeling guilty over what she was doing to her eldest granddaughter and her husband. Sure they were suffering, but it was a good kind of suffering—the kind of suffering that made the resulting joy that much sweeter.

She'd been busy as a whole hive full of bees, but truth be told, she was having so much fun playing cupid, she almost wished her other granddaughters weren't so set on getting married right away to men they knew they wanted. Overcoming obstacles to true love was too pleasurable by half.

Every trick she used produced a good effect.

She ignored Ella's admonitions to stay out of her kitchen and fed them honey and eggs in the morning and when she could, mountain oysters at supper. The cowboys she cajoled into rounding up the calves that had escaped the spring cutting to supply her with the delicate morsels were starting to wonder what she was up to, but she was keeping her lips tightly sealed. It'd never do for it to get back to Sam and Ella she knew they were avoiding the creature comforts of their matrimonial bed. Their efforts to convince her they were as snug as two bugs in a rug continued to aid and abet her own designs. Besides, Sam had one fine singing voice. When he crooned in the evenings to Ella, as he had taken to doing these last few nights, if she closed her eyes, she could almost pretend it was her Nat singing to her. An old woman had to take her pleasures when she may.

The two reluctant lovebirds were out of the house this morning. Ella was tending the garden, and Sam was proving he might be handier than he looked by tinkering with the handle of the well pump which had been acting balky of late. She was busy in the kitchen. Tonight, she planned to serve the reluctant newlyweds a rum pie. She was tripling the liquor called for in the recipe. It wouldn't make them drunk, but it oughta make them plenty mellow before going to bed.

Of course, stimulating the senses involved more than providing passion-inciting foods. Every morning she sent one of the girls to gather fresh flowers for the house. When everyone was occupied elsewhere, she sneaked into the couple's bedroom and doctored their sheets with the musky perfume Nat had given her the last year he was alive. She made certain the two were under each other's noses day and night and arranged for them to brush up against each other whenever she could.

It shouldn't be much longer now. No, sirree. The tension in the air was so thick she could cut it with a knife and spread it on a biscuit. And, once they succumbed to their natural inclinations, Sam and Ella were gonna fall on their knees and thank her for not giving up on them.

Sam coughed and gasped for air when he swallowed the first fork full of the huge piece of pie Mrs. Singleton had set before him. He blinked back the tears pooling in his eyes.

During his incarceration in the Singleton household he had experienced a steady stream of afflictions justifying bitter complaints, but one thing he had never found fault with was the food.

When he recovered, he pasted a wan smile on his face and discreetly lay his fork aside. He did not take it up again.

"Is something wrong with my pie, Sam?" Grandma Jo asked, her brow knit with concern.

"No, no," he answered. "I'm afraid I ate too much dinner."

"I made the pie especially for you," she coaxed. "It was my Grandma Elizabeth's favorite recipe. Been handed down for generations."

"Really?" He continued to maintain his smile. Lifting his fork, he tried another bite. This time he was prepared, and he swallowed it with a minimal display of discomfort. He politely forked in three more mouthfuls before covertly casting Ella an agonized look.

She picked up her fork and tasted her own pie. "Merciful heavens!" she sputtered when she was able to catch sufficient breath to produce intelligible words. "What did you do to this pie!"

Grandma Jo puckered up her face. "I know I ain't got the gift for baking you have, Ella, but that's no cause to insult me. I'm a fine cook in my own right, and you've said so many times yourself."

"Taste it yourself," Ella demanded.

Grandma Jo did just that. "Hmm, I see what you mean," she stated smoothly. "I must have accidentally splashed in a little extra when I was measuring out the rum. But it ain't that bad."

Ella gingerly nibbled another bite and made a face. Her sisters tasted their desserts with the same reaction.

"You don't gotta eat it if you don't want to," Grandma Jo huffed. "Just don't be expecting me to be throwing any compliments your way next time you go to extra effort to make a meal special. You gonna hurt my feelings, too, Sam?"

"It is a bit strong for my taste . . . but it's not so bad I can't finish it," he quickly added when her eyes narrowed. After all the trouble he had gone to to get on the woman's good side, he wasn't about to lose ground over a piece of pie.

A satisfied smirk stretched across Grandma Jo's face. "Well, it's good to know somebody sitting at this table has some manners." She folded her arms across her chest and leaned back in her chair. "The rest of you could learn something by emulating this fine gentleman. By my reckoning, you could learn a lot."

. . . Lord, she was beautiful, Sam exclaimed as he watched his wife walk toward him across a meadow. Her feet floated above the ground. A gentle breeze billowed her dark hair off her shoulders, gifting him with enticing glimpses of her pink-tipped breasts. A garland of wildflowers ringed her waist, cascading down her flat belly to tease a nest of dark curls. The flowers perfumed the air. The flowers were all she wore.

Without hesitation, she came into his open arms. Crushing her breasts against him, she hungrily devoured his lips.

Until the moment she pressed herself full length against him, he had not realized he was as naked as she. He welcomed the knowledge.

He felt himself rise up hot and hard.

Lifting her into his arms, he dropped to his knees, cradling her against him while he buried his face in her breasts and breathed in a heady draught of her scent. She encouraged him, pulling his head deeper into the cleft of her bosom. He kissed her everywhere, eliciting satisfying mews of pleasure.

Their lips met and joined. She tasted sweeter than a honey drop and was twice as warm as the sun. Her tongue darted into his mouth and withdrew, then circled his lips. Hooking his tongue with her own, she invited him to enter her mouth, where their tongues imitated the dance of passion he had been yearning to perform with her for ever so long with slow, deep thrusts.

He was exploding with desire. He couldn't wait any longer to have her. Lowering her to the ground, he crushed her with his weight. He parted her thighs with his knees . . .

He took her lips again as she struggled against him and found her hand splayed across his forehead pushing him away with frantic force. Her other hand clamped over his mouth. With a mighty shove to his shoulders, she rolled him onto his back. "Wake up! You're having a bad dream! If you don't stop making so much noise, I'm afraid someone might come in here," Ella hissed in his ear.

The feel of the hard floor against his back and a very real woman sitting astride him jolted Sam fully awake, if not fully aware.

"What?"

Ella lay her fingertips against his lips to remind him of the necessity of keeping his voice low. When he nodded his comprehension, she lifted her fingers and softly answered him. "I said you were having a bad dream. I came down here to wake you, and you grabbed me and . . ." She blushed. "Never mind. It's not important." Ella changed the subject. "What on earth were you dreaming about that upset you so much it set you to thrashing about and crying out with such longing? Were you dreaming about your mother?"

"No! I don't think so. . . . I don't remember," Sam lied, his cheeks becoming every bit as red as Ella's. "Forgive me if I . . ." He drew in a ragged breath. "I think it would be wise, if you got off me and went back to bed before we continue this conversation."

Glancing down and seeing her nightgown had hiked up to

the top of her thighs, Ella immediately complied. When she was safely ensconced under the covers, she hesitated a long while before she whispered, "I didn't mean to pry. I'm sorry if I did. It's just after my mother's death, I used to have the most awful nightmares. I know you haven't been sleeping well on the floor, and . . . it's a pity the one night you're able to fall asleep without any trouble at all, you have your rest disturbed by upsetting night visions."

"It's probably that da—that unfortunate rum pie," Sam mumbled.

"Most likely. I suspect it had more than a little to do with you falling asleep the minute your head hit the pillow. Usually you lay awake for hours."

"As do you."

"We are both in danger of dying of exhaustion if we don't get my sisters married soon." Ella stared at the ceiling, while she scolded her body for refusing to forget how tantalizing it had felt to lie beneath the weight of the man on the floor. "I'm sorry it's taking longer than I thought it would."

"You are falling back into your old habit of apologizing with every other breath. Please refrain from doing so. It is as unnecessary as it is annoying." Sam tensely requested. "I don't think we will have to put up with each other too much longer. Your sisters' dresses are coming together quite nicely."

"Yes, they are."

"So, we have nothing to worry about," he stated, imbuing his words with false conviction.

"Nothing at all," Ella confirmed in a voice as hollow of certainty as his heart.

"Try to get some sleep."

"You, too."

"Yes, I will."

Neither did.

Twelve

"I beg your pardon!" Sam sputtered, sinking until the water filling the bathtub lapped at his chin.

"What for?" Grandma Jo innocently queried.

Groping for the washcloth, he tried to stretch it to a more accommodating size as he spread it over his privates. "This is my bedroom! I am taking a bath!"

"Oh, I see." She bobbed her head in understanding and smiled her sweetest. "You ain't asking me to pardon you, but wanting me to beg it from you."

"I want you out of this room!"

"Sam, you're the shyest boy I ever did meet," Grandma Jo chided. "There ain't no need to get yourself in such a dither. You ain't got nothing I ain't seen before. I won't be in here but a minute."

"I want you out now," he stiffly stated. "I don't care if you've seen scores of men strut *au naturel*. I have a right to my privacy."

"Scores of men? Nah, I ain't seen scores. Maybe half a dozen . . ."

"I asked you to leave."

"That you did."

When she didn't budge, Sam glared at her. "I am demanding you do so, *immediately!*"

"Oh, okay." Grandma Jo pursed her lips into a mock pout.

"I was just looking for a pair of drawers I've been missing. I guess it can wait till you're done."

"It most certainly can."

Sam watched her amble out of the room through narrowed eyes. The door latch clicked closed behind her. He closed his eyes and leaned his head against the back of the tub, willing his muscles to relax.

He understood his solitary upbringing had ill-prepared him for the interminable hustle and bustle of life in a large family, and he was doing his utmost to be tolerant, but some things a man shouldn't have to tolerate. Having an audience at bath time was one of them.

To give himself credit where credit was due, he was willing to admit—to himself at any rate—that he was adapting to the family routine rather better than he thought he would. Though on the surface the excess of activity appeared chaotic, each member performed her assigned chores efficiently, without complaint, and without getting in the way of another family member's duties. Nothing was done in silence, but the chatter was cheerful. If he could forget why he was here, he might judge the atmosphere within the house agreeable.

Of course, he couldn't forget, but he did wonder how different his life might have been had he been raised in a household full of brothers. When his thoughts traveled that path, the images his mind conjured were invariably pleasant. Pleasant enough, he sometimes found himself viewing the well-ordered life he had always lived with a more critical eye, where once he had unequivocally judged it near perfect.

"Ella, honey, I'm glad you're back from the barn. Sam's been calling for you," Grandma Jo enthusiastically greeted her eldest granddaughter.

Ella set the bucket of milk from the evening milking on

the sideboard and covered it with a piece of cheesecloth. "Where is he?"

"In there." She motioned with her head toward the bedroom door. "Says he needs his back scrubbed. I offered to do it, but he won't have no one but you. Been hollering nigh on ten minutes."

"I don't hear a sound," Ella argued.

"That's 'cause I told him if he hushed up, I'd send you in the minute you stepped through the door. Now, hurry on in there and see to your man's needs before you make a liar out of me."

Me make a liar out of you? Ella silently protested. She knew as sure as the sun rose every morning, her grandmother was lying through her teeth, but she couldn't tell her so without admitting she and Sam weren't on intimate terms. Why she was lying was a more interesting question. Ella discarded the notion her grandmother might be suspicious all was not what it seemed between her and her husband. The self-satisfied grin her grandmother habitually wore was proof positive she believed all was well. Probably, it was just her bawdy sense of joie de vivre compelling her to play a joke on them or . . .

"Well, you gonna go in there or are you gonna just stand here like a statue?"

"I'm going in," Ella tersely replied. Marching across the room, she paused before opening the door long enough to call out, "Sam, darling, I'm coming."

Once inside, she stood with her back to the door and her eyes tightly closed until a stalwart, "Ella, how good to see you," signalled her it was safe to open her eyes.

Sam sat in the tub, a towel draped over the edges like a coverlet on a bed. All she could see of his nakedness was his mid torso up, but her wayward imagination filled in the rest of the picture. Her body responded with a prickling to attention of every sense, a quickened heartbeat, and a hot blush.

He motioned her to come closer so they could converse without being overheard. She reluctantly obeyed.

"Grandma Jo said you wanted me to scrub your back," Ella explained her presence before he asked the question.

"I thought it must be something like that."

"I couldn't refuse without . . ."

"Yes, I know." Sam grimaced. "I've heard numerous hair-raising tales of meddling in-laws from friends and business associates, but your grandmother takes the offense to new bounds. I half expect her to send your sisters parading in next. Let me tell you, if we were truly married, I would not hesitate to tell her how inappropriate I find her interest in our intimate affairs."

"Nor would I," Ella assured him. "And you needn't worry about my sisters coming in. They're out . . ."

"Do you hear . . ."

"Approaching footsteps?" She finished the sentence for him.

The creak of the doorknob confirmed their fears.

Sam threw off the towel. Ella grabbed the bar of soap.

When Grandma Jo stepped through the door, Ella was on her knees, energetically rubbing soap across Sam's back. Josephine Singleton smiled broadly.

"Don't mind me. I just stepped in to fetch my medicine box. Nicked my finger with a knife." She held up a finger oozing a droplet of blood as proof. "I'll be in and out of here before you know it."

Ella grit her teeth at the too convenient excuse and continued to rub soap on Sam's back. The tension in his muscles echoed her own. She wished there had been time to reach for the washcloth before her grandmother's untimely entry. Palming bare hands across his moist, naked skin was provoking an intense and all too familiar hot, empty, urgent feeling between her thighs.

She glanced over Sam's shoulder, hoping the washcloth was in easy reach, but instead of the washcloth, her gaze fell directly upon her husband's bold manly appendage bobbing below the water's surface. Ella stifled a gasp.

Ducking her head, she furiously scrubbed on his back.

All of a sudden, the room felt stifling warm, and she had to concentrate in order to draw sufficient breath. In hopes of distracting herself, Ella began to hum a hymn.

Grandma Jo took her time rummaging through the medicine box for the items she required. Ella made killing faces at her back.

It neither lessened her frustration with her grandmother nor muffled her senses all too keen awareness of the naked man sitting in the tub. If only she could stop touching him, but she couldn't. She couldn't stop scrubbing his back until Grandma Jo left, or he might be forced to rise from the tub, which was a possibility she refused to entertain. She was already close to smothering on her own desire.

An eternity later, Grandma Jo turned to face the room, her finger neatly bandaged. "Well, thanks for letting me trouble you," she said. The instant she strolled out of the room and closed the door, Ella dropped the soap and retreated to the far corner of the room.

"When someone next makes a trip to town, we are going to demand the purchase of a lock," Sam spoke loud enough to be heard clear into the next county.

"Yes, I think we should," Ella responded in an equally clarion voice.

Sam sunk beneath the surface of the water. When he emerged, he indicated with a circular movement of his forefinger for Ella to turn her back.

She was all too happy to oblige.

* * *

All four wedding dresses were nearing completion. All that
was left to do was the hand sewing of yards of lace. Ella
wished her sisters hadn't picked so complicated a pattern, but
she had to admit the dresses were beautiful.

Her eyes scanned the contented foursome as they bent over
their needles. She had never seen her sisters so happy. When
they did their chores, they talked of nothing but their coming
marriages. Their beaus were in constant attendance. Their
steps were so light, they danced rather than walked through
each day. Even knowing the intolerable situation in which she
found herself was as much their faults as Grandma Jo's,
couldn't prevent Ella from feeling glad for their sakes. If enduring the misery of having a temporary husband—a body in
good conscience could neither love nor touch—allowed them
to at long last have their hearts' desires, then at least some
good would come from this abominable situation and her suffering would serve a purpose. Her misery, after all, would be
short-lived. Their bliss promised to last a lifetime.

Her gaze settled on Lily, and she wiped her hands on her
apron. Lily still hadn't decided who she most wanted to wed,
but Ella wasn't discouraged. She approved of all the top contenders. And contenders they were. Lily had taken Sam's sci-
entific method of mate selection to heart. Every night this
one or that wasn't courting her, she could be found sitting at
the table, sheets of paper spread before her, adding merits and
shortcomings to her lists.

Now that the word was out she was immediately available,
Lily had received four more proposals. All were from men
she adored, making her decision a bit more complicated. It
didn't help that every time she had her mind halfway made
up, Grandma Jo pointed out some overlooked benefit of marrying someone else. But Lily had privately promised both her

and Sam that by the time the dresses were finished, her heart would be settled.

Ella believed her. Lily just liked the idea of all those men fighting over her, so she was waiting until the last minute to announce her decision. Ella drew a deep breath.

"Relieved" seemed a mild word for what she was feeling now that she knew she wouldn't have to wait much longer for her sisters to marry so her marriage could end. Since Sam had taken it in his head to pass the time by helping out on the ranch, her admiration for him increased on a daily basis.

He really was good at figuring things out, like how to fix the sticking handle on the pump. It hadn't worked so well in years. He knew more about horses than the rest of them put together. He wasn't as fast as she was, but he'd learned to milk the cow as well. One day when Bob was visiting, he took him out on the range to see the herds of cattle. When they returned, Bob claimed Sam had natural cow sense and if her husband was willing to put away his fancy clothes and give him two weeks, he could turn him into a proper cowboy. Coming from Bob's lips, Ella knew it wasn't false praise. Bob had an inborn antipathy for greenhorns.

So now in addition to refined manners, a sharp mind, saintly patience, and impeccable morals she was compelled to add hardworking farmhand to Samuel Carrigan's already over-whelming list of personal virtues.

More than once, for the sake of her beleaguered heart and soul, she had seriously contemplated sitting her husband down and telling him to stop making himself so damned loveable or she wasn't going to let him go, but she could never quite work up the nerve.

Pushing a stray wisp of hair out of her eyes with her fore-arm, Ella frowned as she checked the contents of the basket sitting on the sideboard one last time before covering them with a bright, checkered cloth.

While the others had been outside tending the chores, she had been in the kitchen all morning frying chicken, making a salad of boiled potatoes, eggs, and pickles, and baking brown bread and sweet cakes. Grandma Jo, Sam, and she were going huckleberrying.

Grandma Jo had suggested the outing. Despite knowing she and Sam would be compelled to spend the day playacting for her grandmother's benefit, Ella was looking forward to it.

Walking amongst the beauties of nature always helped clear her head, and her head was sorely in need of help on that score. She couldn't concentrate on anything anymore. Anything that was, except for Mr. Carrigan. Try as she might, she couldn't prevent her mind from engaging in flights of fancy that were an affront to common sense and decency.

She knew the cumulative effects of a lack of even one satisfactory night's sleep since her wedding day was partly to blame for her mind's failure to operate at top form, but she retained enough of her mental faculties to realize it was also caused by the distracting nature of having a husband constantly by one's side who incited one's lust but had no desire to quench it.

"Looks like we're all ready." Grandma Jo entered from the bedroom, a blanket on her arm, at the same time Sam entered the house with the three berry-picking baskets he'd been sent to the barn to fetch. "Mind you other girls behave yourselves while we're gone."

"I wish we was going picnicking, too," Lily sighed.

"Well, you're not. Sam and Ella have got a right to a little privacy every once in awhile, and privacy is mighty hard to come by living in this gaggle of geese. Besides, you girls got your dresses to finish up. With all the extra company we've been having lately, we're in danger of falling behind schedule."

"I guess you're right."

"Always am," Grandma Jo proclaimed.

"Yes, ma'am."

"Y'all have fun." Lily joined the rest of the family in waving them out the door.

"Why don't you and Sam lead the way while me and Hound Dog trail behind," Grandma Jo admonished. She rooted herself to the spot until Sam and Ella were several yards ahead.

Ella turned her face away and rolled her eyes when subjected to the obvious ploy. It seemed to her if Grandma Jo wanted them to be alone, she should have sent them off by themselves, but she had long since abandoned any expectation of logical behavior from her grandmother's quarter. She forced herself not to flinch when Sam reached for her hand.

"I've never gone berry picking," he commented conversationally, his eyes signalling it was time for the play to begin.

"It doesn't take any great skill. It's all a matter of knowing where to look, having patience, and avoiding the bears," Ella sweetly replied.

"Bears?" Sam queried, more curious than concerned.

"Yes. They love huckleberries every bit as much as we do. But there's no reason to be alarmed. They're as keen on keeping their distance from us as we are from them. I'm speaking of black bear, of course. Grizzlies are a different story, but as long as a body doesn't panic, they usually leave you alone, too. It's easy to tell them apart. Grizzlies have a hump on their shoulders."

"What should I do if one decides he doesn't want to leave me alone?"

"If you're attacked, more than likely it'll be a female rather than a male," Ella calmly informed him. "As to what you should do: Curl up on the ground, cover your neck and head, don't move a muscle . . . and pray for all you're worth."

Sam glanced over his shoulder and smiled broadly for Grandma Jo's benefit, before returning his gaze to Ella. "Wyoming seems to have an overabundance of rampaging females, wouldn't you agree?"

Ella ignored the comment.

As they hiked up into the mountains, Sam asked a steady stream of questions about the plants and animals they passed. Ella answered them with the ease of lifelong familiarity. It was a comfortable topic, and before long she was feeling relatively relaxed.

Grandma Jo had allowed the distance between her and them to steadily increase, which eventually allowed them to forego the effort of concocting comments of a romantic nature and strategically interjecting them into the conversation for her benefit. Sam kept hold of her hand, but trudging among the trees, breathing the fresh crisp air, the gesture felt more natural than it did in the house.

They reached a stream and began to follow its path. A short distance later, Ella stopped and pointed out a plant tucked among the foliage. It resembled a blueberry bush, only smaller. "That's what we're looking for," she announced, dropping his hand and moving forward. A dozen blue-black berries dotted the bush. She quickly harvested it, then turned back to Sam. "This whole area is covered with bushes. You just have to hunt for them."

"You two concentrate on picking the berries. I'll keep track of our picnic basket and blanket as we move upstream," Grandma Jo called out when she caught up with them. "I'm hoping to get enough to make two kettles full of jam, and I know Sam will be wanting you to make him a pan of your huckleberry buckle."

With berry baskets in hand, they spread out.

It didn't take Sam long to find a bush of his own. He plucked off its tiny berries, then moved off in search of another.

He had been dreading this outing all morning, but after awhile, he concluded berry picking had the potential to be an enjoyable pastime. It required a minimum of conversation, and there was something oddly satisfying about searching out the elusive berry bushes among the lush forest foliage, especially when one found a bush heavy with large shiny berries as he just had. After popping several in his mouth, he dutifully put the rest into his basket.

The warm summer sun percolated through the trees, painting the ground with patches of light. Hound Dog ranged between him and somewhere in the distance in the direction Mrs. Singleton had tramped off. He couldn't see the older woman, but Ella was up ahead. She looked as at home in these woods as he felt out of place.

Her knowledge of plant and animal life was extensive, but it was more than that. It was the graceful way she moved, and the way her hazel eyes had turned a golden hue when they had stood watching a deer and her fawn cross their path. It was the way she smiled at squirrels and skirted wildflowers so she wouldn't crush them underfoot.

He had to admire the graceful way she was handling their awkward marriage, too. In the beginning he had had strong doubts she could pull it off, but he judged her performance better than his own. She was the epitome of the blushing bride, flustered one minute, gazing at him with erotic eyes the next, not to mention the sensible way she handled the numerous uncomfortable situations that were thrust upon them. That bath incident had to have been an ordeal. And she would have been well within her rights to slap him the other night when he had . . . Luckily, she had no idea what he had been dreaming about, or he probably would be sporting a freshly blackened eye.

The unbidden memory of his prurient dream made an adjustment of his trousers necessary. That hadn't been the only dream he had had about her. It only qualified as the first and the noisiest. He dreamed about her every night now—not sweet dreams but highly improper dreams. He didn't know which was worse, not sleeping at all or buying bits and pieces of sleep at the price of fueling his already overheated blood. She must never know of his feelings, of course. It would only add to her embarrassment. She was a nice woman. He didn't want to do that.

How Miss Ella Singleton had managed to grow up into a nice, intelligent, sensible woman in the atmosphere of outrageous behavior that pervaded her household—and her community for that matter—was a great mystery to him, but that was exactly what he judged her. Before he left, he intended to make sure she understood how grateful he was it was *she* he was coerced into marrying. He could have gotten stuck with one of her featherbrained sisters. Or *God forbid* her grandmother.

In his studied opinion, Ella Singleton had but one glaring defect as a partner in this whole wretched affair, and he judged the fault his not hers. Everything about her roused his ardor like no other woman had ever roused him before. There were times when he feared he might be becoming as mad as the rest of them so intense were his feelings, and it took every whit of his common sense, self-discipline, and sense of honor to rein in his lusts. Many was the day and night he had spent catechizing himself with the admonition it was not good form to indulge in lascivious activities with a woman for whom one held no tender feelings, especially when a man had promised to behave as a gentleman *and* had a fiancée awaiting his return to New York.

He lusted after Ella and loved Clara. Sam felt as though he was betraying them both.

As there was nothing to be gained by allowing his mind to wander down that uncomfortable and familiar path, Sam banished thoughts of all women from his mind. Thinking about his troubles didn't solve them. If it did, they would have been solved long ago. He was here to pick berries. Berries would fill his thoughts.

The baskets were half full when Grandma Jo emerged from the bushes and suggested it was time for lunch. Since it was well past the usual dinner hour, everyone was agreeable.

Their appetites sated with a minimum of conversation, they immediately set back to work.

Several hours later, Grandma Jo announced herself satisfied with the results. "The work is done and now it's time to play. Come here, Sam." She grabbed his hand and led him around a bend, then a hundred yards upstream, before coming to a halt. "I bet they don't have anything like this in the city."

They stood before a large pool of crystal-clear water. Above the pool, water cascaded over a huge granite boulder. The boulder set at roughly a forty-five degree incline. Its surface had been worn as smooth as glass over the years.

"Best swimming hole in the territory," Grandma Jo informed him as she began to unbutton her bodice. "Last one in is a three-legged goat."

Sam threw Ella a startled look. She had been trailing behind them, and from the dread-filled expression on her face, it was obvious she had gleaned her grandmother's intent several minutes before he had.

"You look like a tree that's took root," Grandma Jo chided him. He stood arms at his side, not quite knowing where to cast his eyes as she disrobed down to her chemise and drawers. "No need to be bashful. We're all family."

On that comment, she turned and ambled barefooted up the hillside. Seconds later, she was whooshing down the natural slide, hooting in anticipation of the icy plunge awaiting her at the end of her ride.

When she emerged from the pool, she was laughing like a young girl. "Come on, Ella. Show your husband how it's done."

"I'm not really in the mood for a swim today," Ella demurred.

"Then get in the mood. You look so hot and sweaty, you make me miserable, and I ain't taking any excuses. The two of you are gonna let loose and have some fun if I gotta strip you down and drag you into this water with my own two hands. Sam! You quit looking at your toes. The sight of a few half-naked wrinkles ain't gonna kill you."

Sam looked up, but he looked over her head.

Grandma Jo took another turn down the slide. When she arose from the water and saw they had yet to remove their shoes, she climbed out of the pool and planted her hands on her hips. "Ella Marie, why the way you're hanging back, if I didn't know better, I'd swear your husband ain't seen you without your clothes yet. I know you ain't afraid of the water. You've been swimming in this hole buck naked all your life."

"Ella, dear, I think we should go for a swim," Sam promptly suggested. He threw her a steely glance to be sure she wouldn't endanger the success of their scheme by putting up any farther argument. They were too close to achieving their goal to risk failure now. "It does look like fun."

"You don't know how cold the water is. I do," she retorted. "You've been beat and bit and shot up since coming to Wyoming. If you have your heart set on adding freezing yourself clean down to the bone to your list of adventures, I guess I have no choice but to oblige you." Her voice was saucy, but no teasing light sparked her eyes, and Sam knew she spoke for her grandmother's ears.

He wished he could do something to spare her this new complication, but he could think of little he could do. Her cursed grandmother had come too close to hitting upon the truth. It was imperative they contravene any and all suspicion. Leaning close, he whispered in Ella ear, "I won't look."

"Thank you," Ella whispered back. "Neither will I."

"Good." He planted a quick kiss on her lips to give their whispered assurances the illusion of love talk. Sam withdrew himself from her immediate vicinity and slowly began to remove his clothes. He folded them neatly, carefully tucking his eyeglasses into his vest pocket.

As soon as he was stripped down to his drawers, he slipped into the bushes and climbed to the top of the slide.

Ella had not exaggerated when she described the temperature of the water, Sam discovered when he stepped into the water at the top of the rock slide, but if he was going to be obliged to spend the afternoon cavorting half-naked in the woods with his too tempting wife, he could think of no better ally than a stream full of frigid water. Giving himself a push, he plunged down the slide, landing with a loud splash in the pool below. Sputtering as he surfaced, Sam shook the water from his hair. With genuine enthusiasm he proclaimed, "That was delightful."

"The territories are full of delights for the man who ain't afraid to jump into the water," Grandma Jo schooled. "Turn yourself around. Here comes Ella."

He had promised he wouldn't look, but as his wife came racing down the slide, her breasts bobbing, the water pushing her chemise up her hips, and her wet drawers clinging to her thighs, his eyes would not obey his brain's command to be a gentleman. He gawked like a school boy at a French postcard and despite the chill water, his manhood rose to the occasion.

He was so busy staring, he didn't have the sense to move out of the way. Ella landed atop him. He grabbed her instinctively. Her breasts crushed against his chest. Her skin felt hot enough to melt what little clothes she wore.

The water churned as they hastened to untangle their limbs and escape the pool. Ella made it out first. She sprinted toward the top of the slide.

Too late, Sam realized his mistake in taking up the rear. Her soaking wet chemise and drawers left absolutely nothing to the imagination, and as scrambling up the hill required a bent posture, her hips swayed all too provocatively in front of his face for the entire journey.

The moment she reached the top of the slide, she was down again. Sam waited until she had exited the pool and was half-way up the hill, before he pushed himself down the incline.

Sam found that if he carefully timed his climbs and descents, he could avoid the most severe tests of his strength of character. That was not to say he didn't spend a good amount of time surreptitiously adjusting his drawers in hopes of concealing the most obvious evidence he was not nearly as gentlemanly as he claimed.

Concentrating on the exhilaration of whizzing down the natural slide was his best and only defense. He supposed it was foolish for a man his age to take so much pleasure in such a simple pastime, but swimming in the creek like a native appealed to a primitive part of his nature that had heretofore gone unrecognized.

When he had come to Wyoming, his only purpose was to find his family. He hadn't found them, yet. What he had found was his cherished concept of himself might not be wholly accurate. He had discovered there was a certain satisfaction to be had working with one's hands, and being a member of a large boisterous family was oddly appealing. He found being surrounded by raw nature soothing rather than distressing.

He may have been raised by his mother, but he was beginning to think more of his father's adventuring spirit might be in him than anyone knew. It had just never been fostered. He liked the idea. And he didn't like it. He had always been comfortable with his highly civilized, intellectually predictable, morally correct, well-ordered world. Anything that disturbed his equilibrium was not to be embraced without a thorough weighing of the consequences.

The three of them continued to splash in the creek. The sun shone brightly over head, keeping them sufficiently warm while the cold creek water was seductively refreshing. Sam couldn't remember the last time he had done something for the sheer pleasure of doing it, and despite the obvious drawbacks imposed upon his idyll by his swimming companions, he was having a grand time.

"Well, I've had about all I can take. You two young folks keep on having fun. There's still some chicken in the basket if you get hungry later on. I'll leave it for you and take the berry baskets and Hound Dog with me. See you back at the house when I see you." Gathering her clothes in her arms, Mrs. Singleton was out of sight before the last words left her lips.

Ella was at the top of the slide and Sam was halfway up the hill. Sam quickly decided since they had to stay away from the house sufficient time to create the impression they were two lovers enjoying a lazy afternoon, they may as well have a few more rides on the river.

It *was* a hot afternoon. Sam knew the chivalrous thing to do would be to give up the game and get dressed, but why should he? he reasoned. He hadn't done anything but look and engage in the occasional carnal fantasy. Having resisted temptation night after night *and* all day, no one should begrudge him those harmless diversions. He was in full control of himself and the situation.

True, there was a certain amount of perversity in his willingness to continue to torture himself with enticing glimpses of what he must not have, but his mettle had been tested again and again, and he had proved himself a man of iron will.

Ella was climbing out of the pool below. Since he had discovered timing was everything if a man intended to avoid too much stimulation, he knew now was the best time to take his turn.

When Sam arrived at the bottom of the slide with a masculine bray of elation, Ella was not halfway up the hill where she was supposed to be. She was standing in a patch of sunlight by the edge of the water.

He stayed in the center of the pool. "What are you doing?"

"I'm drying myself out enough so I can get dressed."

"Oh." He tried not to notice the way the wet fabric molded to her breasts. "I'm going to play in the water a bit longer, if you've no objection."

"No. You should do whatever you want."

"We can't go back to the house right away," he offered as an explanation for his decision.

"No, we can't."

He did not want to deny her the refreshment of the creek, especially, when from his own observations, she had been enjoying it at much as he. "There is no reason you, too, can't continue to swim if you are so inclined."

"There isn't?"

"No."

At first her expression was disbelieving, then confused, then slightly affronted. In the next moment it settled into something resembling wistful resignation, but with a determined gleam in her hazel eyes. "Well, if you're sure there's no reason I shouldn't, I might take a few more turns on the slide myself."

Turning on her heels, she started up the hill.

Sam was certain there was some important message in the play of emotion upon her face he was failing to discern, but he had no inkling what it was and an equal amount of ambition to give himself a headache trying to figure it out. If something was bothering her and she wanted him to know what it was, she would have to be forthright about it and tell him.

It was relaxing not to think, Sam concluded as he tromped up the hill after giving her a more than ample head start. He would have to consider doing it more often. A mountain stream, the scent of pine, moist moss tickling bare toes, these were wonderful things. They made a man feel alive.

Ella had just entered the pool with a splash. Most of her hair had come down during the afternoon, and as her head emerged from the water, her image brought to mind myths he had read of river nymphs. She really was quite beautiful. He sighed.

He intended to wait until she exited the pool, but as Sam stepped into the stream at the top of the slide, his foot slipped on the slick rock. He was halfway down the slide before his mind registered what happened. In the next second, he found himself in the pool, his body entangled with his wife's. It seemed the most natural thing in the world to kiss her.

Filling his arms with her, Sam did just that. It was the sweetest kiss he had ever known, and he stole another. She clung to him as tightly as he clung to her. It was all the encouragement he needed.

The water roared in Ella's ears. No, it wasn't water; it was the pulsing of her own blood. Blood heated to the boiling point by too many days and nights of her handsome husband stoking the passionate fire burning within her with no opportunity to find relief. She wanted him too much to think about what she was doing. She was tired of being noble.

Wrapping her arms around his neck, she devoured her husband's lips. They were soft and strong and as hot as her own. His mustache sent tickly prickly sensations dancing across her upper lip. She couldn't get enough of him.

Her fingers raked through the dark, wet, hair covering his chest. They kneaded the muscles of his back. They captured his face and held it to her own so she could drink in the honey of his kisses.

Her breasts hung heavy with desire. When she felt his hand tracing the lace of her chemise, dipping lower and lower until his warm hand was inside her bodice, cupping her breast, she arched to his touch. He caressed her taut nipple with the pad of his thumb, drowning her in ripples of delight.

The woman's skin felt like warm wet silk, Sam mused as he buried his lips against her neck and nibbled at the flesh just below her ear. Flushed pink from his touch and bathed golden by the sun, the color of her complexion was as splendid as its texture.

The hem of her chemise floated up above her hips, but it was the sight of her breasts, shimmering upon the water's surface that captivated his immediate interest. How many times had he wanted to fill his hands with them and denied himself? Too many times. He would deny himself no more.

Her nipples were puckered into firm buttons. At his touch, they became more erect. He pressed his hips against hers, so she would know, he too was firm with desire.

Her eyes widened and darkened, not with alarm but with a longing so intense his mouth went dry.

Neither spoke, as they exited the pool hand in hand. Sam pulled Ella's chemise over her head and dropped it on the rock where they stood. Eagerly, her hands reached for the buttons of his drawers while his loosened the strings binding hers. Together they stepped out of their dripping underclothes.

Sam smiled in approval as he filled his eyes with the vision of earthy beauty displayed before him. Full breasts tapered to a trim waist, a tiny almond-shaped navel, round hips, and a dark triangle of curls. Filtering through the trees, the sun dappled her skin, reminding him of the fawn he had seen. Overhead a bird twittered. The barest breath of a breeze lifted a curl off her shoulder. He caught it, drawing her to him.

Their lips met, tongues caressing as they cleaved together. They sipped droplets of moisture from each others skin. They nibbled the tips of berry-stained fingers. Their hands roamed freely—softly stroking, boldly kneading, desperately clinging. Pent-up passions, impatient after being denied so long, raged to express themselves. Every movement was devoted exclusively to giving and seeking sensual pleasure.

Neither was cognizant when their lovemaking moved from standing upright on the granite shore to lying prone on a soft blanket. Neither cared for any sensation other than those derived from the touch of the other.

Straddling him, Ella kissed Sam's chest, his belly, his thighs.

He lavished her breasts with suckling kisses, trailing his lips from her wrists to the pink peaks of her breasts and back again while she writhed with need against him.

Their cries of passion mingled with the song of the birds as they rolled upon the blanket hungrily feasting upon each new sensation.

Sam ran his hand over the mound of feminine curls pushing up to meet him and found his mate hot and moist. The musky scent of her desire perfumed the air.

The voice of reason whispered in his head to proceed was folly. Their carefully laid plans would be for naught.

Sam brashly shut his mind to reason. To stop now was impossible. He wanted Ella Singleton. She wanted him. He would have her.

Covering her with his weight, he raised his hips and plunged into her. For the barest instant, she stiffened; then, her hips rose swiftly to meet each of his thrusts.

They strained together exalting in the rhythm of the nature surrounding them. Their breath was the wind; their unintelligible murmurs the babbling of the creek; the movement of their hips a primitive celebration of wholesome carnality.

The urge to reach fulfillment consumed them. Their's was not a temperate lovemaking but a frenetic pursuit of sensual release. There was no room for thoughts of civilized restraint. No room for thought at all. There was only room for taste and touch and sight and sound and deep intoxicating breaths of air heavy with the scent of life and passion.

There was no sun above them nor blanket beneath them, only each other's embrace.

Flames of desire licked at their skin as the heat radiating from their coupled loins grew hotter and hotter. Every thrust of their hips wound the coil of need tauter and tauter. Every nerve tingled. Every muscle tensed. Each breath became more labored and shallow than the one preceding it.

Release when it came, pounded their senses like a thundering waterfall, leaving their bodies limp and their minds dazed.

Thirteen

Ella slept.

For hour after hour she slept, a deep restful sleep undisturbed by dreams or fits of half wakefulness.

It was dark when she finally blinked her eyes open. She stared at the bright moon and the stars twinkling over head, for a moment confused as to where she was, but the sound of a very male murmur inches from her ear abruptly cleared her head. She quickly closed her eyes.

Ella was unsure if her husband was as awake as she or merely mumbling in his sleep, and she had no wish to open her eyes and find out—not when they were lying naked together, wrapped in a blanket, and her memory spared her no detail of what had gone on before she had fallen asleep.

Discomfiting as those memories were, her present circumstances were equally disturbing. The blanket wasn't the only thing in which she was wrapped. She was swaddled in her husband's arms. The press of his flesh against hers, the enticing scent of his skin, the silken texture of his hair tickling her skin where his head lay pillowed upon her breasts, stirred fresh desires within her person.

Ella was at once mortified and intrigued. Lovemaking produced the most satisfying sensations she had ever experienced. It was fascinating that two people could—she cut off the thought.

She had not behaved rationally. When Sam had drawn her

into his arms, she should have stopped him. Ladies, by nature, possessed more moral fortitude than men. At least that's what the magazines said. It was her duty to protect him in his moment of weakness. What had she been thinking? Rather than protect him, she had leapt at the opportunity to take advantage of his passion of the moment.

She didn't hold herself entirely to blame. It had been stupid to continue to swim together after Grandma Jo's departure removed the necessity to do so, and they had done so at his suggestion. True, she had not put up much of a fight, but she had grown accustomed to following his lead in these matters. He had earned her confidence.

So now what was she suppose to do? Demand he commit himself to being a proper husband to her? She would be within her rights to do just that, but she didn't want a husband who didn't want her. She had no idea what Sam's feelings toward her were now that they had . . . but she remembered no whispered words of love or undying devotion. The sounds they had been making weren't words at all.

She was finding it impossible to hold onto a logical train of thought more than a moment with his limbs entangled with hers, but Ella had yet to muster the courage to let Sam know she was awake, which precluded retreating to a more expedient distance. She struggled on the best she could where she was.

If he told her he had grown fond of her, she would willingly reconsider her resolve to end their marriage. She was certainly fond of him. Given the least bit of encouragement, she was convinced she was capable of falling head over heels in love with the man. She had absolutely no objections to fulfilling the physical obligations of a wife.

Previously, she had regarded the comingling of the flesh of man and woman with a jaundiced eye, but having engaged in the activity, she had to admit—odd though the whole procedure still seemed when analyzed from the position of an uninvolved party—the Almighty had known exactly what He was doing.

It was a pity she couldn't claim the same was true for herself and Sam. For all she knew, he was lying beside her feeling like an animal caught in the jaws of a trap. Was he cursing himself or cursing her? Did he reckon her no better than a whore? Was he wishing himself a thousand miles away?

The day of their wedding Grandma Jo had said he was everything she had ever wanted in a man and more, and a more true statement had never been spoken. But what did she have to offer him? She had no idea what his notion of an estimable woman was, and even less idea if she possessed any of those qualities. Every man she had ever turned down as a husband paraded across the back of Ella's eyelids. With rare exception, they were all fine men, but she hadn't been inclined to be a wife to any of them. She was a fine woman, but that didn't mean Sam would ever view her as a desirable wife.

Oh, she now knew he found her physically desirable, and the knowledge went a long way toward heartening her. However, a marriage *if it was going to be satisfying* had to be founded on something more lofty than mutual lust.

Ella drew in a slow, deep breath, exhaling it with corresponding care.

The sensible thing to do was open her eyes and forthrightly ask him why he had done what he had done and what did it mean? Then, she could decide how she felt about her part in this complication to their already knotty relationship.

Ella was in the process of alternately devising excuses to avoid doing the sensible thing and bucking up her nerves to face the task when a low, throaty growl caused her to stiffen. At the same moment Sam's arms tightened around her. Rolling, he protectively covered her body with his.

"I believe it's a black bear, but in this light I can't be sure," he whispered in her ear.

Ella twisted her head so she could see the intruder. He was rummaging through the remains of their picnic basket. When he lifted his head, his teeth gleamed in the moonlight as he noisily chewed a chicken leg. "It's a black bear," she confirmed, her lips distinctly forming the barely audible words. Sam lowered his voice to her level as they continued to converse.

"I thought you said they were shy creatures."

"They are unless they smell food. We should have strung the basket up on a rope before we . . ." she left the rest unsaid. "I know better; I just wasn't thinking."

Sam mutely took full measure of the situation. A resolved expression settled upon his face. "When I say 'go,' I want you to get yourself up the nearest tree. I'll play decoy. There is a branch not too far from me. If need be, I can use it as a weapon."

Ella was touched by his willingness to put her safety above his own, but she didn't allow emotion to cloud her judgment. "There's no need for that. If we just lay here quietly, he'll probably go away after he finishes his meal."

"Are you sure?"

"As sure as a body ever can be when dealing with a wild animal."

"All right. We'll do as you say. But if he charges, we do it my way."

Ella nodded her agreement, though she had no intention of following his command. If the bear attacked, she would be right beside Sam, fighting for all she was worth. She was *not* going to sit in a tree and watch him be eaten.

Luckily, she was confident it wouldn't come to that.

What she wasn't confident about was her ability to lie naked underneath the equally naked weight of her husband for an extended period of time without her body betraying her. She almost wished she was more afraid of the bear. A healthy dose of terror might purge her mind of its wanton wanderings.

To her chagrin, she felt her nipples begin to harden against his chest. She prayed he wouldn't notice. The next sensation to catch her attention was a warmth against her leg. The source grew ever hotter and more rigid by the moment. Her cheeks pinkened.

"I really do apologize," Sam mumbled. ". . . for everything."

"Now is not the time." Ella scowled at him. Sam blushed. "I'm not going to ravish you in front of a bear."

Her eyes blinked wide open. "I know that. I meant now is not the time to talk about . . . *our problem*. It's important we don't make too much noise."

They both fell silent, keeping their eyes if not their minds wholly focused on the bear. He took his time with his midnight snack, pausing often to smack his lips and lick his paws. When the basket was empty, he threw it in the air; then, to be certain he hadn't missed a tasty crumb, he proceeded to chew the basket into several pieces.

Lifting his nose in the air, he sniffed in their direction, raised himself on his hind legs, then turned, dropped to all fours, and waddled back into the forest from whence he came.

Sam and Ella didn't move or say a word until he was out of sight; then, as if on cue, they both leapt to their feet. Disregarding the dampness of their undergarments, they pulled on their clothes with the speed of cattlemen rushing to put out a prairie fire.

Not until they were fully dressed did they turn and face each other. Sam was the first to speak.

"Before we go back to the house, I think we should talk."

Ella rearranged a pine needle with the toe of her boot several times before raising her head. "Yes."

"What do you want me to do?"

For an instant their eyes met; then, both looked away. "I don't know what you mean."

After an interminable pause, Sam began to speak. His voice was strong, but Ella sensed the effort he was expending to make it thus. "I take full responsibility for what occurred between us. I shouldn't have let it happen. I promised you I wouldn't. I broke my word and am willing to pay the price of my lack of character. If you want me as a husband, it is my duty to remain by your side."

Clutching the sides of her skirt, Ella pasted a stoic expression upon her face. She hadn't realized just how very much she had been hoping he would offer her some crumb of affection until he dashed her hopes. He had not grown fond of her as she had grown fond of him. His feelings for her hadn't changed one whit since the day they had met. She was glad she knew the truth, but the truth hurt so much her only defense was to retreat behind a wall of indifference. "No."

"No, you don't want me or no, you do not believe it is my duty? If it is the first, I will not argue. Your feelings are your own. But if you are denying the latter, you are wrong."

She raised her chin. "I would reckon your duty to Clara would take precedence over your perceived duty to me."

"I have never bedded Clara."

"If you had tried, I can't help but believe she would have had the moral fortitude to tell you: *no*. I can't let you shoulder the entire burden of blame. I am as much at fault as you."

His mien as somber as Ella's, Sam shook his head. "It's generous of you to say so, but I disagree. For sometime I have been aware of my prurient interest in you. I should have had less faith in my ability to resist temptation and more concern for your future. As much as I dislike our marriage, you are a decent human being. I will not stand by and see you suffer for my sins."

"Our sins," Ella corrected. First she was a duty and now she was a sin. Ella wanted to cry, but she had too much self-respect to give into the urge. "I don't see any reason we can't go ahead with our plans for an annulment. We will have to lie to the judge about this, but by now we've told so many lies to so many people neither of us should flinch at one more."

"What if I got you with child?"

The question caught Ella off guard, and she shuddered. His was a legitimate concern, and one she should have considered herself . . . but she hadn't . . . and she didn't want to. "You didn't," she stubbornly denied the possibility.

"You can't know that."

"Well . . . I will by the end of the week, so I don't think it's worth worrying about yet. I figure we should stick to our original plan unless or until we have concrete evidence we can't."

"Assuming I have not fathered a child, there is still the problem of explaining to any future husband why you are not . . ."

"Any man I marry will know the truth before I let him lead me to the altar," Ella interrupted, cursing him for his insistence they deliberate every possible ramification of their ill-advised behavior. She didn't want to think things through. She wanted to forget they had ever succumbed to their passions. "If he truly loves me, he will understand. If he doesn't, I'll regard myself well rid of him."

Despite the discomfort of their circumstances, a smile curled the corners of Sam's lips. "You are the most sensible woman I have ever met. It is a very admirable quality."

Ella glowered at him. "If I am so sensible, why do I feel like a fool? Sensible women do not cavort with strangers in the woods."

"We are no longer strangers."

"Neither are we properly man and wife. I should have resisted."

Sam's smile drooped into a pensive frown. "Why didn't you?"

"Why didn't *you?*" she countered with the same question to avoid answering him.

He hunched his shoulders and stared at his feet. "I told you before I liked kissing you. What I didn't say is how much I liked it. Living with you under my nose day and night has roused certain rather intense passions in me that I find difficult to reconcile with our situation. It is not natural for a man and woman to share the same bedroom night after night and not . . . and there is the beguiling way your hips sway when you walk . . . and the way your hair glistens in the lamplight when you brush it . . . And you make an extremely fetching sight in your wet underclothes. . . . Evidently, I am not nearly the gentleman I believed myself to be. There is an uncivilized side to my nature to which heretofore I was unacquainted, and I let it overrule my common sense."

"Oh," was all Ella could manage to say. He certainly had given a thorough answer. She prayed he would not require the same of her. Even before she finished the thought, his voice intruded.

"And you? I believe it wisest we both know why the other was motivated to do what we clearly should not have done. It will help us guard against making a similar blunder in the future."

Ella knew he was right, but it didn't make answering him any easier. "I'm afraid I'm afflicted by the same human frailties as you. I, too, have known of my weakness for some time, but I had hoped to keep you ignorant of it . . . because I find it very embarrassing."

Sam nodded his head in understanding. "Obviously, we both should have been more honest with each other."

"Obviously."

"Well, now that we do know, what do you think we should do to avoid making the same mistake twice?"

"Get my sisters married immediately, and get you out of here!" Ella answered a bit too vehemently.

"Yes, I agree—assuming you are not with child or upon reflection do not decide the loss of your virginity requires I remain by your side . . ."

"We agreed not to discuss the possibility of a pregnancy unless possibility becomes fact," Ella tersely reminded him. Indifference wasn't strong enough to shield her panic and pain from his eyes. She was too full of feeling. "Why is it all men have such exalted notions of their potency? Have you never noticed some couples go years without producing a child? And as to your second concern: I will not be changing my mind. I have told you before, I have great hopes for my future and this marriage is not a part of those plans!"

"Why are you shouting at me?"

"Because you don't listen!"

"All right," Sam calmly replied, though his countenance evinced he thought her accusation unjustified. He sat himself down on a rock and folded his arms across his chest. "I'm listening now. Tell me what you think I ought to know."

Ella imitated his gesture, but she did not sit down. "Why do I have to keep coming up with the answers to everything?"

"You don't think I am doing my fair share to bring this marriage to a satisfactory conclusion?" Sam cautiously offered his interpretation of the meaning behind her caustic words.

"No, it's not that."

"Then, what?"

"I don't know."

"You're angry with me for bedding you?"

"Yes," she yelled, but her conscience compelled her to elaborate. "But I'm even more angry with myself. That's not the problem, or rather it is, but . . . I'm just so tired of feeling responsible for everything that goes wrong, and I know most times I am, but that doesn't make me feel better. It makes me feel worse."

Sam rose to his feet. His expression a mixture of consternation and sympathy, he held out his hands. "Everything is not your fault."

"They're my family."

"True, but you're not responsible for their actions." He took a step toward her.

Ella took a step back. "I'm responsible for my own actions. How do you explain away what happened on that blanket? I knew it was wrong and I didn't care."

"Neither did I."

"Wonderful. We *both* behaved like two elk during rutting season. That makes me feel so much better about myself."

Sam fingered the temple of his glasses. "Maybe we should just go back to the house."

Ella didn't answer him.

Though there was more than ample space between them, he backed up three steps as a gesture of good will. "The wedding dresses are almost ready," he encouraged. "We only have to hold on a few more days. We will avoid each other as much as possible without rousing suspicion."

Ella met his eyes. "What about at night?"

"We've managed the nights thus far, and forewarned is forearmed. Now, that we both know we are not alone in our suffering from this physical attraction, we can help each other circumvent temptation."

"You make it sound so easy."

His brooding gaze slowly moved from her moonlit face, down the beguiling curves of her figure, and anchored on the ground at her feet. "It won't be, but what choice do we have?"

* * *

If anyone besides Hound Dog heard them slip into the house in the wee hours, no one said a word the next morning. Sam kept himself busy outside while Ella helped Grandma Jo boil and bottle huckleberry jam. She kept the conversation firmly anchored on the subject of her sisters' marriages.

"I'm sure the dresses will be done by Saturday. After we're finished here, I figure I'll saddle up Alexander and start spreading the word among our neighbors. Frank is suppose to come to dinner tomorrow. He can spread the word to everyone in town and send a rider out to the ranches further north," Ella declared.

"We can't have all the food we'll need baked by Saturday," Grandma Jo quibbled.

"Sure, we can. With all of us working together, we'll have plenty of time."

"How can your sisters help with the baking if they're busy sewing on their dresses? And don't forget all our other chores. Cow don't milk herself. We got a garden-to hoe, livestock to tend, and the berries are just reaching their peak. Summer is our busiest season."

Ella couldn't believe her ears, and her white face proclaimed her disbelief and dismay. She threw down the towel in her hand, her voice raising a full octave. "You can't mean to make them wait until Fall to marry?"

"Ella Marie, sometimes you get the silliest notions in your head. Of course, I ain't gonna make them wait clean till Fall."

"Then, when?"

"I was figuring three weeks from Saturday. That'll give us plenty of time to get what needs doing done. Don't forget, with all you girls married, I'm gonna be running this ranch all alone, and I ain't as young as I used to be."

Ella couldn't protest she would still be around to help, but three weeks! She could never survive another three weeks! Already getting her sisters married had taken far longer than she had ever thought it would, and look where it had led. Down the path to Perdition, that's where! Sam would be furious. He didn't want to be here with her, and she couldn't bear his presence. Not when she knew he would be leaving her. What if she became even more fond of him? Her heart was already too enthralled. She had to do something!

"You can't mean to stay out here on the ranch all alone," Ella proclaimed. "I want you to come to New York and live with Sam and me!"

Grandma Jo shook her head. "I appreciate the invite, but I ain't you, Ella. I'd be like a skunk at a barn dance in a place like New York. You couldn't haul me there with a team of horses."

"Then, you can live with Janie," she argued. "She'd love to have you. So would Marilee, Fern, and Lily for that matter."

"You're the thinker in the family. I can't believe you would even suggest such a thing. Can't you see the wagon load of trouble that'd cause? If I pick any one of them over the others, I'm likely to be accused of playing favorites." She poured paraffin on top of the jam cooling in the jelly jars. "Nope, ain't gonna do it. Besides, I'm looking forward to having the house all to myself. Been so many years since I've had a minute to myself, I've almost forgot what it's like. Been craving a bit of solitude lately."

"But . . ."

"There ain't nothing you can say to change my mind. All I need is a warm fire, Hound Dog by my side, and the pantry shelves stacked high with enough bottles of jams and jellies to see my sweet tooth through the winter. I'm a simple woman with simple needs."

"My sisters and their beaus aren't going to want to wait another three weeks," Ella immediately tried another tack when it was obvious the first was doomed to failure. "And I don't reckon it would be wise to try to make them. I know you raised us to know right from wrong but sometimes, as the Good Book says, though the spirit is willing the flesh is weak. You know Lily settled her heart on Monty Mitchell and ever since she told him so, the two of them can't keep their hands to themselves. You don't want our neighbors counting months on their fingers when your first great grandchild is born."

"I'll give Lily a stern talking to when she comes in," Grandma Jo reassured. "And if that don't appear sufficient to do the trick, I'll put enough fear of God in Monty he'll be afraid to unbutton his pants to pee."

Her account of Lily and Monty's behavior had been largely exaggeration. A pang of guilt prompted Ella to make another change in strategy.

"I'm sure a word whispered in Lily's ear will be enough to save them from the folly of youth; still, the wedding can't wait three weeks. You know my husband must get back to New York. If you want us here for the wedding, it'll have to be held this Saturday."

Reaching into the sugar sack, Grandma Jo began measuring out the ingredients for the next batch of jam. Her tone remained conversational. "I ain't completely convinced Sam has to get back to New York as quick as he claims. Truth is, I'm not convinced at all. You just tell him he can't go until after your sisters are married."

"I most certainly will not! I'm sure he knows his business far better than any of us."

"Then, I'll tell him. I'll tell him if he tries to spirit you off to New York before your sisters have their wedding, I'll send a posse of prospective bridegrooms after the two of you and drag you back."

"I could stay and he could go," Ella proposed.

"Nope, I want you both here. Besides, it's not good for a married couple to be separated so soon after the wedding. I know you and Sam are getting along better than either of you reckoned, but a body can't be too careful when it comes to nurturing new found love." Wiping her hands on her apron, she gently stroked Ella's back. "I'm only thinking of what's best for your future.

"If you have a care for our future, I would think you would have more concern about my husband's ability to support us."

"I have absolute faith in Sam on that count, but if it'll make you feel better, I'll have a heart to heart with him about the matter. Still, I can tell you now, I can't see him saying anything to change my mind."

Ella knew a sinking feeling in the pit of her stomach. She had run out of arguments. Even if she hadn't, she doubted it would matter. Taking out her frustration on the bowl of berries she was mashing through the strainer, she pleaded between pounding blows, "Why are you being so unreasonable?"

"Ain't being unreasonable. There's nothing unreasonable about wanting the whole family together to celebrate such a joyous occasion, especially when it might be years before we're all together again."

"It won't be years."

"Might be. Life has a funny way of being unpredictable. Could be, we might never all be together again. My mind is made up, Ella. I don't care how mad you get at me, or Sam either. An old woman is entitled to indulge herself when it comes to spending the good times with her family, and indulge myself is just what I'm gonna do."

The first excuse Ella could find, she hurried outside in search of her husband. She found him in the barn studying a broken harrow.

"I think I can fix this," he commented when her shadow fell upon him.

"You'll have plenty of time to try," Ella grimly informed him.

He lay the harrow aside. "Something is wrong."

"Do you figure I'd be out here with you if it weren't? Grandma Jo says there is too much work to do and my sisters' wedding isn't to be until three weeks from Saturday. She's adamant. What are we going to do?"

"Damn her!" Sam slammed his fist against the wall of the barn.

"I'm not any happier about it than you are."

"I can see that." He pushed his glasses up the bridge of his nose. His eyes were dark with frustration. "How can she possibly contend it will take that long when the dresses are nearly done? I'll sew on the lace myself if that's what it takes!"

"It's not the dresses."

"Then, what is it?" he demanded.

Ella stood soldier stiff and spoke with dull precision; however, her dismayed expression belied her stoic stance. "Summers are our most productive time, and a unproductive summer means a hungry winter. She doesn't figure we can accomplish the wedding and all our summer chores without the extra time. I told her we couldn't stay because of your business, but she won't listen to reason. She says if we leave before the wedding, she'll have us dragged back."

"Did you suggest I go and you stay until after the wedding?"

"Yes. She won't hear of anything but *everyone* being here. She says it may be the last time the whole family is together for a very long time."

"Hmm," Sam growled.

Ella continued, her shoulders sagging and her voice rising in pitch with each word. "I even fabricated a story about Lily and Monty being in danger of providing her with an early great grandchild if they didn't tie the knot right away, but I'm afraid all I succeeded in doing was getting them in a pickle."

"Lily and Monty's troubles are of no consequence to me," Sam dismissed her last comment. "Getting away from here is." He was thoughtfully silent a long moment. "Since she won't be reasoned with, have your grandmother make me a list. I'll personally see to it whatever she thinks needs to be done is done."

Ella paled. "You can't be willing to stay another three weeks. What about your business?" she asked, reluctant to voice her most compelling objection to the delay.

"It will be fine without me." Sam shrugged. "I only used it as a convenient excuse."

"Oh." Swallowing the hard lump in her throat, Ella forced herself to cease avoiding mention of her overwhelming concern. "What about us? Three weeks is a long time. I wouldn't figure you willing to risk . . ."

Sam met her panic-ridden gaze with one of sympathy and steely determination. "I'm far from willing, and I don't intend to be here another three weeks. We will enlist your sisters and their beaus and dispatch three weeks' worth of work in less than one. With all of us working together and me as task master, your grandmother's latest condition to their marriage will be met in record time."

When they heard of the delay and the reason for it, her sisters and their beaus were more than happy to cooperate with Sam's scheme. Ella had thought they would be. They were almost as exasperated with Grandma Jo as she and Sam were when they learned how far back she proposed to set their wedding date.

Of course, no one knew the true reason behind Ella and Sam's fervent ambition to see them wed as quickly as possible. The reasons they gave for their preoccupation were Sam's business interests, vague statements about the agreeable nature of marriage, and their wish for them to share in that happiness.

Happiness. The word made Ella choke every time she said it. She was miserable.

Rather than relieve her desire for her husband, making love to him had made it a thousand times more intense. The only thing that saved her from believing she had been born with the mores of a harlot was the knowledge she was more than half in love with her husband. Being more than a little in love might make her wanton feelings more palatable, but it didn't comfort her in the least. It only made their situation all the more excruciating.

Her days were an agony, but the nights were far worse. During the day she succeeded in avoiding him at least part of the time. At night, she lay in the bed, clutching the sheets, listening to him breathe, listening to the agitated beat of her own heart, praying—praying for all she was worth, she wouldn't leap from the bed and into his arms and beg him to make her feel all those wonderful sensations he had introduced her to by the creek. She wanted to beg him to love not only her body but her whole person. But she didn't.

She knew how he felt about her. She also knew if he knew how she felt about him, he would feel more duty bound than he already did to stay by her side. Everyday he asked her if she had reconsidered her position. Everyday she told him "no," relief washed over his handsome face.

All marriages demanded compromises be made, but some compromises were not to be borne.

Grandma Jo might know her well enough to have guessed right about *her* feelings for Sam growing into something out of the ordinary, but she was horribly wrong about Sam's feelings growing into anything approaching a consuming love for her. He had made it plain he didn't want to stay with her, and she would go to her grave before she asked him to stay against his will.

They were in the mountains picking berries for more of Grandma Jo's jam this afternoon. It conjured memories of another day, but there were important differences. For one thing, they were not so alone. Janie, Rex, Marilee, Bob, Fern, Frank, Lily, and Monty were with them. No one was going swimming. No one was having any fun. Her husband saw to that.

He wanted the baskets filled to overflowing, and he brooked no idlers. She wasn't sure exactly how he made his money in New York, but Ella was glad she wasn't one of his employees. He had barely let them swallow their lunch before he was prodding them back on their feet. *She* wasn't complaining, but the others were starting to grumble.

Ella moved through the forest in a labyrinthine pattern, efficiently stripping one bush of berries, then picking up her basket and hunting for the next. She paid little attention to her companions. Occasionally, she would catch a glimpse of one or the other through the trees, but she was too busy to bother keeping track of their movements.

Her basket was almost full when the first fat raindrop plopped on the back of her neck. Straightening, she glanced up. Huge thunderclouds blanketed the sky. "We better start back to the ranch, or we're going to get soaked," she called, annoyed the summer storm was calling an early halt to their labors. No one answered and she called again.

"You're right," Sam's voice answered back from somewhere above her. "Stay where you are. I'll be right there."

A flash of lightning lit the sky, and it began to rain in earnest. "Janie, Lily, Fern, Marilee . . ." Ella cupped her hands and yelled in every direction. "Where are you?"

She strained her ears to hear an answering call, but all she could hear was the whistle of the wind in the trees, the patter of rain, and the rumble of not so distant thunder. Another bolt of lightning split the sky.

Sam arrived at her side and answered the question on her lips before she asked him. "Janie and Rex were in a gully below me, but that was twenty minutes ago, and they've since moved on. I lost track of the rest of them over a half hour ago."

Ella sheltered her face from the rain with her forearm. "It's been forever since I've seen anybody."

"I'm sure they have enough sense to make a run for the house."

"They'll be soaked long before they get there."

"So will we." Taking her basket from her hand, Sam started back the way they had come. His strides were long and his pace brisk. Ella matched it. The house was miles away.

Before they covered a quarter mile they were both drenched to the skin. Ignoring the discomfort, they trudged on. A half mile later, it began to hail.

"We're going to have to find shelter," Sam yelled over the unremitting claps of thunder. He pointed to an overhanging rock, grabbed her hand, and began to pull her up the mountainside.

Ella might have been tempted to argue they push on, gambling the hail would stop as suddenly as it began, but the words had barely left his mouth when a marble-sized chunk of ice hit her hard on the shoulder. In the next instant, a bolt of lightning struck a tree less than twenty yards away. She needed no further urging.

Fortunately, it had been raining so heavily, the tree did not catch fire.

When they reached the overhang, they paused to catch their breath.

"How long do these storms usually last?" Sam queried.

Ella squinted at the sky as she wrung what moisture she

could from her skirt and blouse. "Sometimes it's five minutes. Sometimes it's five days. It's impossible to predict, but from the looks of these clouds, I'm not optimistic."

He frowned. "You're shivering."

"I'm wet," Ella stated the obvious.

"I can't do anything about that, but I can get you out of this wind," he pulled her deeper under the overhang. Hidden behind an outcropping was a aperture. He eyed it speculatively. It wasn't large, but it was big enough for a man to squeeze through. "Stay here," Sam ordered dropping to all fours.

"Be careful. It might be some animal's den."

"You'll hear me scream if it is." He disappeared into the opening. Less than a minute later he was back. "It's a cave of sorts. It's so dark I can't tell how large, but I didn't meet the previous owner, if there was one, and it's a lot warmer in there than out here."

Ella followed him inside.

They sat on the floor, huddled together for warmth.

With any other human being Ella would judge it a sensible thing to do, but with Sam, she judged it foolish in the extreme. His touch, even through the filter of wet, clammy clothes, set her heart to beating at an accelerated rate and her thoughts on a path she had forbidden them to wander. She credited the cold with the hardening of her nipples, but she didn't really believe herself. She didn't want to be here, or rather, she shouldn't be here. There was nothing untoward about the way her husband held her, but . . .

Ella tried to concentrate on something else. It was still hailing, and raining, too, by the sound of it. Sudden summer storms were common and this one's fierceness didn't surprise her. In other circumstances, she would enjoy the storm. All her life she had found the flash of jagged shards of lightning and soul vibrating booms of thunder exhilarating. She found them exhilarating today as well, but cocooned within the circle of her highly desirable husband's arms, exhilaration was not a wise sensation to feel.

The rain and hail continued, steady and relentless. Ella stopped counting the minutes. There were too many of them. She closed her eyes.

This cave had a musky odor. It reminded her of the scent of passion. Sam's breath tickled the top of her head. The rise and fall of his chest seduced her into relaxing against him. His arms were so strong, so comforting, so . . . she drifted into a sensual waking dream . . .

"It's too bad I never took up smoking. Some matches would be welcome right now," Sam commented, causing Ella to bolt to attention. "I'm not sure what is all over the floor, but it feels dry enough to burn."

"If we can find a stiff stick, we don't need matches," Ella proclaimed, rapidly disengaging herself from his embrace. "I don't know what I was thinking sitting here like a basket of wet laundry while our teeth chatter like squirrels. I swear, my mind isn't usually this obtuse."

Searching the floor with her hands, she found what she needed. Cleaning away the debris from a workable area so she wouldn't accidentally set the whole cave on fire, Ella made a small pile of dry leaves and twigs, placed the stick between her palms and began to rapidly rub it against the stone floor.

"What are you doing?" Sam asked.

"Making a fire, I hope. An old Indian woman used to live near our ranch when I was a little girl. She taught me. I used to be quite good at it," she paused to blow puffs of breath on the base of the stick, "but I haven't tried it in years."

It was several more minutes before Ella coaxed a spark to life, but once she did, it quickly caught hold. She mindfully fed it more leaves and twigs until she was sure it wouldn't go out. Remembering a dead limb she had climbed over near the mouth of the cave, she crawled outside and dragged it inside. It was dry enough to break into manageable pieces over her knee. Soon a small but cheery fire lit the cave.

"I'm impressed," Sam praised, moving himself out of the path of the smoke as it wafted toward the cooler air of the entrance.

"Don't be."

"Why not?"

"Because, we are too alone in this cave. When you compliment me, it makes me like you, and liking you makes it harder for me to resist making love to you, which I want to do very badly." Ella compelled herself to be frank in hopes Sam would protect her from herself, but the minute the words were out of her mouth, she realized honesty had been a mistake.

She hadn't been able to observe his face in the darkness, but now that she could, Ella could see he was every bit as hungry for her as she was for him. His eyes reflected the fire.

Ella licked her lips.

Sam's fiery gaze mesmerized her, drawing her to his side.

Even as Ella told herself she would do nothing to sate their mutual desire, she found herself pressing him to the floor of the cave and clawing at his clothes.

The buttons of his vest and shirt were no match against her burning need. She buried her face in the dark, curly hair of his chest, kissing him again and again as she mewed with want of him.

She rocked her hips against him, clinging to him, crying out her desire for him.

Ella's lips met his, and she devoured them.

Her blouse joined his shirt, as did her corset and chemise. She rubbed his chest with her breasts.

Sam caught her, lifting her up so he could take a hard nipple

in his mouth. His tongue circled the areola, once, twice, then
flicked across the bud of her breast before latching on and
suckling with such force it caused her to whimper with the
pain of delight.

She squirmed against him, but he would not release her.
Ella felt the pleasure of his mouth upon her in every inch of
her person, it radiated in heady waves to her fingertips, to
her head, to her toes. The pounding of her heart inside her
chest echoed the crashing thunder outside the cave.

Sam's mouth clamped onto her other breast, and he gave it
the same adoring attention he had given its mate, refusing to
be distracted no matter how urgent Ella's cries of passion became. Not until she was near weeping with need, did he stop.
Raising his shoulders from the ground, he trailed his lips down
her bare belly as his hands freed her from her skirt and petticoats and slipped inside her drawers. He dallied upon her
buttock, massaging the twin cheeks until they burned beneath
his hands. He swept her drawers from her hips in a single,
fluid movement.

If it was possible to go mad from desire, Ella judged she
had passed the point of sanity some time ago. Only one thing
stood between her and what she wanted. She barely paused
to tend the buttons before yanking off her husband's trousers
and drawers.

Kissing and caressing her way back up his legs, Ella re-
joiced in the way he quivered beneath her touch. When she
reached the protruding evidence of his desire, she kissed it as
well. There was no part of him she didn't want to love.

Sam groaned his gratification.

Ella tormented him as he had tormented her, her hands
splaying across his belly and up his chest. Her fingers kneaded
his flesh like the paws of a house cat.

Sam grabbed her by the wrist, pulling her up until the heart of her sex lay above his pulsating organ. Without further urging, Ella sheathed him in her womanly warmth.

She rode him with the fervor of the storm. Frissons of lightning hot sensation flashed within her loins. Perspiration ran in rivulets down her face. Her blood surged through her veins. The beat of her heart drowned out the thunder.

She was full of him. She reveled in the hard heat of him filling her. Ella could feel herself tightening around him. She could feel him growing ever harder and hotter within her.

The rhythm of their joining became ever more urgent, more abandoned, more fierce.

A peal of thunder clapped outside. Ella and Sam exploded with the zenith of passion, collapsing into each other's arms.

Fourteen

"You have to go!" Ella buttoned her blouse, then tugged at the damp sleeves. Her boots in hand, she scrambled out of the cave. The overhang provided enough shelter she could finish dressing without getting wet.

How could she have let this happen again? she berated herself. No promises of love had passed his lips. Not one sweet syllable. But that hadn't stopped her from throwing herself at him. Had she no shame? Just because she found herself in a cave didn't give her cause to behave like an animal.

The hail had stopped, but it was still raining. A barrage of thunder echoed Ella's ominous mood.

She had barely pulled up her stockings and was reaching for her first boot, when Sam emerged from the cave. *Thank God he was dressed.*

He sat down beside her. For a moment he said nothing. "I know you aren't very happy with me right now, and with good reason, but I think we should wait out the storm together. If I arrive at the ranch without you, your grandmother is bound to ask why."

"You didn't do anything. I was the one who . . ." She averted her face. "And I wasn't talking about you leaving here. Getting yourself struck by lightning might solve our problem, but I'd rather not have you dead. It's the ranch I want you to leave, *immediately.*"

"What about our plan?" Sam cautiously queried.

"We're abandoning it. It was never supposed to take this long to get my sisters married. I can't handle this! I want you out of my life!"

"I understand your feelings, but . . ."

"No, you don't understand my feelings!" Ella shook with the potency of her wrought-up emotions. She wasn't infuriated with him but with herself. She wanted to be strong for both their sakes, but she wasn't strong. She was weak. She liked making love too much. She liked Sam too much. If he didn't go . . . *she couldn't let him stay.* If he did, she might selfishly accept his noble offer to ignore his lack of affection for her and remain her husband. His lust would wane. He would end up hating her, and she would hate herself right along with him. It wasn't a future she would wish on her worst enemy. It was better he believe she had no more feeling for him than he had for her. "I never wanted you for a husband in the first place. We have nothing in common except lust and a lack of self-control. We can't keep doing this, and you know we will if we don't put more than a few miles distance between us."

He appeared slightly affronted by her blunt words, but his tone remained reasoning. "Perhaps if we stay out of the woods, we will be better served. There is definitely something about a natural setting that seems to compel us to be ruled by our impulses and not our heads."

Ella sighed. "I would love to blame my behavior on the trees, but they are not the problem. We are. Every time we find ourselves alone, we're in danger."

"Then, we won't let ourselves be alone."

"We weren't suppose to be alone today; yet, here we sit."

"But what would my leaving accomplish? You said before, I would only be tracked down and dragged back."

"I know what I said, and it's true; but I've been thinking. They don't watch us as closely as they did in the beginning, and they'll be expecting you to ride to Green River to catch the train. We can arrange for no one to notice your absence for a full day. When they do discover you're gone, I'll feign reluctance to tell on you, but in the end admit that Green River is exactly where you've gone. That should buy you a minimum of another day. You will ride north. You did say you wanted to check out the Rutherford's story about your family's ranch. If they're wrong, your family will protect you. If they're right and your family is no longer there, you can head for Montana and catch a train home from there." She covertly glanced at him to measure his reaction.

He raised a brow. "When did you hatch this scheme?"

"I've been tinkering with it since the first time we 'failed' each other." Ella yanked on the laces of her boots before tying them. "Mostly at night. I judged it a better use of my time than cursing you because I can't sleep."

"I don't like it."

Thinning her lips, Ella persisted to hide her pain behind a cross countenance. "Why not? A few weeks ago, we could never have pulled it off, but now *everyone* believes we're a contented couple. I'm sure of it. If not for my sisters' pending wedding, we could pack our bags and say we were off to New York without rousing the least bit of suspicion."

"I'm not questioning the merits of your plan. I agree it has a better than fair chance of success." He rubbed his head as if it hurt. Several emotions—confusion, remorse, frustration—contorted his features before he resumed speaking. "The reason I don't like it is: I can't help but feel it is wrong to abandon you now that we have . . ."

"I know what we have done, and I know it was wrong," Ella broke in. Drawing her posture erect, she shifted her position so she faced him. "If I'm willing to pay the price of conscience; then, you should be too. Our staying married will not cancel out our previous transgressions. It will only add to them. And I will not have you pretend to be abandoning me when I'm the one insisting you go."

His backbone as stiff as hers and his expression stern, Sam replied, "I know you won't appreciate me mentioning this today anymore than you did the first time I did, but I feel it must be said. What about the possibility we inadvertently have created a child?"

"You will give me your address in New York before you leave. I will contact you if the worst has occurred."

He stared at her a long time. "It still feels wrong."

"Our marriage is wrong! It is not really a marriage at all, and every time we give in to our passions we betray decency," Ella snapped. "If you won't leave for my sake or yourself, then do so for Clara. She may be the most forgiving woman in the world, but I know if I were in her shoes, I wouldn't want my fiancée lying with another woman."

A guilty blush stained Sam's cheeks.

"I hadn't thought of Clara."

"Well, you should. You're in love with her."

"Yes, I am," he gruffly confirmed.

"Then, it's settled. You will leave first thing tomorrow morning. All we have to do is think up a reason to explain your absence."

Capturing her chin in his hand, he forced her to meet his gaze. "Are you certain this is what you want?"

"Absolutely certain," Ella lied.

From where he sat atop his horse, Sam judged their plan to have been close to perfect. He was less than a day's ride from the ranch where he would either find his family or confirm they had moved on to another area. He was certain he wasn't being followed. He hadn't seen another human being in days.

Of course, avoiding all contact with humanity was part of their plan, as was traveling in stream beds whenever possible to cover his tracks. Ella had given him a long list of dos and don'ts to help him elude capture before he left. Some were so obvious they called into question her assessment of his intelligence, but others were quite ingenious. All bespoke of a sincere desire to have him gone from her life.

He didn't blame her. He had proved himself a cad not once but twice. If he stayed, he probably would have done it again. Fortunately, they had escaped the steepest price of their folly. She had gifted him with the news her monthly had arrived on schedule the morning he left. He had greeted the news with the same relief with which she whispered the glad tidings.

Sam pushed his glasses up the bridge of his nose, and continued to let his mind wander.

Getting away from the ranch had proved far easier than he thought it would. They simply had packed a picnic lunch and a blanket, saddled two horses, and announced they intended to spend the day alone together. Old Mrs. Singleton had been delighted with the plan.

The only hard part was when it came time to say goodbye.

Ella might be certain he was doing the right thing, but he was not. A man owned up to his actions. He believed that with every fiber of his being. His anger at being coerced into their marriage remained like a lump of smoldering coal in his gut, but that didn't mean the wrongs done to him justified him wronging another. He wanted out of the marriage. She said she wanted him to go, and he believed her. But he hadn't been able to shake the feeling he was betraying her.

To make matters worse, he had kissed her goodbye. Why he still hadn't been able to figure out, but he had done it. He had meant it to be a cordial kiss—a parting of two soldiers who side by side had fought the good fight and were now returning to their separate lives. It hadn't turned out that way.

He had kissed her with the passion of a lover, and she had responded with matching fervor. If he was a man looking for a mistress, Ella Singleton would be his first choice.

Thankfully, he wasn't in the market for a mistress. Clara would never approve, and he had too much respect for Ella to ask her to take on the role of his *petite amie*.

So, that left him exactly where he was. Logically, he accepted their choice as a very sensible one. Intuitively, he sensed it was flawed. He felt guilty for leaving, but glad to be gone. He was riding away, but at night just before he fell asleep, an insistent voice murmured in his head he should turn around and ride back. At long last, he had won his freedom; yet, he felt no rush of joy. He only felt dreary and confused.

It was an uncomfortable position for a man to be in, but not as uncomfortable as his marriage. He kept on riding.

Sam could see the house, a large barn, and several outbuildings. His heartbeat quickened. They were exactly where his map said they should be. He accepted there was a chance his family no longer lived there, but he couldn't help believing after so long a delay, he had arrived exactly where he wanted to be.

A half dozen men were scattered about the yard. Three were in the corral. One was hanging laundry. The other two were doing something in the doorway of the barn. He was too distant to see what or to discern what any of them looked like.

If he had been eager to meet his family before, Sam was even more so now. Living in the Singleton household had made him realize how subdued his own childhood home had been. He had no idea how a household of men conducted themselves, but if they were half as lively as a household of women, there was little risk of him being bored during his visit.

Spurring his horse to a gallop, he crossed the last stretch of sage-covered prairie.

"Howdy," a man—Sam guessed to be in his late fifties—emerged from the house and greeted him as Sam reined to a halt before the porch. "What can we be doing for you, stranger?"

Sam doffed his hat and dismounted. The man was the right age. They shared the same height and same chin. Though the older man's hair was grey, they both had thick, curly hair. It looked promising. Wearing a warm smile and standing tall, he replied, "My name is Samuel Carrigan. I'm looking for Barnett Carrigan and his sons, Adam and Joshua."

"I'm afraid you're about ten years too late."

Sam's face fell. "You're not Barnett?" It was as much a statement as a question.

"Nope. Name is John Sawyer. The fella you're looking for died the year before his sons sold this ranch to Dexter Wyatt. Wyatt sold it to me two years after that."

"Barnett Carrigan is dead," Sam dully repeated the news. Lowering his gaze to the ground, he closed his eyes and took a deep breath. It wasn't that the possibility had never crossed his mind, but it still came as a shock and a bitter disappointment.

"I'm sorry. You having the same name and all, I suspect you're a relative of his. I oughta have broke the news more gentle. You okay?"

Sam slowly raised his head and stiffened his shoulders. "I'm all right," he stated resolutely.

"Are you a relative?" Sawyer asked.

"Yes. Barnett Carrigan was my father."

Sawyer eyed him speculatively. "And you didn't know he

was dead all these years? Now, don't that beat all. Seems like somebody oughta had the decency to write you a letter or something."

The wound of his father's death was too fresh for Sam to wish to discuss him or the circumstances surrounding their separation, and he determinedly changed the subject. "Do you know where Adam and Joshua Carrigan went after they sold the ranch?"

"Nope. Never met them."

"Do you think this Mr. Wyatt might know?"

"Probably does."

"Do you know where I might find him?"

"Nope."

Mr. Sawyer was obviously not going to volunteer any information. Sam had a niggling feeling Sawyer didn't completely trust him. "Can you give me any clues to where I might start to look?" he asked, hiding his growing impatience.

"He used to rent a room over a bar in Sheridan, but I wouldn't waste a lot of time trying to hunt him down. He ain't been right in the head ever since that horse kicked him betwixt the eyes. That's why he sold the place to me. Kept seeing things out on the prairie that weren't there. Gave him the spooks."

"I see."

"Well, I don't," Sawyer complained. "How come if you're a close relative to the Carrigans that use to own this place, they don't let you know nothing about them? You sure you ain't some kinda troublemaker?"

If he was going to learn anything useful, Sam knew he would have to explain, but he did so grudgingly. "My father and mother were separated before I was born. Neither my father nor my brothers ever met me. I'm looking for them at the behest of my mother's will. Each of my brothers have inherited a sizable sum."

Sawyer's eyes widened. "How sizable?"

"I don't believe that is any of your business."

"You got the money on you?" he pressed.

"No. It's in a bank in New York," Sam answered him truthfully, but if he had had the money on him, he knew he would not have been candid. He was inclined to believe Sawyer merely curious, but . . .

"There's no need to be looking at me so suspicious like," Sawyer counseled. "I only asked 'cause it ain't smart to be riding alone if you're carrying a lot of loot, and I thought I oughta tell you so. You being a greenhorn and all."

Sam nodded. "I apologize for questioning your motives."

"Hell, no need to be apologizing. At first, I weren't inclined to trust you further than I can spit either, but after looking you over, I've decided you're being square with me." He grinned broadly. "Out here, it's just good sense to have a suspicious nature. It's also good sense to carry a gun. How come you ain't got one?"

"It was stolen."

"By who?"

"The ringleader of the gang of outlaws who were holding me prisoner," Sam commented dryly.

Sawyer raised his brows. "Reckon they're headed this way after you?"

"No, I'm reasonably certain I eluded them."

"They hurt you?"

"Only my pride."

Shrugging at his answer, Sawyer rubbed his chin. "If they're headed this way, I've a right to know. Me and my boys will hunt them down and string them up so fast they won't know what hit them. Can't have marauding thugs bothering law-abiding folks." He abruptly changed the subject. "You want some dinner? I was just about to sit down when you came riding up."

Sam smiled. He had eaten the last of his food yesterday. "I appreciate your hospitality."

"Glad to be neighborly. If there's anything else I can do for you, just let me know."

"As a matter of fact there is," Sam didn't hesitate to let his needs be known. "I'd like to know the quickest route to the nearest train station with a telegraph office. Green River City is not an option. Also, I need to buy enough food to see me through until I get there, and a gun. As you say, it's not good sense to ride without one."

"You got money?" Sawyer's raspy voice crackled with confusion.

"Some."

"What kinda outlaws take your gun but leave your money?"

"Misguided ones," Sam proclaimed.

It wasn't suppose to hurt this much, Ella angrily swiped at a telltale tear with the back of her hand. And she wasn't supposed to cry. Crying was for babies.

She stared out the window at the pouring rain. It had rained everyday since Sam had left. The rain reflected her mood. She didn't mind it, it felt right. What she did mind was the afternoon thunder and lightning storms. They reminded her too much of the last time they had made love. . . . Ella slammed the door on the thought, sniffed back another tear, and planted a stiff smile on her face.

Everything had worked out exactly as they had planned. She and Sam had outwitted them all. By now he was either joyfully reunited with his family or on his way back to New York and Clara. He had gotten what he wanted. She had gotten what she wanted. She should be happy.

So where was the sense of smug satisfaction?

Realizing she was beating the air out of her muffin batter,

Ella dropped the spoon on the sideboard and dusted her hands on her apron. She glared at the dense batter in disgust.

She wasn't much use to anyone these days.

As she had done every day since he had left, Ella began to methodically list all the reasons why Sam's leaving was for the best. She listed all the reasons she was eager for an annulment. She lectured herself that she had known from the moment she had laid eyes on him there was no hope of a future together.

It was the truth, plain and simple. Her logical self accepted the reality of the situation. Her logical self was proud she had done the right thing and sent him away. He belonged in New York with Clara. She belonged . . . she wasn't sure where she belonged, but she knew it wasn't by the side of a man who not only didn't love her but was in love with another woman.

As long as her sensible self was in control of her thoughts, Ella was fine. It was the whimsical side of her nature that destroyed her peace of mind. It kept trying to rearrange the facts to suit her fancy. Whenever they occurred, she sternly rebuked these errant mental meanderings. . . . Then, her eyes would set to leaking. The pattern repeated itself at least a thousand times a day. Nights were even worse.

She wanted to move back to her old bed and her old bedroom, and pretend she had never met Samuel Carrigan, but Grandma Jo would hear none of it.

The room seemed so empty without him.

She was sleeping more now that he was gone, but her sleep was haunted by dreadful dreams. Sometimes, she dreamed Sam was lying on a cobblestone street badly hurt. He kept calling for her. She tried to help him, but no matter how far she ran, he was always out of reach. Other nights, she *would* reach him. As she knelt by his side, he would jump to his feet and, laughing, run away from her. Then there were the dreams of drowning in a raging river while her friends and family *and her husband* stood on the banks smiling and waving as she was swept to her death. Most mornings she woke up feeling more exhausted than if she hadn't had any sleep at all.

"I'm as hungry as a bear," Grandma Jo interrupted her dark musings when she entered the house with her egg basket. She paused to shake the moisture from her bonnet before hanging it and removing her rain slicker. "If your sisters don't finish their early morning chores and get in this house right quick, I'm gonna be compelled to start eating breakfast without them. . . . How them muffins coming?"

"They're going to be as heavy as stones," Ella somberly informed her.

"Still taking out your bad mood on our food, are you?"

Ella pressed her lips together and concentrated on spooning the abused batter into a pan. She could feel Grandma Jo staring at her.

"I keep telling you, he'll come back," the older woman comforted.

"No, he won't. And I don't want him back."

"Yes, you do."

"No, I don't," Ella insisted, banging the spoon on the edge of the pan. "How many times do I have to explain to you, neither of us ever regarded our marriage as a permanent state of affairs? We only pretended to grow to like each other, so you all would let down your guard and he could get away."

"And your watery eyes are 'cause all of the sudden you're suffering from an allergy to something, only you don't know what. Yep. I heard it all before. You can stand there lying to yourself all day long for all I care, but don't ask me to believe your moonshine."

Ella starched her shoulders and continued to fill the pan. "The important thing is he got away."

"Nope, the important thing is: he's coming back."

"Stop saying that."

"But it's true. He's a good man. He won't be able to stay away."

Ella wished her grandmother would see her stubborn refusal to face the fact that Sam was gone for good was causing her more pain not less, and leave her be. She wished everyone would leave her be. She had half a mind to find the cave she and Sam had sheltered in during the storm and hide herself away. If the cave didn't hold so many memories, she would be gone in a minute. "If you truly believe Sam is coming back, then let my sisters get married now instead of insisting they can't until he does," Ella curtly proposed.

"Can't do that," Grandma Jo protested. "Sam's worked so hard helping us get ready for the wedding, I wouldn't feel right having it without him here."

"But you're making them and their beaus miserable, and they in turn are making *me* miserable. All except Bob who is so mad he won't even set foot on the property. As far as they're concerned, everything is all my fault, and it isn't. I only did what was right. If you were in my place, you would do exactly the same thing."

"Might," Grandma Jo admitted. She poured herself a cup of coffee and sat down at the table. "We're like two peas in a pod, you and me. Both too stubborn for our own good. But that don't make it right. And it ain't right for two young people to part company just 'cause their courtship was a bit out of the ordinary. Seems to me, your sisters' yammering at you is just punishment, seeings how you and Sam keep on insisting on making a simple thing like falling in love so blasted complicated."

"I refuse to let you blame Sam or me for failing to cooperate with your designs for our lives. I know you're disappointed you were wrong about us, but you ought to have realized people can't be forced to fall in love just because you think they should. And don't ask me to excuse my sisters' behavior toward me. They have no call to abuse me. I'm the one who has been cheated. They were allowed to fall in love and choose who they will marry."

"So, they were. But there's nothing wrong with switching the usual order of things when circumstances call for it. There's no reason you and Sam can't be enjoying a love every bit as satisfying as your sisters' and their beaus except that you're both too muleheaded to admit your feelings."

Her hands trembled as she carried the muffins to the oven, but Ella made her voice strong. "I know Sam's feelings—and he is in love—with Clara."

"Nope."

"Yes, he is. He told me so himself."

"Then, he's lying."

The battle to maintain the iron grip she had on her self control was lost. This conversation was killing her, and her grandmother knew it. The cruelty of her grandmother's indifference to her agony, hurt almost as much as Sam's leaving did. "You're the one who is lying!" Ella shouted, tears streaming down her face. "You lied about letting Sam go! You lied about letting Hound Dog kill him! You lied at our wedding! You lied about allowing my sisters to marry once I did. Now, you are lying about my husband's feelings for his fiancée, and if we stand here long enough, you'll make up more lies about my feelings for him and his for me!"

"The pot is calling the kettle black, ain't she?" Grandma Jo calmly sipped her coffee. "But I'll forgive you. I know you're missing Sam so much, you ain't capable of thinking straight."

Fifteen

"Kinda strayed a long way from home, don't you reckon?" Bob McNaught stepped into the circle of firelight.

Sam reached for the gun strapped to his hips, drew, and centered the bore on McNaught's chest.

Bob smiled back at him, his own firearm instantaneously leveled in the reciprocal position. "Not bad for a greenhorn. We gonna shoot each other?" he asked.

"That depends," Sam stated stone-faced.

"On what?"

"How determined you are to drag me back to the Singletons' ranch."

Bob adjusted his hat with his free hand. "Oh, I'm mighty determined . . . but I ain't gonna drag you anywhere. I figure you got enough troubles without me adding to them."

"Then, why are you here?"

"Grandma Jo sent me."

Sam kept his eyes firmly moored on his uninvited guest's gaze and his finger curled around the trigger. "And she didn't order you to drag me back?"

"Yep, she did. Told me stay out of sight, let you get where you were going so you'd be satisfied in your own mind about your family not being here, then haul you on home."

McNaught might say he didn't intend to wrest him back to the ranch, but Sam didn't trust him. Why else would he be here? "How did she know about why I came north? Did Ella tell her?" he coldly questioned.

"Nah. Ella said you was headed for Green River."

Sam's lips twitched into a tighter line. "Then, how did she know?"

"When you first got there, she went poking in your gear. Found a map, some diaries, and a copy of your mama's will. When you turned up missing, she put two and two together and came up with four."

A splenetic growl rose from Sam's throat. "Mrs. Singleton is without doubt the most meddling woman ever to plague the planet. You can tell her for me: I do not appreciate her rummaging through my belongings."

Bob raised a brow. "You figure she's gonna listen to me? Hell. I'd have been married years ago if she paid a mind to anything I gotta say."

"She does have a penchant for ruining people's lives."

Bob shifted his weight from one foot to the other. His gaze and his gun remained steady. "She ruin your life?"

"Yes."

"Don't look that way to me. Unless, I miss my guess, you're on your way home. I suspect, some big city lawyer can fix things up so you ain't saddled with Ella no more, and you can pick up where you left off."

"That *was* my intention," Sam confirmed.

"It ain't now?"

"Yes . . . and no." He didn't know why, but Sam found himself speaking his doubts aloud. "I want to go back to my old life, but I feel like a cur leaving Ella. I know she says she doesn't want me for a husband, and I have no reason not to believe her. I do believe her. We were both forced into the marriage. But . . ."

"But?"

Sam ran the fingers of his left hand through his hair. "I

was raised to believe a man's word is his bond. I broke my word to her concerning something very important. It was her idea I go, and she insists I'm not deserting her; however . . ." Whatever else he was going to say, he left unsaid.

"Do you want to stay married to her?" Bob commiserated.

"No. But she is a decent woman, and I don't want to wrong her."

"Hmm." Bob looked thoughtful. "I don't know nothing about this promise you broke, and I reckon you prefer it that way, but I do know Ella. We've had our disagreements, but she's a fine woman and don't deserve to be treated badly."

Sam's eyes darkened. "That's exactly my point."

"Yep. Underneath all that sass, she has a heart of honey."

"Yes."

"Pretty, too."

"Yes."

"Wonderful cook."

"Yes."

"Ain't stupid."

"No, she is not."

"Women sure are troublesome creatures, ain't they?"

"I didn't used to think so, but yes, I've come to that conclusion."

The two men stared at each other. Both wore pensive frowns. Bob cleared his throat. "I don't know about you, but I'm getting mighty tired of holding this gun on you. How about we both put away our firearms and you offer me a cup of that coffee you got boiling on the fire?"

"No tricks?"

"No tricks."

Sam nodded his agreement. Relaxing his arm, he put his gun away after Bob did the same. Bob poured himself a cup of coffee and sat down cross-legged by the fire. Neither said a word for the space of several minutes.

Sam nursed his own coffee and stared into the fire. He hadn't needed Bob to remind him of Ella's virtues as a human being. He hadn't been able to stop thinking about her since he left, and his list was far more extensive than McNaught's. Sam cursed her for being so damned *nice* as a fresh tidal wave of guilt washed over him. He was doing what she asked. He had thought his mind made up. He was going to New York. He *had* been on his way. But now, with McNaught sitting across the fire from him . . .

Maybe he should go back and talk to Ella one more time before he left her. . . . When Bob had first stepped into the firelight, for the briefest of moments, Sam had almost been glad he had been caught.

He didn't want to go back. He wanted to return to his orderly, uncomplicated life in New York. But his conscience kept telling him he *should* go back. If Bob compelled him back to the ranch, the decision was out of his hands, and he couldn't make a wrong one. He didn't want the responsibility that had been thrust upon his shoulders. Be an honorable idiot and stay, be a guilt-ridden wise man and go? How he longed for the comfort of burying himself in his business dealings, where decisions could be made based on fact and messy emotions never came into play. . . .

"So, you coming back?" Bob asked, after pouring himself a second cup of coffee.

"What if I say no?" Sam charily replied.

"I lose my respect for you."

"But you'll let me go?"

"Yep."

"What will you tell Mrs. Singleton?" he pressed.

"I'll figure up something."

"What about Marilee?"

"We discussed it before I left. We're getting hitched when I get back, no matter what. Grandma Jo will just have to learn

304 René J. Garrod

to live with it. The lot of us have been letting that old woman push us around long enough."

"Why are you willing to defy her now, when you wouldn't before?" Sam dolorously demanded. "None of this would ever have happened if you had married Marilee a few months ago."

Bob shrugged. "I guess 'cause since you and Ella got together, I come so close to being a married man, I can taste it on my tongue. Kinda run out of willpower to resist Marilee's abundant charms. Choice has come down to courting Grandma Jo's wrath or dishonoring the woman I love. I don't know what you'd choose, but I gotta do right by Marilee."

Sam scowled.

"So you coming or going?" Bob repeated his question.

Sam's gaze remained lost in the flames. "I wish I knew."

"It's a hard decision, ain't it?" Bob sympathized. "Why don't you sleep on it? It's too late to be going anywhere tonight, anyhow. You can give me your answer in the morning."

"Well, look who's coming home just like I told you he would," Grandma Jo called Ella out onto the porch.

Ella almost tripped on her skirts dashing outside, but when her eager gaze fell upon Sam *and* Bob McNaught riding over the horizon she stopped cold. "You sent him after him, didn't you?" she accused.

Grandma Jo straightened the strings of her bonnet. "What if I did?"

"How could you!" Her eyes wide with anguish and flashing with fury, Ella balled her hands into fists.

"I did it 'cause I love you."

Knowing if she stood there another second, she was in danger of strangling her own grandmother, Ella lifted her skirts and bolted down the steps. She didn't slow her breakneck pace when she disappeared into the barn.

Moments later she reappeared on horseback. With a powerful kick of her heels, she set her mount galloping off in the opposite direction of her returning husband.

"How could she? How could she? How could she?" Ella railed. "All that talk about Sam coming back because he was a good man. She knew he was coming back because she sent Bob to shanghai him back!" It had been so long, Ella had been certain he had gotten away. Secretly, she wanted him back more than anything, but not like this. Not as her grandmother's prisoner. She only wanted him back if he wanted to be back.

Spurring her horse to an even faster pace, Ella let her tears fall freely. She had no idea where she was going, and she didn't care. *As long as it was far far away.*

"He give you any trouble, Bob?" Grandma Jo addressed her words to her future grandson-in-law.

"Nah."

"Good. Sam, why don't you come inside, and I'll pour you a cup of coffee? We got some important talking to do."

"Where's Marilee?" Bob peered over her shoulder.

"Out looking over our herd with her sisters. Thought we might have heard a pack of wolves last night. If you ride south, you ought not have any trouble finding her."

"Thanks." Tipping his hat, Bob remounted his horse and rode off.

Grandma Jo waved him on his way and sauntered back into the house. Sam followed her. She poured them each a cup of coffee, then sat down at the table. Sam accepted the coffee, but remained on his feet.

"So, what do you gotta say for yourself, Sam?"

"Nothing to you."

"Well, I've got a lot to say to you." Grandma sat her coffee cup down with a thud and pinned him with her censorious gaze. "Running off was a plain mean-spirited thing to do. Why you like to broke my sweet Ella's heart."

Sam met her steely eyes without flinching. "She told me to go."

"Never said she didn't, but that's no excuse. A man your age oughta have acquired enough sense to know how often a woman says one thing and means the opposite."

"Ella is too sensible for that."

"Then you explain to me why she's been crying her eyes out since the day you left."

He might be here of his own volition, but Sam was in no mood to play the old woman's games. "Ella doesn't cry."

"True, she don't cry. She don't cry unless someone hurts her so bad she can't dam up the pain no matter how hard she tries."

Was she lying? Mrs. Singleton appeared genuinely furious with him and concerned for her granddaughter, but he knew better than to trust her. But if she was telling the truth . . . his expression as grim as the old woman's, Sam stiffened his shoulders. There was only one way to find out. "Where is she?" he demanded.

"Caught sight of you and ran like a rabbit."

"I need to find her," he stated crisply.

"Yes, you do, but you ain't going nowhere till I'm through with you." The volume of her voice raised with each word. She paused to draw in several deep breaths. "I'm starting to feel too riled up inside, so we best change the subject till I get control of my temper. You find that family of yours?"

"Obviously not, or I wouldn't be here, at least not alone anyway." Sam remained thin-lipped, his posture tense. "What I can't fathom is why you told Bob to let me get as far as their ranch?"

"It's been eating at you."

"What would you have done if my family had been there?"

"Told them the situation and trusted in the good Lord to guide their actions."

He slid his glasses down the bridge of his nose an inch and stared at her over the rims. "It seems quite a gamble on your part."

"You telling me I shouldn't trust in the Lord?" she queried.

"No. But if I were you, I would consider the possibility the Lord's opinions and my own are not necessarily always one and the same."

"That's interesting advice, Sam, but we're getting mighty close to talking religion, and I make a point of never talking religion with close relatives. Best way I know to start a feud that can't be settled till everyone involved has gone to meet his Maker and checked out the right and wrong of their opinion personally." Picking up her cup, she took a long sip. "Anyhow we got more important matters to discuss."

"You keep saying that, but I have yet to hear anything worth keeping me here listening to you." Sam gave the door a meaningful glance and took a step in its direction.

"Okay. I was trying to ease into it, but if you're getting itching feet, I'll quit beating around the bush. You best sit down." She indicated the chair across from her with a weathered hand.

"I will stand, thank you."

"Suit yourself."

"Well, what is it?" Sam inquired impatiently.

"You're gonna be a daddy."

"What!" He choked on the word. "That's impossible. Ella told me . . ."

"I don't know what she told you, but the time for her monthly has come and gone with nary a rag on the line," Grandma Jo interrupted him with the information.

"But before I left she said . . ." Sam tried again to say

what he had attempted to say before he was interrupted, but he was only allowed to make it halfway through his sentence before Grandma Jo answered him.

"Maybe she said what she thought *you* wanted to hear."

"She wouldn't lie about something so important," he argued.

"She might if she thought it wouldn't matter. She's late sometimes, only she ain't never been this late. I wasn't absolutely sure about the baby myself till two days ago when she started turning green cooking breakfast."

"Perhaps she has a touch of flu," he offered the alternative without conviction.

"Don't reckon so," Grandma Jo declared. "I've seen that baby sick look on the face of too many women not to recognize it when I see it on the face of my own granddaughter."

"Damn," Sam murmured, deciding to take her up on the suggestion he make use of a chair after all. He propped his elbows on his knees and braced his head in his hands.

"Kinda puts a kink in your plans for an annulment, don't it?"

He jerked up his head and stared at her.

"Oh, don't look so startled. After she thought sure you were safe, Ella told me you two have been planning an annulment all along. Not that it was any surprise to me. I kinda figured it out on my own after I cottoned onto the fact you two weren't giving each other no marital physical satisfaction."

He dropped his head back into his hands and closed his eyes against his reeling thoughts. "You knew all along?"

"It took me a few days to figure it out," she confessed.

"And you didn't say anything?" Sam continued to speak in a muted voice.

"Couldn't. Had to sit back and let nature take its course. Mind you, I couldn't resist giving it a little nudge now and then. Like feeding you them mountain oysters and getting Ella to scrub your back and . . ."

Sam abruptly jumped to his feet and strode toward the door. "I don't want to hear this!"

"Fine with me." Grandma Jo called after him, "I ain't eager to share my secrets."

Sixteen

"I've been looking for you for hours," Sam stated as he reined in his horse and dismounted. Leaving the animal to graze beside Ella's, he approached her with steadfast strides.

Ella turned her back and stared off into the distance. She had missed him so badly. She was afraid she would debase herself and embarrass him by flinging herself into his arms. Her heart was beating so hard it made each breath an effort. What was she going to say to him? What could she say? She wished he would disappear, but no matter how hard she wished, she could feel him standing a few feet behind her.

"I didn't want you to find me," Ella finally managed to reply.

"Why?" Sam demanded.

She ignored his question. "I'm going to kill Bob McNaught. He had no right to hunt you down and make you come back. He didn't hit you over the head or shoot you or anything, did he?" Glancing over her stiff shoulders, her eyes surveyed him for injuries.

"He didn't hit me or shoot me or *anything*. He didn't have to use force. I came back on my own."

"Right. And I'm the queen of England."

"I hear the queen of England is carrying my child."

Spinning to face him, Ella gaped at him. Then, her expression turned irate. "Is that how he got you to come back without beating you to a pulp first? I can't believe he would stoop so low as to tell a rotten lie like that! I really am going to kill him."

"Bob didn't tell me, but that's not the point, is it?"

"It is if that's why you're here, because I am not with child," Ella declared.

"Your grandmother says differently," Sam informed her without raising his voice. Instead he used his somber countenance to lend burdensome weight to his words. "We just had a very interesting discussion over a cup of coffee."

"Well, she's wrong," Ella insisted.

"Are you saying you didn't lie to me about the arrival of your monthly? Your grandmother claims it is long past due."

Laying her arms across her belly, Ella raised her chin. "She's an old busybody who would tell you anything if she thought it would make us stay together."

Sam caught her chin in his hand and compelled her to meet his eyes. "You didn't answer my question."

"Yes, I lied, but it was only a little white lie. And just because I lied doesn't mean I'm with child. I'm late that's all." Ella could feel the heat rising in her cheeks, but she didn't abandon her speech. "It happens all the time. If I'm not worried about it, you shouldn't be either. And another thing, I really don't appreciate having my private bodily functions discussed over coffee."

"And I don't appreciate being lied to. It makes me wonder if you would have ever told me."

"I promised I would write you, and I would have *if it became necessary.* Despite what you may think, I'm not bereft of a sense of integrity."

Sam released her chin and dropped his hands to his side, but his gaze remained intense and scrutinizing. "Forgive me if I'm skeptical, but I was intimately acquainted with a woman who concealed the existence of a child from her husband— something I would never have conceived could happen outside of maudlin novels—and I knew that woman far better than I know you."

"I'm sorry for what your mother did, but ours is a totally different situation." It was, Ella reassured herself. His parents had lived years together in an authentic marriage. She and Sam had merely shared weeks of a counterfeit one. Her lie had been meant to ease his fastidious conscience, not deceive him. *And there wasn't a child.* She would know if there was. Preferring any subject to the one they discussed and sincerely caring, Ella asked, "Speaking of your mother, what did you find out about your family?"

"The Rutherfords were right. They weren't there. The present owner says my brothers sold the place ten years ago, after my father died."

"Your father is dead? Oh, no." Ella reached out to comfort him, but before she touched him, she jerked back her hand and clasped both hands behind her back. "And after you have come so far and suffered so many indignities. What are you going to do now?"

"Since the only clue I have to my brothers' whereabouts is poor at best and my personal circumstances are rather complicated at the moment, when I return to New York, I will hire a detective to continue the search for me. Hopefully, a professional will be more efficient and effective than I have been. I can't imagine him making a worse job of it," Sam solemnly explained. "Which brings us back to our original topic, and I repeat: I don't appreciate being lied to, and I especially don't like being lied to about a matter as important as whether or not I fathered a child."

"You lied to me about why you're here," Ella countered, hoping to distract him. "If Bob hadn't caught up with you, we both know you'd be on your way to New York by now."

"It is a fair accusation," he admitted. "I might not be here. Then, again, I might. The thought of returning crossed my mind more than once since I left. I have never felt right about leaving you to face the disgrace of our misdeeds alone. Now that I know you carry my child, I realize I should have listened to my instincts from the start."

Ella glared at him. "I refuse to stand here and discuss fiction as if it were fact."

"I'm sorry, but I think this conversation is necessary."

Anger and agony were not that far apart. They were both overpowering and incompatible with rational thought. It was becoming a habit, and not one Ella judged as admirable; nevertheless, she embraced the former to hide the existence of the latter, preferring to be judged peevish rather than pitiable. "No, it is not! I want you to go away."

"Will you cry if I do?"

The softly spoken question caught her off-guard, and it took a moment to muster enough presence of mind to school her expression to one of annoyance and give answer. "Why would I do that?"

"Your grandmother said you've been crying a lot lately and I'm the cause." Sam's eyes riveted on hers and narrowed. "Your eyes definitely appear slightly red-rimmed, so I am asking you . . ."

Ella presented her back. "Are you really a successful New York City businessman?" she interrupted, suffusing her voice with biting sarcasm.

"Yes, of course."

"Well it's a wonder you are if you go around believing everything everyone tells you without regard for their motives."

"I don't believe you when you say you are not with child," he defended himself against the charge of gullibility.

"Why not? *I'm* telling the truth."

"You are telling what you hope is the truth."

Ella couldn't believe her ears. The man was positively obsessed. Why couldn't he see they had enough trouble without borrowing more? She brusquely changed the subject. "If Bob didn't make you come back, and he didn't trick you with lies, what *are* you doing back here?"

"I already told you. I am not a man who takes his responsibilities lightly. I wanted to talk to you again . . . to make absolutely certain going ahead with the annulment was what you wanted me to do."

"It is."

"*Was*, possibly—but it is no longer an option now that we are to be parents."

Ella sighed loudly. "How many times do I have to tell you I'm not carrying your child before you will believe me?"

"You don't possess enough breath to convince me with words." Sam's cold, commanding tone evinced he had come to the end of his patience. "Someone is not telling me the truth. Whether it is your grandmother or you, remains to be seen. Neither of you have proven particularly trustworthy. I will be watching you closely and determine the truth of the matter myself. If you are carrying my child, we will remain man and wife and learn to live with each other in harmony for the sake of the babe."

"Don't you think we ought to wait and see who is right and who is wrong before we make any decisions about our future?" Ella tried to match her tone to his and failed miserably.

"No. There are some things in life that are not negotiable."

The only good thing to come of Grandma Jo's erroneous belief her first great grandchild was in the making was her sudden willingness, after so many weeks of dragging her feet, to let her other granddaughters wed without further delay. The wedding invitations had gone out the day after Sam's return.

Allowing time for the guests to receive their hand carried invitations and make the trip to the ranch meant they had to wait a few more days, but with the date firmly set, no one was complaining. They were too busy seeing to last minute details.

Ella remained adamant in her insistence her grandmother was wrong about her being pregnant. She might have some of the symptoms, and every day her monthly failed to arrive she found it more difficult to maintain her position, but maintain it she did.

In a tiny, relentlessly rational corner of her mind, Ella knew there was more than a slim possibility her grandmother was right; however, she wasn't going to believe it until the evidence became overwhelming.

She didn't want to believe it.

Ella knew Sam was willing to stand by her side no matter what the personal cost to himself, and she admired his sense of honor, but she wasn't going to delude herself into hoping there might be more behind his decision to stay than a sterling sense of duty. How could she nurture such delusions when the words "duty," "responsibility" and "obligation" punctuated his every sentence.

If there was a baby, the only thing she could do to free Sam from the shackles of their marriage was divorce him, and divorce was not a simple matter. A body had to have compelling evidence of a gross breach of the marriage contract to divorce, which she did not, and even if one could prove nefarious misdeeds, divorce was far more scandalous than an annulment.

Then, there was the child to consider. She didn't want her son or daughter to grow up in a house where tolerance rather than love reigned. Neither did she want her child to grow up without a father.

It had taken every fiber of her moral fortitude to send Sam

away in the first place. Now, it took every fiber of moral fortitude to pretend she was angry at him for coming back. She wasn't angry, at least not at him. She was scared. More scared than she had ever been in her life.

If he stayed, she might beg him to take her to his bed. If he stayed, she would fall more deeply in love with him than she already was, which would make his polite indifference all the more agonizing to bear and her guilt for the part she had in ruining his happiness all the more acute.

Oh, she knew they would contrive to get along for the sake of the baby, but she didn't want to settle for "getting along." What she wanted for herself was a marriage filled with love and laughter and friendship and passion. The only qualification she and Sam could claim was passion, and satisfying though it might be, they both deserved so much more.

If her feelings were the only ones that counted, Ella knew they could achieve the kind of marriage she wished for them, but marriage was a partnership. No matter how expedient it might be to do so, one could not control with whom one did and did not fall in love. She was confused about many things, but she was not confused about Sam's feelings for her. He felt a strong sense of responsibility. He felt passion. On rare occasions, he might feel mild admiration. But he did not love her.

Love. She had refused to marry many a man for lack of that essential emotion on her part. It was not in her to ask Samuel Carrigan to do what she herself would not.

If a baby was in the making, every scenario Ella's mind could conjure led to nothing but disappointment for everyone involved. So, she told herself there was no baby.

She preferred to forget her own life and throw all her energy into her sisters' wedding.

* * *

"Y'all look as beautiful as a bouquet of flowers," Ella proclaimed as she adjusted the ribbon in Lily's hair.

"We do make a fine sight, don't we?" Marilee seconded her opinion.

"This is the most euphoric day of my life," Janie warbled. "Thank you, Ella for making it possible."

"It wasn't my doing," Ella demurred.

"No, it wasn't," Fern agreed. "It was ours, but I'm so joyful today, I don't mind giving you the credit. You done good, Ella. You done real good."

For the briefest instant an expression of pain darkened Ella's eyes, but it was immediately overlaid with the light of genuine happiness for her sisters.

Never had there been four more winsome brides. Their dresses flattered their fine figures with high-necked, close-fitting bodices and multi-layered, draped, blue faille skirts. The skirts were covered with large fabric bows, and from the knees down, row after row of cream colored lace cascaded to the ground. The sleeves were puffed at the shoulders, then snug to the wrists, and constructed of matching lace. Velvet, azure ribbons graced their throats. Each wore a coronet of velvet ribbons and wild flowers upon their freshly shampooed and lavishly crimped curls. Felicity painted their complexions rosy and radiant.

"You girls about ready?" Grandma Jo stuck her head into the bedroom. "I got four handsome bridegrooms getting mighty fidgety out in the yard. Don't know how much longer I can hold them off from coming in here and hauling you out."

"We're ready," they trilled in unison.

"I'll tell them you're coming."

Ella followed her grandmother out the door. She glanced up at her husband as she took her place beside him at the front of the gathering of friends and neighbors. He was watching her. He always watched her these days. She knew why he did, and she wished he wouldn't, but she wasn't going to think about it today. Today belonged to her sisters.

Sam took her hand. His hand felt warm and comforting against the cold of her icy fingers.

Pete Wilson put his fiddle to his chin and began to bow the slow, sweet notes of the wedding processional.

The front door opened wide, and one by one her sisters stepped into the sunlight, first Janie, then Fern, then Marilee, then Lily. Their heads held high and smiles so broad they threatened to outshine the sun, they marched as regal as four queens down the porch steps and across the yard to take their places before Judge Barkley and beside their respective bridegrooms.

A hush fell over the wedding guests.

"Friends and family, we're gathered here today to share in the jubilation of the joining in holy matrimony of these four loving couples," Judge Barkley commenced the ceremony.

Ella was pleased to note he was absolutely sober. She knew they had Rex to thank for that. Sheriff Rex Johnson had had the judge under twenty-four hour guard for the last three days.

Rex had bought a new suit for the occasion, and he looked as handsome as she had ever seen him. All of the bridegrooms looked as natty as their brides were beautiful.

As Ella listened to Judge Barkley deliver a long-winded lecture on the duties and blessings of the marriage contract, her gaze drifted among the crowd. There were more grins than leaves on a tree in June. Many of the women were dabbing their eyes with lace handkerchiefs and sniffing discreetly. Some of the men were shedding a few sentimental tears as well.

All but one of Lily's forsaken beaus were here. George Carson wore a wistful expression. Ralph Kincaid stood soldier straight, his lips screwed into a rigid smile. The others showed no outward sign of their disappointment.

By Ella's count everyone who had been at Sam's and her wedding party was here and dozens more. If Grandma Jo had her heart set on a grand affair, she certainly had gotten her wish.

Ella's gaze settled upon her grandmother. She doubted God himself had worn so proud a smile when he sat back to rest from the labors of Creation. Ella didn't begrudge her her pride, but she considered it more than a little amusing since, until this last week, Grandma Jo was more hindrance than help when it came to her sisters achieving their matrimonial ambitions.

Grandma Jo had stitched a new outfit for the wedding, too—a simple but smart tailor suit of light-weight, burgundy wool. Upon her head she wore a black velvet bonnet, trimmed with fabric roses and loops of gaily-colored ribbons. It complemented her silky, snow white hair and brought out the golden twinkle in her hazel eyes. Old and wrinkled she might be, but her youthful beauty was still much in evidence. She made a fetching sight in all her finery.

Judge Barkley had finished his speech. Rex was speaking his vows. Next it was Janie's turn. Janie's voice rang out confident and clear as she promised to forever love and honor the man by her side.

Of all her sisters, Ella was closest to Janie. Though Janie tended to let others form her opinions for her, a body couldn't help loving such a kind-hearted soul.

Ella's mind wandered back to her own wedding. The crowd who had attended her wedding had been exclusively male, and though they wore grins, they were the grins of merry mischief-making not well wishing. No smiles had graced Sam and her faces. No light of adoration sparkled in their eyes. She wondered what it felt like to speak wedding vows willingly with a heart full of love. It must be a glorious feeling. She glanced at Sam. He was watching her. He smiled wanly.

Ella smiled back. His lips settled back into a straight line, and he shifted his gaze forward to the wedding couples. Ella covertly studied him. She could feel the tension in the muscles of his arm, but he didn't appear resentful of the other couples' joy. He didn't appear salubrious or melancholy or bemused either. His face was like a blank mask. She wished she could read his mind.

Was he thinking of their wedding as she was? If he was, what was he feeling? Was he wondering what she was thinking?

Having no hope of obtaining the answer to any of her questions, and not wishing to sink into a gloomy mood, Ella returned her attention to her sisters.

Judge Barkley was just finishing up with Marilee and Bob. He took a sidestep and positioned himself before Fern and Frank. The eager "I do" that leapt from Frank's lips sent a chuckle rippling through the crowd. Fern gifted him with a coquettish wink.

Before the last syllable of Fern's vows had left her lips, Lily and Monty stepped forward and were nodding their readiness.

It wasn't long before Judge Barkley bellowed out, "Ladies and gentlemen, I now pronounce y'all man and wife. Gentlemen, you may kiss your brides!"

The bridegrooms threw their hats in the air. The brides squealed with glee. A resonant roar rose from the assembly as the brides and grooms hurled themselves into each others arms and kissed each other so thoroughly it caused more than a few of the female onlookers to blush scarlet.

Ella's cheeks flushed as well, but the warmth of her cheeks was caused not by prudishness but by joy.

The couples willingly entertained the congregation with

their profuse and protracted kisses, and the guests encouraged them with a steady barrage of applause and hoots of appreciation.

Grandma Jo tolerated their antics for several minutes before she puffed out her chest and stepped to the front of the crowd. "There'll be time enough for that, you randy young'uns." She waggled her finger at the embracing couples. "Y'all straighten yourselves up into a line so your guests can shake your hands and offer their congratulations. We've got enough food to feed an army to gobble up, a table groaning with wedding gifts to open, and before this day is over, I expect every one of my grandson-in-laws to take me for a spin on the dance floor."

Ella was first in line to offer her congratulations.

The wedding celebration spilled over into the wee hours of the morning. The dance floor creaked under the strain of countless pairs of prancing feet. Plates were filled and emptied again and again. The din of cheerful chatter at times was close to deafening. Laughter floated on the air.

Everyone was having so much fun, no one noticed when the newly wedded couples slipped off two by two to carry on the revelry of the afternoon and evening in private.

It was a blessed wedding day.

Seventeen

"I am tired of sleeping on the floor," Sam announced, rising to his feet. He lit the bedside lamp.

"I'll be happy to change places with you," Ella magnanimously offered. Sitting up, she swung her feet to the floor.

Sam sat on the bed beside her, capturing her hand and holding her in place when she would have bolted. His gaze slowly moved over her nightgown-clad figure.

"That isn't what I mean, and I think you know that. It has been a week since your sisters' wedding. Since my return, I have lain on the floor night after night without complaint, because I knew it was what you wanted, and *I* wanted to be absolutely certain in my own mind our marriage could not end before I asserted my husbandly rights. More than ample time has passed to remove all doubt. I have stayed out of this bed as long as I intend. We both know forbidding each other the pleasures of our marriage bed serves no purpose when you are already carrying my child."

Ella opened her mouth to vigorously deny his last statement but knew she could no longer deny the truth to herself or him. Her monthly was *too* late. The mere thought of breakfast made her stomach roil. Her breasts felt larger. She was wearing a rut in the path between the house and the necessary. A humble, "I'm so sorry," rose out of her throat.

Sam stiffened his spine and stared straight forward. "Don't be. Before I was torn, not knowing what was the correct thing to do. With a baby coming, there is no question. I will stay by your side and be a proper husband and a good father."

Her thumb nervously rubbed against his. "I can't help being sorry when I know you were forced into marrying me."

"I was not forced to take advantage of your physical charms the day we swam in the creek. That was my doing, and no one else's."

"I should have stopped you," she insisted.

"Even if you had tried, I doubt you could have."

The resignation in his voice fell like a ponderous weight upon Ella's shoulders. She knew his words were meant to make her feel better, but they did not. "If you insist on assuming full blame for the first time, then I must for the second. We don't know which time . . . was our undoing."

"The accurate assignment of blame is of benefit to neither of us. If blame must be decided, then we should leave the task to a Higher Power. We have but one legitimate concern and that is what is best for the child you carry."

"Do you want this child?" Ella asked, dreading the answer but having a need to hear it.

His gaze remained focused across the room, and his vacant expression unchanged. "Would I have chosen to have a child under these circumstances? *No.* But that doesn't mean I will love it any less. I expect you to try to do the same. A child deserves the benefits of growing up with the love and guidance of both parents. For the sake of our child, we will both learn to love each other as well."

"Can we learn to love each other?"

"I don't know." Sam tightened his grip on her hand. "I only know it is our duty to try, and if we find we cannot, to spare our child the knowledge we have failed."

"I agree," Ella stated, because she truly did. The more compelling the evidence of her pregnancy had become, the more time she had spent contemplating their various options. What she wanted and what Sam wanted no longer carried the weight it once had. They had the needs of another to consider. "An innocent child ought not suffer for the sins of his parents."

Sam's eyes met hers. "Strictly speaking, I don't believe what we have done is classified as a sin now that we are committed to remaining married."

Her lips twitched into a weak smile. "I suppose that is some small comfort."

"We should take our comfort wherever we can find it," he solemnly advised.

"What about Clara? Who will comfort her?"

His gaze shifted back to the wall. "Clara will understand we are only doing what we have to do. My mother's death prevented us from publicly announcing our engagement, so she will be saved that humiliation. I can't say I'm eager to tell her, but it is something that has to be done. As soon as we arrive in New York, I will go to see her. I don't want her to hear the news of our marriage from a third party."

When we arrive in New York, the phrase filled Ella's breast with both dread and delight. She was going to live in a city. She could go to the theater. She could join a ladies' society dedicated to the advancement of the mind. She could invite her neighbors over for tea. There would be whole stores filled with nothing but books. Her child would attend the finest schools. She was achieving her dream. But the price she would pay, Ella feared, would be steep. "When are we leaving?" she asked numbly.

"I thought the day after tomorrow, if you can be ready."

"I can be ready."

"Good."

The steady tick of Sam's silver pocket watch on the bedside table counted out the minutes. Ella clutched the edge of the mattress with her free hand. She was glad her father and mother weren't alive to see her today. They had always had such high hopes for her. She had always had such high hopes for herself. Now, look at her. She sat on the bed that had once been theirs like a frightened child—married, pregnant, and worried the one thing that made life worth living—*to love and be loved*—might be forever beyond her grasp. The only way her situation could be worse was if Sam refused all responsibility for their child. But she knew he would never do that. He was too good a person.

"How are you feeling?" His question caught Ella off guard and she startled.

"Fine."

"You're not queasy?"

"No." It seemed to Ella an odd moment to be inquiring after the state of her stomach, but she gave him a complete answer. "I only feel that way early in the mornings. The rest of the day I feel wonderful."

"Are you sure?"

"Yes."

His eyes roamed over her, giving her person a thorough perusal. "I'm pleased to hear that . . . because as I said before, I am tired of sleeping on the floor."

"Oh." Ella's galloping heartbeat brought a blush to her cheeks. Her hazel eyes met his blue ones, strayed to the mattress, then returned to his face.

Lifting the blanket, Sam stretched out upon the bed, carrying Ella with him. He gathered her in his arms. "We are man and wife. From this night forward I intend we behave as man and wife in all ways. *Especially in this way.*" He trailed his lips along her jaw and kissed her throat. "This aspect of our marriage we will both enjoy to its fullest. It will help us forget how we were brought together. It will help us forget many things."

"Yes." Ella trembled with anticipation. "Make me forget."

* * *

All her life Ella had dreamed of living in an exciting, so-phisticated city, but with the fulfillment of her dream immi-nent, it didn't feel nearly as appealing as it once had.

For one thing, she had never stopped to consider how far away from her family she would be. It was silly she hadn't, but when dreams had little possibility of becoming reality, a body didn't waste time contemplating bothersome details.

She told herself she should be relieved to be ridding herself of their meddling presence. They had made a mess of her life. Two thousand miles was barely a safe distance. She would be better off without them. But, no matter what they had done, she couldn't help loving them, or worrying about them. Par-ticularly Grandma Jo.

When she had told Sam her grandmother was an old busy-body, it was the absolute truth. But she was a happy busybody. How would she get along without anyone but Hound Dog to boss about? She might say she was looking forward to the peace and quiet, but Ella just couldn't picture it.

Then, there was herself to think about. In Heaven she was the undisputed leader of the intellectual set—because the in-tellectual set consisted of one person, *her*. In New York City, everyone had access to as many books as they wanted and all the time in the world to read them. They had real schools. They grew up attending teas and balls and the symphony and rubbing elbows with poets and the like. Half the population had probably been to Europe. What if they thought her stupid? What if she humiliated her husband?

Her husband. Ella sighed. She still had trouble thinking of Sam in that way. Now that a child was involved, she was absolutely committed to doing all that she could to make their marriage a success, but . . . she wasn't sure how to finish the thought. She only knew there was a hollow place in the pit of her stomach that had nothing to do with the fact she had lost her breakfast this morning.

"Do you need any help packing?" Grandma Jo stepped into the bedroom where Ella sat on her knees on the floor, staring into her empty traveling trunk.

"No."

Grandma Jo peered into the empty trunk. "Looks to me like you do."

"I'm just having trouble getting started."

"It's natural to be a little anxious. It's a big step you're taking. But don't be fretting yourself into a tizzy. Everything is gonna work out just fine."

"I wish I had your confidence."

"So do I, and if I knew some way to make the trade, I'd gladly do it." Grandma Jo ambled to the dresser and returned with a stack of Ella's undergarments. "You know, Ella, sometimes a body can think too much. My advice to you is to just live life as it comes your way."

Ella rose to her feet and walked to the shelves that held her books. Surveying the titles, she selected enough to make a comfortable arm load, walked back to her trunk, and began to arrange them in a layer on the bottom. "But too many things have changed too fast. This spring when the snow melted, I was plain old Ella Singleton. I milked the cow, tended the horses, cooked the meals, argued with my sisters, and had grand adventures between the pages of my books. Now, I'm *Mrs*. Carrigan; I'm going to have a baby; my sisters are all married; and I'm moving to New York City."

"And you're scared," Grandma Jo added. "Listen, Ella, when I agreed to move out West with your grandpa, I was so scared I couldn't keep food down for a week, and I didn't have no baby in my belly to give me a good excuse."

"But you loved Grandpa."

"And you love Sam." She clamped her hand over Ella's

mouth before she could deny it. "You love Sam," she repeated. "You wouldn't be carrying his baby if you didn't. A man might lust after a woman just 'cause she's a woman, but a woman don't hanker after a man unless she's in love with him."

"What if I do love him?" Ella straightened back to her full height. "He doesn't love me."

"You sound mighty sure of yourself."

"I am."

"Just 'cause a man don't say he loves you, don't mean he doesn't."

Ella returned to the bookshelf and reloaded her arms. "In this case, it does. We have discussed our feelings for each other thoroughly. I know exactly where I stand with him."

"So, you told him you love him, did you?"

"No," she admitted.

"Maybe he's holding out on you, too."

Her brows screwing into tight knots, Ella pleaded, "Grandma Jo, he isn't. I know you want it to be true. *I* want it to be true. Do you think it's easy for me to accept the death of my long cherished romantic dreams? I wish Sam could fall in love me, but he can't any more than I could force myself to fall in love with any of the men who came courting me. A body's heart cannot be ruled by expediency. I intend to do everything in my power to make this marriage the best it can be, but I'm not going to delude myself with false hopes and neither should you. My husband will be kind to me. He says he will love our baby. I don't expect more."

"Well, I still do, but I'll not argue with you about it." She changed the subject. "Are you taking all your books?"

"Only a few of my favorites." Glancing at the volumes in her arms, Ella shook her head. She returned three to the shelf and replaced them with two others. "I thought I'd leave the rest here for you. Feel free to loan them out if anybody wants to read them."

"I'll do that. Can't let folks around here stay ignorant just 'cause you ain't gonna be around to prod them into bettering their minds. They're big boots you're leaving me to fill, but I believe I'm up to it." Grandma Jo opened another dresser drawer and pulled out its contents. She carried a fistful of hair ribbons to Ella and laid them in her hands.

"If *you've* taken it into your mind to convince folks around here to read more, Heaven is likely to be the most educated town this side of the Mississippi in no time at all."

"I'd accuse you of flattering me, Ella, but true is true. When I set my mind to something, I ain't one to let anything get in my way."

"There's no need to remind *me* of that," Ella muttered under her breath.

Grandma Jo snorted. "I know you're still sore at me about the way I brung you and Sam together, so you may as well say what you're thinking out loud. I've got a hide like a buffalo, and I don't regret a thing I've done for the two of you. "It's all gonna work out just like I always said it would. You've finally admitted you love Sam, and that's a start. It won't be long before Sam realizes he's in love with you. You just gotta have a little faith and patience."

"I'm trying to, but I can't."

"Yours will be a first-rate marriage, Ella," Grandma Jo stated resolutely.

Would that she could ignore reality and embrace her grandmother's optimism Ella wished. She could believe her marriage would be civil; she could hope it would be genial; but even those wan expectations required an immense effort on her part

Wrapping the Bible her parents had given her for her twelfth birthday in a chemise, Ella carefully packed it into the trunk. "We have less than a day left together. I'm not going to spend it quarreling with you."

"That's a wise decision. Someday, I reckon you're gonna be as wise as me. By then, I'll be long dead, but I promise I'll raise a glass of huckleberry cordial to you in Paradise."

Ella smiled. "I doubt they have huckleberry cordial in Paradise."

"Then, I ain't going."

"You're incorrigible."

Grandma Jo began to laugh and Ella joined her. Once started, neither had the will to stop. They giggled their way through the packing of stockings and petticoats, blouses and skirts. The last item to be packed into the trunk was Ella's green silk dress. Tears were streaming down both of their cheeks.

"I'm gonna miss you, honey." Grandma Jo opened her arms and snuggled Ella against her breast like a small child. Ella hugged her tightly.

"And I'm going to miss you."

"Well, it looks like you're all ready," Grandma Jo announced when she finished surveying the wagon one last time. She was flanked on both sides by Ella's sisters and their new husbands who had come to see them off. Despite her grandmother's cheery proclamation, the mood in the yard was somber.

Rex stepped forward and shook Sam's hand. "Good luck to you, Mr. Carrigan." Moving to Ella he gave her a quick hug. "You, too, Ella. You take care of yourself, you hear."

"I will," Ella replied.

Monty was next to offer his well wishes, then Frank.

"Maybe we'll come visit you some day," he said. "Fern is real excited about becoming an aunt."

"You're welcome to visit anytime," Ella responded; then, realizing she may have overstepped, she cast a questioning glance at her husband.

"All of you are welcome to visit," Sam certified. "Though we would like a little time to get settled first. Ella and I . . ."

"We ain't gonna invade your home like a hoard of field mice, anytime soon," Grandma Jo reassured him. "Be at least a year or two. We all got our own lives to fuss with."

"You don't have to wait a year, but I would appreciate a little advance warning."

"Need to stock your cupboard with a few extra bottles of brandy to survive a visit from your in-laws, do you?" Grandma Jo teased.

Sam's expression remained strained. "No. I am merely stating my preference for living a well-ordered life, and such is achieved by planning ahead."

"I'm a fan of planning ahead myself," Bob McNaught said. "It's a necessity if you're gonna run a profitable ranch. Mr. Carrigan, it's been a pleasure." He offered his hand. "I hope someday there won't be no hard feelings between us."

Sam nodded and shook his hand.

"Ella, you remember how much we all love you," Bob admonished. "And don't be picking up too many fancy notions living back East with those city folks."

Ella smiled wanly. She had never been fond of farewells, and she was even less fond of crying. Already, she could feel her eyes welling with tears, and she had promised herself she wouldn't cry. It was not a good omen. These were the easy goodbyes.

"Well, step up and give your sister a hug." Grandma Jo ushered her sisters forward. They all crowded around Ella. None of them made any pretense of holding back their flood of tears.

"Now, I wish we hadn't made you marry Mr. Carrigan,"

Lily whimpered into her handkerchief. "I never reckoned on you having to go so far away to live."

"Me neither," Marilee sniffed. "In my mind, I kinda figured Mr. Carrigan would take up ranching or something."

"I know we ain't always got along as well as we oughta." Fern drew herself up. "But before you go, I want you to know Frank and I talked it over and we're gonna name our first daughter after you. We was gonna give you the privilege of naming her, but I told Frank you might come up with something real strange like you do for the livestock, so we best play it safe. Anyhow, I know I don't always show it, but I do love you, and I want you and Mr. Carrigan to be as happy as Frank and me."

Before Ella could respond, Janie threw her arms around her neck. "Bye, Ella," she wailed.

"Bye, Janie."

"Tell him you don't want to go."

"You know I can't do that."

"I know, but I still don't want you to go. I oughta have stayed a miserable spinster. It would have been better than having to say goodbye to you."

"No, it wouldn't." Ella patted her back. "Rex is going to make you so happy, you won't have time to miss me. You'll see."

Janie gulped back a sob. "He is a fine man, ain't he?"

"Yes, he is."

"But I'm still gonna miss you."

"I'd be hurt if you didn't; just don't miss me too much, okay?"

"Okay."

She had succeeded in blinking back every tear before it had a chance to fall, but the lump in Ella's throat was coming close to choking her. Her sisters moved on to Sam—and her grandmother took their place.

"You're holding up real good, Ella, and I'm proud of you," she whispered, wrapping her in her arms. "But you're gonna have one vicious headache if you keep damming up all those tears."

Ella kissed her grandmother's weathered cheek. "I know."

"But you're willing to suffer for the sake of your pride and your husband's comfort," Grandma Jo accurately assessed her reasons.

"Yes."

"It won't kill Sam to see a few tears, but that's neither here nor there. That stubborn pride of yours will likely be your best friend till you make some new ones in New York City." Grandma Jo's embrace tightened. "Don't let life's challenges get you down, Ella. Your name may be Carrigan now, but you're a Singleton to the very marrow of your bones, and Singletons are born to be happy. You remember that."

"I will."

"Good girl. I'll be expecting a nice, long, newsy letter at least once a week. Now, give me another kiss and climb up on that wagon seat."

Ella did as she was told.

Grandma Jo sauntered up to Sam and gave him a bear hug. "I don't know who is gonna miss having you around here most, me or Hound Dog," she declared as she released him.

"You are a fascinating woman, Mrs. Singleton."

Her eyes narrowed and her lips set in a hard line. "You want to get off this ranch and return to your home in New York, Sam?" she queried, a menacing note in her voice.

"That is what I am doing, isn't it?" he warily replied.

"Nope." Shaking her head, she latched onto his wrist. "You ain't going nowhere till you call me Grandma Jo."

The muscles of Sam's face relaxed. "You are a fascinating woman, Grandma Jo."

"That, I am. Now, get yourself up on that wagon and get

my granddaughter out of here before I change my mind about letting you have her."

"You're awfully quiet," Sam commented after they had been on the road for a full two hours and Ella had spoken less than a half-dozen words.

She sat a little straighter and congenially queried, "Is there something you would like to talk about?"

"No. I was merely expressing concern."

"I'm fine."

"You keep rubbing your head."

"I have a headache."

"Then, why did you say you were fine?"

Ella shrugged. "It'll go away eventually."

Sam reined the wagon to a halt. "Well, in the meantime I'm going to make a bed for you in the back of the wagon. You will lay down and close your eyes. I prefer to keep driving, but if the jostling bothers you too much, you will tell me immediately. Is that understood?"

"I don't want to be a bother."

"Then, don't be." He came around to her side of the wagon and lifted her down. "Don't argue with me."

"Okay, I won't," Ella replied, not because he had ordered it, or because she thought herself in need of his ministration, but because if she lay in the back of the wagon and feigned sleep, he wouldn't expect her to carry on a conversation.

It wasn't that she didn't want to talk to her husband. It was just she didn't know what to say. Too, it was taking all her energy to keep the tears of parting from her family at bay. After triumphing over her emotions when she had said her goodbyes in the yard, she wasn't about to give into them now.

She wanted to start her new life off on the right foot, and sobbing like a baby would not achieve that end.

It only took a minute for Sam to make a pallet of blankets. Ella climbed into the wagon bed and dutifully lay down. After taking a moment to dampen his handkerchief and lay it over her eyes, Sam returned to the front of the wagon.

Though Ella only intended to feign slumber, within the half hour, the rocking of the wagon lulled her to sleep.

It took several long days to make the journey to Green River City. It was the first time she and Sam had been alone for an extended time. They filled their nights with lovemaking—an activity they both embraced with enthusiasm—but their days were a different matter.

Ella was positively bursting at the seams with questions about her new home, but she was reluctant to ask too many for fear of annoying her husband. It wasn't that he complained. He didn't. He answered each and every one of her questions, supplying details when she requested them. It was just, more often than not, his thoughts seemed far away. She could only guess what he was thinking about, and her speculations were not conducive to promoting a blithesome state of mind.

Upon arriving in Green River City, they stabled the wagon and horse at the livery and took a room at the hotel. Bob had business in town and would be picking up Alexander and the wagon in a few days. Sam's horse was sold back to the man at the livery from whom he had originally purchased it.

After seeing her settled in their hotel room, Sam left for the telegraph office.

They had eaten a supper of steak and potatoes in the hotel dining room and were getting ready for bed when a telegram arrived from New York.

"Good news," Sam announced when he finished reading the message. "My friend, Robert Whitney, was in my lawyer's office when my telegram arrived. His sister has recently traveled to California, and as luck would have it, his private railroad car will be coming through with the next train East. Since it will be empty, he has offered it to us."

Ella's eyes lit. "I've never been on a private railroad car."

"You will find it far more comfortable than sitting up all night or sandwiching yourself into a berth," Sam informed her.

Comfortable didn't say the half of it, Ella mused when she stepped onto the train car the next day. "Opulent" was the word she would have chosen. Never in her life had she seen such splendor.

She had always known her husband's world was different from hers, but the sudden realization of just how different hit her like a blow, stealing her breath away.

Chandeliers hung from the frescoed ceiling. The upper half of the walls were lined with red velvet; the lower half wainscotted with dark mahogany paneling. The windows were framed in gilded trim, and the floor covered with a rich array of intricately patterned carpets.

She was standing in an area that resembled an elegant parlor. As Sam led her through the car, Ella discovered an equally grand sleeping room, a small kitchen, and a water closet.

When he had finished the brief tour, all she could say was, "Mercy's sake!"

"I assume that means our traveling accommodations meet with your approval."

"How could anyone *not* approve of this," she gestured with both arms. "It's like a castle on wheels. Your friend must be a very rich man."

"As a matter-of-fact he is."

"Are all your friends this rich?"

"A good number of them."

"Oh, dear. I was afraid you were going to say that."

He frowned. "You disapprove of my having wealthy friends?"

"Not at all. I just don't have any idea how I'm ever going to fit in. I don't want to be an embarrassment to you."

"You'll do fine," Sam assured her. Ella thought she detected a fleeting glimmer of uncertainty in his eyes, but she wasn't sure if she was accurately reading his feelings or assigning her own anxiety to him.

"The train is starting to move. You best sit down," he directed. "It will take a little while to get your train legs."

"Yes." Ella sunk into the nearest seat.

They sat in silence for a long while, each watching the scenery roll by through windows on opposite sides of the rail car. Ella's thoughts were filled with nostalgia for her home. She loved these sagebrush prairies and the mountains and the people. She knew she would be coming back for visits, but it wouldn't be the same. It would no longer be her home.

She would have a new home, with Sam and their baby. Could it be as happy as the one she had known here? She would try to make it that way. She would try every way she knew how. . . .

Sam cleared his throat. "One of the many advantages of traveling by private car is the privacy it affords the occupants."

Ella turned her head from the window and met her husband's gaze. One look into his deep blue eyes and she knew exactly what he was thinking.

Lovemaking had been on his mind a lot, lately. Ever since he had declared their marriage irrevocable and the need for restraint a thing of the past, he seemed determine to make up for lost time. Not that she found his determination the least bit objectionable. The opposite was true. There was nothing she would rather do to pass the time. When they made love, they came together as equals. They were too preoccupied with physical sensations to feel concern for the less satisfying aspects of their marriage.

Rising to her feet, she placed her hand in his.

Sam smiled in approval.

Leading her to the bed, he paused beside it to pull the pins from her hair. As it fell about her shoulders, he combed his fingers through the silken locks, arranging them to his liking.

Removing his glasses, he kissed the top of her head, then her eyes, then gathered her in his arms and kissed her breath away. His lips trailed from her lips down her throat, his fingers forging the way to tend the buttons of her blouse, so his mouth could have free access to her flesh. Ella shivered with carnal delight.

If only all of their marriage held as much promise of rapture as the promise of her husband's hands and lips, their lives would be heaven on earth, Ella yearned, as she eased his jacket from his shoulders. He removed her blouse. She removed his vest.

They fell into another embrace, thighs pressing thighs, hips thrusting against hips, full breasts crushing into a broad expanse of chest. Their lips mated.

Slipping his tongue into her mouth, Sam stroked the inside of her cheeks and teased the tip of her tongue with fervid, furtive flicks. Ella lavished his mouth with like caresses, matching his boldness when he moaned his pleasure.

Sustaining the intimate kiss, Sam's hands kneaded her back, slowly moving to her waist. He unbuttoned her skirt, dropping it around her feet. Untying her petticoat, he used the ribbon to pull her hips tighter against his, before he let the petticoat join her skirt on the floor.

Ella could feel the hardness of him through his trousers, and it heightened her own arousal.

Tugging his shirt from his trousers, she worked the buttons from the bottom up, taking advantage of the opportunity to tickle his smooth skin to gooseflesh as she did so. When she reached his neck, Ella lay open his shirt and snuggled into the hair of his chest. She blew her hot breath across his skin. She kissed his passion hard nipples. She massaged his shoulders and arms as she slid his shirt from his torso.

Leaning low to kiss his belly, Ella found her breasts cupped in his hands. Tenderly, he compelled her upward; then, his fingers moved to the strings of her corset.

"Women . . . wear . . . too . . . many . . . clothes," Sam murmured against her mouth as he methodically unlaced the garment. He pulled her chemise over her head and floated her drawers to the floor. "Better . . . much better." His hands roamed freely over her exposed flesh, reacquainting themselves with every soft inch.

Ella loosened his belt and ran the tip of her forefinger under the edge of his waistband. One by one, she undid the buttons holding his trousers and drawers in place, feigning clumsiness to give herself excuse to stroke his bulging manhood. Sam let her play her game for a delicious minute or two before he pushed her hands away and made quick work of discarding both garments.

Shoes and stockings followed in rapid succession; then, they fell upon the bed.

"These are the loveliest sight I've seen all day," Sam uttered as he showered her breasts with attention. He kissed the pink tips again and again, fondling the fullness of her breasts with his warm hands. He brushed them with the tip of his nose, until they stood in firm peaks, then gently pulled one breast into his mouth, drawing it in deeply, as if he would swallow it whole.

His tongue did titillating things to her senses. Ella arched against him. He suckled harder, his intensely blue eyes taking on a dreamy, glazed, faraway hue.

The hum of the train wheels against the track was echoed in

every nerve of Ella's quivering body. Every where he touched her, she felt on fire and twice as alive as she had been moments before. Her conscious mind knew love and physical desire were not one and the same, but Ella was beyond conscious thought, and the pleasure her husband found in her body made her feel cherished.

His mouth sought out her other breast. He rolled the super sensitive nipple between his lips, playfully nipping, kissing caressing, laving it with his hot tongue until Ella writhed beneath him.

She opened her thighs, and he settled between them, but he didn't enter her. Instead, he rocked his weight against the nub of her desire, causing her to cry out her need for him to fill her.

"Please," Ella pleaded.

"Please, what?" he growled. "Please this?" He dragged his mouth slowly down her abdomen. Pinning her hips so she couldn't escape him, he nibbled on the edges of her navel and lower . . . and lower still, until his tongue danced upon the apex of her core of sensual delight.

Ella's heart was beating so fast, the edges of the room dissolved into a black haze. Sparks radiated from the lowest region of her belly, exploding into shards of white hot sensation. Her muscles began to convulse.

Raising himself, Sam plunged into her and stroked her contracting muscles to an even more powerful response. Ella's legs wrapped around him, pulling him deeper within her, as she carried him with her into the realm of marital ecstasy.

Ella lay basking in the warmth and wonder of her husband's arms. If she never had to stir from where she was, she knew she would live her life the happiest of women.

She didn't stir for a long time. When she did, Ella rolled atop her husband and loved his welcoming body as thoroughly as he had loved hers.

Eighteen

A carriage was awaiting them when they arrived in New York City. The driver greeted his employer deferentially. Tipping his hat to Ella, he saw them comfortably seated and loaded their luggage on the back of the carriage with such smooth efficiency Ella was in awe of him.

"Take the long route home, Cedric. I believe the lady may enjoy seeing a bit of the city," Sam ordered.

"Yes, sir. Will there be any place special you would like her to be seeing?"

"No. You may use your own discretion."

"Very good, sir."

Her husband had explained a servant was to meet them. A man dressed in a high hat, fine black suit, with manners as polished as a prince was not what Ella had expected.

She didn't linger on the matter; however, because her attention was caught by a thousand sights and sounds at once. There were people and horses and carriages everywhere, so many she couldn't begin to count them. As they rolled down the street, they passed pedestrians garbed in every manner of clothing, boys on bicycles, trolley cars filled to overflowing with passengers. It seemed everyone in the whole city was in a hurry to be somewhere.

The noise greeting her ears brought to mind the Biblical story of the Tower of Babel, only these people hadn't built one tower. They had built thousands and were still building more from the looks of things. The buildings they passed were as tall as mountains, three, four, five stories—she tried to count the floors before another building blocked her view.

And the decorations! A plain building was the exception not the rule. Arched windows, turrets, porticos, colonnades . . . there were flat roofs, mansard roofs, domed roofs, and others whose shape she couldn't begin to describe.

Ella couldn't contain her excitement. She peppered Sam with questions about each building that caught her interest, craning her neck in every direction to make sure she didn't miss any of it. If he was growing annoyed, she was too pre-occupied to notice.

"What language are they speaking?" she queried when they paused at a street corner to allow two chattering women, their heads covered with scarves, to cross.

"Hungarian, I believe."

"What is that church?"

"Trinity Church."

"And that building? The one with all the steps."

"The Subtreasury Building."

And so it went until some time later they turned onto a street and Sam announced, "This is Fifth Avenue. Most of my friends live here. My home is on up the street."

Ella's eyes popped open even wider than they already were. The street was lined with huge, ornate structures. "These are private houses?"

"Yes."

"I figured they must b public buildings of some sort."

"No. Society has many passions but two rise above them all: horses, and as you can see before you, houses."

"And you live on this street in a house as big as these?"

"Actually, mine is one of the smaller homes. . . . Ah, here we are. You can see for yourself."

The carriage pulled to a halt in front of a three-story, brick building with a tiled mansard roof and multi-paned windows. Wrought iron decorated the roofline. Window boxes filled with brightly colored flowers sat below the sills of the first story windows. Heavily carved, double, wooden doors gave entry from a five step high porch centered on the rectangular front. The house *was* smaller than the homes on either side of it, but it was easily as large as the hotel Ella had stayed in when she had made her trip to St. Louis. She closed her eyes and opened them again. The house was still there as imposing as ever.

She had no objections to being married to a rich man, but this rich? On the train she had had an inkling that his measure of a successful businessman might be higher than her own, but never in her wildest speculations had she ever considered that Sam lived in a style anywhere approaching this. Surely he must share the building with other families, Ella seized hold of the comforting thought.

"You don't live here alone?" she stated the question as if it were fact.

"No," Sam assured her. "I have the usual assortment of servants."

"Nobody else besides servants lives here with you?"

"My mother did before her death."

Clasping her trembling hands tightly in her lap, Ella stared incredulously at the building that was to be her home. "All this house for two people. How does a body keep from getting lost?" she spoke her thoughts aloud.

"We carry compasses."

"What!"

"I'm twitting you. Your jaw is so low, I couldn't resist the temptation to see how much further it could drop."

Ella snapped her jaw closed. "I'm sorry. I didn't mean to act like a country bumpkin."

"I didn't think that at all." He squeezed her hands. " Actually, it is rather flattering and certainly good for my soul. Sometimes, a man gets so accustomed to living in luxury, he forgets how truly lucky he is. Thank you for reminding me."

"You're welcome" did not seem like an appropriate response, so Ella said nothing.

"Are you ready to go in?"

She hesitated. "I think so."

Cedric had been standing patiently at the carriage door, and he opened it, then stood aside as Sam helped her down. Placing her hand on his arm, Sam led her to the door of her new home.

"Mr. Carrigan, it's good to see you, sir," a tall woman in a starched white apron and mop cap greeted as they stepped through the door. Their trunks followed at their heels.

"It's good to see you, too, Mrs. Potter. Have my rooms been prepared?"

"Yes, sir, but I'm afraid I didn't prepare one for the young lady. When Mr. Gentry came round to say you had wired him you were coming home, he didn't say you would be bringing a guest. I'll send Annie to make up a guest room right away."

"There is no need for that," Sam instructed, his tone formal and his expression unreadable. "I would like you to gather all the servants in the foyer. I have an announcement to make."

"Yes, sir."

Ella was not surprised the housekeeper didn't know who she was. Sam thought it best no one but his lawyer know of their marriage. Servants gossiped liked everyone else, and he didn't want the news to reach Clara before he did. She agreed.

As she waited for the servants to assemble, Ella nervously rubbed her hands on her skirt. She tried not to look too overwhelmed as she surreptitiously glanced about the entry. An ornate gas chandelier dangled over her head. The walls were covered with pale gold chintz. A huge mirror hung over the hall table. Her feet were standing on a floor of white marble.

Ella schooled her face to an amiable, and she *hoped,* confident countenance. She was wearing her green silk dress at her husband's suggestion, so she knew she looked her best, but looking her best on the outside did little to mitigate the apprehension she felt on the inside. Her arrival in this gilded world was bound to create a stir.

Sam had told her servants didn't demand explanations, but she couldn't imagine they wouldn't ask some questions. She didn't want to start off her new life with a pack of lies, but she wasn't all that thrilled with the notion of telling the truth either.

Ella counted the servants as they entered the foyer. There were eleven in all, six men and five women. When they were lined up in a row, her husband began his speech.

"Ladies, gentlemen, I have asked you here to share some important news. It may come as a shock to you, so you may want to prepare yourselves." He paused before continuing. "During my travels in Wyoming I acquired a wife. May I present the former Miss Ella Singleton, now Mrs. Samuel Carrigan, your new mistress."

The ladies bobbed a curtsey, and the gentlemen nodded their heads. No eyebrows shot heavenward. No hands rose to calm flabbergasted hearts. Not a murmur escaped one set of lips.

"You may congratulate us if you like," Sam directed.

One at a time, in an order Ella quickly surmised had something to do with their rank within the household, they did just that. When they had finished, Sam dismissed all of them except Mrs. Potter. He turned to Ella.

"Mrs. Potter will show you to our rooms so you can freshen up. As you know, I have a matter to attend to that requires my immediate attention. I suggest you rest while I'm away, but if you grow restless, Mrs. Potter will give you a tour of the house. Otherwise, I will show it to you myself when I get back."

Ella put on her bravest face and quietly questioned, "How long will you be gone?"

"At least an hour, maybe more."

"You'll tell her how very sor—"

Sam pressed his finger to her lips and sternly shook his head. His eyes, however, told her he comprehended what she had been about to say and he would do as she asked.

Without further comment, he quit the house.

"Excuse me, ma'am. If you'll wait here, I'll take you up." Mrs. Potter disappeared through a door. She returned a moment later with a younger woman who had been introduced to Ella as Annie. Annie scurried up the stairs. Mrs. Potter addressed Ella.

"The master's suite is this way," she informed her as she led the way up the stairs.

"Thank you."

With the housekeeper's back turned, Ella was able to gawk to her heart's content. The stairway they ascended was wide with a massive, dark-stained banister and carpeted steps. Paintings covered the wall. Most were landscapes but a few were portraits of persons bearing a more than slight resemblance to her husband. Upon reaching the second floor, they traveled a long hall. Near the head of the stairs, one side was bordered by a railing that overlooked the foyer. Later, walls and doors lined each side.

Mrs. Potter opened one of these doors and stood aside for Ella to enter. She found herself in a large sitting room. Luxurious Aubusson carpets covered the floor. Dark green velvet upholstered furniture—two biscuit tufted chairs, a settee, and an ottoman—were arranged tastefully before a large marble fireplace. A small desk and bookcase sat against one wall. Bold floral drapery edged with golden tassels flanked win-

dows that took up most of another wall. Rosewood tables of
various sizes and shapes were conveniently located throughout. There were two additional doors on opposite walls.

Mrs. Potter led the way through the sitting room to one of
the doors.

"Here we are." She opened it and ushered Ella inside. "This
will be your bedroom. The master's is across the way."

Annie was just finishing putting fresh sheets on the bed.
She smoothed the bedspread in place, bobbed a curtsey, and
exited the room.

"Your bathroom is in here." Mrs. Potter opened another
door, leaving it ajar. "Would you like me to turn down the
bed before I go?"

"There's no need for you to go to any trouble on my account. If I feel the urge for a nap, I can do it myself."

"Should I help you unpack your trunk now or later?"

Glancing about the room, Ella saw her trunk had already
arrived. How she couldn't fathom, but she was fast learning
her husband's servants were miracles of efficiency. "I can take
care of my things myself," she stated.

"Is there anything else I can do for you?"

"No."

An injured mien pinched Mrs. Potter's heretofore expres-
sionless face. "Do you find my services unsatisfactory,
ma'am?"

"Mercy, no!" Ella exclaimed. "Where would you get a notion like that?"

"You have rejected my every offer of help," Mrs. Potter
stiffly stated.

"Oh, dear. I've hurt your feelings, haven't I? I didn't mean
to. I'm just so new at this."

"New at what, ma'am?"

"Having servants and the like. Why our whole house would
fit into what you all call the master suite with plenty of room

to spare. I said I didn't need your help because with a huge house like this to take care of, I'm sure you have far more important things to do than wait on me. I'm used to waiting on myself and see no reason why I shouldn't keep on doing it, but I don't mind at all if helping is what makes you happy." She smiled sincerely. "I hope you'll be patient with me, and give me time to learn everything I'm suppose to know."

Mrs. Potter stared at her. "Ma'am, may I speak frankly?"

"Please do."

"Well, one of the things you need to learn right off is you shouldn't be having conversations like the one we're having with the servants. Being too friendly can get you in trouble."

A perplexed expression settled on Ella's face. "How so?"

"It might get out you married above your station."

"Is that very bad?"

"Yes, ma'am," Mrs. Potter gravely informed her. "Some folks can be very cruel about that sort of thing."

"I'll remember that. Thank you for telling me."

"You're welcome, ma'am. I'll be downstairs if you change your mind about needing my help. Just pull the bell cord."

Ella's brows knit as she glanced about the room.

Mrs. Potter strode across the floor and pointed to a tasseled cord hanging near the bed.

"Yes, thank you. If I need you, I'll pull the bell cord."

Alone in the room, Ella abandoned her efforts to contain her enthusiasm for her new home. True all this luxury was intimidating, but it was also gorgeous. She had seen drawings of rooms like this and even a photograph or two, but they didn't do justice to their subjects.

She danced around the room, inspecting everything from the gilded mirror hanging over the dressing table to the satin and lace curtains to the intricate carving of roses and cherubs on the headboard.

Removing her boots, she wiggled her toes on the thick Persian carpet beneath her feet. Her head swiveled from side to side as she tried to take in everything at once. She had her own fireplace, an Eastlake chair, a wardrobe twice as big as the one she had shared with her sisters back home. Her bed had four fluffy pillows and a satin spread.

Ella circled the room several times touching every item.

Then, her gaze settled on the door Mrs. Potter had left ajar. She had purposely saved the best for last, savoring the anticipation like one savored the final bite of a rich dessert. Skipping across the room, Ella threw open the door.

"Indoor plumbing," she rhapsodized. "I have died and gone to Paradise." No more chamber pots or trips out back in the bitter cold or buzzing flies or malodorous fumes wafting up to assault her nose. Her gaze moved from the commode to the sink, then lingered on the long, deep bathtub. A grin split her face as she envisioned herself stretched out in the tub, soaking away the aches and pains of the day. She could close her eyes or count the flowers on the wallpaper or . . .

It was a good long while before she was able to tear herself away from the wonderful room.

Though she was a little weary from their travels, Ella wasn't the least bit sleepy. She was too wound up to be sleepy. Preferring to wait for her husband for her tour of the house, she used her excess energy to unpack her belongings. Her dresses appeared lost in the cavernous wardrobe, and she couldn't begin to fill half the dresser drawers, but it didn't bother her in the least. Considerable time was spent arranging her toiletries on the dressing table. Standing back, she surveyed the results, rearranged the items, repeating the procedure again and again until she was satisfied with the results.

The next task she set for herself was writing her grandmother and sisters. Their eyes would pop out of their heads if they could see the room in which she sat, and she described it in great detail. She described everything she had seen.

* * *

Three hours had passed since her husband had left to break the news of their marriage to his former fiancée, and Ella was growing restless with worry. She had run out of things to do to occupy her hands and more importantly her mind.

Her anxiety was not authored by a lack of trust in her husband. If ever a moral man walked the earth, it was Samuel Carrigan. He had her absolute trust. She just couldn't imagine what was taking so long, or rather she could, and visions of a heartbroken Clara unable to stem her hysterical sobs caused Ella to shudder with remorse.

The longer he was gone, the more vivid and tragic her fantasies of the encounter became, until in her minds eye she could see both of the unjustly parted lovers weeping in unbearable misery locked in each other's arms. In self-preservation Ella decided to have Mrs. Potter give her the tour of the house after all.

The rest of the house was as elegantly appointed as the rooms she had already seen. Mrs. Potter led her through a drawing room, two parlors, a morning room, a dining room, a music room, a library, a conservatory, a smoking room, a ballroom, a large modern kitchen, a pantry, and at least a dozen bedrooms, many with adjacent sitting rooms. The third floor belonged to the servants, and they didn't venture there.

Every room elicited Ella's interest and her amazement that people lived their everyday lives surrounded by such grandeur. This was her life now. She didn't know whether to laugh with joy or cry from the weighty responsibility of it all. Her husband's joke about the compass was closer to the truth than he reckoned.

Of the many rooms she toured, Ella liked three above the others. The library was her favorite. It was lined floor to ceiling with books of every description. She had already read many of the titles, but there were enough she had never even heard of to keep her busy turning pages for years.

The second room to fascinate her was the ballroom. It was beautiful with its shining wooden floor, cream and gold wallpaper, potted plants, and lush oil paintings of moorish bathers and woodland nymphs, but what she liked best about it was its purpose. A whole room, in one's very own house, used exclusively for dancing seemed unreal. But she knew it was real because she had seen it with her very own eyes. If Sam was willing, Ella hoped the room would see much use.

The last room to garner special affection was the first on her tour. It was her husband's bedroom. The idea of separate bedrooms didn't please her, but Ella knew from the books she read it was a common custom among the very rich. Sam's room she liked because from the Renaissance bed centered on one wall to the roll-slat window blinds to the intricately tiled fireplace with its uncluttered mantle to the walnut wardrobe and dresser, the room reflected the personality of its owner. Since she loved the owner, it was natural she loved the room.

When Mrs. Potter finished showing her around her new home, Ella wandered back to the library, picked out a book on architecture, and retired to one of the parlors to await her husband's return.

Ella ate her supper at the huge dining room table alone. She barely tasted it and an hour after the meal couldn't remember what she had eaten.

Not wanting to display her distress in front of the servants, she had gone to her bedroom, where she alternately had been pacing and staring out the window ever since.

What could be keeping him? she asked herself for the hundredth time. Had something even more horrible than she could imagine happened to him? This house was too big and empty without him. He must know she was worried. Was it too much for her to expect a note explaining his prolonged absence?

When at last her ears detected the heavy footfalls of a man followed by the click of the latch of the door leading from the hall into the sitting room, she came to an abrupt halt.

Sucking in a half dozen deep breaths, Ella pinched her cheeks and stepped out of her room.

"I'm glad to see you are still up. I wanted to talk to you," Sam greeted.

Ella searched his face for the telltale signs of unbearable agony or recently fallen tears. He looked tired, but there were no other visible signs of distress. "How is Clara?"

"As well as can be expected under the circumstances. She was shocked, of course, but she accepted the news with grace, as I knew she would."

"Did you tell her how sorry I am?"

"Yes."

The compulsion to ask why he had been away so long had placed the question on the tip of Ella's tongue the moment she had heard his footsteps, but she steadfastly resisted the urge to ask it. If he wanted her to know, he would tell her.

"You said you wanted to talk to me about something?" she measuredly queried.

"Yes."

"What is it?" Ella questioned when he did not elaborate.

Discomfort darkened his eyes. "Clara has asked to meet you."

Nineteen

She had said Clara could come. How could she have said anything else after she had taken so much away from the woman, but Ella was dreading the encounter so much her hands had not stopped trembling all morning.

Her husband, the wretch, had gone to his office. He told her not to expect him home before the evening meal. It was unkind of him to desert her even if Miss Clara Harrington had specifically requested he not be present at their meeting. True, she had agreed to the arrangement, but he ought to have seen through her guise of stoic compliance and insisted he stand by her side regardless of what Clara preferred.

She was wearing her green silk dress again today, because Sam had apprised her it was the only garment she owned that came close to being suitable. That had certainly given her confidence a needed boost. Ella scrunched her face at her reflection in the windowpane. He had promised to arrange for a dressmaker to visit and make her a proper wardrobe as soon as possible, but it did her little good at present. Besides, though she loved new clothing as well as the next woman, his offer felt more like an insult than a generous gift.

Ella told herself her pregnancy was making her overly sensitive, that naturally clothes made to withstand the rigors of country life were unsuitable in an elegant city and he had merely been making a statement of fact and was not indicting her tastes, but telling and believing were not necessarily the same thing. And she was too preoccupied to make the effort to be logical just now.

Ella glanced at the clock on the wall of the drawing room. Her guest was due at three o'clock. That meant she had thirty more minutes to fret herself to a frazzle.

What could Miss Harrington hope to accomplish by this visit? If it was designed to make her squirm, she had already accomplished her goal. Perhaps she merely wanted the opportunity to vent her spleen. . . . Though from his descriptions of her, Clara didn't seem the type of woman given to violence, maybe she intended to right the wrong done her by eliminating her rival with poison or a knife. That would explain why she wanted their meeting to be private.

"I'm starting to reckon like a crackbrain," Ella lamented. Deciding what she needed was something constructive to do while she waited, she fished her handkerchief out of her pocket and began to dust the furniture and bric-a-brac. There wasn't a speck of dust to be seen anywhere, but she didn't care.

When the awaited knock at the door finally came, Ella stuffed her handkerchief into her pocket. Clasping her hands behind her back so no one would see them shaking, she meekly called out, "Come in."

"Miss Harrington is here to see you, ma'am," Mr. Creswell, the butler announced.

"I'm as ready as I'll ever be," Ella blurted out before she could stop herself. Blushing, she immediately amended her statement to a decorous, "Please show her in, Mr. Creswell."

When Clara Harrington entered the room, for the space of several minutes, the two women simply stared at each other.

Clara was not just beautiful, she was *extremely* beautiful. The miniature Sam had showed to her didn't come close to capturing her loveliness. Wisps of pale blond hair framed her angelic face. Her eyes were the blue of cornflowers. Her lips as pink as a rose and heart-shaped. Her figure was every man's notion of perfection. She was shorter than Ella by several inches, adding to her aura of delicacy and grace.

Ella felt like she had swallowed a stone.

"This is hideously awkward, isn't it?" Clara broke the grim silence. "I suppose you are wondering why I am here."

"Yes," Ella charily replied.

"You needn't look so anxious." Clara took a step toward her. Holding her head high, she continued to address Ella in clipped tones. "I am not here to wreak vengeance upon your person. I'll admit the thought of tucking my father's pistol into my reticule did enter my mind, but it was a fleeting thought. I never seriously considered it as a sensible option. Samuel has explained the situation to me, and though I don't like it one bit, it appears you are not to blame. Your family is the culprit and that awful sheriff. Them I would gladly shoot, but they are not here, so I will have to forego the pleasure."

Ella was unsure what to think of her speech. Though it was difficult to do so, she made herself meet Clara's intent gaze. "Miss Harrington, I really am sorry . . ."

"Yes, I know. Samuel told me." Clara persisted to stare at her.

Ella bore her keen regard with a rigid spine and a countenance carefully schooled not to reveal her chaotic emotions, but she couldn't do so forever. "Why are you here?" The question came out sounding far more plaintive than she intended.

"Two reasons, actually." Clara tugged at the fingers of her gloves, but she didn't remove them. "The first is curiosity. Samuel and I have been planning to marry since we were children. Ours is, *was* a gentle, civilized romance. When one grows up loving someone as if they were a member of one's family, it is impossible for one not to want them to be happy.

Samuel deserves a superior wife. I needed to see for myself
if you possess the necessary qualities."

"And if I don't?"

"I shall have to think of a way to rescue him from your
clutches."

"I see." Ella nervously rubbed the back of her lips with
her tongue. Miss Harrington certainly didn't mince words. Ella
appreciated her plainspokenness. It saved her the trouble of
sifting her true meaning from a tangle of nebulous prattle, but
she couldn't help believing it highly unlikely she would pass
Clara's test. She didn't possess the nerve to ask what "necessary qualities" she would be required to exhibit, so instead
she queried, "And what is the second reason?"

"I would like to give a dinner party to introduce you to
Society," Clara disclosed.

Ella couldn't prevent her eyes from growing wide with disbelief. Was Clara some kind of saint, or was she out of her
mind with heartache? Either scenario compounded Ella's chagrin. "That's very generous of you," she mumbled, "but I can't
imagine why you'd want to do such a thing."

"I am not being the least bit generous. My motives are
purely selfish, I assure you," Clara coolly informed her. "Even
though Samuel and I never publicly announced our intentions,
all the world for years has been whispering we would someday
wed. When news of your marriage gets out, there will be new
whispers all prefaced with 'Did you hear about poor little
Clara Harrington?' " Her gloved hands clenched into fists, and
her delicate features took on a furious mien. Her expression
gradually smoothed, but the fire of determination remained in
her eyes. "Losing Samuel I can tolerate, but I refuse to be
made the object of pity. By showing my support for your
marriage by giving the dinner party, I'll outmaneuver the gossips. They will be forced to conclude their long held opinion

of the nature of Samuel and my relationship was incorrect—
that all along we were dear friends and nothing more."

That Clara valued her pride above her fiancée was incomprehensible to Ella, but she refrained from commenting on it.
Her plan appeared to be well thought out. Ella judged Clara's
ability to think clearly under such trying circumstances enviable. It was an outrageous plan to be sure, but the very outrageousness of its nature was exactly what made Ella think it
might work. "I'm in awe of your foresight," she gave voice
to her thoughts. "I never would have conceived doing such
an insightful thing."

Clara accepted the compliment with a succinct nod. "I have
played Society's games all my life, and I know what I'm about."

"I certainly hope so."

"Oh, I will triumph," Clara declared with steely-eyed confidence. "When I am through, I'll have my own father and
mother believing I personally arranged the match between the
two of you. All I need is your permission to go ahead with
my scheme."

"It's yours."

Clara sighed with relief. "Excellent. I was hoping I could
count on your cooperation."

"Anything I can do to ease your burden, I will gladly do,"
Ella vowed with heartfelt sympathy.

"Really?" A speculative gleam lit Clara's eyes. As she
watched, Ella could almost see the wheels of cogitation spinning
in her head. Only a moment passed before Clara resumed speaking. "If you sincerely want to help me, then I would like for us
to be seen around town together. Taking tea, shopping, chatting
each other up like old friends, that sort of thing."

"You wouldn't find my company too distasteful?"

"I don't believe I would," Clara replied, her perplexed moue
showing her to be as surprised as Ella by her statement. "I
know it makes absolutely no sense at all. I came here fully

prepared to hate you with every fiber of my being for the rest
of my life, but . . . there is something," her hand fluttered
like a butterfly, "about you. I really can't say what it is. Maybe
it's the look of remorse in your eyes or your willingness to
help me in my hour of need. Who knows? I certainly don't.
But, if I must lose Samuel to another woman, I think I am
not completely opposed to it being you."

"It's very kind of you to say so."

Clara shrugged. "I suppose it is, but it is also the truth, or
at least it is at the moment. Who knows? On further acquaintance we may find we loathe each other after all."

Despite the awkwardness of the situation, Ella found herself
smiling.

"You're much prettier when you smile. You should do it
more often," Clara advised. "Do you have any plans for this
afternoon?"

"No."

"Good. We can make our first public appearance. Where
would you like to go?"

"I really haven't any idea," Ella answered truthfully. Her
mind was still consumed with trying to assimilate Clara's willingness to accept her marriage to Sam without rancor. "Why
don't you decide? Since I want to see everything, anywhere
you choose will suit me."

At that moment, Annie entered bearing a tray with a pot
of tea and a plate of cucumber sandwiches.

"I know," Clara exclaimed. "Instead of having tea here, we
will have it at the Brunswick Hotel. Everybody who is anybody goes there at least once a week. We're sure to be seen
by all the right people."

"Where have you been?" Sam demanded when Ella stepped
through the front door. Ella winced at his brusque tone.

"I was having tea with Clara. Didn't Mrs. Potter tell you?"

"Yes, she did, but tea doesn't last four hours."

"Have I been gone that long?" Glancing at the clock in the hall, she confirmed she had. Her cheeks flushed a rosy pink. "I'm sorry. I guess I lost track of the time. I thought you wouldn't care how long I was gone as long as I was here when you returned."

"You weren't here when I returned," he submitted.

"You said you wouldn't be home until supper which is at eight. It's only a few minutes after seven. If I'd known you were coming home early, I would've made the effort to be here."

Sam frowned at her.

Guiding her into the nearest parlor, he closed the door behind them. "Before this conversation goes any further, I would appreciate it if you explain why you were having tea with Clara in the first place."

"To silence the gossips." Ella laced her fingers and met his gaze directly. She had no idea why he was so vexed with her, and she was inclined to deem his behavior unfair, but she was determined to humor him. "Clara is as smart as she is beautiful, and she has a charitable heart as well. Having met her, I can fully appreciate why you're in love with her and find me such a poor substitute."

He glared at her. "Whatever my feeling for Clara, they are no more. I am a married man." His tone remained terse. "As to you being a poor substitute, I think you judge yourself too harshly. In the future, when we discuss Clara and I, we will speak of friendship not love."

"Clara said the same thing, but I just can't comprehend how a person can turn off their feelings like water at a spigot." Ella reached for his hand. Her eyes were full of compassion. "I know you've promised to be a proper husband to me and a good father to our child, but you don't have to pretend your feelings for Clara have evaporated. I accept it will take a very long time for you to get over her, assuming you ever can."

"Do not presume to know my mind or my heart. I am their master and no other."

She opened her mouth to reply, but before she could, he stopped her.

"That subject is closed." He disengaged his hand from hers. "Tell me why you believe having a four hour tea with Clara will silence the gossips."

"We didn't have tea for four hours," Ella patiently clarified. "We took a stroll in the park and went . . ."

"Fine. You may tell me everything you did later. What does any of it have to do with the gossips?"

She waited for him to interrupt her again. When he didn't, Ella took a deep breath and attempted to explain. "Clara doesn't want people pitying her because you married me, so she's asked me to act as though we're old friends, so she can pretend she is delighted we've married. She also wants to give a dinner party in our honor for the same reason. I hope you don't mind, because I told her she could. It seemed the least I could do."

Raising a brow, Sam stroked the ends of his mustache while he reflected upon her words. When he spoke, his voice wasn't quite as strident as before, but his expression remained rigid. "It is a worthy plan, but I am astonished either of you are comfortable with the arrangement."

"I don't think we are comfortable," Ella corrected the misconception. "Clara says she doesn't hate me, which is far more than I've a right to expect from anyone in her position. For my part, I'm too plagued with guilt to be comfortable."

"So you didn't enjoy her company," he somberly asserted.

Shifting her weight from one foot to another, Ella pleated her lips. "That isn't true. I did enjoy myself and I didn't all at the same time."

"What you say makes absolutely no sense."

"I know. I'm beginning to wonder if life ever makes sense."

His frown deepened. "Of course it does, if one conducts one's life in a sensible manner. That is all I ask from you. I don't like surprises. I was surprised to find you not at home when I returned."

"But it was you who arranged for me to meet with Clara, and I told Mrs. Potter where I was going before I left. I thought you'd want me to cooperate with Clara's scheme," Ella contended. "Truly, I don't want to do things to make you unhappy with me, but how can I avoid them when I don't understand why you're upset?"

He turned from her, casting his gaze upon the wall. "I was worried. That is why I came home early. In case your meeting with Clara went badly. That is why I am upset."

Ella's heart skipped a beat. It was her experience a body only worried about those for whom they felt some affection. "You were worried about me?"

"Yes. You are my wife. I am responsible for your welfare. Naturally, when I found you gone, I was concerned."

The pleasure Ella found in his initial statement vanished. "I'm perfectly capable of taking care of myself. I've been doing so all my life," she retorted. Sam returned his gaze to her, pinning her in place.

"That may be, but this is not Wyoming. This is New York City. You are new here. You do not know your way around. You are unaccustomed to both the physical and social dangers of city life," he lectured. "Now that I know the reason for your long absence, I am willing to concede it may have served a useful purpose. If Clara suggested it, I'm inclined to believe she knows what she is about. However, in the future, I expect to be informed *before* you go traipsing about town the purpose behind the excursion and precisely how long you will be gone. Is that understood?"

It took every whit of Ella's mettle to compose a polite reply. "Yes."

"Thank you. I am used to living an orderly life. Order gives me great comfort."

"I'll try to remember that."

"I know you will. Now, tell me where else you went."

Twenty

The dressmaker and her assistant arrived at eleven o'clock. With them came the latest French pattern books and fashion plates and so many fabric samples it took the assistant a dozen trips to carry them all upstairs. They also brought a generous assortment of readymade dresses.

"Your husband wishes you to choose three of these to see you through until I finish the first gowns of your new wardrobe," Miss LaVoie apprised Ella as she lay the dresses upon the bed.

"I'm to choose three *and* you're to make me more?" Ella's eyes widened as she surveyed the gowns. Every one was far finer than anything she had ever owned. She reached out a hand, reverently stroking the fabric of the one nearest her.

"Yes, ma'am."

"But it seems to me three are more than enough."

"No, ma'am. Three will barely get you through the week."

Ella stared at her. "You can't be serious."

"Yes, ma'am, I am." Having finished arranging the gowns to her satisfaction, Miss LaVoie faced her squarely. "Naturally, the standards for day clothes are less stringent, but as a rule, a lady shouldn't be seen in the same evening gown more than once. Twice is permissible. Three times the very limit."

"You mean, I'm not to wear a gown overmuch in the same week," Ella sought clarification.

"No, ma'am. I mean in the same year, and after that it's out of style so it's of no use to you."

Ella's brow knit in consternation and her lips pursed. Obviously Sam had told the seamstress she was new to New York and the woman hoped to take advantage of her naivete. "I can't believe you're being square with me. I may be new to the city and eager to make a good impression, but I'm not without sense," she curtly informed her. "I'll not be duped into spending more of my husband's money than is required."

Miss LaVoie didn't appear to take offense. She merely smiled politely. "Mr. Carrigan has given me a list. He says you are free to add to it, but not to subtract."

Skeptical, Ella held out her hand. "Give me the list."

"Yes, ma'am." Miss LaVoie fished it out of her pocket.

As she read the list, Ella sucked in her breath. She didn't doubt it was in her husband's handwriting, but she did doubt his sanity. The list stretched into infinity. Not only was he clothing her from the skin out, he had ordered gowns to be made for every possible circumstance. There were walking dresses, carriage dresses, dresses for mornings, dresses for afternoon tea, and that just began to cover what she was to wear during the daylight hours. The number of evening gowns he had ordered was even more outlandish. While she appreciated his generosity, to her mind his extravagance was positively sinful.

"You say I'm only to wear each of these gowns three times?" she numbly queried.

"Yes, ma'am. More than three times would be an insult to your hostess. It would tell her you didn't think her affair important enough to bother looking your best."

"I see," Ella responded, even though she really didn't. She straightened her spine. "What am I suppose to do with the gowns when I can no longer wear them?"

"Some of the ladies give them to their servants at Christmas time, others to charity, still others have them destroyed. The choice is yours."

"What I'd choose would be to wear them till they've outlived their usefulness, but from the looks of this list I don't believe that is what my husband wants me to do," Ella said with a determined murmur as she read the list again. While she definitely was going to talk to Sam about this when he got home. She didn't want to inadvertently hurt any of his friends' feelings, neither could she bring herself to believe the dressmaker's claim. If Miss Lavoie wasn't being completely truthful, they could cancel all or part of the order later. For now, she thought it prudent to accept her word and cooperate fully. "Since you plainly know more about fashion than I do and every gown upon my bed is lovely beyond description, I'd be grateful for your advice as to which ones I ought to select."

Miss Lavoie ran an assessing gaze over her. "With your coloring I would suggest the bengaline silk and the heliotrope foulard for day wear and the crepe de chine for evening."

Ella gave the gowns a second study. She certainly couldn't fault the woman's tastes or her skill with the needle. "Then they will be my choices," she amenably replied.

"I appreciate your confidence in my opinion, ma'am. If you will allow me, I'll help you out of the dress you're wearing, so you may try on the gowns and I can measure for any alterations." She draped a measuring tape over her neck, and her silently efficient assistant stood at the ready with pincushion in hand. "While Mary tends to your new gowns, you and I can review the pattern books and materials and make the necessary decisions for the rest of your wardrobe."

It was nearly five o'clock before Miss LaVoie left with a promise to be back in three days for a fitting of the first garments she planned to complete.

Sam returned thirty minutes before the dinner hour, retiring to his room to change. He stepped into the dining room as the clock chimed out eight o'clock. Ella was waiting for him, wearing her new crepe de chine gown. He nodded his approval.

"Did you have a nice day?" she asked.

"Yes, and you?"

"Yes, but I would like to talk to you about it."

Guiding her to her chair, he saw her seated, then took his own place. Annie carried in the soup. Sam waited until she was gone before he broached the subject. "What is it you would like to discuss?"

Ella folded her hands in her lap. "Miss LaVoie says it isn't, but I feel the number of gowns you have ordered for me is extreme."

He thought a moment and shook his head. "She is correct."

"But it's so much money."

"I can afford it."

She gave him a wry look. "I assumed you could afford it or you wouldn't be buying them."

"Then, what is the problem?" Sam sipped a spoonful of soup.

"There isn't a problem. I just wanted to confirm the necessity to order so many. Is it true, what Miss LaVoie says? That I'll give insult if I wear a dress too often?"

"Yes."

"It seems like a terrible waste."

"Not really. After you are through with them, the gowns will be put to good use by some less fortunate woman." He glanced at her bowl. "Aren't you hungry?"

"Yes."

"I suggest you eat your soup before it gets cold."

Ella silently ate her soup. When her bowl was empty, she lay down her spoon. "Miss LaVoie says some women have their gowns destroyed."

"I consider it vanity to destroy a dress so no other woman will be seen in it, but it's your clothing, and you may do what you wish with it."

He seemed more interested in his soup than her concern, and his willingness to accept spiteful behavior, if it was her inclination, appalled Ella. "Well, I certainly don't wish to see perfectly good clothing destroyed! You can call it vanity, but I would call it infamy. If I had my say, I wouldn't buy a tenth of what you say I ought to in the first place."

"I will sleep better now that I know there is no danger you will spend me to the poorhouse."

Ella thought he was trifling with her, but she wasn't sure. How could she be sure when he persisted in maintaining a calm facade under every circumstance save lovemaking? Since arriving in New York, he was even worse than before. If he was harboring such suspicions, she had to know. "Do you think I married you for your money?"

"No. You married me because you believed I would be killed if you didn't."

"Yes, I know. But I don't want you thinking . . ."

He set down his spoon. "I know you are not a fortune-hunting female, and except for a brief period at the beginning of our acquaintance, it never was a consideration."

The urge to sigh her relief was great, but Ella resisted, and tried to match the tone of her response to his imperturbable deportment. "Good, because I'd never marry a man for money, and I swear I won't spend any of yours without permission."

"There is no need to seek my permission to make purchases you deem necessary for your personal comfort. That includes any redecorating of the house you would like to do."

"But the house already is so beautiful it's like something out of a picture book. Why on earth would I try to improve upon perfection?"

Annie entered with a platter of artfully arranged salmon

and a small pitcher of sauce. She cleared away the soup bowls, saw them served, and exited. While they both applied themselves to the fish, Sam picked up the conversation where they had left off.

"I'm gratified you like your new home. I want you to be comfortable here," he stated without any show of emotion. "Speaking of which, I have arranged for several candidates for your private lady's maid to arrive here beginning at nine o'clock tomorrow morning. I hope that isn't too early."

It wasn't too early. She was used to rising at dawn and had yet to break the habit. The time didn't concern her in the least, but his purpose did. "I don't need my own maid," she earnestly informed him.

"Every lady has her own maid."

"We already have more servants than I know how to deal with. What would I do with a maid whose sole purpose is to see to my whims?"

"Enjoy the luxury of having someone else wait on you," he recommended.

"But I'm used to waiting on myself."

"Ladies don't wait upon themselves."

"Then, what do they do?" she asked.

"They dress in pretty clothing, visit each other, plan and attend social affairs, and provide winsome company for their husbands at the end of the day."

"Oh."

"You do not look pleased."

"There's nothing wrong with what you say I must do. I'll do all of it, and gladly. But surely there's more that's required of me."

"No. The great advantage of money is that one can pay others to attend to the mundane chores of life. I daresay, you'll quickly get used to the idea and come to enjoy the freedom from labor as much as the other ladies of our social circle."

Ella wished she had his confidence in her ability to readily adapt to the requirements of her rich surroundings. She *would* adapt, because she was determined to do so, but she had no idea there would be so many peculiar rules. Ella pinched her lips. It seemed every time they were together, she was the topic of conversation. It made her self-conscious. "May we change the subject?" she civilly requested.

"I will be happy to as soon as you confirm or deny nine o'clock is agreeable to you for the first interview." He smiled, but the smile did not reach his eyes. "If you are uncomfortable making the decision, I can have Mrs. Potter assist you."

"I'm sure I can manage on my own," Ella asserted. "Nine o'clock will be fine."

"You won't feel too ill?"

"No. I seem to be done with the morning sickness. For the past three mornings I haven't even felt a twinge at the sight of breakfast."

"I'm pleased you're better." Another smile curved his lips, this one appearing to be genuine. "Perhaps the life of a lady is more agreeable to your system than you believe. I always thought you worked too hard."

"I didn't work harder than anyone else," Ella contended.

"Maybe not, but I'm glad you no longer have to do so."

The main course—a leg of roast mutton—arrived. Accompanying it were bowls of onions, creamed potatoes, carrots, and two vegetables Ella didn't recognize. She wasn't accustom to seeing so much variety at one meal unless a party was in progress, but she forwent comment.

Sam took a sip of his wine. "Since we have agreed to change the subject, what would you like to discuss?"

"Have you hired the detective to find your family yet?" She asked a question of sincere interest to her.

His eyes darkened, but a hint of a smile curved his lips, suggesting he regarded her interest as gratifying rather than intrusive. "Yes. He will be leaving immediately to pick up the search where I left off."

"I hope it doesn't take him long to find them."

"I share your hope. He comes highly recommended, and he gave a good impression when we met, so I do not think our hope unfounded."

Our hope. Ella liked the sound of the word. Our hope, our home, our family, it didn't feel real yet, but . . . someday . . . soon, she sent a silent prayer heavenward . . . that's the way she hoped they would both feel.

The rest of the meal passed pleasantly. After supper they both retired to the parlor to read. Though they sat in chairs on opposite sides of the fireplace and didn't speak, Ella enjoyed the quiet companionship. She also looked forward to what she knew would come when they ascended the stairs.

She and Sam might have separate bedrooms, but thus far every night since they had arrived, he slept in her bed. Of course, sleep wasn't what he had in mind when he quietly knocked on her door. Love making consumed his thoughts. Slipping under the covers, he gathered her in his arms and loved her so thoroughly, by the time they floated off into satiated slumber, she felt like the most cherished, desirable wife in the world. He never disappointed her . . . except in the morning. In the morning, he was always gone.

The next week passed in a whirlwind of activity. It took two mornings to interview all the candidates for lady's maid. Ella settled on a girl named Katie Dunphy. Though Ella was finding it difficult to accustom herself to being fussed over, Katie was working out well otherwise.

Most afternoons, Ella spent in the company of Clara *being seen*. They strolled in Central Park, shopped together, and took tea in all the best restaurants.

It wasn't hard to act the part of Clara's friend, because Clara was a genuinely nice person. Ella admired her immensely for many reasons, but most especially for her ability to accept the loss of her fiancée with such grace. Sam had said she would do so, but Ella would never have believed such self-possession possible if she hadn't witnessed it with her own eyes.

They often spoke of Sam. There was no doubt in Ella's mind, of Clara's fondness for him. She always asked how he was and what he was doing. If he came home before she had left, her angelic face lit up like a sunbeam. But she never sighed wistfully or bemoaned her fate or exhibited even a hint of bitterness. All her considerable energies were devoted to assuring the success of the coming dinner party.

Ella looked upon the dinner party with equal measures of anticipation and trepidation. So as not to steal any of Clara's thunder, Sam and she had agreed to decline all invitations until after her dinner party formally introduced them to Society as a married couple. For the same reason, they spent all their evenings at home.

Since it would be the first time she met any of her husband's friends, Ella was anxious to make a good impression. She was also determined the dinner serve the purpose Clara intended and didn't want to do anything that might thwart her ends. She would never forgive herself if she did.

But her anxiety aside, Ella was looking forward to the evening. Clara kept her constantly apprised of the details, and it promised to be a grand event, grander than anything she had ever attended. Yesterday, Miss LaVoie had brought by the gown she planned to wear, and it had proven even more stunning than she had imagined it would be. When she had shown it to Clara, Clara clapped her hands with delight.

"Tell Samuel to let you wear his mother's pearls. They will be perfect with your gown," she recommended.

"I could never ask him such a thing," Ella protested.

"Then I will," Clara announced, with a nod of her head.

The day of the dinner, Ella was so full of energy she couldn't sit still. It was hours before she needed to start getting ready, and she longed for some useful occupation to keep her from pacing the floor.

She had been behaving exactly as everyone told her to all week long. Surely, she deserved some reward.

Deciding, lady of the house or not, today she was going to help with the morning cleaning, she changed into one of her old dresses and searched out Mrs. Potter. "Where do we keep our broom?"

"In the cleaning closet, ma'am." Mrs. Potter took in her appearance with a jaundiced eye. Ella purposefully ignored it.

"Where is that?"

"Off the kitchen."

"Thank you."

Fetching the broom, Ella immediately set to work in one of the parlors. It felt good to be doing something physical; it helped her feel more like her old self; and she hummed while she swept.

"Ma'am."

Ella glanced up. The housekeeper was standing in the doorway staring at her. "Yes, Mrs. Potter."

"What are you doing?"

"I'm sweeping the parlor," Ella replied with a defiant grin.

"Yes ma'am." Mrs. Potter's expression was starched. "If the maids aren't performing their duties to your satisfaction, I will call them here at once and give them a thorough scolding, but under no circumstances are you to be doing the work yourself."

"The maids do a first-rate job, but I'm sure they'd welcome a little extra time to call their own. I'm just lending them a hand," Ella blithely responded.

"But you can't, ma'am."

"Why not?"

"You're the mistress of the house."

"That's right, I am, so I ought to be able to do as I please sometimes, and it pleases me to do something besides sit and stare at my reflection in the mirror."

"But the scandal."

"I can't believe it's scandalous for a woman to help clean her own house. Perhaps it's frowned upon, but I believe scandalous is an exaggeration. Besides, who's to know?"

"Word has a way of traveling, ma'am."

"Then close the door and say I'm not to be disturbed. Nobody but you and I will know I'm being *scandalous,* and I won't tell if you don't."

"Ma'am, this is not a matter for joking. You'll do your reputation irreparable harm if you persist in this foolishness. People will call you common."

Ella planted a hand on her hip. "But I am common."

Mrs. Potter gasped. "Never say that aloud again! There'll be the devil to pay." She snatched the broom from Ella's hand. "You are the mistress of the house and at all times must conduct yourself accordingly inside and outside these walls. The master will not be at all pleased when I tell him of this."

Unsettling the housekeeper didn't bother Ella overmuch, but unsettling her husband did. She hadn't counted on her every activity being reported to him. It annoyed her to think they might be, but she couldn't in good conscience allow her vexation to override her desire not to cause him trouble, especially today. "If it really makes you so distraught to see me sweeping, I won't do it," she acquiesced.

"Thank you, ma'am."

"You in return will not go tattling to my husband."

"Yes, ma'am."

Ella turned to leave the room.

"Ma'am."

Halting in mid stride, Ella glanced over her shoulder. "Yes, Mrs. Potter?"

"Please go upstairs and change into proper clothes before someone sees you. If you'll have Katie gather up your old things, I can have them taken to a charity box at one of the churches, so they won't be a temptation to you."

Ella sighed. "If you reckon I must."

"I do, ma'am."

Ella was greatly relieved when it was time to begin getting ready for the dinner party. She had spent most of the morning and early afternoon pacing the floors, looking for something she could do that would meet with Mrs. Potter's approval. Her offer to bake a pie was met with the same enthusiasm as sweeping the floor. A brisk walk was frowned upon. "A lady mustn't be seen out and about too early in the day," to quote the stuffy housekeeper. She filled one hour writing a second letter to her grandmother; another she attempted to fill by reading a book, but her mind would not be still and she gave up.

Katie drew a hot bath and helped Ella undress and ease herself into the scented water. The water felt wonderful, but it was difficult to enjoy its soothing effects with someone hovering over her.

"Why don't you go into the next room and lay out my clothes," Ella gently suggested.

"Yes, ma'am. I'll listen for your call so I can help you wash your hair."

When she was alone, Ella closed her eyes. She didn't need someone to help her wash her hair. She wasn't a child; she was twenty-five years old. She had fretted about most everything under the sun on the trip to New York, but being reduced to the status of helpless infant in her own home was not one of them.

She knew she would have to call Katie back when the time

came to scrub her hair, or no doubt she would ruffle the girl's feelings, but she wasn't in any hurry to do so. Perhaps a long soak was just what she needed to relax enough so that she would be able to graciously surrender herself to the overly helpful household staff.

When she finished with her bath and her hair was squeaky clean, Ella insisted on drying herself. Afterwards, she submitted herself to Katie's hands.

While Ella lay upon the bed, a slice of ice cold cucumber over each eye, Katie fluffed her hair dry. She then led Ella to the dressing table where she picked up the brush and gave all her effort to styling Ella's hair. . . .

"I've never looked better." Ella gazed in awe at her own reflection. She barely recognized the woman gazing back at her, she looked so elegant. "Thank you, Katie."

"You're welcome, ma'am." Katie bobbed a curtsey.

Ella continued to smile at her reflection.

Miss LaVoie had had to rush to finish her gown on time for the occasion, but she hadn't cut corners on quality. From the round skirt covered with pointed flounces of rose-colored faille to the pleated silk drapery of rose and green to the puffed sleeves to the green velvet trim, the gown was a delight. Her gloves reached above her elbows and were the color of fresh-butter. She wore silk stockings whose color matched the rose pink slippers upon her feet. Around her neck she wore Sam's mother's pearl necklace. The matching earrings decorated her earlobes. Katie had fashioned her hair into an intricate chignon, teasing wisps of hair into tiny curls to frame her face and dangle at the nape of her neck.

A knock at the door brought her attention round. Katie scurried to open it.

"Are you ready?" Sam queried as he stepped through the door.

"Yes," Ella replied, taking in his dark evening suit in a

sweeping gaze. Her heart fluttered. Surely, he must be the most handsome man alive.

Offering his arm, he escorted her to the waiting carriage. When they were settled in the carriage and on their way, he asked, "Are you nervous?"

"A little. Are you?"

"Yes, but we will survive the evening. Clara told me she has been schooling you on what you should and should not say?"

"Yes. All questions about our courtship are to be answered with mysterious smiles and poetic statements about the nature of true love. I'm to say absolutely nothing of my family unless asked a direct question and even then under every circumstance I'm to follow Clara's lead. She was very firm about that. She doesn't want me inadvertently saying something that might contradict her story." She took a breath and continued to outline her instructions, "Clara and I are the best of friends, and I give her much of the credit for our marriage, only I'm to say she's too modest to allow me to reveal the details. Again, she wishes to supply them herself."

Ella fingered a curl at the nape of her neck. "It's vexing to be obliged to tell half truths and outright lies. It seems that's all we've done since our marriage, and I'd hoped we were done with it," she murmured as much to herself as to him. "I don't like it."

"Neither do I, but it is necessary."

"If Clara wasn't involved . . ."

"But she is involved," Sam reminded. He couldn't explain the other reason behind his willingness to cooperate without bludgeoning his wife's unsophisticated hopes, and he was determined not to ruin her first evening out. A flicker of regret marred his varnished countenance, but he masked it with a short speech. "If this is what she wants, I will bear the protestations of my conscience without complaint."

"As will I," Ella assured him. "Clara is adamant and I haven't the heart to deny her."

The windows were ablaze with light when they arrived at Clara's family home. Though similar in size to Sam's house, the walls were sandstone and the architecture leaned heavily toward gothic.

Cedric opened the carriage door. Sam alighted and assisted Ella in doing the same. When they knocked at the front door, the butler was waiting to take Sam's hat and guide them to their host and hostesses. Clara was standing beside a middle-aged couple, Ella surmised to be her parents. On her left stood a fair-haired, nattily dressed gentleman closer to her own age. He wore a self-satisfied expression.

"Samuel, Ella, dear," Clara greeted effusively. "Ella, you have yet to have the pleasure of meeting my parents." She indicated the couple standing beside her with a sweep of her hand. "Mother, Father, this is my dearest friend, Ella of the Wyoming Singletons. I'm sure you've heard of them. Why I've heard her grandmother rivals Mrs. Astor in influence in her region of the country. Ella, these are my dear parents, Mr. and Mrs. Emmet and Isabel Harrington."

"I'm glad to meet you." Ella offered her hand.

They accepted it with only a slight hesitation.

"Have you had time to settle comfortably into your new home?" Mrs. Harrington politely queried.

"A body couldn't help but be comfortable in a house like my husband's."

"It is a lovely home. When he showed us the plans, I knew it would be perfect for Cl . . . oh dear, please pardon the slip of my tongue." Mr. Harrington blushed. "We had thought . . . but Clara has disabused us of the notion. There is no accounting for the fickle hearts of youth or the delusions of their parents. But we love our Clara anyway, don't we Isabel?"

"Of course, we do." Smiling bravely, she squeezed her husband's hand.

"There's no need to beg my pardon," Ella assured him. "I know Clara and my husband have been close friends for many years. It's I who ought to beg your pardon for distressing you by marrying without advance warning a man Clara tells me you regard almost as a son."

"We would so have liked to attend the wedding," Mrs. Harrington confirmed.

"I wish we could have invited you," Ella sweetly rendered.

"You are as charming as Clara says. I am glad for the opportunity to see for myself Samuel is in good hands. I feel I owe it to his dear departed mother." Mrs. Harrington sniffed. "Congratulations, my dear. You have married yourself a fine man.

"I told you she was wonderful," Clara brightly declared. "If ever two people were made for each other it is Samuel and Ella."

"Yes, we are," Sam added for good measure. Ella glanced at him hoping to catch a glimpse of the certitude she heard in his voice in his eyes, but they were unreadable. She suppressed a disappointed frown.

The man standing beside Clara cleared his throat.

"Oh dear, I have been neglecting you, haven't I, Mr. Livingston? How naughty of me. Ella, this is Mr. Randall Livingston, my partner for the evening. Mr. Livingston, this is Mrs. Carrigan."

"Charmed." He bowed over Ella's hand.

"I'm glad to meet you as well," Ella reciprocated.

"Mother, Father, why don't you continue to greet our guest while I take Samuel and Ella inside to meet the early arrivals," Clara suggested. Before they could give answer, she clasped Ella by the hand and towed her toward the drawing room where the other guests had gathered to await dinner.

Pausing at the threshold, Clara whispered in Ella's ear, "Pinch your cheeks and smile."

Ella complied.

Upon stepping into the drawing room, Ella was immediately aware every head had turned her way. Her smile felt rigid and her hands were icy cold. In her estimation, she had barely held body and soul together during her introduction to Clara's parents. The trusting look in their eyes made her feel wicked. It was all she could do not to fall on her knees and confess the truth. How she was going to successfully finesse the entire evening was beyond her ken.

Telling herself if she failed the test this evening, she failed Clara and Sam as well as herself, Ella called upon a reserve of inner strength and banished every defeating thought from her head. She replaced them with positive thoughts. *She was Mrs. Samuel Carrigan and proud to be so. Tonight, her friend Clara was honoring their marriage. She was dressed as elegantly as a queen. She was an intelligent woman who was capable of conversing with anyone.*

"I'm glad to meet you." Ella extended her hand to yet another couple and smiled graciously, when Clara introduced them. After the usual exchange of congratulations and social pleasantries, the inevitable question came up.

"Tell me, dear, how did you two meet?"

"I declare, we've told the tale of our romance so many times, I fear we're becoming boorish. Let me just say 'love is strong as death.' Upon laying eyes on each other, try as we might, we couldn't pull ourselves apart. Don't you agree, husband?"

"Absolutely," Sam suavely replied.

"It was like something out of a fairy tale," Clara interjected her opinion. "And to think I had a part in bringing it to pass. Why it gives me gooseflesh." She promptly ushered them on to the next couple.

When this couple made a similar inquiry Ella's eyes took on a mysterious light and she responded, " 'Love comforteth like sunshine after rain.' " Another was gifted with, " 'Better is a dinner of herbs where love is, than a stalled ox.' "

Clara raised a brow at that one, but she carried the conversation admirably.

At first opportunity, Ella whispered a brief apology for sounding more countrified than poetic. When Clara reassured her no harm had been done, Ella sighed with relief. In all honesty, every word that had left her lips this evening made her feel either like a fool or a fraud, often both, leaving her bereft of the comfort of her own powers of discernment. She was reduced to judging the effect of her words by Clara's and Sam's reactions. Besides, she was running out of quotes.

The announcement that dinner was to be served was extremely welcome. Ella knew she was to be seated between Sam and a cousin of Clara's.

Entering the dining room on Sam's arm, Ella was taken aback by the splendor of the room. Covering the center of the table the entire length a virtual garden of cut roses and orchids perfumed the air. Golden candelabras with tapered white candles gleamed in the candlelight. The table linen was snow white with intricately embroidered edges. Expensive china, crystal, and silver made up each place setting. From an adjacent room, soft music provided by a hidden orchestra floated on the air.

Sam gallantly seated her and took his place beside her.

Ella covertly surveyed the plethora of forks and glasses before her. Tomorrow, I'm going to the nearest bookstore and purchase every magazine and book on etiquette I can find, she promised herself as she was assailed by a fresh wave of anxiety.

Clara's cousin was a man in love with the sound of his own voice, and he was more than content to carry the weight of conversation. Ella listened to him with one ear, smiling and nodding politely at the appropriate times. With her other ear she listened to the other conversations going on round the table.

There were twenty couples in all. With the exception of Sam and herself, none of them were seated next to their spouses. Earlier, Clara had explained it was a social custom universally practiced by hostesses who valued harmony at their tables.

The unmarried couples in attendance were allowed to sit together. Clara, who naturally was sitting next to Mr. Livingston, was flirting with him so convincingly, Ella was positive everyone at the table must believe him a favorite beau.

Ella discreetly moved her gaze around the table, matching the names in her memory to faces. She was gratified when she remembered them all.

Most of the conversations she eavesdropped on consisted of who had done what the day before, entertainments planned for the next evening, or the latest fluctuation of the stock market and what it meant to whom. Sam was engaged in discussing the latter with the man across the table from him, a Mr. Belmont.

If her husband was displeased with the progress of the evening thus far, he gave no outward sign. He appeared perfectly comfortable among his friends. Of course, she couldn't be sure he was. She was never sure of his feelings no matter what the circumstances. Tonight, she considered his talent for masking his feeling exactly that—a talent, but when they returned home, she knew she would not be so admiring of his ability.

Because she was not required to contribute more than the occasional nod, Ella was able to relax and enjoy the meal more than she had assumed she would. By carefully observing those around her, she caught onto which glass and what piece of silver she was to use with a minimum of errors. Her wobbly confidence gradually returned.

The dinner consisted of eight courses which Mr. Harrington announced by name with great flourish as they were carried into the room. First a clear soup was served, then terrapin, followed by filet of sole. Next three entrees—filet of beef in black sauce, veal, and cold turkey—were offered with a choice of asparagus and artichoke. Some diners chose one dish over the other, but many took generous helpings of each dish. The next course was Canvasback duck. This was followed by a salad smothered in thick dressing, a cheese course, and finally Nesselrode pudding. Each dish was accompanied by wine or champagne. Between each course sorbet was served to cleanse the palate.

The dinner lasted hours, and though she took reasonable portions, by the end of the meal Ella feared she would burst her skin. How Sam contrived to keep so trim if this was the way he and his friends ate was a mystery to her.

When the pudding dishes were cleared away, Clara rose to her feet and announced the ladies would retire, so the gentlemen could enjoy their coffee and cigars. Even though Clara had warned her this would be the most taxing part of the evening, Ella gladly pushed herself away from the table.

"Mrs. Carrigan, now that we have unburdened ourselves of our husbands, we ladies can have a little tête-à-tête. I want to hear every detail of your inspiring romance," Mrs. Mabel Tarbett cooed as she seated herself next to Ella on the settee.

The ladies sitting round the parlor seconded her request.

Ella glanced about for Clara. She was dismayed to find her absent. "There isn't a lot to tell." She searched her mind for something to say that would satisfy the women and not cause complications for Clara. The ladies stared at her expectantly. Lacking brilliant inspiration, she offered a grain of truth. "My husband became lost and ended up in our town."

"What town is that?" Mrs. Baxter queried.

"Heaven."

"What a quaint name."

"Yes, I've always liked it myself. It sounds so serene."

"Is it a large city?" Miss Gerry asked.

"Quit interrupting so she may continue. I don't want to hear about some town I've never heard of. I want to hear about how she met our dear Mr. Carrigan," Mrs. Tarbett scolded.

"My sisters met him before I did. Wishing to be hospitable, they invited him to supper. After that events just seemed to be out of our control. We married each other and here we are." Ella smiled broadly rather proud of how well she had managed to stick to the truth without revealing too much.

"But what about Clara? I thought she was the one who brought you together," Mrs. Mills questioned.

"Oh, but I did." Clara swept across the room and wedged herself on the settee between Ella and Mrs. Tarbett.

Ella hadn't seen Clara reenter the room, and she breathed a sigh of relief when Clara proceeded to answer the question for her.

"Ella and I have been friends of the pen for years. When she wrote me telling me she had made the acquaintance of a Mr. Samuel Carrigan and hinted at her fondness for him, I instantly knew fate had intervened to bring my two dearest friends together. I wrote her back that very day promising my friend the object of her affection was worthy of her regard and expressing my absolute delight should they decide to wed which I encouraged them to do." She lowered her eyelashes and grinned sheepishly. "Naturally, my motives were not entirely unselfish. I didn't like Ella living so far away, and I knew if she married Mr. Carrigan she would be coming to the city to live near me."

Clara leaned close, whispering in Ella's ear, "Sorry to have deserted you, but I absolutely *had* to visit the water closet," before she continued, "Since Samuel has always been like a brother to me, now I feel as though I have a sister as well."

"But Clara, we thought you and Mr. Carrigan were about to announce your engagement," Miss Cutting spoke her thoughts aloud.

A nervous twitter flowed round the parlor.

"Been listening to the gossips again, haven't you, Melissa? You know our families have been friends for years. Though I love Samuel dearly," Clara brought her hand to her bosom and giggled gleefully, *"Me marry him?* Never in a million years. We are suited to be friends. We would never suit as man and wife. We know each other too well. Ella, we must be sure to tell Samuel what Miss Cutting said to me. I'm sure he will be as amused as I."

"Oh, please don't tell him," Miss Cutting pleaded.

"But it's so hilarious. I just know he would . . ."

"Is your grandmother really as influential as Mrs. Astor?" Mrs. Harrington interrupted her daughter. "All my life I have dreamed of being invited to one of her dinner parties."

"Having never made Mrs. Astor's acquaintance, I can't say," Ella chose her words carefully. "But I can say with complete confidence my grandmother wouldn't hesitate to invite you to her table. She loves company, and I'm sure she would love you."

"Clara tells us your family achieved its social eminence and made its vast fortune by speculating on cattle," Mrs. Knickerbocker commented.

Ella struggled not to appear startled. "Yes."

"Did you have a large wedding?" Miss Gerry asked.

"Almost everyone in town attended," Ella confirmed.

"It doesn't quite seem proper with his mother so recently laid to rest," Mrs. Tarbett opined.

"Mrs. Tarbett, you are so old-fashioned," Clara accused.

"They fell madly in love. Did you expect him to leave her in Wyoming and send for her after some arbitrary time requirement had elapsed? I for one am glad he has someone to comfort him in his hour of distress, and you should be, too!"

"Now, Clara, I'm sure Mrs. Tarbett didn't mean to give offense," Mrs. Harrington soothed. "There is no need to raise your voice."

"I'm sorry, Mother, but when someone implies my two dearest friends . . . well, I just can't help coming to their defense."

"Do you have connections in the East, dear?"

"England," Clara proclaimed. "Ella's great uncle is a baron."

Ella kept her spine stiff and her hands folded on her lap as she continued to listen to the conversation. Clara was clearly more adept than her at parrying questions, and she was more than happy to abdicate the task to her.

Having plenty of pride herself, Ella understood Clara's need to foster the belief she was not a jilted lover, and she was willing to play along because in her mind this was a case of the ends justifying the means. . . . But pretending her family was something it was not was a different matter. Clara hadn't told her she intended to represent her as coming from a rich, socially prominent family. From some of Mrs. Potter's comments, she could guess why Clara might believe she was doing her a favor, but Ella didn't view it as such. However, she didn't dare correct the misrepresentation, or she would expose Clara.

The longer the evening wore on the more uncomfortable Ella became with the whole situation. She couldn't help but believe this a poor way to begin her acquaintance with Sam's friends. But she had promised Clara. She couldn't go back on her word. As she continued to smile and lend support to Clara's fabrications when required, Ella began to wonder how many lies a body could tell before they endangered their immortal soul.

By her reckoning she and Clara had already passed over the line, and it was only half past eleven o'clock.

Twenty-one

The evening was a disaster, and the worst part was Ella had no idea how badly it had gone. It wasn't her fault. It had been doomed from the start.

Sam sat at his desk in his office—*hiding*. There was no better word for his cowardly retreat to his office, and he wasn't going to coddle himself with soothing words. He hadn't told his wife the unpleasant truth he had known before they left Wyoming, and he didn't want to tell her now.

Ella would never be accepted.

He had agreed to the dinner party last evening, because his wife's introduction to society was unavoidable, and because he believed the evening would benefit Clara. He had also hoped, against reason, it might be of benefit to Ella.

He had told her he intended to be a proper husband and a good father and he had meant every word. Unfortunately, at the moment, he was at a loss as to how to deliver on his promise. Ella truly was a remarkable woman, and the more time he spent in her company the less resentment he felt about the boorish way they were brought together. She was his intellectual equal. She was warm-hearted, generous, sweet-natured. It was fun to watch her eyes grow wide with amazement when she was confronted by new sights and experiences. A man could never hope to find a woman more able to set his loins on fire *and* with genuine enthusiasm gift him with the lusty remedy.

She would soon be giving him another gift as well—a son or daughter. He was pleased about that, far more pleased than logic dictated he should be. In part, his feelings of pleasure arose from a masculine pride in his own creative abilities. In part, he knew his emotions stemmed from a need to give to his own child what he himself had been denied. But it was more than that. He couldn't put a name to it, but the feeling was undeniably there.

He raked his fingers through his hair as his thoughts returned to Ella. *His wife.*

She really had done quite well last night, and he was proud of her, but she hadn't done so well she could scale the restrictive wall New York Society erected around itself. It wasn't the fabrications they had told that would be her undoing. It was the truths. Too many truths had passed their lips. It was inevitable they would. Refusing the information would have caused immediate harm; whereas, presenting it in a modified form gained them short term advantages. Clara had given him a detailed account of what had occurred in the parlor. It didn't help to know even if all of them had remained mute as stones, the end result would be the same or worse.

Armed with a maiden name, the name of his wife's home town, and her family's connection to cattle, it was only a matter of time before some bored busybody investigated and discovered Ella lacked the three essential qualities necessary for entrance into his elite circle of friends: birth, background, and breeding.

"The Three Bs" they were called. Already there were whisperings. No amount of money could compensate for their absence, and despite the generous fantasy Clara promoted on Ella's behalf, it would also be discovered Ella's family lacked wealth as well as a desirable family tree. She was doubly condemned.

It wasn't fair, but it was the way things had been for as

long as he had been alive. He had never questioned the system before because its strictures hadn't effected him. Now, it made him angry . . . and ashamed by his silent consent he had sanctioned the practice of excluding those deemed less than worthy.

His entrance into Society had been gained through his great grandfathers' names and wealth. If he had made his own money, he wouldn't be welcome either. The truth was: he was looked upon as a bit of an eccentric because he chose to spend his days increasing his inherited wealth rather than riding his horse in the park or sitting in his club. But he was allowed to be a little eccentric because he was born into his place in Society.

Ella had no such advantage. She was an outsider. She would always be an outsider. How was he suppose to tell her that? How could he tell a proud woman like Ella the elegant, urbane life she craved would forever be out of her reach?

Sam grit his teeth. He wasn't going to tell her. Hadn't he made that decision on the train trip home? He wasn't going to tell her—not until he absolutely had to do so, not until he had something worthy to offer her in exchange for her girlhood dreams.

His income wasn't dependent on the social acceptance of his wife, or himself for that matter. He had several options, but none he was able to embrace with genuine enthusiasm at the moment. For one thing, he was waiting to see what came of finding his brothers, if they could be found. For another, he was still mourning the loss of the well-ordered, uncomplicated life he had once known. Even though he was not so certain he admired it any more, it was comfortingly familiar. He hadn't had to lay awake at night wondering if he was saying and doing the right thing. He hadn't had a wife and baby to worry about.

At times, he resented the burden. Other times, he was half

glad his life had taken this unexpected turn. But most of the time, he didn't know what he felt about anything or anyone.

Clara was numbered among those who confused his emotions. Ella was accurate when she said a person couldn't turn off their feelings for someone like turning off water with a spigot. He still loved her, but the love he felt was different than the emotion he had carried in his heart when he left for Wyoming. He cared for her. He wanted her to be happy. But . . .

Because he couldn't neatly sort them out, he banished his thoughts of Clara and returned his thoughts to Ella and how best to protect her from harsh reality. Sam raked his hand through his hair again.

There would be plenty of invitations for a month or two. He could count on curiosity to overcome suspicion at least that long. He could take her to the symphony, the theater, every place she longed to see. With any luck, by the time her family background was revealed, her pregnant state already would have become obvious, forcing her to enter her period of confinement, and he could further shield her. Then the baby's arrival would keep her preoccupied . . .

By the time the baby had arrived, he would have come to a decision regarding their future. Until then, he would provide her as much entertainment as he could while he could. The more he thought about it, the more Sam was convinced this was the kindest course.

She was almost content, Ella concluded, when she had time to think about it, which wasn't often these past two months. Even when she had the time to sit and contemplate her new life, she was invariably too exhausted to make the effort.

Since the night of Clara's dinner party, they never spent an evening at home. The first night, Sam took her to dinner at

Delmonico's and to hear the New York Philharmonic play. The next, they attended a program put on by the Oratorio Society. By the third, they were receiving a stack of invitations every day.

Ella spent part of each morning sorting and answering them. Sam gave her leave to choose which affairs they would attend when two occurred on the same night. She made her decisions with care, never choosing one family over another too often lest she hurt someone's feelings.

Afternoons Ella spent driving in Central Park with Clara, shopping, and attending teas. Clara and Mrs. Potter helped her arrange two teas of her own, and though they weren't quite as well attended as some she had gone to, she wasn't overly disappointed.

On afternoons she was free from the demands of social obligations, Cedric drove her all about town on delightful exploratory expeditions. Some days she just liked to lean back upon the carriage seat and gaze upon the endless variety of people and buildings they rolled past. Other days she had a specific destination in mind. Two of her favorites were Robert Carter & Brothers Bookstore and the Metropolitan Museum of Art. She could happily wile away hours at both establishments.

Evenings, Sam and she attended dinner parties, soirees, musicales. On the rare night they didn't have an invitation to a private home, they frequented the Metropolitan Opera or dined out at any one of a dozen elegant restaurants. Ella was surprised to learn that theater was considered beneath the notice of the wealthy class, but her husband graciously escorted her to the Fifth Avenue, the Park, and the Casino theaters whenever one of their offerings caught her fancy.

Yes, she was almost content, but not entirely. The reasons were many and varied. None of them were solid reasons; rather, they were vague feelings of disquiet. Whole weeks passed that Ella managed to convince herself, she was inventing trouble that wasn't there.

Though she truly enjoyed all the gay parties and elegant evenings out on the town, there was an emptiness of purpose in her life. She was used to doing productive work. Now, she was forbidden to lift a finger. All she did all day was answer invitations and dress for one affair or another. Sam had advised her to savor the luxury of being rich enough to be idle, but her nature was just too practical to allow her to do so with any amount of satisfaction.

Then, there were her husband's friends.

Ella couldn't shake the feeling she was the focus of inordinate and not always benevolent interest at every social function they attended. Ofttimes, the conversations she had with her fellow guests struck her as thinly disguised interrogations. She was treated politely, and she certainly didn't lack for invitations, but it seemed to her the warmth of sincere friendship was missing in all her relationships with her new acquaintances with the exception of Clara . . . and Clara was the last person in New York City Ella would have thought would be her friend.

Though she found Clara a warm, witty, and thoroughly agreeable human being, and Clara never said or did anything the least bit untoward concerning her husband, it bothered Ella to have Sam's ex-fiancée be so frequent a visitor at their home. She also was present at every social affair they attended. It was a constant reminder to her that she was not her husband's first choice or any choice at all. It was a constant reminder she was living the life that ought to have been Clara's.

But how could she say anything? She couldn't, unless she was willing to be mean-spirited.

Whenever she thought of Clara, Ella couldn't help but reflect upon the lies she had told and still preserved at Clara and her husband's bidding. Pretending Clara had a hand in bringing Sam and her together didn't bother her that much. She certainly wasn't eager to share how they really had come to be married, and it eased her conscience concerning Clara to do this small thing for her. But lying about her family seemed terribly wrong, and the longer she did it, the worse she felt.

It probably had more than a little to do with why she was having such difficulty feeling accepted by her husband's friends. Honesty, after all, was the foundation of true friendship. However, whenever she hinted it might be prudent to gently correct the misrepresentations concerning her family, she met which such forceful opposition from both Clara and her husband, Ella invariably abandoned the idea.

It was Wednesday and as yet not a single invitation had arrived for the following week. Rather than feeling disappointed, Ella was relieved. She was starting to worry about her husband.

She might have nothing to do all day but dress for the next social occasion, but he worked long hours everyday but Sunday at his office. Though they went out every night at his insistence, he didn't appear to be having all that much fun. Oddly, the attention he paid her as he escorted her here, there, and everywhere had an urgent undertone, as if he was working against some unseen deadline. When she questioned him about it, he declared she was imagining things and made jokes about the frantic pace of city life.

But she knew she wasn't imagining things. At night, when they made love, she could feel the knots in the muscles of his neck and shoulders.

More than once she had suggested they stay home so he could rest, but he would hear none of it. Now, he would have to stay home, at least a few nights. . . .

"Ma'am, Mr. Carrigan would like to see you in the library." Annie delivered the message to Ella's room where she was listening to Katie's suggestions for how she should wear her hair at the dinner party they were to attend at the Baxter home this evening.

Glancing toward the window, Ella confirmed it was still mid afternoon. "He's home already?" she voiced her surprise.

"Yes, ma'am, and he'd like to see you in the library as soon as it's convenient."

"I'll go to him at once."

When she entered the library, Ella immediately noticed the tension in the room. Her husband sat behind his desk, looking as somber as a pallbearer. "Is something wrong?"

"No."

It obviously was. It was also obvious she would have to pry the information out of him. It was discouraging but not unexpected. "You haven't heard bad news from the detective you hired to find your family?" Ella ventured a guess.

"No. The last telegram I received from him was a week ago and nothing significant has changed."

"Are you ill?"

"No."

"Have I done something wrong?"

"No."

"Then, what is it?"

He cleared his throat and laced his fingers together. "Ella, I know you won't be pleased to hear it since you take such delight in the variety of experiences available to you now that you reside in a city, but it is time for you to enter your period of confinement. Miss LaVoie may be a genius with a needle, but even she cannot hide your condition any longer."

Thoroughly perplexed, Ella asked, "My time of confinement?"

"Yes." Sam nodded. "It is considered in poor taste for a

woman who is with child to be out and about town once the evidence of her condition cannot be disguised."

Her eyes widened. "Why?"

"It is seen as an unwelcome reminder of the less than dignified activity that got her in her condition in the first place."

"But I'm a married woman. Surely, all married couples . . ."

"I'm sure they do else there would be no children in the world, but that is not the issue. The issue is one of good taste and good taste dictates you are not seen in public until after the baby is born," he patiently explained.

"I'm not to go out at all?"

"I'm afraid not."

In all her life Ella had never heard anything so ridiculous, but from his demeanor she knew he was absolutely serious. Now that he mentioned this new rule she was expected to follow, she realized she *hadn't* seen a single pregnant woman at any of the social affairs they attended. City customs were strange, indeed.

Though she was loath to do so, Ella knew she had no choice but to acquiesce with as much grace as she could muster. "When is this confinement to begin?"

"Immediately."

She took a step back. "What about the Baxter's dinner party tonight?"

"I have already sent our regrets," he informed her. "The other invitations you have already accepted have been taken care of as well."

Twenty-two

Confinement. After three long months of being closeted within the walls of her own home, Ella thought *imprisonment* a far more accurate word.

Sam had meant it quite literally when he said she was not to be seen in public. She hadn't been allowed to step so much as a big toe outside the front door.

It was disappointing and depressing. The holiday season had come and gone, and she had had to sit at her window and watch the world make merry while she celebrated quietly and alone.

Occasionally, Clara came to see her, and Miss LaVoie stopped by every few weeks to let out the seams in the gowns she had made to see her through her pregnancy, but no one else ever came to call. Ella had had a difficult enough time accepting decorum dictating she wasn't to be seen outside her own door. Accepting that no one was permitted to visit her was even more difficult, but her husband said such was the case. Clara supported his opinion, explaining the only reason she was allowed to bend the rules was because she was a close family friend.

Ella was persuaded the entire population of New York City thought being with child synonymous with some grave infectious disease. Not only was the world sheltered from her expanding figure, she was sheltered from the world. She wasn't even permitted to read the daily newspapers lest some bit of news unbalance her vulnerable constitution. It was a lot of crock as far as she was concerned, and she told her husband so. Voicing her opinion, gained herself nothing. Neither had bribing the servants to buy her a newspaper and sneak it into the house. She had only succeeded in making Sam furious with her.

Each day, Ella grew more and more restless. She had absolutely nothing to do.

She sent Katie out to purchase fabric, notions, and yarn so she could make her baby's wardrobe. That kept her occupied a few weeks, but she couldn't keep making clothing day and night. Already, she had sewn and knitted her baby twice as many clothes at it would need.

Each day, she read until her eyes began to burn with fatigue.

Lately, she had taken to stealing a mop and feather duster from the closet and slipping upstairs. Mrs. Potter always found her out. Ella was convinced the housekeeper had a set of eyes in every room of the house. A lecture on the proper conduct of a lady inevitably ensued. This was followed with a scolding admonition that she must vigilantly guard her health now that she was in a delicate condition. When she argued with the housekeeper, maintaining that the secret of her affinity for housework need never leave the room in which they stood and that her health had never been better, Mrs. Potter threatened to report her sedition to her husband. Since Ella didn't want Sam informed she wasn't cooperating as a proper wife should, Mrs. Potter always won their argument.

The results were the same when she attempted to help out in the kitchen. Though they looked nothing alike and were different ages, Ella was half convinced Mrs. Svensen, their cook, and Mrs. Potter were twin sisters so alike were they in their stiff-necked refusal to let her make herself useful.

The forced inactivity was driving her to distraction, but the feeling of not being needed was even more insufferable. And she wasn't needed. Not a soul in the house needed her, including her husband.

More often than not, he spent long hours at his office. He was usually home by eight o'clock, but some evenings he stayed out so late she fell asleep before he came home. Even when he was home, he was inclined to shut himself away in his library, politely hinting he preferred not to be disturbed.

It was partly her fault, she knew. He was avoiding her. She talked too much, or rather she asked too many questions. She didn't mean to annoy him, but if convention forbid her to have a life of her own while she was with child, she desperately desired to be included in the outside world through detailed accounts of *his* day. Even if she was allowed to leave the house, she would want him to share his thoughts with her. A husband and wife were suppose to share their thoughts. How else could they grow closer?

They couldn't.

He no longer visited her bedroom as frequently as he used to which frustrated her as well. It was the one aspect of her marriage, she had never had to worry about. Now, she was worried, and more than a little. She wasn't sure if her burgeoning figure made her less attractive to him or he was simply growing bored with her.

When she screwed up her courage to ask him, he claimed the only reason for his inattentiveness was he didn't wish to cause her any physical discomfort. Ella didn't believe him. There was something more he wasn't saying. It was the same something that made his shoulders sag and his brows pinch whenever he thought he was alone.

If he only would talk to her . . . *honestly.* But he wouldn't. He didn't want to share his innermost feelings with her. Instead, he pasted a hollow smile upon his face and banally asserted all was well with him.

Ella was not so adept at putting on a brave face as he.

Every day her heart felt heavier; every day another chunk of the fragile hope—given time—they could build a good marriage was chipped away. Her once rosy cheeks were now pale. Her eyes lost their sparkle. She gave up trying to smile altogether.

The only way Sam knew to protect his wife from discovering the truth from which he sought to shield her was to avoid her. She was too keen witted for her own good. He lived in constant fear she would see through his mask of false cheer, or read the truth in his eyes, or one of her many questions would cause a disastrous slip of his tongue.

It was exhausting being ever vigilant *and lonely,* but he could see no help for it. A proper husband protected his wife and he had promised he would be a proper husband.

He missed the quiet evenings they had once spent together. He missed making love. But he didn't trust himself to keep his guard up while engaged in so intimate an activity. Occasionally, carnal urges overwhelmed reason, but the risk he took was enormous. Afterwards, he always felt like a selfish lout for putting his own needs above the need to protect his wife.

He knew he would persevere, because having studied the situation from every possible angle he felt he had no better option, but he fervently wished circumstances allowed him some other choice.

"I can't stand to see you looking so downcast," Clara grimly announced, after she had been trying with little success to engage Ella in cheerful conversations about nothing in particular for over an hour. "I don't care what Samuel says. I think you should be told."

That Sam and Clara were having private discussions concerning her startled Ella, but she masked her dismay behind quizzical mien. "Told what?"

"The truth."

Those two words, following on the heels of Clara's first disclosure, filled Ella with such foreboding, she felt a tremor shudder through her body. "What truth, Clara?" she asked softly.

"I want you to know I did everything I could for as long as I could, but even I cannot work miracles. As it is, I'm surprised we managed to pull it off for as long as we did. I should have known Ernest and Mabel Tarbett would be the spoilsports. I swear, I shall never invite either of them to any affair I give for as long as I live."

Ella gave up all pretense of composure. "Clara, please, if you're trying to break whatever this awful truth you have to tell me gently to spare my feelings, it is having the opposite effect. Just say it and get it over with."

"Please understand I am telling you this for your own good, and Samuel's good. His happiness is very important to me." She hesitated. Leaning close, she confided, "Your confinement is a ruse."

"What!"

"Oh, I'm not saying a lady in your condition is free to go where she will. She isn't. What I'm saying is: Samuel has been using your confinement to protect you from the knowledge Society considers you a Shoddy."

She had overheard the term before, mentioned in connection with other names in conversations in which she was not included. At the time, Ella hadn't paid attention. Now, she wished she had. The word didn't conjure pleasant mental images. "What is a Shoddy?"

"An unworthy, a social climber, to be blunt—a poison personage," Clara explained. "It was inevitable they would find out you are nothing but an ordinary farm girl.

Ella cringed. "I knew I ought to have told the truth about

my family from the beginning. I don't blame them for being furious with me."

Clara raised her brows. "If you had told the truth from the beginning, then you would have been an outcast from the beginning, and think of all the gay parties you would have missed."

Ella found Clara's words difficult to credit, but Clara had met her gaze steadily and with eyes full of compassion. "Are you saying just because my family isn't rich there was never any chance of my husband's friends accepting me?"

"Yes and no. Money is vital, but a blue bloodline is even more so. You, unfortunately, cannot lay claim to either essential, and Samuel marrying you did not confer his stature to you. Neither you nor your children will ever be countenanced. Possibly after you are long dead and forgotten, your grandchildren—if they marry wisely—will be, but I can't even say that for certain."

"There must be something I can do," Ella numbly stated.

"No. You could be the most charming woman in the world and it would make no difference. Mixed marriages cannot be condoned else Society would soon be overrun with common people and we would lose our claim to privilege. We must protect ourselves or cease to exist."

"But you're my friend." It was more question than statement.

"Privately, yes, but publicly, no. Publicly, I had to distance myself as soon as the truth became known. I was willing to sponsor you for a time for Samuel's sake and I do like you. Too, I enjoy thumbing my nose at Society on occasion, but I am no fool. I have had to tell everyone you deceived me about your family's social standing."

"Why didn't Sam tell me?"

"He wanted to protect you for as long as possible." Clara sighed. "Men are such silly creatures. They believe women the weaker sex, so they go out of their way to protect us from matters we can invariably handle far better ourselves. Person- ally, I think he should have told you the truth from the be- ginning. You are an intelligent woman. Think how much better you could have played the game if you had known the rules, and you wouldn't be so long-faced now because knowing the truth all along would have afforded you the opportunity to deal with it more effectively."

"He was trying to protect me?" Ella was still too stunned to muster more than a sentence at a time.

"Yes. He planned to tell you after the baby is born."

"Not till then?"

"That is what he told me. Why do you think he won't allow any newspapers in the house?"

Ella's eyes widened in horror. "It's in the newspapers?"

"Of course. There is nothing our local journalists like to report more than a juicy Society scandal. When the truth was first uncovered, every paper in town ran the story with weekly updates. They dropped the story when it became old news, but after today . . ."

The dread filling Ella's chest swelled. "What happened to- day?"

"There was a fresh story. Someone, and I suspect it is the Tarbetts again, took it upon themselves to hire a detective to investigate you more thoroughly. Their initial information was gleaned courtesy of a cousin who happened to be traveling through Wyoming on his way to San Francisco and was per- suaded to stop a day or two and make inquiries into your family's fortune. He discovered your lack of wealth and breed- ing. Regrettably, the detective also discovered the circum- stances surrounding your marriage."

Ella covered her face with one hand. The other she lay protectively over her belly. "And the details were printed in all the papers?"

"All but a handful of the less prominent rags."

She didn't want to know, but she had to ask. "What did they say about me?"

"I'm afraid they painted you quite the villainess," Clara unhappily reported.

"What about Sam?"

"They were kinder to him. Some cutting things were printed about his powers of discernment, but mostly he is portrayed as an innocent. The most popular explanation for his willingness to stay married to you is he was suffering from a crushing grief for his mother and unable to think clearly. His sin is regarded as forgivable. Yours is not." Though she was brutally honest, Clara plainly took no joy in being the bearer of bad news. She touched Ella's hand. "But that is of little consequence to you. You were already regarded as an undesirable."

The numbness in her limbs was gradually giving way to rigidness as Ella compelled herself to ask the necessary questions. "And you?"

"If I am mentioned at all, I am just a footnote. I have been seen laughing gaily on the arms of so many different men, I am regarded as a family friend of the Carrigans, no more."

"I'm glad of that at least."

"So am I," Clara declared with utter sincerity.

It was difficult to think with so many emotions assailing her at once. Ella was grateful to know the truth, but she was also angry, hurt, confused, frustrated, and worried. Clara's revelation explained a lot and at the same time crowded her head with questions. She forced herself to focus her thoughts. "I want you to tell me what all this means for my husband."

"He is no longer invited into the homes of the elite, of course. I didn't think it my place to ask him how it is effecting his business dealings, but it can't be doing him any good. I'm sure you have noticed how haggard he looks lately."

"Yes, I have."

"Well, that is why I told you the truth. You don't look any

better than him, and if a person is going to be miserable, they may as well be miserable for the right reasons. My hope is now that you know the truth, you will be able to help Samuel."

"What can I do?"

"I don't know, but something must be done. You're his wife. He needs someone to share his burden."

"Why didn't you tell me about this?" Ella greeted Sam at the door, a stack of newspapers in hand. His lips thinned and paled.

"Who gave you these?" he demanded.

Her tone remained high-pitched. "That's not important. Why you kept me ignorant is."

Sam snatched the newspapers out of her hands. Gently but firmly grabbing her by the elbow, he ushered her into the library and closed the door behind them. Discarding all but one of the newspapers on the top of his desk, he stared at her disgruntled face a long moment before he spoke. "I can understand why you are upset, and I'm sorry you found out. I'm sure this is a terrible blow. It was my intention to keep the news from you until after the baby was born."

"So I heard."

"From whom?"

Ella ignored his question. "I'm still waiting to hear why you didn't tell me. Apparently, you aren't sorry for that. You're only sorry I found out."

"No, I am not sorry I didn't tell you," Sam confirmed. "What good would it have done? None at all. As your husband, it is my duty to protect you from as many of the unpleasantries of life as I am able. I was able to protect you from this, at least I was able to until some unknown malefactor interfered." He twisted the newspaper tightly, as if he wished it was someone's neck. "Which ever of my servants let this trash into the house shall be punished severely, I can assure you. If you will not tell me who did it, and I cannot ferret out the Judas, I shall fire the entire staff."

"No one on the staff is to blame. If you must know, I induced Clara to smuggle it into the house."

His jaw went slack. "Clara?"

"Yes, she figured I had a right to know what's been going on. I agree with her completely, so please don't hold it against her. After she told me, I convinced her to buy me the newspapers, so I could read the truth myself."

"What good does knowing do you?" Sam protested. "There is nothing I can do to improve the situation at the moment."

"It is my understanding there *is* no remedy. That before I even stepped foot in New York my fate amongst your friends was sealed."

He grimaced. "All problems have a remedy. Some just take longer to divine than others. For instance one of the remedies I am contemplating is moving to another city, one with less rigorous requirements for entrance into Society."

"But what about your business?"

"It may not be as convenient, but I can conduct it profitably elsewhere."

"Your beautiful home?" she pressed.

"I will build another."

"And your friends?"

"If the people I used to call my friends are not willing to accept my wife in their midst, then I can no longer consider them my friends."

"I don't want to come between you and your friends." Ella could feel her eyes welling with tears, and she crossly blinked them back. He lifted a hand to console her. She stepped out of reach.

"I just told you I no longer consider them friends."

"But they *are*. If I hadn't come here, you would still regard them as such."

"Probably," he reluctantly admitted. "It isn't you personally they abhor. It is what you represent."

"I have committed the sin of being born of common stock." Ella supplied the words he would not.

"Yes."

"I can't change what I am, even if I wanted to, which I don't. I love my family. I'm proud of my ancestors. They took risks, they worked hard, most of them died poor, but they were good people. There is no shame in that."

"No, there isn't." He twisted the paper in his hand even tighter. "But I cannot reorganize Society to suit your democratic vision, and I *have* tried. My efforts have been met with nothing but shock and derision. . . . So, I must come up with some other, less than ideal solution."

"And it didn't occur to you I ought to be a part of finding this solution?"

He refused to meet her penetrating gaze. "It occurred to me, but I discarded the notion. It is my responsibility."

"But . . ."

"It is my responsibility," he repeated. "It isn't good for you to distress yourself. If you will not think of yourself, think of the baby. Let us not speak of it again until I can offer you a satisfactory answer to our dilemma."

"But . . ."

"I am a man who prefers to keep his own counsel," he interrupted her again, his voice and expression stern. "We will not speak of it again."

Sam watched his wife exit the library, her shoulders stiff and her head held high. The self-possessed expression he had pasted on his own face crumpled the moment she closed the door behind her.

He knew he hadn't managed the encounter well, but other than keeping a tighter control on his temper, he had no idea how he could have handled it differently.

Clara had no right to tell Ella about her rejection by Society. He had specifically forbidden her to do so. He knew she hadn't revealed the truth to Ella out of spite. Not only had she forgiven him for marrying Ella and not her, she said she was glad he had, and he believed her. They had known each other too long and too well to be able to deceive each other. Both Clara and he had come to realize the affection they shared for each other was not what they had once thought it was. They were lucky not to have made the mistake of marrying each other. So why had she done it?

The only reason that came to mind caused Sam to clench his teeth to steel his churning emotions. Clara was a keen observer of the foibles of her fellow man. She was probably as aware as he of his inadequacies as a husband.

Though his efforts to shield Ella from the ugly truth had been successful in the sense he had saved Ella the hurt of knowing her dreams of living a gay, cultured life in New York City were not to be, thus far he was proving a total failure at producing an acceptable substitute. Not that he wasn't trying. He was spending long hours at his office, pursuing dozens of different possibilities for their future.

He was determined to succeed not so much for his own sake but for Ella's. She deserved the best life could offer. Sam dropped his head into his hands.

Unfortunately, he knew he wasn't giving her the best. Here she was being a near perfect wife, and he had nothing to offer in return except his sincere desire to make her happy.

The twist and turns his well-ordered life had taken since the day he had ridden into the town of Heaven may have made a chaos of his life and left him groping in a darkness of frustration and indecision, but there was one thing of which he was certain. Despite everything, he had no regrets concerning their marriage. He was glad Ella was his wife and was soon to be the mother of his child.

He wanted Ella to feel the same, and the only way he knew how to do that was to provide for her comfort and protect her from the cruelties of an unfair world.

He considered it not only his duty but an honor. An honor, at present, he didn't feel he deserved, but one of which he was desperate to prove himself worthy.

Twenty-three

After her conversation with her husband, Ella shut herself away in her room, and she didn't come down to breakfast the next morning. She hadn't handled telling him she knew about the newspaper articles, and what they meant, well at all. She shouldn't have reacted with anger. But she was angry. He ought to have told her.

He must think her a sorry excuse for a friend if he didn't think he could share his troubles with her, and she'd thought their relationship had progressed enough that her husband at least regarded her as his friend. Her eyes flashed with fiery sparks of green and gold. What more did he expect of her that she wasn't already doing? She was trying in every way she knew how to be what she thought he wanted her to be!

Ella spent all of the morning and half the afternoon wallowing in frustration and self-pity. By then she had had more than enough.

Since she was already a social outcast, Ella could see no reason she shouldn't do exactly as she pleased. It didn't please her to be shut up in the house. She needed to think and she thought best on her feet.

Ignoring the protestations of the household staff and Mrs. Potter's threats to tell her husband, Ella pulled on her cloak and marched out the door. Her destination was Central Park. It was the closest thing in New York City to the wilds of Wyoming.

It felt liberating to be surrounded by trees, breathe fresh air, and exercise the stiffness from her limbs. It helped her feel more like her old self, and she hadn't felt like her old self for so long she had almost forgotten who she was. For too long she had let herself languish under the thumb of others. Her husband, Clara, Mrs. Potter, Mrs. Svensen, Katie, Miss LaVoie, everyone she met had been telling her what to do ever since she arrived in New York.

And what good had it done? None at all that she could see. It was past time she started listening to herself and doing what she thought was best.

Ella judged it good advice she gave herself except for one small hitch. She hadn't the slightest idea what she ought to do and even less what she wanted to do. Oh, she knew what she wanted. She wanted Sam to love her. She wanted him to respect her. She wanted him to be more like the man she had known and come to love in Wyoming. In Wyoming they had worked together to solve their problems. Working together hadn't done them a whole lot of good, but it was better than his refusal to discuss the mess they were in now with her.

He had said he was a man who preferred to keep his own counsel, but she noticed he didn't have any objections to discussing their situation with Clara. That hurt. It hurt a lot. She didn't believe he was betraying his marriage vows. He wasn't that sort of man, and Clara wasn't that sort of woman. She only knew he and Clara shared a congenial intimacy they did not.

Clara didn't seem to have any trouble telling him what she thought; whereas, she choked on every word if she tried to discuss something important with him. Most times she didn't even try. She was too reluctant to distress him.

The only subjects Sam and she were able to discuss with any degree of comfort were impersonal—politics, a favorite book, the merits of the lastest invention. These conversations satisfied the mind but not the heart.

"Look, there she is!"

The words were spoken in a loud whisper. They jarred Ella out of her thoughts. Looking up, she recognized Mabel Tarbett and Eunice Baxter coming her way down the path. Mrs. Tarbett was pointing at her.

"Can you believe her gall? Walking in *our* park, as if she had a perfect right to be here," Mrs. Baxter hissed. The two women lifted their chins and their skirts and made a wide circle as they hurried passed her.

Ella scowled and raised her own chin a notch. This was a public park and she had as much right to be here as they did, she argued with herself. She accelerated her pace to discharge her vexation and felt better.

It wasn't long, however, before two more women she recognized appeared on the path. Upon spying her, they presented their backs, marching off in the same direction they had come.

Ten minutes later, Miss Melissa Cutting and her cousin Candice came strolling her way. "Why she's as big as a horse," Candice proclaimed. "I bet she's carrying twins. Mother always said *her kind* make good breeders."

It was the same all afternoon. Every time she passed a person she knew, Ella was met by cold stares, spiteful remarks, the broadside of a back, or a combination of all three. Clara clearly had not been exaggerating when she said she was a "poison personage."

Ella knew matters were bad, but she hadn't realized they were this bad. Still, she refused to be intimidated. She needed a walk and a walk she would have.

Against the well-meant advice of her husband, Clara, and every servant in the house, resentment at the injustice being done her kept Ella going to the park every afternoon for a week. It sustained her halfway through the next. By then, constantly being subjected to glares and icy comments had become too wearing on her nerves, and she took to walking in the early morning hours before anyone who knew her was out and about.

It wasn't long before she learned ordinary citizens read the Society columns with avid interest and were every bit as inclined to point and stare. Ella bravely bore up under the disapproving public eye, but she took no pleasure in her daily walks. Only her stubborn pride kept her from retreating to the shelter of her house.

If Singletons were born to be happy, then she had defied her birthright. Ella wanted to go home.

She needed Grandma Jo. She needed her sisters. She needed the people of Heaven.

The only bright spots in the relentlessly dull and lonely days she endured were when a letter arrived from her family or friends.

All her life she had dreamed of living in a sophisticated city, and now that she did, she dreamed of living back on their simple ranch.

She didn't belong here with these people. Even if they had been willing to accept her, she wasn't made to spend her days preening and her nights attending dinners and soirees whose sole purpose seemed to be to provide an opportunity to parade the results of one's private preening before an audience in hopes of gaining their regard.

Behavior she considered perfectly rational and responsible, Society regarded as a crime against itself. Why shouldn't she be able to take a walk whenever and wherever she liked? Why shouldn't she be able to speak freely about her family? If baking a pie or sweeping the floor brought her pleasure, it was her business.

Her relationship with the serving class wasn't any more felicitous. From birth, they had been taught not to socialize with their betters, and even though she was no longer welcome among the privileged, her position as Sam's wife placed her in that category. They were willing to wait on her hand and foot, but none of them wanted to be her friend. They tolerated her because they were paid to do so.

Ella's thoughts drifted back to the wealthy people who had once invited her to their homes. For herself, she had to confess, while she might bemoan Society's harsh judgment of her, her opinion of them was not much better than their's of her. She found them shallow and cruel. They might have fine clothes and a sophisticated mode of speech, but underneath their skin their hearts didn't match the golden lives they led.

No, now that she knew their true colors, she had no desire to call them her friends. If she only had herself to consider, she would gladly wipe her hands of them. . . . But for her husband's sake, Ella minded what they were doing terribly. She might not like them, but these were Sam's lifelong friends. He must admire them or he would never have regarded them as friends in the first place. That they would turn their backs on him because he had married outside their elite circle, when anyone who read the papers or listened to gossip knew he hadn't done so by choice, made her at once furious at them and riddled with guilt for her own part in his downfall.

Whenever she tried to discuss the problem with him, he insisted everything was being taken care of and she shouldn't worry. He claimed his business was fine. He claimed his only concern was for her injured feelings.

Her feelings. Whatever her opinion of Society, if Ella was honest with herself, the people of New York were not the root cause of her prodigious discontent. Her relationship with her husband was.

If they loved each other, they would be able to weather the storm of social stigma, and be the stronger for it. They would make new friends here or elsewhere. But they didn't love each other. It was no use pretending that they did.

Sam had said he would learn to love her. If he had, he had coldly neglected to tell her, and he wasn't a cold man. He was a kind man. He said and did all the proper things. But that wasn't love speaking. It was his unswerving sense of responsibility and duty, and worse yet pity.

She made him a totally unsuitable wife. She knew it; he knew it; the whole world knew it.

Why else would he be gone so much of the time?

Ella believed him when he said he was at his office. That wasn't her concern. It just seemed to her that a man who had been successful in his attempt to fall in love with his wife would have no need to bury himself in his work. . . . But it made perfect sense for a man who was still—despite his valiant efforts—in love with his ex-fiancée to do so. When the mind and hands were busy, the pain of the heart could be more easily ignored.

Ella sighed. It would certainly make her life less complicated if she could hate her rival, but she was even denied that small solace. Clara Harrington was the best friend she had in New York. She was her only friend. Clara was a consummate creature of Society, but Clara never mocked her. Clara tried to help her understand the labyrinthine rules of Society. Clara still came to call when no one else would. As a friend, Clara had but one glaring fault. Ella believed as firmly as she believed there was a God in heaven Clara would have made Sam a perfect wife.

The more time she spent with her, the more convinced she became of the truth of her dreary opinion. Clara possessed impeccable manners. She instinctively knew how to navigate the choppy waters of New York Society. Where Ella found

Society's endless rules tedious and cruel, Clara viewed them as part of an elaborate and highly amusing game. She fit into Sam's world.

Then, there was the matter of her character. Whatever flaws she had, if she had any, she kept them well disguised. Given the chance, she would see to all Sam's needs. Given the chance, she would love him well.

Ella swiped at the tears rolling down her cheeks with the back of her hands and frowned so fiercely it made her face ache. She loved Sam. She loved him every bit as much as Clara ever did, maybe even more. But she didn't love him well. Clara had spoken of the need for her to share Sam's burden, but how could she? She was his burden. She would always be a burden. His lips told her courteous comforting lies, but his eyes . . . his eyes revealed his true feelings. *He was not a contented man.*

Ella tried and failed to blink back another torrent of tears. She had tried so hard to be what she thought he wanted her to be, to make this marriage work, but it wasn't working at all. Sam might possess the intestinal fortitude to keep a smile firmly pasted on his lips and pretend all was well, but she did not. It was too exhausting.

Here she sat, a thoroughly desolate human being, in love with a man who couldn't love her, who in all likelihood was in love with the only real friend she had in all of New York City, and believing with all her heart the two of them deserved the happiness she had denied them.

This was no way to live. This was no situation in which to bring an innocent babe.

Ella honestly didn't know what she was going to do about the future. She was torn between loving Sam so much she wanted to let him go and her strong sense of responsibility to their child, whom she loved equally dearly. Could she, for the sake of the father, condemn her child to grow up without him? Could she, for the sake of the child, condemn the father to a hollow existence with a wife he never wanted to begin with? Ella didn't waste time considering her own desires, because they were impossible to fulfill. All of her desires, save one.

There was no reason she couldn't go home to have her baby. She was useless here. No one would miss her.

She didn't intend to stay away forever. She would just stay away until she had the baby and she could determine what she should do. The first requirement would be fulfilled in a month's time. The second might take much longer. How long she had no idea, but surely the separation would do both Sam and her some good.

She would be free to be herself again. No one would tell her how to dress or act or think. She could have her baby surrounded by love. With her gone, Sam's old friends might accept him into their homes again. He could be alone with Clara. He could decide if the price he had offered to pay for their actions last summer was perhaps too high after all.

It was not what she wanted, but if he asked her for a divorce, she would give it to him. She would give him anything he asked.

The more she thought about it, the more persuaded Ella became that going home to Wyoming was what she must do.

In the most secret place of her heart, she harbored the hope, when faced with her imminent departure, Sam would wrap her in his arms and beg her to stay, but she regarded the possibility as so remote, she felt ridiculous for entertaining such thoughts. It did neither of them any favors to live in a fantasy world, praying for love where none existed. It was what they had been doing these past months. It was slowly killing them both.

* * *

When Ella broached the subject of returning to Wyoming that evening with her husband after dinner, the only evidence of her inner turmoil was an unnatural paleness in her cheeks and an imperceptible trembling of her fingers.

"I'd like to talk to you about something," she began with a steady voice.

"Yes."

"I want to return to Wyoming to have my baby."

Sam raised both brows and gifted her with a curious, incredulous stare. "Surely, you can't be serious."

Ella folded her hands in her lap. "Yes, I can."

"You are eight months pregnant."

"I've been waddling around here long enough to have cottoned onto that fact, and even if I didn't possess enough wits to discern the obvious, everyone else is only too eager to point it out to me and order me about."

Sam smiled sympathetically. "I know you are hurt about not being well received in New York and frustrated by the restrictions put on your freedom by your condition, but that is no reason for you to contemplate doing something so unwise as traveling all the way to Wyoming."

"I'm not being unwise."

"You most certainly are, but don't let it alarm you. I have heard from a reliable source, women in your state are prone to being plagued by odd notions."

"There's nothing at all odd about my wanting to go to Wyoming," she argued, not at all pleased he was exacerbating an issue she found difficult enough to discuss in the first place with his patronizing attitude and gloomily guessing Clara as his source of information concerning pregnant women.

"All right," Sam condescended. "It isn't odd to wish to abuse your body with the rigors of travel when you are already so uncomfortable you can't sit in a chair for five minutes without shifting your position."

Since Ella was in the process of doing exactly that, she couldn't contest the point, so she offered a solution to it. "I'll book a private compartment on the train."

"You still won't be comfortable."

"I'll be fine," she persisted. "If I was sickly, I could understand your objections, but I come from sturdy stock. I daresay, I could walk to Wyoming if not for the time involved."

"I am grateful for your good health, but . . ."

"There are no 'buts.' "

"Yes, there are. Even if I agreed it would do you no harm to make the trip, which I do not, now is not a good time for me to be away from my business. I am in the process of ascertaining the details of what I hope has proven a very lucrative investment, and . . ."

"The trip wouldn't interfere with your business. I realize how busy you've been and would never ask you to jeopardize a business venture on my account. I'd not even considered the possibility of you coming along," Ella stated the truth, praying the anxiety she felt at the thought he might insist it was his duty to come with her did not come through in her voice. "I planned to go alone."

He averted his gaze and shook his head. "Alone. You absolutely will not be traveling anywhere alone. You will not be traveling anywhere."

"I want to see my grandmother," Ella insisted.

"It is natural you would be especially homesick at this time, and I do sympathize, but *no.* I cannot in good conscience allow you to take a trip at this time. Everything has been arranged for the baby to be born here. The nursery is ready; the midwife hired; you have servants to take care of all your needs. Here you have all the modern conveniences, and you would have none in Wyoming."

"I don't care about modern conveniences. Modern conveniences are no substitute for companionship."

"You are feeling neglected," Sam stated his interpretation what she was really trying to say. "I have a bad habit of concentrating on business to the exclusion of all else when I am in the midst of deal making. You should have spoken up sooner. I will try to be home more."

"That's not what I want at all."

"Then what do you want?"

"I want my Grandma Jo." Ella cringed when her voice came out sounding too much like the child he was treating her as if she was.

"If you would like, I will wire her the money for a ticket and have her come here," he offered with only a trace of reluctance.

"No." Ella couldn't believe he was making her simple request so complex. Surely, he could see as clearly as she did things could not go on as they were, that the separation she suggested would benefit them both. Her spine was beginning to feel as limp as her spirits and she stiffened it. "I want my Grandma Jo and my sisters and Hound Dog and the ranch. I want the mountains and the wide open prairie. I want wildflowers at my feet and trees towering over my head. I want to wake up to the sound of roosters rather than the clang of trolley cars. Tell me how you are going to put all that on a train!"

Sam sighed, pushing his glasses up the bridge of his nose. "You know I can't. After the baby is born and you have had time to recover from the birth, I will be glad to make arrangements for a visit. I'm sure your family will want to see you and the baby as much as you want to see them."

Ella remained adamant. "I want to go now."

"I know you do, but it is not a rational request. You may

be angry with me if you like, but I'll not ignore common sense. My answer remains: *no*."

They continued the same argument, in various forms, over the next week.

True to his word, Sam immediately began to spend more time at home, making a special effort to engage Ella in conversations he thought would be of interest to her. His new attention to her only made her feel worse.

She didn't want to be humored. She already felt enough of a cumbersome millstone about his neck without him neglecting his business for her sake.

If once during their many "discussions" of the subject he had even hinted at the three words: "I love you," nothing could have dragged her from his side. If he had said he didn't want her to go because he would miss her, she would have agreed to stay. Even if all he had professed was a desire to share in the birth of their baby, she might have been persuaded to remain where she was. But he said none of these things.

All he talked about were plans already made and long train rides and the many advantages civilization could provide a woman in her delicate condition. Ella didn't contend his reasons were without merit. They were imminently practical. She, however, was in no mood to be practical. She was in the mood to go home.

He was never going to say the words she longed to hear— words that would provide her some hope, any hope, given more time, they were capable of building a tolerable future together. Everyday that passed, her despair deepened and her need to return to the one place she could be assured of receiving the love she craved became more compelling.

Two days into the next week, Ella gave up trying to persuade Sam he should let her go. Even she was not so confident in her exceptional good health to delay the trip any longer. Ella preferred to go with his permission, but since she had failed to secure it, she would have to go without it.

Having made the decision, the next thing she did caused her almost equal agony. She played the coward.

Because she couldn't bear to see the pity in his eyes or to hear him speak of his responsibility and moral duty to her, there were two arguments she hadn't used to convince him to let her go. The first was that she loved him. Because she loved him she wanted him to be happy. It was as necessary for her well being as it was for his. Because she loved him, everyday she spent in his company, knowing he could never return her love, was a torment beyond description. The second argument was related to the first. She had never told him she wanted to go away to give them both time to decide what they should do about their marriage, or that she felt a long term separation would be best for them both.

Pen in hand, she told him these things now in a letter. She told him everything. She told him the absolute truths she couldn't bring herself to speak when he was in the same room with her.

She owed him the truth, so he would understand why she wanted so desperately to go, so he would understand all the noble sacrifice in the world couldn't overcome his lack of feeling for her. He needed to know she didn't blame him that he hadn't learned to love her. He needed to know she was granting him his freedom and her blessing to be with Clara. He needed to know, no matter what he chose to do, she would never deny him whatever contact he wished with their soon-to-be-born son or daughter.

It took Ella three days to compose the letter to her satisfaction. When it was finished, she hid it under her mattress. While she had still been trying to persuade her husband to give permission to let her go, she had obtained a copy of th train schedule. Katie was given the next two days off as an early birthday present. She was ready to leave.

The moment Sam departed for his office, Ella left word with Mrs. Potter she was going to lie down and was not to be disturbed for any reason; then, she hurried upstairs to retrieve the carpetbag she had packed with the minimum necessities for her journey. She had to hurry or she would miss her train, and her emotional state was such that a day's delay might be her undoing.

The hard lump in her throat forewarned tears, but she fought them off. She didn't have time for tears this morning. Later, she promised herself, when she reached Wyoming, she could cry a river of tears. Right now, she needed to be strong.

She had managed to sit through breakfast with a vacuous smile planted firmly on her face, when her heart was in peril of shattering every time she glanced up at the man sharing her table. She would manage now.

Arranging her pillows under the blankets in a shape approximating a human body, in case someone decided to peek in to check on her, Ella pulled her letter from its hiding spot and placed it on the top pillow. After covering the whole, and fluffing up the middle pillow to a size more in keeping with her belly, she stepped back and took one last glance around the room. Everything was in order.

Avoiding detection by the household servants while she made her way to the front door was her next and most daunting challenge. Ella held her breath, listening for footsteps. When she heard none, she cautiously poked her head out the ˌ ˌˌˌom door. The sitting room was empty, and she proceeded ˌ ˌ ˌor leading to the hall. Again she paused to listen. ˌ ˌeeted her ears.

ˌ ˌˌˌˌperformed their daily duties on a rigid schedule, and she mentally placed each one before advancing into the hall with carpetbag in hand.

Stepping as quickly and as quietly as her awkward figure allowed, Ella traveled the hall and descended the stairs. She paused to catch her breath, then dashed across the foyer and slipped out the door.

Once outside Ella walked—at a sedate gait designed to call as little attention to herself as possible—down the block and over two streets before hailing a cab. She met no one who knew her along the way.

Traffic cooperated and the trip to the train station was accomplished with the same economy of effort as her escape from the house. Ella bought a one-way ticket to Green River City and immediately boarded the train.

When, five minutes later, the wheels of the train began to roll beneath her, Ella leaned back against her seat. It had all gone so smoothly, it was as if Providence had willed her to be here. Providence wanted her to go home. She squeezed her eyes tight against the stinging threat of tears. Providence wanted her to leave her husband.

When she had awakened this morning, Ella had surmised it impossible for the human heart to bear a greater weight than hers and still go on beating, but her last thought caused the crushing weight to increase tenfold.

Twenty-four

A very unbusinesslike whoop burst from Sam's lips when he finished reading the telegram. He read it again and again, his smile becoming broader with each reading.

His agent had located his brothers in Montana. After so many months of disappointment, he had begun to despair this day would ever come.

What made the long awaited news even better was his brothers lived near the town of Helena. Years ago he had been persuaded to invest in a mine in the area, and recently the mine had proven more than well worth the risk of his capital. He had planned to travel there later in the year already. If that wasn't an auspicious coincidence, he didn't know what was.

Finally, he had some good news to share with Ella. He could hardly wait to tell her. He knew she would be happy for him, but what he was really looking forward to was: now that his brothers were found, there was no longer any reason to delay selling his house and establishing his family in another community.

He had been investigating several cities, compiling information on advantages and disadvantages. Helena wasn't on his list. It didn't qualify as a city. But if things worked out with his brothers and Ella was agreeable . . . perhaps, they should consider it.

Under no circumstances would they be staying in New York City. After the way his wife had been treated, the city had

lost the charm it once had held for him. He could no longer
esteem people he had once admired. He was sick of defending
a woman who needed no defense. Ella was a far finer human
being than those who belittled her.

He was tired of asking Ella to behave in ways contrary to
her nature. He did so to protect her from further ridicule, but
he didn't like it any more than she did.

Though the urge to board the next train west and make his
brothers acquaintance was strong, Sam knew he would have
to wait. He wanted to wait until after the baby was born. Ella
needed him here. Besides, becoming a father was a momen-
tous event in a man's life. He wouldn't miss it for all the
brothers in Christendom.

According to the telegram, his brothers had bought a ranch
in Montana a few months after selling the one they had owned
in Wyoming. Neither were married, but they were established
members of the community. They would be there for him to
meet after the baby was born and Ella had recovered enough
to travel comfortably.

Sam immediately began to make his plans. First, he would
take Ella to Heaven to visit her family. From there he would
travel on alone. Since he had instructed the detective he hired
not to reveal his purpose, his brothers still didn't know of his
existence. He wasn't sure why, but it was important to him
that he be the one to tell them. Also, he didn't want them to
learn of their mother's death from the lips of a stranger. The
pain of hearing the news of his father's death in that manner
was fresh enough in his memory, he preferred to avoid inflicting like pain on them.

The initial meeting was bound to be awkward, and he continued to fashion his plans. If he found himself welcome, he
could return to Wyoming for Ella and the baby. If he was not
welcome, he could spare her the discomfort of an icy recep-

tion. In either case, she would have her longed for visit with her family.

Sam rose to his feet and picked up his hat to go home to share his news; then, he reconsidered and returned to his desk. If they were going to Montana in two to three months time, possibly to stay, he best keep his mind on business now. Several matters required his attention, and he preferred to dispatch them today rather than tomorrow.

His news would wait until the dinner hour.

The efficiency with which Sam dispensed with his business obligations amazed even him, and he was able to lock up his office a full hour earlier than was his custom. He stopped to purchase flowers for his wife on the way home.

Mr. Creswell greeted him as he stepped through the door.

"Where is Mrs. Carrigan?" Sam asked while shedding his hat and coat.

"I believe she is still upstairs napping, sir. I'll fetch Mrs. Potter at once. She'll know for certain."

Mrs. Potter appeared momentarily.

"I'm trying to determine Mrs. Carrigan's whereabouts," Sam brightly informed her. "I have favorable news to share with her."

Mrs. Potter didn't return his smile. "I'm glad you're home early, sir. I'm a bit concerned about her. She went back to bed right after you left and hasn't been up since. That's not like her."

"Have you checked on her?"

"She left orders she wasn't to be disturbed. I didn't dare do more than crack the door and take a peek. Every time I did, she was sleeping soundly."

"I'll look in on her myself." Sam took a step toward the stairs. "I'm not surprised she slept all day. Her expanding figure makes her uncomfortable. More often than not these days, she has trouble sleeping during the night. Last night I heard her pacing again. It's no wonder she is exhausted. I'm sure you noticed she appeared a little paler than usual this morning."

"Yes, sir, I did."

"If she isn't yet awake, I believe I shall let her continue sleeping. Mrs. Svenson can prepare a tray for her later."

When Sam reached Ella's bedroom, he quietly eased the door open. Crossing the room on tiptoe, he stood by the bed, looking down on her.

Panic gripped his chest. His ears detected no whisper of breath. The bed covers were as still as a shroud.

Dropping the flowers in his hand, he yanked back the blankets. Sam stood stunned with relief she wasn't dead and shock that where he had expected to find his wife were four pillows and an envelope bearing his name.

When he recovered himself enough to command his limbs, Sam picked up the envelope and lit the bedside lamp. He sat down on the bed.

This letter is to inform you I have gone to Wyoming. As he read the first sentence of her letter, his eyes darkened and his bottom lip protruded. Had she lost her mind? He continued to read.

I know you said I could not go, and I always try to do what I believe will please you, but in this I find it impossible. It is necessary that I go. I am doing this for myself. I am doing it for you.

Please do not worry. . . . Slapping the letter against his thigh, Sam blew out an exasperated breath. He wasn't suppose to worry? She may as well have told him not to breathe. Of course, he was going to worry. She was in no condition to go traipsing across the country.

His eyes dropped to the next line of the letter, then the next.

When he finished reading the entire letter his hands were trembling so violently the paper cracked against the air.

He stood, walked to the window on leaden feet, and drew

open the drapery. Returning to the bed, he sat down to reread the letter. . . .

"Damn her! She doesn't want to visit her family! She wants to stay away forever!" he cursed when he had finished the second reading. "How dare she leave me! I tried to do right by her! I did everything I could to protect her! I may not be a perfect husband, but I did try! I tried my damndest!"

Sam argued with the empty room until he was hoarse with the effort and his fist was sore from the many times he had slammed it against the bedpost. Having vent his fury, a more melancholy mood settled over his heart.

Removing his glasses, he closed his eyes and massaged the bridge of his nose. He may have tried his damndest, but he had been aware for some time of his own failings and denying it was pointless. However, her stated reasons for leaving him had nothing to do with his inability to provide her with the high-toned life she desired and deserved.

Her letter claimed she was leaving him because he didn't love her. But he did. He did love her. How could she write this letter saying he didn't? He thought she knew. She was an intelligent woman. She was usually so sensible. How could she not have known?

Just because he wasn't given to grandiloquence, romantic declarations was no excuse. She knew his nature. He thought he knew hers.

If he didn't love her, why would he defend her when others made disparaging remarks? If he didn't love her, why would he work so hard to make sure he could provide her and their child with a good future? If he didn't love her, why would he care about her health or the baby's? He wouldn't. When she had asked, he would have packed her off to Wyoming with a merry grin and a heartfelt "good riddance" on his lips.

If anything happened to either of them . . . Sam couldn't finish the thought.

He persisted to argue his case. From the moment they had decided their marriage was going to be a permanent state of affairs, he had devoted himself to falling in love with his wife. It had been far easier than he had expected it to be—possibly because, though he was loath to admit it at the time, he was already more than a little enamored with her.

What rational man wouldn't be? She possessed every virtue a man could hope to find in a wife. She never complained or nagged or made unreasonable demands—save her behest to go to Wyoming. She made love with abandon. *And* she was beautiful.

Certainly, he had spoken more than once of duty—which she perversely insisted was his only reason for keeping her by his side. It *was* his duty to provide for her and their child. But a man could love his duty.

So, he had learned to love his wife just as he had said he would do. He had expressed that love through his behavior on a daily basis. And his reward was to be confronted with this letter claiming he felt nothing but obligation?

And what was all this rubbish—a full page and a half—about freeing him so he and Clara could be together? He shuffled the pages of the letter until he came to the offending passages and jabbed his finger at them. What he had felt for Clara was a thing of the past. He and Clara were friends, nothing more. They had never been more than friends. It was just neither of them had recognized the lack in their relationship until Ella had come along, and he learned the difference between loving a woman and being *in love* with a woman.

Sam scowled. Something else Ella said in her letter left him equally frustrated and even more angry. In one sentence she claimed she loved him with all her heart. In the next, she used her love as an excuse for leaving him, saying he would be better off without her. She had even offered him a divorce, suggesting he charge her with abandonment as just cause.

Another woman had made that same argument many years
ago. She too had been pregnant, only her husband didn't know
she carried his child. Ella had no more right to presume she
knew what was best for him, than his mother had had to presume she knew what was best for his father.

Why his father had allowed his wife to desert him, never
making any effort to get her back, was a puzzle he might
never solve, but his own actions were not in question.

He had no intention of letting history repeat itself.

In her letter, Ella promised him he could be with his child
as often as he liked. Well, that was every day of every week
of every month of every year. He had been deprived of the
love of his father, and he was not about to let a child of his
suffer the same misfortune.

And why should he, *or she,* he amended? He loved Ella. Ella
said she loved him. They would both love their baby when it
came. They would love their baby *under the same roof.*

They were a family and a family belonged together. He was
furious with Ella right now, but not so furious he was willing
to let his ire prevent him from pursuing her. When he caught
up with her, he would sit her down and make her listen to
reason. If reasoning didn't work, he would order her to stop
behaving like a hysterical female. And if *that* proved ineffective, he would adopt her family's mode of getting what they
wanted and carry her home by force.

A check of the train schedules revealed he would have to
wait until morning to leave. Sam spent most of the night at
his office, making sure he left nothing undone that couldn't
be delayed indefinitely. It needed to be dealt with, but mostly
staying busy helped keep his anxiety at bay.

It was pointless to even pretend to sleep. He could catch
up on his sleep on the train.

A predawn visit to his lawyer's home with a list of instructions took care of the remaining details. Sam returned home to oversee the packing of his luggage.

A survey of Ella's room revealed she had taken precious little with her, and he had Mrs. Potter fill a small trunk with items he thought Ella might find either useful or pleasant to have until they were able to return home.

Arriving at the train station an hour early, Sam paced the platform impatiently until the boarding call was sounded.

Not until he was in his seat and the train was speeding down the tracks did he force himself to try to relax. For the most part, the effort was futile, but the knots of tension in his shoulders slackened a bit.

The days spent on the train were long and filled with worry. They afforded him ample opportunity to think.

Having gotten over the initial shock of Ella's departure, he could contemplate the contents of her letter more logically. In an effort to understand, he tried to put himself in her shoes. When he did, he saw his own behavior in a different light.

He had complained Ella had no right to decide what was best for him, but hadn't he been doing exactly that to her? The more he thought about it, the more Sam realized he had. . . . And he *hadn't* told her he loved her. It was such a gradual process, and he had so many other concerns on his mind, he didn't even know when he had first become cognizant he loved her himself. He should have said the words. He realized that too now. . . .

Sam had brought several books with him, but none of them could hold his attention. Likewise, visits to the smoking car to engage in conversation with other gentlemen traveling on the train proved nothing but an embarrassment. No matter how intriguing the topic, his mind kept wandering back to Ella. He would have to ask his companions to repeat themselves, and after he had done this a half a dozen times, they began to become annoyed.

So, Sam passed the time sitting in his seat, staring out the window and wondering how Ella was feeling, and what she was doing, and if when he caught up with her, he would know what to say to her.

He wasn't sure which train she had taken, but he knew she couldn't be more than twenty-four hours ahead of him. He was counting on her being tired enough from her journey she would take a room and rest a day or two in Green River.

The thought of bundling her up and putting her right back on the next train to New York occurred to him more than once. Reason said the train trip would be less arduous than the wagon ride to her family's ranch, but his heart counseled him not to deprive her of the comfort of her family.

She could have waited to leave him after the baby was born. If she was willing to risk so much to be with them, he would not deny her.

Sam was the first passenger off the train when it stopped in Green River City. Leaving his luggage on the platform, he headed to the hotel. Ella had not checked in.

He inquired at every establishment in town that rented rooms and received the same answer. His next stop was the livery.

There he was greeted with the news his wife had hired a horse and buckboard. He also learned she was exactly one day ahead of him.

Making arrangements for the majority of his luggage to follow him to the ranch by wagon, and paying handsomely for the service, Sam hired a horse for himself.

It took him less than a half hour to see it outfitted with saddle and saddlebags, retrieve a change of clothing from his luggage, and buy enough food for the journey.

Mounting his hired horse, Sam spurred it into motion, setting the quickest gait he dared without hazard of overtiring the animal and rendering it useless. Even at a measured pace, a horse traveled faster than a wagon, and he calculated he should catch up with Ella long before she reached the ranch.

Sam cursed a string of oaths that would have earned him the respect of every longshoreman on both shores as he kicked the horse beneath him hard in the ribs.

The horse had been an admirable mount the first day out, but the second day, it balked at keeping up a mile-eating pace. For the first couple of hours, he coddled the beast. When he ran out of patience and insisted on a gait faster than a slow plod, the horse had reared, taken off at a dead run, and used a low lying branch to scrape him off his back. He had wasted nearly a full day trying to catch the hateful animal.

Once caught, the horse still refused anything but grudging cooperation. Sam intended to suggest a trip to the glue factory when he returned the animal to its owner.

With the wasted day and the snail's pace, Sam feared he wouldn't catch up with Ella until after she reached the ranch. Though he knew her to be more than competent, he didn't like the idea of her being out in this wilderness all alone. The nights were bitter cold, and though the days had been sunny, they were still far from warm.

He was not the kind of man who was in the habit of borrowing trouble, but his mind couldn't be prevented from playing the "what if?" game. What if she got sick? What if she fell off the buckboard? What if she was attacked by wild animals? What if her horse bolted and the wagon careened into a gully? The scenarios in his mind became more gruesome by the mile.

Ella might not believe he loved her, but he had had long, lonely days on the train and longer, lonelier days on the trail to contemplate just how much he did love her. He had never missed another human being so much in his life.

True, her mood had been melancholy of late, but all that was going to change. He realized the error of his ways and would make amends. He would make her smile again.

The thought of seeing Ella smile caused his own lips to curve upward. Sam continued to contemplate his feelings for his absent wife.

It wasn't anything in particular but everything in general he missed about her. The way her eyes lit up when something sparked her interest. Her pluck. Her passion for books. The way she warmed the bed at night. He even missed the comic way she now waddled when she walked across the room.

She would be indignant if she knew how amused he was by her cumbersome physical state, but he didn't care. The sound of her voice, whether soft or strident, would be music to his ears. He just wanted her to be safe.

It was approaching late afternoon when Sam spied the driverless buckboard. The horse had been unharnessed and left to graze.

Sam kicked his mount hard enough, it immediately understood this was one contest of wills it had no chance of winning, and it provided the demanded burst of speed.

When he came abreast of the abandoned vehicle, the first thing Sam noticed was the broken wagon wheel. The second was that the traveling bag in back belonged to Ella.

Every misfortune to her person his overwrought imagination had conjured since he had discovered her gone returned full force. His muscles tensed.

Shading his eyes, Sam searched the horizon in all directions. He could see no sign of her.

He cupped his hands and shouted her name.

There was no answer.

Twenty-five

Sam's heart began to thud and he broke into a cold sweat, but he didn't waste precious time by giving into his panic. Only one thought filled his head. He had to find Ella.

Giving up his search of the horizon, he studied the ground. It only took a moment to locate her footprints. Leading his horse by the reins, Sam followed them.

He followed them for a mile and then another and another. His progress was steady but of necessity slow. If he traveled too fast, he risked losing her tracks altogether.

It was apparent to him, she had decided to walk the remaining distance to the ranch. It was the only logical thing for her to do, but in her condition, he couldn't fathom how she had managed to make it as far as she had.

He trudged on.

Already it was getting dark, and with the sun going down, so was the temperature. Sam hunched in his overcoat. Was Ella warm enough? He had no idea what she was wearing. Was she carrying a gun to protect herself? Could she find her way home in the dark?

Sam tried to comfort himself by arguing as long as her footprints kept going, she had to be fine. It helped a little, but as the sun continued to sink behind the western mountains, the panic he had kept under tight rein rose in his breast.

* * *

Ella pressed her back against the trunk of the tree and moaned as another contraction seized her belly. Despite the chill air, her face flushed and perspiration ran in rivulets down her forehead. The contraction seemed to last forever. When it finally loosened its grip, she sagged against the tree and gasped for breath.

"Please stop," she pleaded with her belly as she rubbed it with the tips of her fingers. "Everybody knows first babies come late not early. I'm almost home. Just give me a little more time."

Her entreaty was cut short by another contraction.

After it was over and she could relax a little, she tried to reason her way out of the mess she had gotten herself into. She had two choices: stay here and have her baby alone or attempt to travel the remaining distance to the ranch.

Neither choice was a good one.

She had heard of Indian women going off into the woods to bear their children alone, so a woman must be able to do so. She admired any woman who could perform such a feat immensely—they deserved a medal in her estimation—but the thought of giving birth to her baby all alone terrified *her*. She was not one to shrink from a necessary task, but . . .

Her thoughts were cut short by yet another contraction. Its intensity was an unwelcome reminder of the chief drawback to getting back up on her feet and walking again. She didn't know if she could do it. What if walking made her contractions come faster or stronger? What if she lost her bearings from the mind numbing pain and became lost?

As if to lend credence to her concerns, another contraction engulfed her.

The contractions were coming closer together now, and Ella knew she would have to come to a decision soon or she no longer would have a choice.

She didn't know how far she would make it, but she knew she had less than a mile to go. She was going to try to walk.

Closing her eyes to concentrate her strength before rising to her feet, she abruptly blinked them open at the sound of her name being called. It sounded like Sam's voice, but she knew it couldn't be. He was in New York. She must be imagining it was him. Maybe, she was imagining the voice.

"Ella!"

She heard the voice again, louder this time as if it wasn't coming from so great a distance, but before she could answer, a contraction snatched her breath away.

"Ella!"

"I'm over here!" she shouted the instant she could.

"Ella! Is that you?"

"Yes! I'm over here beneath this tree!" It was a poor description of her location since she was surrounded by trees, but it was the best she could do. She could hear the snapping of twigs, as if someone was riding toward her; then, Sam came galloping into view, reined his horse to a halt, and was standing before her. "It *is* you," she mumbled in disbelief.

"Thank God, I found you. Are you all right?"

"I'm . . ." Before she could finish, she doubled up with pain.

Sam fell to his knees beside her and cradled her hand in his. "My God, you're not having the baby now, are you?"

Ella answered him with a grim-faced nod.

"What should I do? Can you ride a horse? No, of course, you can't. I'm sorry I asked such an idiotic question. Don't worry. I'll think of something . . ."

"Get on your horse and ride for help. Grandma Jo can help you hitch the wagon and come back with you," Ella advised after the contraction had eased.

"I can't leave you here alone."

She didn't want to be alone anymore than he wanted to

leave her. She was still half afraid she was hallucinating his presence. But reason and determination to do what would be best for her baby overrode her fears. "It's not that far."

"Then, I'll carry you."

"You can't. I'm too heavy. You'll hurt yourself."

Ignoring her protests, Sam scooped her up in his arms. He had only gone a few steps when another contraction came. Ella's face contorted with pain. "I . . . can't . . . breathe . . . like . . . this. . . . You . . . have . . . to . . . put . . . me . . . down."

Sam quickly eased her to the ground. When the contraction was finished, he distraughtly repeated the question he had asked before, "What should I do?"

"Go fetch a wagon."

"I told you, I can't leave you."

"Then, help me up and hold me while I walk on my own two feet. I'll be fine until the next contraction."

Sam did what she asked. They didn't cover much distance before the anticipated contraction brought a halt to their progress. This time, Ella remained on her feet. Sam supported her weight with his encircling arms. Ella wrapped her arms around Sam's chest, her embrace tightening in concert with the muscles of her womb.

When it was over, she smiled wanly. "That one didn't hurt as badly as the others," she reported. "Let's keep doing it this way."

Though his ribs felt as though they had been crushed in a vise, Sam readily agreed.

Without the need to lower Ella to the ground with every contraction, they made better progress between them, even though they kept coming closer and closer together. At first, Sam kept up a steady stream of encouragement, but before long he realized Ella was too absorbed in her labor to be cognizant of anything he said, and he fell silent. His physical presence seemed to be all the support she needed. . . .

"We're almost there," he joyously announced when at last he spied the silhouette of the ranch house up ahead. He measured the remaining distance by the contractions Ella was obliged to endure. By the fifth, Sam was simultaneously holding her up and kicking at the door.

Inside, Hound Dog set to barking furiously.

"Whatever varmint is trying to kick my door down better have one good reas . . ." Grandma Jo's grumbling came to a halt when she opened the door to find her granddaughter and Sam on her doorstep.

"She's having the baby," Sam frantically explained.

"I can see that." Grandma Jo clucked her tongue. "Let's help her get into bed."

With Josephine Singleton in charge, Ella was stripped of her clothes, dressed in a borrowed nightgown, and tucked into bed before the next contraction took hold.

"Sam, fetch a bucket of water and set it to boiling on the stove," Grandma Jo ordered.

"Why?"

"Don't ask questions. Just do it! When you've got the water heating, grab some clean linen and start tearing it into strips."

He didn't like leaving Ella, but Sam did as he was instructed. He was allowed into the bedroom to bring in the linen strips and later to carry in the boiling water; otherwise, he was banished from his wife's side. Hound Dog sniffed at his heels as he paced back and forth. Absently, Sam reached down to pat his head.

He could hear Ella moaning in the next room, and it was driving him out of his mind not to be in there with her. He should be with her. He might not be of much use, but he wanted to offer her what little comfort he could. He strode to the door only to be met by a stern, "Sam, now you stay out of here!" before his hand touched the doorknob.

He approached the door several more times with the same results. Each time his frustration burgeoned.

Every sound coming from the room caused him to shudder. He knew they hadn't been in there that long, that it was supposed to take a long time, but he couldn't stand it. He had to know what was going on, to see for himself that Ella wasn't suffering more than she should.

Sam burst through the door, just as his daughter burst into the world with a lusty cry of protest. He stared at his daughter, then at her mother. Ella was laughing and crying at the same time.

"Is she all right?" he asked.

"Both mother and daughter are fit as a fiddle," Grandma Jo assured him.

Sam smiled at Ella.

"I did it. I can't believe it. I did it," she kept babbling over and over.

"You sure did, honey. You done real good," Grandma Jo praised. After cutting and tying the umbilical cord and wrapping the baby in a blanket, she turned her attention to Sam. "Well, now that you've barged in here, you may as well make yourself useful. Come hold your daughter while I deal with the afterbirth and clean your wife up."

His muscles tensed and his cheeks paled. "You want me to hold her?"

"No, I want you to stand there like a statue with your mouth hanging open. If you're afraid of babies, you oughta have stayed put when I told you." Striding across the room, she unceremoniously lay his daughter in his arms. Without waiting to see if he knew what to do, she returned to Ella.

Sam nestled his daughter to his chest. She was so tiny, he was afraid to hold her too tightly lest he break her. He was afraid if he didn't hold her tightly enough, he might drop her. It took several minutes for him to gain sufficient confidence, he could study her individual features.

His daughter's head was covered with wisps of downy black hair. She had dark blue eyes, a dainty nose, puckered bantam lips. He counted her fingers, then her toes. They were all there. Despite her wrinkled, ruddy complexion, he judged her the most beautiful child he had ever seen. Pride swelled in his breast. She was his child. She was his little girl to love and protect and teach all the things she would need to know to flourish. It was an awesome responsibility, but it didn't weigh down his heart. It buoyed it up

They were a family, a real family complete with mother, father, and child. Nothing and no one would ever tear them apart. He would make Ella believe they should be together. He kissed his daughter's forehead. "I'll make her believe," Sam whispered to his daughter. "Just watch."

When he glanced up at her mother, she was sound asleep.

"So you gonna tell me what in tarnation you two are doing here?" Grandma Jo asked as she poured them both a cup of coffee. "I'd have thought you'd have more sense than to go dragging a pregnant wife halfway across the country this close to her birthing time."

Sam tucked the blanket under his daughter's chin as she peacefully slumbered in the old wooden cradle he had retrieved from the loft in the barn and added a log to the fire in the fireplace, before joining Grandma Jo at the dining room table. "I do have more sense," he informed her. "Ella ran away."

She pursed her lips. "That don't sound like the Ella I know."

"I'm afraid I haven't been a very good husband to her."

"Why not?" she asked without rancor.

Sam stared at the coffee in his cup. "How should I know? Stupidity, inexperience, confusion, take your pick."

"Do you love her?"

"Yes."

"You told her?"

"No, not yet."

"Stupidity," Grandma Jo succinctly named the cause of his troubles. Taking a long sip of her coffee, she cocked her head and commanded his gaze. "So, you gonna keep on being stupid forever, or are you planning on wising up some time soon?"

He straightened his shoulders. "I am going to talk to her just as soon as she wakes up."

"Glad to hear it. You want the settee or the bedroom?"

"What?"

"We both could use a little shut eye. Ain't no one around here gonna be getting much sleep for some time. First thing you gotta learn about babies is when they sleep you sleep; otherwise, they'll run you ragged."

Sam glanced at his sleeping daughter. "You take the bedroom."

"Good enough." Yawning, Grandma Jo rose to her feet. "See you when I see you."

A high-pitched squawk startled Sam out of a fitful sleep. As soon as he regained his bearings, he looked down at his daughter and grinned. "Your great grandmother warned me about this." Picking her up, he cradled her to his chest. Her mouth found her fist. She calmed for a moment, then let loose a series of indignant wails.

"What's wrong, sweetie?" Sam cooed, rocking her in his

arms in an attempt to calm her so she wouldn't wake the entire household.

She turned toward the sound of his voice, her tiny lips making smacking noises as she rooted against his chest.

"Oh." His eyes illuminated with comprehension. "I'm afraid I can't help you with that."

Just then Ella appeared at the door.

"What are you doing out of bed?" Sam remonstrated, hurrying to her side.

"I heard my baby crying."

"Our baby," he gently corrected. "Get back into bed, and I'll bring her to you."

Ella nodded and padded back to bed. She was too tired and sore to argue with him. As soon as she was comfortably settled, he handed over her daughter. Unbuttoning the top buttons of her nightgown, she put her squalling little girl to her breast. Instantly, the baby quieted.

"What do you want to name her?" Sam softy asked as he gazed at mother and daughter.

She didn't look up. "I thought Margaret, after your mother."

"Margaret is a nice name, and I am touched by your wish to honor my mother, but I'm more inclined to name her Josephine, after your grandmother. She is the one who brought us together."

Ella's brow wrinkled. "I would think she'd be the last person on earth you'd want to name our daughter after.

"Why?"

"Because she is the one who brought us together." She used the same reason as he did to support her contradictory opinion. For added emphasis, she stated, "She ruined your life."

Sam shook his head. "No, she didn't. If not for her dogged determination, I might never have had the opportunity to get to know you well enough to realize I love you."

Ella's eyes darkened and her lips trembled. "Sam, please,

haven't more than enough lies already passed our lips? I know why you're here. You're here because you think it's your duty to be here. You don't need to do this."

"Yes, I do." Sitting down on the edge of the bed, Sam captured her shoulders in his hands. "I need to tell you I love you. It isn't a lie. It is the truth. The *unadulterated, unabridged, unvarnished* truth. I would have told you sooner only I thought you already knew. Obviously, from your letter you didn't, so I came here to set you straight."

Her heart pounded against her ribs. Ella wanted to believe him, but she couldn't. What he said made no sense. "What about Clara?" she made herself ask.

"Clara is a friend, nothing more. My feelings for her were never what I feel for you."

"But you talk to her," she argued.

"I talk to you."

"Not about anything important. Not about us." She tried to turn away, but Sam refused to release her.

"You're right, but I didn't mean to hurt you by it. I was trying to protect you. I wanted you to have the refined life you told me you have always dreamed of having, and it angered me I couldn't give it to you. I knew I could for a short while, so I didn't tell you the truth about my friends. Later, I wanted to have something creditable to offer you in exchange for the grand life you thought you would be getting in New York, before we discussed our options. I realize now it was neither wise nor fair to exclude you from decisions about our future. You told me as much, but I was too proud to listen. I'm sorry."

Ella stared at him.

"Are you going to forgive me?"

"You don't need to ask my forgiveness," she counseled him. "I've never believed you did any of the things you did to hurt me. You did them because of your sterling sense of responsibility."

"I did them because making decisions on my own was the way I have always done things. It was the way I was raised to be. I did them because I never have been truly in love before and was an inexperienced fool," he argued. "I love you, Ella. Honestly, I do."

"How can you? You didn't want to marry me in the first place."

"You're right, again. I didn't. But I didn't know you then." He refused to let her turn from his steady gaze. "When I was a little boy, my mother once set a bowl of tapioca pudding in front of me and told me to eat it. I balked. I didn't like the way it looked. I didn't like the way it clung to my spoon. But do you know what happened when she finally coaxed me into tasting it? I loved it. Now, it's my favorite dessert. I wouldn't want to live without it. I feel the same way about you."

He sounded so sincere, he was confusing her. Ella glanced from him to their daughter to him again. "But what about your fine life in New York? Without me, you could have it all back again."

"Possibly, but I don't want it back. I'll admit I took far too long to come to the realization the well-ordered life I had before I met your family no longer appealed to me. It's hard for a man to change his way of thinking about the world. But I have. Having broadened my horizons with travel, I find I prefer my wife's Western-style friendliness to my old friends' Eastern-style snobbery."

Ella scrutinized him through narrowed eyes, but she couldn't extinguish the spark of hope flickering to life in her breast. "Are you sure you aren't telling me this because you think it's what I want to hear?"

"Absolutely," he forcefully stated. "From now on neither of us is ever going to tell another lie to each other or anyone else. I have found even if one has admirable motives, it only leads to disaster."

"Will you swear you will always tell me the truth?" Ella deliberately demanded.

"I swear."

"The whole truth?"

"I swear."

"Okay . . ." Ella took a deep breath. "Do you love Clara?"

He didn't flinch. "Yes, but only as a friend. And you needn't worry about Clara's feelings. She is having so much fun being seen on the arm of a different man every night, she told me she wished we had broken off our engagement years ago."

"When did you decide you loved me?"

"I don't know. It happened so gradually, I cannot name a specific time and place, but it occurred months ago. I have always liked you, even when I acted as though I didn't." He paused before amending, "Except for the first time I met you, when you were wearing trousers and were filthy. You stank, too. I didn't like you then."

Her lips threatened to quiver into a smile, but Ella refused to be distracted. "If you had no one's needs or desires but your own to consider, where would you choose to make your home?"

"Helena, Montana," he answered without hesitation. Dumbfounded, Ella blinked at him.

"Why there?"

"Because the detective I hired found my brothers, and that is where they live."

"He found your brothers? Why didn't you tell me?" Her voice was no longer that of an interrogator, but that of a bemused and concerned friend. Sam answered with unswerving honesty just the same.

"Because when I came home to share the news with you,

you were on a train running away from me. I only just found out that day."

"And you wouldn't mind living in a place like Helena?"

"Would you mind living there?" he asked.

"No." Ella didn't need to take time to think about her answer. "I've learned the hard way it isn't so much where you live but who you live with that determines a person's happiness."

"Do you think you could be happy living with me for the rest of your life?" Sam diffidently queried.

"Do you really love me?" she countered with a question of her own.

"Ella, I swear I do. I love you with all my heart. If you want, we can have another wedding, and I'll marry you all over again. I'll marry you a thousand times if that is what it takes to convince you." Gathering her in his arms, he kissed her passionately.

Ella responded with equal ardor, at last believing the words of love he spoke were true. Her spirit soared. They continued to cling to each other until their baby cried in protest.

"Sorry, sweetie." Ducking his head, Sam gifted his disgruntled daughter with a fatherly kiss. "But I think you will forgive me when I tell you I believe your mother has just agreed to give me a second chance." He addressed his next words to Ella. "You will, won't you?"

"Nothing would give me greater pleasure," Ella fervently promised.

"Good, because on the way here I decided if you said no, I would be compelled to give you no choice in the matter."

"Already falling back into your old habits, are you?" Ella teased.

"I'm afraid so." Sam expelled an exaggerated sigh. "It may take me awhile to get the details of this marriage business right. Perhaps another kiss would help me learn faster."

Their lips embraced again, speaking wordless vows each would stand steadfast in their commitment to face both the joys and disappointments of life as loving partners.

"I love you, Mr. Carrigan."

"I love you, Mrs. Carrigan."

A noisy squeal rent the air.

They both laughed and gazed down at their daughter. "We love you, too, Josephine," they assured her.

The white-haired old woman standing in the next room with her ear pressed to the door tilted her face heavenward, nodded her thanks to the Almighty, and grinned.

Dear readers,

Samuel Carrigan isn't the only one of the Carrigan brothers to have woman trouble.

In TWO OF HEARTS, coming in March 1995, Sam's oldest brother, Adam finds a piece of land promised to him sold to a woman who is every bit as determined to keep it as he is to buy it back from her. Both are willing to use every trick in the book to achieve their goals.

The romantic misadventures continue in THE CROWDED HEART, March, 1996. Joshua Carrigan goes looking for a wife to warm his heart and his bed . . . and gets a whole lot more than he intended in the bargain.